Praise for Cheryl Holt's
Nicholas

"A Cheryl Holt novel is something I always impatiently anticipate, and NICHOLAS reminds me exactly why. Fabulously enticing characters along with a storyline that will get the reader's blood pumping equals a book that is a must read."
~ *Book Wenches*

"VERDICT: An exciting plot complicated by Emeline and Nicholas's roller-coaster relationship keeps the pages turning. A great weekend read."
~ *Library Journal*

"NICHOLAS, by Cheryl Holt is in one word, 'Captivating'! A perfect read for snuggling down with your favorite blanket and a nice glass of wine at the end of the day. But be warned that you will not be able to put it down until the last page is read."
~ *Novels Alive TV*

Nicholas

Cheryl Holt

SAMHAIN PUBLISHING

Samhain Publishing, Ltd.
11821 Mason Montgomery Road, 4B
Cincinnati, OH 45249
www.samhainpublishing.com

Editing by Heather Osborn
Cover by Angela Waters

First Samhain Publishing, Ltd. electronic publication: August 2011
First Samhain Publishing, Ltd. print publication: July 2012

Chapter One

London, May, 1814...

"Are you sure about this?"

"Very sure."

Emeline Wilson forced a smile as she leaned across the wagon seat and patted Mr. Templeton's hand.

He was an older gentleman, an acquaintance from her rural village of Stafford. He'd offered to drive her to London as he brought a load of hides to the tanner. Since she hadn't had the money to travel any other way, she'd accepted.

The trip had been bumpy and lengthy and fraught with uncertainties. She was worried over whether she should proceed with her plan, and still hadn't convinced herself that she was doing the right thing.

Nervously, Mr. Templeton pointed to the ostentatious mansion that towered over them. It belonged to Nicholas Price, the new Lord Stafford, a mysterious personage who'd been earl for a year and who no one at the Stafford estate had ever seen or met.

"The house is awfully grand, isn't it?" he said.

"Not as grand as Stafford Manor."

"How will you gain entrance?"

"I'll simply knock on the door."

"Do you think his staff will admit you?"

"Why wouldn't they?" she firmly replied.

Two days earlier, when they'd left home, she'd been brimming with indignation, aggrieved on her neighbors' behalves, and prepared to slay any dragon as she sought a paltry crumb of justice for them.

But now, with their having arrived, her confidence was flagging.

Why had she assumed she could make a difference? Why was she always so eager to carry the burdens of others? Perhaps she should have stayed in the country and kept her mouth shut.

Unfortunately, it wasn't her nature to be silent or submissive. She was forever arguing when she shouldn't, fighting unwinnable battles, and cheering on the less fortunate. Usually to no avail. There were few rewards to be gleaned by heroics, but she couldn't stop herself.

Life was so unfair, catastrophe so random and typically heaped on those least able to withstand the onslaught. If she didn't comment on inequity, who would?

Her dear, departed father—the village school teacher and best man she'd ever known—had educated her beyond her needs. She saw problems and the obvious solutions too clearly, and she couldn't comprehend why the easiest remedies were the hardest to attain. Especially from someone as rich and powerful as Lord Stafford.

His tenants were suffering egregiously. Crops had failed and conditions were desperate, yet he couldn't care less. He'd never bothered to visit Stafford. Instead, he'd installed Mr. Mason as his land agent. Mason was a bully and fiend who had been given free rein and unfettered control.

His sole objective was to put the estate on a sound financial footing, by any means necessary. He implemented his draconian measures without regard to the human cost. Families had been thrown out on the road. Acreage had been confiscated.

No one was safe from his harsh edicts, not even Emeline. Despite her father's three decades of loyal service, she—and her two sisters, ten-year-old twins, Nan and Nell—were about to be evicted.

Mr. Mason had already forced them to relinquish their comfortable house, located next to the manor, in which Emeline had been raised. They'd been relegated to a dilapidated cottage in the woods, and they had to start paying rent or leave, her dilemma being that she had no way of paying the rent and nowhere to live if she didn't.

"Should I wait for you?" Mr. Templeton asked, yanking her

out of her furious reverie.

"There's no need," Emeline said. "Go make your deliveries, then pick me up at four o'clock as we planned."

"It doesn't seem as if anyone is at home."

Emeline studied the mansion. The curtains were drawn. No stable boy had rushed out to greet them. No butler had appeared.

"Someone will be here," she asserted. "I have an appointment, remember?"

It was a small lie, but she told it anyway. She'd written to the earl three times, requesting an audience, but hadn't received a reply. Finally, in exasperation, she'd written a fourth time to inform him that she was coming to London—whether he liked it or not.

She couldn't abide snobbery or conceit, and considering Lord Stafford's antecedents, why would he exhibit any?

Twelve months ago, he'd simply been a captain in the army. When the old earl had died without any children, it had been a huge shock to learn that title would pass to Nicholas Price. In an instant, he'd gone from being a common soldier to a peer of the realm. What reason had he to act superior?

"You asked for an appointment," Mr. Templeton counseled, "but that doesn't mean the earl will keep it. His kind doesn't have to be courteous."

"Maybe he should recall that he's not all that far above us."

"Oh, Missy, be careful with your disparaging talk. If you're not here at four o'clock, I'll likely be searching for you at the local jail."

"Don't be silly. He wouldn't have me...*jailed* merely for speaking out."

"He's dined at the palace with the king. That sort of experience tends to alter a fellow. He might do anything to you."

"He won't. He's an officer in the army. He wouldn't harm an innocent woman."

"You just never know," he ominously warned.

"I'll be fine," she insisted as a shiver of dread slithered down her spine.

Afraid that her courage might fail her, she leapt to the ground before she could change her mind.

"Good luck," he said.

"I don't need any luck," she boldly retorted. "I have right on my side, and *right* will always prevail over injustice."

She marched off, and he clicked the reins, his horses plodding away. As he departed, she felt terribly alone, as if she'd lost her last friend.

She gave in to a moment of weakness, to a moment of doubt, then she straightened with resolve.

"You can do this, you can do this," she muttered over and over.

There had been a neighborhood meeting, and in a unanimous vote, she'd been elected to present their grievances to Lord Stafford, to seek some relief from Mr. Mason's oppressive decrees. She would *not* return to Stafford without garnering concessions from the earl.

She climbed the steps and was about to knock, when suddenly, the door was jerked open.

"It's about bloody time you arrived," a man barked. He grabbed her and yanked her inside.

"What?" Emeline stammered, taken off guard by the peculiar welcome.

"You were supposed to be here two hours ago."

"I was?"

"He's probably not sober enough to entertain you now. If he's foxed to the level of incoherence, don't expect to be paid."

"Paid for what?" she asked, but he didn't answer. He stormed off, her wrist clasped tightly in his hand, and she stumbled along behind him.

After being out in the bright sunshine, the vestibule was very dark, and she blinked and blinked, trying to adjust her vision. Before she could get her bearings, she was across the floor and being dragged up the stairs. To slow their progress, she dug in her heels, but the brute who'd accosted her was very large and very irked. She was only five foot five, and she weighed a hundred-twenty pounds. She'd have had more success, attempting to stop a charging bull.

They reached a fancy hallway and started down it. There was a bit more light, and she caught glimpses of a red coat, a dangling lapel, gold buttons. He was wearing a soldier's uniform, so he had to be one of Lord Stafford's cohorts.

The earl had inherited the earldom, but he hadn't resigned

his commission in the army, and Emeline hadn't heard that he intended to.

Evidently, his position in the military was so glamorous that he'd rather continue at it than worry about his responsibilities to the people at Stafford.

The notion made Emeline's blood boil. Her life, her sisters' lives, the lives of everyone she knew, were hanging by a thread, but Lord Stafford was totally unconcerned.

"Excuse me." She fought the man's strong grip but couldn't pry herself loose.

"Excuse me!" she said more sternly, tugging hard and lurching free.

The man halted abruptly, and he appeared the type who might commit violence. She took a hesitant step back.

"What is it?" he snarled.

"I'm...I'm...here to see Lord Stafford."

"Well, of course you are. Why else would you be here?" He frowned, scrutinizing her tattered hat, her worn traveling cloak. "We've waited all this time, and this is how you've dressed yourself? You could be a fussy governess."

"What's wrong with being a governess? I'm not hoping to impress with my attire."

"You're not? For pity's sake, don't you know anything about men and what they like?"

At his insults, her temper sizzled. She couldn't help it if she was poor, if she was a week away from being tossed out on the road by Mr. Mason. Through no fault of her own, she was in dire financial straits, and she wouldn't grovel or apologize for her reduced condition. "Of all the rude, uncivil, offensive—"

He blew out an aggravated breath. "What kind of girls is Mrs. Bainbridge hiring these days? She's aware of his preferences; he won't like you."

"Why not?" she sneered.

"Because you're a frump—"

"A frump!" she huffed.

"—and you're too skinny. And you're *blond*. He hates blonds. Mrs. Bainbridge has been apprised that he does. Why she would send you is beyond me."

"Who is Mrs. Bainbridge?" she inquired, but he snagged her wrist again and took off.

Quickly, and despite her best efforts to pull away, they were at the double doors at the end of the corridor.

"Can you at least try to look pretty?" he implored. "Pinch your cheeks. Let your hair down."

"I don't wish to look...*pretty*," she claimed, oddly incensed that he didn't think she was. "I wish to be listened to and...and...heeded."

"Oh, Lord, spare me. Just what I need—a philosopher!"

He spun the knob and pushed her over the threshold. As she passed, he made a hasty grab at the combs keeping her neat chignon balanced on the back of her neck. Her tresses tumbled down in a golden wave.

"Are you insane?" she seethed, twirling to confront him.

"I'd better not hear any complaint from him," he snapped in reply. "Now get on with it and get out of here."

He slammed the door in her face and turned the key in the lock, trapping her.

What sort of asylum had she entered?

She jangled the knob, then pounded on the wood, hissing, "Release me! At once!"

But she received no answer.

Bending down, she peeked through the keyhole, and she could see him retreating. She threw up her hands in exasperation, then whipped around to survey the space where she'd been imprisoned.

Immediate escape was necessary, and she had to either maneuver the lock or find another exit. Since she had no mechanical inclinations, locating an exit was her only option.

She was sequestered in the sitting room of a grand suite, complete with several inner rooms. Hopefully, there would be servants' stairs at the rear, and she could flee down them.

She tiptoed over to the bedchamber, and it was empty. Breathing a sigh of relief, she hurried into it, but she shielded her eyes so she wouldn't glimpse the enormous bed in the middle. It was large and ornate, designed for a king. The blankets were on the floor, the pillows strewn about, so the maids hadn't been in yet, or perhaps there were no maids.

What self-respecting female would work in such a madhouse?

Cautiously, she approached the next door that led into a

washing room. There was a bathing tub full of water. Bars of soap and a scrub brush were stacked on a stool.

She was about to sneak in, but before she could, she was horrified to note that there was a man inside. Was it Lord Stafford?

He was a few feet away, his back to her, which she could clearly see because he wasn't dressed. With just a towel wrapped around his waist, he was naked as the day he'd been born, and much too eagerly, she took stock of his attributes—broad shoulders, lean hips, long, long legs.

His skin was bronzed from the sun, his hair dark as a raven's and in need of a trim, his arms muscled from strenuous endeavor. He had a perfectly formed anatomy, the type of flawless shape a sculptor might copy when chipping away at a block of marble.

She studied him, transfixed and confused by the sight.

Her neighbors at Stafford had gossiped about him so frequently and in such derogatory terms that she'd developed an image of him that corresponded with their disparaging remarks. Though she knew he was thirty years old, in her mind, she'd painted him as aged, fat, and ugly, but the reality didn't match the fantasy.

He was strong and youthful, vigorous and fit. His blatant personality oozed outward, his arrogant confidence wafting over her.

She hovered behind him, too terrified to move. Her heart thudded against her ribs, urging her to *do* something, but what? She couldn't return the way she'd come and she couldn't proceed.

He reached for a decanter of liquor, pulled the cork, and swallowed down the amber liquid—swigging directly out of the bottle. The ease with which he gulped it proved that he was well acquainted with intoxication. He was drinking and he was naked, and she was tempting fate.

Any bad thing could happen to her, and unless she found an escape, it probably would.

Why, oh, why had she sent Mr. Templeton away? Why had she visited on her own? Would it have killed her to bring a companion?

He set the liquor on a nearby dresser, then—stunning her—he bent over the bathing tub, palms braced on the rim, and dunked his head under the water. For several seconds, he was submerged, then he stood.

Like a wet dog, he shook himself, droplets cascading everywhere. Rivulets glistened on his shoulders, streaming down to disappear under the towel.

His hair was drenched, and he pushed it off his forehead, then, without warning, he spun and grinned at her. It was an evil, wicked grin, informing her that she hadn't been furtive in the slightest. He knew she'd been lurking just outside; he knew she'd been spying.

She was mortified and wanted to run, but she was held in place by the mesmerizing indigo of his eyes.

He was incredibly handsome. He had a face that brooked no argument, that would have women swooning and men happy to follow wherever he led.

For an eternity, they stared and stared, and they might have tarried forever, but he shattered the interlude by speaking. His voice was a rich, soothing baritone that made her knees weak, that made her keen to do whatever he asked.

"I am Captain Nicholas Price, Lord Stafford."

She blanched with dismay.

This wasn't the appointment she'd envisioned at all. She'd pictured a stuffy library, uncomfortable chairs, stilted conversation, tea on a tray. How would they engage in a rational debate about the crops at Stafford when she'd seen him without his trousers?

She gave him the fleetest curtsy in the world. "Hello, Lord Stafford. I am Emel—"

He cut her off. "I don't need to know your name."

"Well!"

He grinned another wicked grin. "Are you impressed by me?"

"Not particularly."

"I hate your outfit. It's too dowdy."

"I don't care."

"You're not arousing me in the least."

"Arousing you!"

"Take off your cloak. Let me see what you're hiding underneath."

"Absolutely not! What a rude request!"

"How will you entice me with such a dour attitude?"

"I'm not...*dour*. My attitude is quite pleasant—when I'm in pleasant company."

He laughed. "Don't you know the rules? You're supposed to fawn over me. You're supposed to feign excitement and tell me I'm the manliest man you've ever met."

He *was* the manliest man she'd ever met, but she wouldn't admit it in a thousand years.

"I've never been much of a one for fawning."

"Good. I can't say I enjoy it much myself. Have you looked your fill?" He gestured down his body, as if he'd been deliberately displaying it for her. "Would you like to continue admiring me? Or shall we get down to business?"

"Yes...ah...business would be fine." She waved at all that bare skin. "Would you put on some clothes?"

"Why would I want to do that?"

"I can't imagine discussing any topic of significance when you're undressed."

"I'm not interested in *discussion*. At the moment, I have more important things on my mind. Such as how quickly we can get the dirty deed accomplished."

"I can't possibly proceed when you're in this condition."

He raised a curious brow. "You are the strangest whore ever in the entire history of whores."

"The strangest...*what?*"

He lunged for her, and she shrieked and raced into the bedchamber, but she tripped on a pillow. As she hastened to right herself, he was on her.

He scooped her into his arms and sauntered to the bed, and though she kicked and complained, she couldn't stop him. He dropped her onto the mattress, and he fell on top of her, her wrists pinned over her head, his torso stretched out the length of hers.

While she'd planned to keep fighting, she was astonished by the intimate positioning. She could feel him and smell him, and even though she was fully clothed, it didn't seem as if she was. She yearned to be closer to him in a very naughty fashion.

Her interactions with men had been few and fleeting. She'd never been courted, had never had a beau, so she had no experiences by which to measure what was happening. She should have been incensed—and she was—but she also should have been petrified, and she wasn't.

Though he was obviously a rake, she sensed no overt menace. Her virtue was certainly in peril, though what would have to transpire in order for her to *lose* it, she couldn't say. She was clueless as to the physical conduct between men and women.

Still, she perceived details about him that she had no reason to know. He wouldn't hurt her. He wouldn't do anything she didn't wish him to do—the trick being to snag his arrogant attention long enough to make him listen.

"Let me go," she demanded.

"No."

"I mean it. Let me go!"

"No."

"If you don't, you'll be sorry."

"I doubt it. I've never been sorry my whole life."

"I'm sure that's true."

He untied her cloak and pushed it off so he could glance down her body.

"That is the ugliest dress I've ever seen," he said.

"I guess I don't rise to your incredibly high standards," she sarcastically retorted.

"Are you new at this? You don't have any flair. Couldn't you have borrowed a fancier gown from one of the other girls?"

"Honestly, you are a vulgar, annoying cur."

"Yes, I am," he agreed, seeming proud of the fact.

"And I am not a—"

Her tirade was cut off by his leaning down and kissing her. The same instant, his roving hand shifted to her breast and rested there. The illicit touch made her nipple harden into a taut nub. It nudged against his palm, as if begging to be petted.

His lips were warm and soft, and she inhaled a shocked breath, and it only encouraged him. He slipped his tongue into her mouth, and he stroked it in and out as he massaged her breast.

The outrageous contact was so unexpected—and so thrilling—that for a delicious second, she forgot to protest. Then she remembered herself, her mission, her place, and she yelped and shoved with all her might.

She managed to slide out from under him and scurry across the mattress. Clutching at her cloak, she scrambled to the floor.

"What the devil?" he muttered, his confusion plain. "What kind of whore are you?"

"I am not a whore!" she fumed.

He narrowed his gaze and focused on her so intently that she understood how the soldiers under his command had to feel when they'd committed an infraction. She wondered if she was about to be flogged.

"If you're not a whore," he asked, "what the hell are you?"

"I am Miss Emeline Wilson."

He cocked his head; he scowled. "Why do I know that name?"

"Perhaps because I've written you four times, requesting an audience. We have an appointment today at two."

"We do not."

"We do."

"About what?"

"About the condition of the tenants at your estate. If you'd ever deigned to visit Stafford, you would have discovered that—"

In a fluid move, he leapt from the bed, the towel gripped at his waist. Murder in his eye, he stormed over, grabbed her and dragged her to the door.

When they reached it, it was still locked, and he was so angry that he was flummoxed as to why it would be or how he was to open it.

He hammered on the wood, shouting, "Stephen! Stephen! Get your ass in here!"

She hissed and wrestled, trying to free herself, as he continued to bang and bellow. Eventually, footsteps winged toward them. A key was jammed and turned. The door was flung wide. The man who'd initially seized her—the one with features she now recognized as looking very similar to Lord Stafford's—was standing there.

She recalled that he had a brother, Mr. Stephen Price, who was two years younger. Stephen Price was also in the army. They served together.

"What is it?" Mr. Price snapped. "What did she do? I warned her that she wouldn't be paid if she caused any trouble."

Lord Stafford hurled her at his brother, and Mr. Price caught her.

"She's not a whore," Lord Stafford explained.

"She's not?" Mr. Price frowned. "Who is she then?"

"She's that fussy scold from Stafford."

"Emeline Wilson?"

"Yes. Why is she in my house?"

"She walked in—bold as brass."

"Well, get her the hell out! It's bad enough that I have to put up with her nonsense through the mail. I shouldn't have to tolerate it in my own home. Is this my castle or isn't it?"

"May I say something?" Emeline interrupted.

"No, you may not," Lord Stafford barked.

He gave a curt nod to his brother. Mr. Price spun on his heel and marched down the hall, Emeline's arm tight in his fist.

She struggled with him, but she was too small and too easily manhandled to have any effect.

"But...but..." Emeline mumbled, "I haven't said what I came to say."

"Believe me," Mr. Price replied, "you've said plenty."

He stomped down the stairs, as Emeline staggered after him. In a thrice, they were across the vestibule, and she was tossed out onto the stoop.

With a firm slam, the door was shut and locked behind her.

Chapter Two

"What were you thinking?" Nicholas demanded of his brother, Stephen.

"I thought she was the whore Mrs. Bainbridge sent over from the brothel."

"Did you see what she was wearing?" Nicholas asked.

"I couldn't miss it, could I?"

"Then why would you presume she was a prostitute? She was dressed like a scullery maid."

"I assumed she was naked under her cloak. Or that she'd stripped down to corset and drawers."

"You didn't check?"

Stephen rolled his eyes. "I'm not about to fumble around under the cloaks of the doxies who service you. If you don't like the caliber of girls I let in the door, you can answer it yourself when they knock."

They were in the earl's library, with Nicholas seated behind the massive oak desk and Stephen in the chair across. They were both drinking, and to emphasize his testy remark, Stephen slammed his glass down on the desktop. The loud thud made Nicholas's head throb. He flinched and massaged his temples.

After two weeks of parties that had included too much debauchery and intoxication but very little rest, he was hungover, tired, hungry, and grouchy. He wanted breakfast and a hot bath and a shave. He wanted the mess from the prior evening's festivities removed. He wanted clean sheets on his bed so he could crawl back under them and sleep until the next morning.

Generally, he wasn't so slothful. At age thirty, he'd spent the past sixteen years in the army, so he was used to discipline and restraint. But it was the first time he'd been in England since he'd been installed as earl of Stafford. To his surprise, the visit was extremely stressful, and tension had him acting in unusual ways.

He was no longer an ordinary citizen. People sought boons from him that he wasn't inclined to give. He was fawned over and lied to. Strangers were anxious to be chums.

When the lofty title had been dumped on him, he'd been stunned—he hadn't even realized he was the heir—and the elevated status was like a dream. Or maybe a nightmare. He hated Stafford and had no interest in the riches it had bestowed, so he'd never even traveled there. He didn't care about it, and no one could make him care.

His lawyers had nagged him to return to London, to handle pressing business, and it had taken a pleading letter from them to his commanding officer before he'd been ordered home on a two month furlough.

He'd never previously had a holiday. As a lowly soldier, he couldn't have afforded a vacation, but as an aristocrat, he actually had money to waste on frivolities. He was doing his utmost to enjoy himself, but he was exhausted by the constant revelry.

He owned one of the grandest houses in the city, but there were no servants to attend him. They hadn't been paid in an eternity, so they'd quit and left. He'd considered hiring a staff for the short eight weeks he was scheduled to be in town, but it seemed silly to go to so much trouble.

There were dreadful stories circulating—that he was an uncivilized barbarian—but they weren't true. He knew how to behave; he just didn't want to.

His father had been a cousin of the earl of Stafford, but he'd fallen in love with an actress and had had the audacity to run off and marry her. It was a transgression for which he'd been promptly disowned and disinherited.

Until the very sad afternoon he and his wife had died in a carriage accident—Nicholas had been six and Stephen four—the poor man had never been forgiven by his judgmental kin or their arrogant friends. In a misguided tribute to his deceased father, Nicholas relished the chance to rudely insinuate himself among his new peers. They loathed him, and the feeling was mutual.

Despite his title of earl, he didn't and never would belong in the *ton*. The snooty members anticipated base conduct from him, and he was happy to live down to their expectations.

Wondering what time it was, he made the mistake of gazing over at the window, and he winced in agony.

"Would you pull the drapes?" he asked. "I have a terminal hangover. I can't bear all that merry sunshine."

"You really should clean yourself up."

"If I decide I'd like you to be my butler or valet, I'll let you know."

"This place is disgusting."

"Your opinion has been noted."

"What if Lady Veronica stops by?"

Lady Veronica Stewart was a duke's daughter, the quintessential debutante, a flawless example of groomed womanhood. And Nicholas was engaged to her.

As with so much of his life, it didn't seem possible that he was betrothed, especially to such a beautiful, conceited—very rich—eighteen-year-old girl. She was young and immature, and they had nothing in common, but he had purposely picked her.

In another misguided effort, this one an attempt to avenge his father, he was determined to wed as high as he was able, to throw his low birth status in the faces of those who had been awful to his parents. His marriage to Veronica, scheduled for the end of August, was the perfect solution.

The snobs of the *ton* would forever fume over his having absconded with their little darling. He had climbed over the walls and taken what shouldn't have been his.

"Don't worry about Veronica," he insisted. "She'd never come here. She knows better than to visit a bachelor's quarters—even if we are engaged."

"What if she got a wild hair? What if she grew a spine and showed up unannounced? What if she did?"

"She won't," he snapped, "now close the damned drapes."

Stephen stomped over and was tugging at the heavy fabric, when a sight outside made him halt and curse.

"Oh, for bloody sake," he grumbled.

"What is it?" Nicholas asked.

"It's Miss Wilson. She's pacing out in the drive."

"I could have sworn you tossed her out."

"She didn't leave!"

"What is wrong with her?" Nicholas groused.

"Do you think she's crazy? Literally. Could she be insane?"

"Yes."

"Perhaps she's the village lunatic."

"I wouldn't be surprised."

"Might she be dangerous?"

"Ha!" Nicholas scoffed. "She's too small to be dangerous."

He rose and went over to join his brother. Together, they stared at the petite virago. She spun toward them, and she couldn't help but notice them watching her.

An awkward moment ensued, with Nicholas trying to intimidate but having no effect. Though she was a tiny sprite, her disdain made him feel petty and pathetic.

She had the biggest, prettiest green eyes, and they bored into him, delving straight to the center of his cold, black heart. Under her intense scrutiny, he lurched away.

She was the first and only tenant he'd met from Stafford. What did she want? More importantly, what stories would she tell when she returned to the country?

While he detested the estate, he had his pride. In London, he was working hard to offend, but—oddly—he was incensed at the notion of having his character sullied at rural, provincial Stafford.

He whipped around and stormed outside. Wrath wafted off him like a cloud, yet she was unfazed and unafraid. On noting her fearlessness, he became even more angry.

Didn't she understand how powerful he was? Didn't she realize how he could crush her? How he could ruin her family? With the stroke of a pen, he could beggar her, could have her jailed or hanged or transported.

He never would, but still!

"Miss Wilson," he growled as he approached, "why are you loitering in my driveway?"

"We had an appointment at two o'clock." She flashed what—if he'd been a more superstitious fellow—appeared to be the evil eye. "It's almost three. You're late."

"We do not have an appointment."

"Yes, we do."

"In order to have an appointment, both parties must agree

to the meeting. I've been abundantly clear that I have absolutely no desire to speak with you."

"You have not been 'abundantly clear'. You've been rude and juvenile. I've written you four times, and you never replied."

"Has it occurred to you that there is a reason I didn't reply?"

"Well, of course it has. You're a discourteous boor, but you're behaving like a child. You're *Lord* Stafford now"—she pronounced the word *Lord* as if it were an epithet—"and you can't shirk your responsibilities. There are too many people counting on you."

A muscle ticked in his cheek.

She was very short. Her head came up to the middle of his chest, and she was so thin, a stiff wind would blow her over. But there was an aura about her—of righteousness and rectitude—that made her seem much larger than she was.

She was a veritable ball of umbrage, rippling with indignation over his conduct—and she didn't even know him. If they ever had the misfortune to be better acquainted, she'd never survive the affronts she'd suffer at his behest.

After his parents' deaths, he'd had to care for his brother, so he'd grown up very fast. He'd bluffed and blundered his way to adulthood, and even before being named earl, he'd been spoiled and impossible.

He never did what he didn't wish to do, and he never took advice or listened to complaints—particularly complaints from women.

He endured their company for one thing and one thing only, that being sexual congress. He loved their shapely mouths, but he felt they should be used for a deed other than talking.

Out on the street, an open barouche rattled by. It was filled with young ladies going for a ride in the park. They saw him and waved, calling out flirtatious hellos.

He supposed he was a peculiar sight, dawdling as he was and arguing with the diminutive shrew. He didn't like the image it created: of himself being chastised and not in control of the conversation.

He yanked his furious gaze to Miss Wilson.

"You!" He pointed a condemning finger. "Inside. Now."

"With how you've treated me," she snottily said, "I don't know if I should—"

"Miss Wilson, you've demanded a meeting, and you're about to get it." He bowed mockingly and gestured to the door. "After you."

She studied him, then relented—as he could have predicted she would. He was a master at issuing commands and having them obeyed. Her pert nose thrust up in the air, she marched by him. She smirked with triumph, but he'd drum it out of her soon enough.

He herded her to his library and indicated the chair where she was to sit. Then he went around to his seat behind the desk.

Stephen was lurking over by the window, having watched their pitiful escapade in the driveway. He raised a curious brow, as if to ask if Nicholas was insane, and Nicholas decided he probably was. A brief hour in the irritating woman's presence and he was stark raving mad.

"Miss Wilson"—he tossed a thumb toward Stephen—"may I introduce my brother, Mr. Stephen Price."

"I've already had the displeasure of making his acquaintance."

Ignoring the barb, Stephen was overly polite. "Hello, Miss Wilson."

"She is here," Nicholas said, "to...to..."

He stopped, having no idea what she wanted. He'd never bothered to read her letters.

"Why precisely are you here?" he inquired.

"I've come on behalf of the tenants and villagers who have been affected by the deteriorating conditions at Stafford."

"Stafford is fine."

"You've never been there. How would you know?"

He actually had been there once. Shortly after his parents' funeral, a kindly minister had tracked down his relatives, had written to them to request assistance, but he'd never received an answer. He'd then paid for coach fare, had accompanied Nicholas and Stephen to Stafford, wrongly presuming that the family would relent and welcome two orphaned boys.

To Nicholas's undying mortification, they'd been detained at the gate and denied entrance, as if they were beggars pleading for scraps.

He'd never forgotten how he'd felt that day, had never forgotten the shame and embarrassment of being disavowed. As they'd trudged back to London, he'd sworn he would make something of himself, that they'd be sorry for how they'd shunned him.

Finally, he'd been elevated above them all, just as he'd often envisioned, but to his consternation, he garnered no satisfaction from the outcome.

He'd never returned to Stafford, and he never would.

"I don't need to visit Stafford," he informed Miss Wilson. "I have hired Mr. Mason to manage the property for me. He's had extensive experience, and he sends me regular reports."

"If he's telling you all is well, then he's lying."

"Miss Wilson"—Nicholas struggled to control his temper—"I realize that you have some bee in your bonnet, and it's left you cantankerous, but—"

"Don't you dare belittle me or my complaint."

"I wouldn't dream of it," he sarcastically said, because of course he *was*.

He didn't like bossy females, and he didn't think they had any reason to conduct business. Why was she a *miss* anyway? Why wasn't she at her home in Stafford, tending the hearth fires and chasing after her dozen children?

Obviously, with that disagreeable attitude and sass, no man would have her.

"You're being deliberately condescending," she charged. "Is it just me you don't like? Or do you treat everyone this way?"

Her impertinent remark stirred Stephen's ire. "Miss Wilson, you have some nerve, insulting the earl. We don't have to put up with it."

"You don't scare me," she blithely responded, "and I'm not afraid of either of you."

Stephen looked as if he might determine if her boast was true, as if he might march over, pick her up, and throw her out again. Nicholas didn't want any bickering. He had to let her state her case, for he was quite sure that if he didn't, she would become a squatter on his stoop.

He held up a hand, urging Stephen to restraint.

"Miss Wilson," Nicholas asked, "what is your position at

Stafford?"

"My father was the schoolteacher for thirty years."

"A school! How very modern."

"Yes, it was. The old countess was very devoted to the project."

"What is your father doing now?"

"He's deceased."

"Oh. And you? You seem like a very...ah...bright individual. Have you taken over his post?"

"No." She glared as if he was stupid. "You had the school closed, remember? You claimed you wouldn't waste your money teaching the offspring of peasants."

"I said that?"

"Yes."

"Oh," he mumbled again.

He recollected no such decision and no such comment. He himself had been educated at the very progressive orphanage where he and Stephen had been reared. He was a great believer that everyone should learn to read and write.

Would he have closed the school in such a haughty manner? He was disturbed that she might be raising a point he didn't wish to hear.

"Continue," he demanded, wanting her to finish her harangue, then go away.

"I'm presenting our grievances."

"Your grievances?" He oozed skepticism.

"Yes. We have many."

"Who is *we?*"

"I told you, the entire village, plus the tenants and the servants at the manor."

"The *entire* village? *All* the tenants and servants?"

"Yes."

"So you're some sort of...spokeswoman for the whole town?"

"Yes."

She was sitting very still, her back straight, her hands folded in her lap. A ray of sunlight was cast across her, making her golden hair glow. She looked placid and serene but filled with energy, a Joan of Arc, without fear and ready for battle.

The strangest sensation slithered through him, that by her

arrival, their fates had been twined together. A frisson of dread wended down his spine. He didn't want their fates connected; he didn't want anything to do with her, at all.

"Why would they choose you?" he snidely queried.

"Because I know right from wrong."

"There is no *wrong* occurring at Stafford."

"Mr. Mason is a cruel bully."

"He is not," Nicholas insisted without reflecting.

He wasn't overly familiar with Mr. Mason. The man had impeccable references, and during their sole interview, he had proved himself knowledgeable and competent.

The old earl had been a gambler not a farmer. Nicholas had inherited a place careening toward bankruptcy, with too many employees, too few crops harvested, too few animals sent to market, and not enough income generated.

Mason's mandate was clear—Get the accounts into the black. The large property wasn't a charity, and Nicholas couldn't treat it like one. People at the estate had to be essential to its financial survival or they had to go.

"Since you've never been to Stafford," Miss Wilson taunted, "how would you know if Mr. Mason is cruel or not?"

"I don't need to be there. As I mentioned, I receive full reports."

"I'm here to give you a different view."

"And I've been more than patient in listening to it."

He stood, indicating the meeting was over and she should leave, but she was very obstinate and she didn't move. Instead, she began citing a list of transgressions, and short of walking over and clapping a palm over her mouth, he had no idea how to make her shut up.

She described a parade of outrages—a widow with six children tossed out on the road; elderly servants fired without pensions; the park closed to hunting so tenants couldn't stock their larders with meat as they always had in the past.

She hurled words like famine and starvation and catastrophe. Surely, the situation couldn't be that bad?

Could it?

The longer she talked, the more animated she became. Her cheeks flushed a fetching pink, her eyes blazed with moral fervor. She was pretty and vibrant and persuasive, a martyr on a mission, a savior bent on success.

He was starting to feel ashamed, starting to regret that he was such a sorry excuse for a landlord, when one of her criticisms had him jerking to attention.

"What was that?" he asked. "Repeat your last sentence."

"If you don't rein in Mr. Mason, I've been authorized to inform you that we'll strike."

She grinned, as if they'd been playing cards and she'd drawn an ace.

"You'll...strike?"

"Yes."

"In what fashion?"

"The tenants will plant no crops, so you'll have no income."

"Then *they* will have no food to see their families through the winter."

"You've pushed them to the brink. They're willing to risk it."

"Really?"

"Yes."

His temper exploded.

He'd thought she was a harmless scold, that she would merely reprimand him as if she were his nanny or tutor. He'd planned to humor her, then send her on her way, ignored and forgotten the instant she was out the door.

Due to her small size and her female gender, he hadn't recognized the danger she posed. She was a bloody menace, a radical troublemaker who idiotically assumed she could thwart him with her foolishness.

She'd intruded into his home, had disturbed his peace and quiet, had insulted and offended, and now had threatened.

What sorts of revolutionaries was he harboring at Stafford? What sort of mischief was fomenting?

He wondered about Mr. Mason. Did Mason know about the tenants' plotting? Was he aware that Miss Wilson was in London at their instigation and behest?

Nicholas would brook no rebellion. If Miss Wilson and her cohorts believed he would, she was insane.

He had spent a goodly share of his life commanding men. He'd learned how to mold them, how to coerce them, how to lead them. Miss Wilson presumed she'd bested him, that he would meet her demands rather than suffer the indignity of a mutiny.

My, wasn't she in for a surprise!

"Thank you for your stirring presentation," he mildly said. "Your concerns have been noted, and I will take them under advisement. You may go."

She frowned. She'd expected theatrics, shouting or denials of guilt, so his calm dismissal confused her.

"That's it?" she asked. "That's all you have to say?"

"Yes."

"But if they don't plant any crops, you'll be bankrupt."

"I certainly will be."

"You're not worried?"

"Oh, I'm *worried*, Miss Wilson, but not in the manner you suppose. Please rush to Stafford and notify your cabal that I shall personally arrive on Wednesday to investigate their complaints."

"You'll visit the estate?"

"Yes."

"You mean it? You're not jesting."

"Trust me, Miss Wilson, I never jest."

His easy capitulation had her perplexed. He'd called her bluff, had given her what she wanted, and she was afraid it was a trick. And it was. He would travel to Stafford, but he would never forgive her for forcing him to make the journey.

"Well then"—she stumbled to her feet—"I appreciate your time. I'll see you on Wednesday."

"You definitely will."

"You won't regret this."

"I already do."

Stephen ushered her out, and Nicholas listened, breathing a sigh of relief as the front door was shut behind her.

He went to the window and watched her walk to the street. As Stephen returned, a teamster's wagon pulled up, an older man at the reins. Miss Wilson climbed aboard, and they lumbered off. She was chattering a mile a minute, apparently regaling him with her success. They disappeared from view, and Nicholas spun around.

"What in the hell are you up to?" Stephen inquired.

"I can't let that little termagant provoke an insurgency, can I?"

"No, you can't. Her bravado is galling."

"Yes, it is."

"So...we're finally going to Stafford?"

"We finally are," Nicholas fumed, "and Miss Wilson will be very, very sorry that she asked me to come."

Chapter Three

"What do you think is happening in there?"

"We'll know soon enough."

Emeline heard the men grumbling behind her, and she spun and flashed a confident smile.

"Lord Stafford is here to set things right," she insisted.

"According to *you*."

"Yes, according to me. He promised he'd come on Wednesday, and he has. He'll straighten out this mess."

"Not bloody likely," someone mumbled, and another said, "Mr. Mason's in there with him—alone—telling tales. He'll screw us further. Just see if he doesn't."

Emeline ignored them and studied the manor. They were in the driveway, Emeline at the front of the crowd, with old Mr. Templeton beside her. There were dozens of people hovering, all of the tenant farmers, most of their wives, many of the shopkeepers and tradesmen from the village.

No one was sure when Lord Stafford and his brother had arrived at the estate. Eight o'clock that morning, word had spread that they were present and sequestered in the library with Mr. Mason. Everyone had raced to discover what was occurring and what the result would be once the earl emerged from the meeting.

Emeline's trip to London was the talk of the neighborhood. Lord Stafford was viewed as a rogue and an ingrate, and it was commonly assumed that he'd duped Emeline, that he'd never show his face where he was so thoroughly despised.

Emeline herself had been a tad skeptical. Yet he'd traveled to Stafford as he'd agreed he would. At that very moment, he was inside and conferring with his land agent. She was an optimist and always had been, and she refused to accept that he had come with malicious intent.

If she was anxious, it was only because he'd spoken with Mr. Mason before anybody else. Mason was such a convincing liar, and he would distort the facts so that he looked reasonable and *they* looked like recalcitrant complainers.

Emeline would have to counter whatever falsehoods Mason told, and she was certain the earl would heed her. Contrary to the despicable reports that had drifted to Stafford, he had a conscience, and she would play on his sympathies—regardless of how deeply buried those sympathies might be.

They had forged a bond, and they were allies, both wanting what was best for Stafford. Together, they would move the estate in a new direction. Mr. Mason would be restrained and lives would vastly improve.

She *had* to believe it. It was too depressing to consider any other conclusion.

The door opened, and Emeline could feel the tension rise.

She turned and urged, "Remember—Stay strong. We've issued our demands, and we've warned of a strike. We have to let the earl know we're serious."

"Mr. Mason will have filled his head with drivel." The shouted comment provoked a wave of nodding. "We don't stand a chance."

"Yes, we do. *I* will correct any misperceptions that Mr. Mason has created. The earl is a rational man, and we'll get what we want. We merely have to exhibit a united front. We can't waver."

Lord Stafford walked out, flanked by his brother on one side and Mr. Mason on the other.

The two brothers had dressed in their army uniforms, their red coats blazing against the tan stone of the house. Their trousers were a blinding white, their black boots polished to a shine.

With their dark good looks, tall height, and broad shoulders, they were handsome and intimidating. The earl in particular was magnificent, his sleek hair pushed off his forehead, his arresting blue eyes sweeping across the huddled throng. He meticulously assessed them, making them shuffle their feet with concern.

The brothers towered over Mr. Mason. He was short and

portly, with thinning gray hair, overwhelming muttonchops, and unremarkable brown eyes. He seemed small and harmless while they appeared unapproachable, tough as nails, ready for a skirmish and destined to win it.

As if posing, they tarried at the top of the grand staircase, letting the mob gape up at them. A subtle message was conveyed: Nicholas Price had risen from humble antecedents, but he was far above them all.

It was everyone's first glimpse of the dynamic siblings, and people were agog with shock and admiration. Emeline, too, was gawking, pining away as if she was a love-struck girl, and at the realization, she flushed with chagrin.

For the briefest instant, the earl's gaze locked on hers, then he shifted his attention to the crowd, scrutinizing each individual. He was taking their measure, tallying their worth, and Emeline could sense them standing a bit straighter.

He stepped away from his brother and Mr. Mason, separating himself, but powerfully flanked by them nonetheless. Emeline ignored her surge of panic.

"I am Captain Nicholas Price, Lord Stafford." His voice boomed out over the assembly. "I have proudly served king and country for the past sixteen years. Now I am your lord and master. Do you acknowledge my authority over you?"

Men doffed their hats and bowed. Women curtsied. He was an imposing figure, and it was impossible not to respond with deference. Only Emeline was brave enough to show no sign of respect. She glared, and he glared right back.

"I have been informed by Miss Wilson," he continued as she blanched at being singled out, "that some of you are unhappy with how the estate has been run since I was installed as earl." There was an embarrassed muttering in the ranks—with her name being disparaged. "I have also been informed that you might join in a strike and not plant any crops. Is this true?"

Emeline strode forward. She was trembling and couldn't hide it.

"We don't wish to quarrel, Lord Stafford. We simply ask for fair treatment."

"The old earl was a gambler," he said to the gathering, rather than Emeline, "and he didn't value your contributions to Stafford. The fiscal condition of the estate is ominous. I need you to help me put it on a sound financial footing. I need your help *and* your hard work. Will you give it to me?"

There was an awkward silence. He was tremendously eloquent, a leader to be obeyed, his request for assistance difficult to resist.

"We're eager to aid you," Emeline said, "but we must be assured that our toil is not in vain."

"This property is not a charity"—he replied to the crowd—"and I will brook no insurrection. If you would like to stay, you may, but on my terms. If you can't abide my rules, implemented by Mr. Mason, leave immediately."

No one moved. No one breathed.

After a dramatic pause, he added, "For those who choose to remain, I offer a free bag of seed and a jug of ale. They're in a wagon out by the barn."

Feet shuffled again, then one man, and another and another, shrugged and started off to collect the bounty he'd tendered.

Emeline shook herself out of her stupor.

"Wait!" she called to them. "We haven't earned any concessions."

"Don't need no concessions," someone grumbled.

"A free bag of seed!" a second gushed. "And ale! You'd have to be an imbecile to refuse."

"He's toying with us," she pleaded. "Don't let him win without a fight!"

Mr. Templeton patted her on the shoulder. "He's bested us, missy."

"No, he hasn't!" she implored. "Don't take his...bribe!"

"You did what you could, but a fellow has to recognize when he's been beaten."

"Beaten!" she huffed. "The battle hasn't even begun and you're defeated?"

Mr. Templeton lumbered off, following the horde to the barn. She watched as he deserted her. Soon, she was alone, and she felt stupid, ill-used, and very, very foolish.

They had beseeched her to intercede with the earl. They hadn't known how to save themselves, and they'd pushed her to lead their charge.

Go to London, they'd begged. *Get us some justice.*

She'd listened to their entreaties, had accepted the mantle, and this was her thanks?

Lord Stafford and his brother looked smug, delighted with how they'd played on the fears of the poor and desperate. Mr. Mason simply looked malevolent, and Emeline understood that he would retaliate and that she would bear the brunt of his vengeance. But what else could he do to her that he hadn't already done?

He'd closed her father's school and wouldn't permit Emeline to keep it open. He'd expelled Emeline and her sisters from their home. He'd relocated them to a dilapidated cottage in the forest, and now their eviction had been ordered, the hovel scheduled for demolition.

The previous year, when he'd initially arrived at Stafford, he'd developed an interest in Emeline that she hadn't reciprocated. Her father had still been alive, and Mr. Mason had approached him about courting Emeline. In those days, Emeline had been cocky and confident, naively assuming that the world would continue on as it had been.

She hadn't comprehended how quickly things could change or how badly Mr. Mason would view her rejection of his suit. Since she'd spurned him, his every act toward Emeline seemed executed for the sole purpose of reminding her how she shouldn't have crossed him.

Lord Stafford was arrogantly appraising her. He appeared to expect an indication of surrender, but she wouldn't be cowed, wouldn't grovel. She wouldn't let him see how terribly his behavior had wounded her.

"Will that be all, Miss Wilson?" he snidely asked.

"Yes, Lord Stafford, that will be all."

"Your neighbors aren't quite as concerned as you imagined them to be."

"No, they're not."

"I presume I won't have to hear any complaints from you in the future."

"No, you won't have to."

"Don't pester me. Don't knock on my door. Don't ever again harass me with your frivolous grievances."

She wanted to say, *they're not frivolous,* but what would be the point?

"I won't, milord. I apologize for bothering you." At having to beg his pardon, she nearly choked.

Having sufficiently demonstrated his authority, he gave an imperious, benevolent nod. "Why don't you help yourself to the seed and the ale before it's gone?"

If he'd slapped her, he couldn't have been any more insulting.

Anger washed through her, and she wished she had the temerity to march up the steps and shake him till his teeth rattled. But as swiftly as her fury had flared, it fizzled out, replaced by a desolate sense of betrayal.

Her burdens pressed down on her, so heavy that she felt as if she couldn't breathe. She was just a woman—with no skills or abilities worth mentioning.

The life she'd known, the life she'd wanted for Nan and Nell, had vanished, and she had no idea how to get it back. Was he aware that they were about to be tossed out on the road? Did he care?

She was sure he didn't.

Because he'd kissed her, because he'd gazed at her with lust in his heart, she'd imbued him with honorable traits he didn't possess.

He wasn't the man she'd believed him to be, and the despair she was suffering over her mistake was all out of proportion to the facts of the situation. He was a brute, not a champion. Why had she anticipated a different result?

She was awfully close to crying, and she could barely keep from falling to the ground in a bereft heap.

Mute and defiant, she peered up at him, refusing to be the first to glance away. For a short, fraught interval, he met her stare, and apparently, he was capable of some shame.

He whipped away and went into the house. His brother and Mr. Mason tagged after him. As they departed, Mason glared down at her, his threat and menace clear.

What would happen now? In light of how easily her protest had been quashed, her trivial stand was pathetic. She had no power or influence to wield, so there'd be no stopping any further calamity.

From out by the barn, she could hear laughter and camaraderie, the ale jugs uncorked. There would be hours of merriment, then reality would sink in. She might have joined them, but at that moment, she didn't want to see any of them ever again.

And when Mr. Mason evicted the next family, when people were outraged and they came knocking...well...

She turned the other way, toward the woods and the cottage that would be hers for a few more days, and started the long walk home.

"She always was a troublemaker," Benedict Mason was blathering.

"Was she?" Nicholas asked, not really listening.

"Just like her father. He complained constantly."

"Good thing he's deceased then." Nicholas was being sarcastic, but Mason didn't recognize his mockery for what it was.

"Yes, his death was a blessing in disguise for us," Mason rudely said. "He never should have taught her to read and write. It's made her feel superior."

Stephen chimed in, "There's naught worse than an educated woman."

"No, there isn't," Mason concurred.

It was only the second occasion that Nicholas had spent any time around Mason, and he had a brusque, curt personality that was grating. Nicholas had quickly figured out why his tenants were so upset. It was bad enough for an employee to be let go, but when the words were delivered in such a harsh fashion, by such a gruff, unpleasant individual, it had to be doubly hard to accept the consequences.

They were strolling down the hall, headed for Nicholas's library, when he passed a window and could see down into the drive. Miss Wilson was still there. What was wrong with her? Why hadn't she left? He yanked away, not anxious to view the dismal picture she painted.

He hated to admit it, but he'd been extremely proud of how she'd dared to confront him. She was so passionate, so devoted to her cause. It was rare to witness such blind, potent determination.

He'd known that he could crush her revolt in its infancy. But he was sorry for how he'd embarrassed her, and he was incensed at how she'd been deserted by her cowardly allies.

What kind of men were they? What kind of neighbors? They'd pushed her to be their leader, but at the first hint of conflict, they'd abandoned her.

He was glad none of the spineless oafs served in his regiment. He wouldn't want any of them guarding his back.

In the library, he sat at the ostentatious desk, struggling to focus as Mason spewed numbers about crops and harvest and austerity measures, but he couldn't concentrate. Miss Wilson kept distracting him. There at the end, she'd been so forlorn. For a wild instant, he'd thought she might burst into tears, but she hadn't, and he was very relieved.

If she'd begun to weep, he'd have felt as if he were kicking a puppy.

"Where does Miss Wilson live?" he asked, interrupting one of Mason's speeches.

"Miss Wilson?" Mason appeared confused, as if she—having been vanquished—was so far from his mind that he didn't remember who she was.

"Is she still residing on the estate?"

"Yes, but not in the house her father occupied. I've supplied them with other quarters away from the main buildings."

"*Them?*" Nicholas inquired. "She has family?"

"Her twin sisters, Nan and Nell."

"How old are they?"

"They're girls—ten or so."

Nicholas let the subject drop, and he wasted another hour pretending he was paying attention. Thankfully, Stephen was interested in Mason's accounting, and he asked the questions Nicholas should have.

Eventually, the butler announced the noon meal, and Nicholas was able to slip away. Pleading fatigue, he proceeded to his suite, but once he was out of sight, he sneaked down the servants' stairs and went to the stable to saddle his horse.

It was easy to obtain directions to Miss Wilson's cottage. She was notorious, and the stable boys knew where to locate her.

Though it was insane, he had to find out if she was all right. Strangely, he wanted to explain himself to her, wanted her to understand why he'd behaved as he had. Gad, he practically wanted to apologize. For hurting her. For shaming her.

Except that he never apologized, and he wasn't about to start. Yet he couldn't get beyond the impression that she could benefit from some wise advice and that he should be the one to give it to her.

She was too optimistic, and she needed to toughen up, to be more shrewd and cunning. She had to stop being so damned trusting and gullible. He was a renowned scapegrace. Why had she assumed he'd help her?

She was mad to have thought he would, and he felt compelled to set her straight.

He rode out of the woods and into a clearing, and he could see her cottage. It was tiny and decrepit, with boarded-up windows and a sagging roof that probably leaked like a sieve when it rained. Behind it, there were foundations of several other ramshackle structures that had been torn down, the aged lumber piled in stacks to be burned.

It was a sorry, dismal spot, and he couldn't imagine how she managed.

She and her sisters were extremely isolated, miles from the village and from the manor. There was no sign of a horse or carriage. How did they get around? How did she feed her sisters? How did she support them?

The concerns flew at him, demanding solutions, and he shoved them away. There were many, many poor women in England, and he wasn't anybody's savior.

He dismounted and walked to the door as it was opened from the inside. Two pretty girls emerged, younger versions of Miss Wilson, with the same blond hair and big green eyes. They were wearing identical dresses that had been mended too many times and were too small.

He was overcome by the worst impulse to purchase new ones for them, but he never would. Any gifts would be foolish and inappropriate and most likely tossed in his face by Miss Wilson.

"Hello. I am Lord Stafford."

Their brows rose with surprise, but they knew their manners and they curtsied.

"I am Nan."

"I am Nell."

"I'm delighted to meet you." He gave a theatrical bow that made them giggle. "Is you sister home?"

"No," they replied in unison but provided no more.

"Where is she?" he asked, and a visual exchange passed between them.

"We oughtn't to say," Nan hesitantly responded.

"Why not?"

"We wouldn't want you to be angry," Nan mumbled as Nell added, "More angry than you've already been."

He huffed with fake indignation. "Emeline said I was angry? I was not. She shouldn't fib like that."

"So...you're not mad?" Nell cautiously ventured.

"No. She's being ridiculous."

"She told us you shouted at her."

"I have never shouted at a woman in my entire life. Shame on her for claiming I did." There'd never been a female who could resist him. He squatted down and flashed his most charming smile. "Where is she?"

They hemmed and hawed, then Nan admitted, "She's fishing."

It was the last answer he'd expected. "Fishing?"

"For supper. But she's not very good at it, so you don't need to worry. She doesn't ever catch very many."

Nell asked, "You're not upset, are you?"

"No."

"You won't tell Mr. Mason?"

"Why would I tell Mr. Mason?"

"We're not supposed to fish. It's against the rules."

At his confused frown, Nan clarified, "The fish in the river belong to you. We're not allowed to have any of them."

"Oh..."

"Sometimes, though, we don't have any other food, and we get very hungry. We don't know what else to do."

"Well..." he murmured. His heart turned over in his chest.

"Emeline says there are plenty of fish, that you won't miss them if we take a few."

"No, I won't miss them. You can have as many as you want. I'll notify Mr. Mason."

"Thank you," Nell solemnly said. "It will ease Emeline's mind. She's been terribly vexed over it."

He stood, and he rested his palm on the top of Nan's head, then Nell's.

"Where is the stream?" he coaxed. "I need to speak with her."

They pointed to the woods, and he marched off in the direction they'd indicated, but not before slipping a shiny penny into both their hands. As he stepped into the trees, he glanced back.

They were huddled together and closely studying the pennies as if they'd never previously seen a coin. Perhaps they hadn't. How long had they been in such dire straits? If the fish in the river all swam away and Miss Wilson couldn't pilfer any more of them, would her sisters starve?

Oddly, he was furious with her. He felt as if he'd been tricked, as if Miss Wilson had been lying to him. He wanted to shake her; he wanted to paddle her shapely behind.

Visions assailed him, of future visits to the cottage. Suddenly, he was desperate to improve their lot. Whenever he called on them, he'd bring treats for the twins: ribbons and bonnets and dolls and frilly dresses and...and...

He pulled himself to a stop, and as abruptly as the peculiar urgings had swept over him, they drifted away.

He didn't know Nan and Nell Wilson, and what he knew of their sister, Emeline, he didn't like. Their difficult situation was not his to rectify, and he had no interest in immersing himself in their troubles.

He was their new lord, and he planned to leave first thing in the morning. He'd traveled to Stafford, he'd seen the manor house and the tenants and the farm, and he'd had his fill. The place and people were just as dreary as he'd imagined they'd be.

Only Miss Wilson had brightened his stay. He would scold her for her folly. He would explain a few facts of life, then he'd go away and never come back.

Chapter Four

"Are you stealing from me, Miss Wilson?"

Nicholas stood on the bank of the river, fists on hips, trying to appear stern but failing. Though he didn't like her sassy attitude, he couldn't deny that she was very pretty, and it pleased him to look at her.

She was out in the stream, the water up to her knees, the bottom of her skirt sodden and heavy. She wore a man's hat—her father's?—the brim torn, the fabric faded. Her beautiful golden hair was stuffed haphazardly into it, but the tresses couldn't be constrained and various ones drooped down her back.

She hadn't heard him approaching, and at his severe query, she squealed with alarm and whipped around.

Her fishing pole was a paltry stick, a piece of string tied to the end, and he couldn't imagine what she was using for hook or bait.

From the condition of her cottage, her sisters, and her fishing gear, it was obvious she hadn't a clue how to fend for herself. She was a walking disaster. Previously, he'd wondered why she wasn't married, with a husband to protect her, and the question was becoming ever more relevant.

She had a sharp tongue and quick wit, but she had no practical qualities. She couldn't care for herself or her sisters—she probably couldn't even cook or clean—and he'd never stumbled on a woman who was more in need of male guidance and support.

For the briefest instant, he almost wished he was staying at Stafford so he could provide what she required. Almost.

It was amusing to think about an extended acquaintance,

but he would never pursue one. She was exhausting. She'd slay him with her foolishness and constant speechifying. In a week, he'd be dead from exasperation.

"What did you say?" she asked.

"You're fishing. Are you stealing from me?"

"I wasn't fishing." Surreptitiously, she dropped her rod, and it floated away.

She peered up at him, her gaze firm and unwavering, and he laughed.

"You, Miss Wilson, are a bald-faced liar."

"I am not. Do I seem like the sort of person who would know how to...*fish?*"

"No, you don't, but your sisters spilled the beans."

Panic flashed in her eyes. "What have they told you?"

"That you regularly dine off the bounty from this river—despite Mr. Mason's specific prohibition that you not."

"They're just girls," she gamely retorted. "They're easily confused."

"A suggestion, if I may?"

"No, you may not," she snapped, but he offered it anyway.

"You don't have to do it like that."

"Like what?"

"You can fish from the bank. You don't have to wade in and dampen your gown. Simply tie a longer string onto your pole."

"If I was fishing—which I *wasn't*—I would take your method under advisement."

She started toward him, but her skirt tangled around her legs, and she pitched one way, then the other, and she tumbled to the side. She was about to suffer a complete dunking—could the madwoman even swim?—but she merely fell to her knees, wetting herself to her waist.

She struggled in the current, and he couldn't bear to watch her flail. It was like seeing a turtle on its back. He marched into the water, soaking his boots in the process. Without asking her opinion, he picked her up and hauled her out.

"Don't touch me!" she fumed.

"Should I have let you drown?"

"Yes."

"Your sisters would miss you if you perished."

"They'd be the only ones."

"Perhaps I'd miss you, too."

"You're too selfish. You'd never notice I was gone."

"I stand corrected: If you vanished, I wouldn't be concerned in the least."

"I'm sick of you manhandling me."

"Mind your manners and thank me for saving you."

"As if I'd *thank* you for anything," she complained as he set her on her feet. "You're a menace. I wish I'd never begged you to come here."

"No, you don't. You're delighted to see me."

"You're so vain that I'm surprised your head can fit through a door."

He released her, but not too swiftly. He liked buxom, fleshy, dark-haired trollops, so he'd deemed her too blond, too thin, and not his type, but there was no mistaking the shapely breast that had just been pressed to his chest. Rogue that he was, he reveled in the naughty contact.

An image flared, of her stretched out on his bed at his London house. He hadn't thought the fleeting moment had registered, but apparently, his body remembered the prurient interlude. To his amazement, his cock stirred.

Was he physically attracted to her? How hilarious! But then, he was enticed by any female in a dress. He wasn't fussy, and Miss Wilson's irritating traits hadn't yet grown so irksome that they'd overwhelmed his salacious urges.

She had scrambled up the bank and stomped off. He'd expected her to stop and insult him again, but she kept going. On realizing that she'd had enough of him and was leaving, he was extremely annoyed.

She was correct that he possessed great vanity. He was the center of his universe; he was heeded and flattered. He barked out commands, and underlings jumped to execute them.

They didn't storm off in a huff. It wasn't allowed. The entire world was aware of this fact—except her.

"Miss Wilson!" he bellowed, infuriated to find himself chasing after her, his drenched boots squishing with every step.

She whirled around. "What now?"

"I'm not finished speaking with you."

"Well, *I* am finished speaking with you."

"You may not depart until I give you permission."

"Oh, please." She rolled her eyes. "Just go away!"

She started off again, and he trailed after her like a spurned suitor. In a few strides, they were walking side by side.

"Why doesn't Mr. Mason let you fish?"

"Why would you think?"

"I haven't any idea."

"He's a cruel bully. I told you he was."

"You don't like him, but that doesn't mean he's—"

"People are hungry and crops have failed three years in a row, but we can't hunt or fish in the park. Mr. Mason claims it was *your* decision."

"I never issued any such order."

"I don't believe you."

"So...am I overrun with poachers?"

"Yes, and I've tattled about it, so what will you do? Will you have everyone at Stafford arrested? Will you throw the last remaining families out on the road? Then you and your awful brother can have the place all to yourselves."

She'd hurled so many slurs that he couldn't figure out where to begin with countering them. He didn't care about poaching or Mason or any of the rest, and in answer to her accusations, he chose the only topic that interested him.

"My brother isn't awful."

"You couldn't prove it by me."

"He's actually quite noble. If you had a chance to become better acquainted, you'd like him more than me."

"I'm sure that's true. I'd like any man in the kingdom more than you. I'd like a criminal more than you. I'd like a heretic more than you. I'd like a...*dog* more than you."

She humored him beyond measure, and he laughed again, but his merriment left her even more aggrieved.

"I hate you," she seethed.

"I have that effect on women."

"You're a cur, an unrepentant, unremorseful cur."

"That's the best denigration I've heard in ages."

She halted and spun to face him, an angry finger poking his chest. "This is a game to you, isn't it?"

"What is?"

"This estate and these people. You've strutted in here and tossed around your bags of seed. You've demonstrated that you can humiliate me in front of my neighbors. Job well done, Lord Stafford."

"It wasn't difficult to humiliate you. Not when you act like such a fool."

"I assume you'll be leaving shortly. What will happen then?"

"What do you mean?"

"You're not stupid," she said. "Why are you behaving like this? Why are you pretending you can't see the reality?" She studied him, her astute gaze digging deep. "You don't care about anything, do you?"

Her barb aggravated him. He cared about things—his brother, his regiment, his sudden infusion of cash so that he never had to worry about feeding himself.

But he didn't care about Stafford, and she couldn't make him feel guilty.

He loomed in, hoping to intimidate her, but she didn't retreat. They were next to a tree, and he pushed her back against it.

His torso was crushed to hers—breasts, bellies, thighs forged fast. At the contact, his body came alive. There was an energy flowing from him to her, and he was practically dizzy with elation, as if he'd arrived right where he'd always belonged.

She sensed it, too, and her consternation was obvious. Dismayed, she shoved at his shoulders, but he wouldn't move until he was good and ready.

"You don't know anything about me," he charged.

"I know enough."

"You waltz into my home and my life, and you fling allegations as if I'm a monster. I can't save the world for you. I wouldn't presume to try."

"You don't have to save the whole world. You can just focus on this little corner of it."

She was so livid, so upset and so lovely. When she stared at him, she seemed to see someone else, the honorable fellow he might have been had circumstances carried him down a different, easier path.

Oddly, he wished he could be the man she envisioned, that he could vanquish her demons and fix what was wrong, but he never would.

He was an untrustworthy scapegrace. Early on, he'd learned that there was no benefit to standing on principle or seeking the high ground. He'd scrapped and fought to eke out a spot where he was safe, where he could survive and protect his brother. In the process, he'd discovered that he was capable of any notorious conduct.

Words bubbled up inside him. He wanted to tell her how it had been when he was small. He wanted to describe the horrid forces that had shaped him into such a despicable lout, but he never talked about those dark days.

Yet he couldn't pull himself away. The strange power surging between them was like a magnet holding them together. Though he knew he shouldn't, though it was mad and ridiculous, he couldn't stop himself from bending down and kissing her.

With his bold advance, he shocked her into submission. She inhaled a sharp breath and collapsed against him. He took advantage of her confusion to grasp her waist and draw her even closer. Her silly, floppy hat was in his way, and he pitched it off and slid his tongue into her mouth.

She was soft and yielding, and very quickly, he was in over his head. He recognized that he was, but he couldn't desist. He craved boons from her that she would never relinquish, that he could never have, and he might have tarried forever, but she was wiser than he, and she wiggled away.

"Are you insane?" she hissed.

She wiped a hand across her lips as if to rid herself of his taste. The rude gesture severed any fond feelings, and his haughty attitude returned with a vengeance.

"You enjoyed it in London, and you enjoyed it now. Don't deny it."

"I *enjoyed* it? You grope and maul me—against my will, I might add—and you think I'm happy about it?"

"Any woman in the kingdom would give her right arm to be kissed by me."

"Not this woman. You're obnoxious, and I detest you."

"Consider yourself lucky that I took the time."

She scoffed with disgust. "Since I met you, I've suffered nothing but trouble. Go to London and leave me be. If I never see you again, it will be too soon!"

She stamped off, and he hollered after her, "I'm sending

you a basket of food."

She hollered back, "We don't want your charity."

"I'm sending the basket anyway. Deal with it."

She continued on in one direction while he stormed away in the other. His horse was still grazing in the clearing at her cottage, but he'd have somebody from the stable come and fetch it.

She was an ungrateful shrew, and he wouldn't risk walking into her yard where she might appear and accost him anew.

He kept on toward the manor, cursing his stupidity every step of the way.

"We had services this morning."

"What for? It's Wednesday."

Stephen Price gaped at the vicar, Oscar Blair, but couldn't manage any cordiality. Blair was age forty, fat, pompous, and pious, and Stephen wondered why he'd been granted the living. The old countess had been extremely devout, so perhaps she'd had the temperament to put up with the arrogant buffoon, but Stephen certainly didn't.

"We have services *every* morning at nine," the vicar intoned like a threat. "The earl didn't attend."

"No, he wouldn't have."

Nicholas hated Stafford and wouldn't pay any social calls. Nor would he condescend to chat with someone he didn't like. Stephen at least tried to be affable and make the required overtures, but Nicholas didn't possess the character trait that imbued tact and civility. He'd never waste his time on such a sanctimonious boor.

"He's not a churchgoer? Well!" The vicar huffed indignantly. "I'll have to speak with him about his absence."

"I wouldn't if I were you."

"But he must set an example for the community."

"You shouldn't count on it."

Stephen rose, indicating that their conversation was over.

"Must you go?" Blair inquired. "I'd like to give you a tour of the church and grounds."

Stephen would rather be tortured on the rack. "Sorry. I have several other appointments."

"I understand."

Blair escorted him to the door, and as they entered the vestibule, a woman hurried in. She tugged off her cloak and hung it on a hook.

She was twenty-five or so, thin and pretty, with big brown eyes and luxurious brunette hair that was pulled into a neat chignon. It was a cool, windy afternoon, and the cold temperature had reddened her cheeks with a healthy glow.

As far as Stephen was aware, Blair was a bachelor, so who was she? Blair was an ass and didn't deserve her company.

"You've finally arrived," Vicar Blair snapped with impatience.

"I apologize, Oscar." She smiled, but it was a tired smile. "I was delayed in the village. I couldn't get away."

"This is Mr. Price," the vicar haughtily informed her, "the earl's brother."

"Hello, Mr. Price." She extended her hands in welcome. Stephen clasped them and bowed.

"You were not here to greet him," the vicar complained. "I had to entertain him myself. You are my hostess, but what good are you if you can't perform simple tasks?"

It was a horrid comment, and an awkward moment might have ensued, but she politely smoothed it over.

"I heard that you and the earl were at the manor," she said to Stephen. "It's lovely that you were able to visit the estate. Everyone will be so pleased to make your acquaintance."

"Mr. Price," Blair said, "may I present my sister, Mrs. Josephine Merrick?"

"How do you do, Mrs. Merrick?"

"She's a widow," Blair continued. "For how many years now, Josephine?"

"Almost three, Oscar."

"Her husband's relatives sent her back to me after his death," Blair started to explain, but Mrs. Merrick interrupted him.

"It's an old story, Oscar. I'm sure Mr. Price isn't interested."

At her halting of Blair's tale, Stephen was so grateful that he could scarcely keep from hugging her.

"It was very nice to meet you, Mrs. Merrick." Stephen nodded at her brother. "Vicar Blair, I appreciate your courtesy."

He should have invited Mrs. Merrick to the manor for supper—it was the appropriate gesture—but he couldn't have her as a guest without asking the vicar, too, so the invitation wasn't tendered.

There was an uncomfortable second where they realized they'd been snubbed. Then Mrs. Merrick smiled again and held the door so he could escape.

He hastened to the lane as the vicar poked his nose out and called, "I'll need to talk to the earl about his lack of piety."

Stephen couldn't think of anything more pointless, and with the wind blowing, he motioned as if he couldn't hear. He waved and plodded on.

The vicarage was situated next to the church, the cemetery in between the two buildings. He entered through a gate and strolled the paths, reading the aged headstones. When he was positive the vicar couldn't see him, he went into the church and sat in a rear pew.

It was dim and quiet, and it smelled of polish and prayer. A single candle burned at the front, producing a magical glow.

As a boy, he'd spent a lot of time in churches. The orphanage where he'd been raised was run by a religious organization, so he'd endured his share of services. After he and Nicholas had enlisted, he hadn't had much occasion to visit one, and he liked having the chance to silently ponder.

On Sunday mornings, the neighbors would fill the seats, dressed in their Sunday best, as they assembled to worship, chat, and socialize. He'd never experienced that sort of life.

He was twenty-eight, and he'd never planted any roots. The decades had passed with him trailing after Nicholas, thwarting his worst schemes and keeping him out of trouble.

Now that they were at Stafford, Stephen was so happy. Nicholas loathed his inheritance and had no idea what the words *home* and *haven* meant, but Stephen knew.

He craved the ties that would bind him to Stafford, where he would settle down, marry, and have a family. He'd already sired a daughter, Annie, who was ten and growing up at a convent in Belgium. Her mother had been a camp follower who'd died in childbirth.

Annie would be brought to Stafford, sooner rather than later, which was the reason he'd sought out Vicar Blair. He'd gone to inquire if there was a kindly widow in the area who might have room for one small girl so that Annie could travel to England immediately. Of course, after his encounter with the vicar, he hadn't asked.

Still, Stephen was eagerly devising a plan of action.

Eventually, he would muster out of the army, and he would join Annie at Stafford. He hadn't worked up the courage to inform Nicholas, but he would.

Nicholas couldn't understand Stephen's desire to belong. Nor could he understand Stephen's affection for Annie, and Stephen couldn't explain it to his brother. He'd given up trying.

Off to the side of the altar, a door opened and Josephine Merrick came in, carrying two large vases of flowers. He was hidden in the shadows in the back and didn't want to startle her.

"Hello, Mrs. Merrick," he said, announcing himself but startling her anyway.

"Ah!" she shrieked.

The flowers swayed, and he raced up the aisle to assist her before she dropped them.

"Let me help you with those."

"Mr. Price, it's you. You scared me."

He reached for the vases and put them on the floor as she laughed and patted a hand over her heart.

"I'm sorry," he told her. "I was attempting to make my presence known, but I botched it."

"No need to apologize. I never expect anyone to be in here, but there often is, and when I find I'm not alone, I always jump like a frightened rabbit." She leaned nearer and whispered, "I'm afraid of the dark."

"I won't tell."

With her being so close, there was a pleasant intimacy surrounding them that he enjoyed. He felt as if they were old friends reunited after a lengthy separation.

She, too, perceived a connection. Her gaze narrowed as if they might have met previously and she couldn't recollect where or when. She moved away, grabbed the vases and took them to a table in the vestibule.

He balanced his hips on the rail, watching until she returned. She sat in the front pew and peered up at him.

"Were you praying?" she queried. "Have I interrupted you?"

"I don't ever pray."

"Really? How sad. What sustains you in times of despair?"

"I don't despair," he blithely said, "so I'm never melancholy."

"How lucky for you."

"Yes, I have been lucky."

Not in his younger years, but definitely in his more recent ones. After all, how frequently did your only sibling inherit an earldom?

"If you're not overly religious," she ventured, "I don't imagine you'll get on with Oscar."

"He's a tad...*pious* for my tastes."

"He's very devout."

"My brother and I aren't."

"I've heard that Captain Price—I mean, Lord Stafford—is a bit of a heathen."

He snorted. "You're too polite."

"I've been wondering how he and Oscar will fare."

"Badly, I can guarantee. Let's make a secret pact to keep them apart."

"That's a good idea," she concurred. "I'll shall keep Oscar silent and at home."

"And *I* shall keep Nicholas busy at the manor and far away from the vicarage."

They grinned a conspiratorial grin, and he was struck again by the impression of fond acquaintance.

There was an unusual attraction between them, and it would be hard to ignore it. He'd quickly grow bored at Stafford and would crave female companionship. He was curious as to how she'd view a dalliance.

She was a widow. Was she missing her husband? Was she a teeming cauldron of unbridled passion that was begging to be assuaged? Or was she chaste as a nun? She was a prim, proper lady, and he'd had scant experience with her type. How did a man suggest an affair to someone like her without having his face slapped?

It was probably impossible. The rules were different in a rural village than they were at an army camp. At Stafford, if he so much as danced with her twice at a neighborhood party, a marriage proposal would be due shortly after.

Rudely, he inquired, "What happened with your husband's family after he died? How is it that you ended up living with your brother?"

"Why, Mr. Price, shame on you for posing such indelicate questions."

She didn't look offended. She was still smiling, which he took as permission to continue.

"Would you rather I gossiped about you behind your back? Should I learn of it from the servants?"

"I'm sure you'd hear plenty."

"If I want to know something, I ask."

"How refreshingly annoying." She declared, "It's a very sordid tale."

"Will I be shocked?"

"Yes. Your manly self might not be able to bear it."

"Try me. Let's see how I hold up."

They both chuckled.

"I was married for seven years, but I never had any children." Her courage flagged, and she glanced away. "I oughtn't to be embarrassed, but I guess I am. It's still difficult to talk about it."

"You can tell me," he coaxed. "I have my own squalid past, so I'm not in a position to judge."

"He'd filed for divorce, claiming I was barren."

"What a disloyal ass."

"I certainly thought so, and of course, it had nothing to do with the fact that his cousin had just come of age and she was very rich."

"Oh, of course not," he sarcastically agreed. "I'm liking him less and less by the minute."

"He had the grace to perish before the divorce was finalized."

"Thank heaven."

"After he passed away, I hadn't the funds to stay in London. He wasn't wealthy, and what little there was to inherit, his mother seized." She sighed. "I didn't have anywhere to go."

"It must have been hard for you to move in with your brother."

"Very hard," she admitted. "He's always blamed me for the debacle. The 'sins of Eve' and all that. He says if I'd been a

51

dutiful wife, God would have blessed me with many babies. It's a constant harangue."

The words rushed out of her as if it was a confession she'd been yearning to make. Her shoulders drooped, and she appeared smaller, as if she'd been deflated by it.

"My dearest Josephine," he murmured, improperly using her Christian name. "I'm so very sorry."

Tears flooded her eyes, and he dawdled like an idiot, knowing he should comment but perplexed as to what his remark should be. He couldn't stand to see a woman abused. Should he offer to pound her brother into the ground? To whip him? To have him fired? And then what?

Stephen wasn't inclined to support her financially, and he wasn't about to marry her himself, so he was worthless as a defender. Oscar Blair was her elderly male family member, and he had full authority over her. He could beat her or lock her in a closet or starve her, and Stephen couldn't intervene.

"I can't believe I told you so much about myself," she said.

"I'm glad you did."

"I'm usually so reticent. How could you have pulled it out of me?"

"I inspire confidences."

"Then I'm in trouble, for there's very much I'd like you not to discover."

He walked over and sat down beside her, and he clasped her hand in his, linking their fingers. Her skin was warm and soft, and though it seemed harmless and friendly, it seemed wicked and dangerous, too.

For an eternity, they tarried, not speaking. He stared at the altar while she stared at the floor. Ultimately, she straightened and turned toward him. She studied his mouth, and he was overcome by the strangest notion that she was thinking about kissing him. She didn't, though.

He could have leaned in and done it for her, but he was terribly afraid that he might have mistaken her intent. They remained transfixed, frozen in place.

"I'd better go," she eventually said. "Oscar will be wondering where I am."

She stood and went to the door by which she'd originally entered. As she stepped through, her gaze locked on his. To his astonishment, he didn't have to struggle to decipher her meaning.

Her look was filled with such hot, searing desire that he felt it to the tips of his toes. His balls clenched, his cock stirred, and the holy church nearly sizzled with their untapped passion.

She raised a brow in invitation, but as he rose to chase after her, her burst of bravado fled. In an instant, she vanished like smoke.

Chapter Five

"Remember what I told you," Emeline said to her sisters.

"We're to be very brave," Nan answered.

"And very polite," Nell added.

"Yes. No matter what, we mustn't let him see that we're upset."

Nan and Nell were such good girls, and it broke Emeline's heart to watch as they were reduced by the slings and arrows life had shot at them.

With each step down society's ladder, they'd had their world torn into tinier pieces, but they'd weathered the descent better than Emeline. She supposed—as children—they adapted more swiftly. Or perhaps it was because she was older than they were. As an adult, she'd built a larger store of memories and was suffering more over her losses.

When she'd first realized her father's health was failing, she hadn't grasped the extent of the calamity that was approaching. They had both assumed the school would continue after his death, that Emeline would teach in his stead. The school had operated at the estate for thirty years, and she'd never imagined that Nicholas Price would refuse to keep it open.

She'd staggered to the end, which had finally and fully arrived. She would face it down boldly, unwavering in her defense of her sisters and unafraid of the future and what it might bring.

Horses' hooves clopped out on the dirt track leading to their cottage. They glanced over to observe Mr. Mason riding up on one of the earl's mares. There were men behind him in a wagon, their axes at the ready, a torch ablaze so the fire could be quickly ignited after their home was demolished.

Mason halted in front of Emeline, and as he dismounted, she studied him. At age forty, he wasn't unattractive, but there was a cruel gleam in his eye. When she stared at him, she always had to fight off a shudder.

The smartest thing she'd ever done was decline his courtship, but it was the stupidest thing, too. After she'd spurned him, he'd put her on his vengeance list, and once a person was on it, he or she could never get off.

"Miss Wilson," he said, "why are you still here? You were to vacate the premises by eight o'clock."

"I'm asking one last time—for my sisters. Have mercy on them, Mr. Mason. We have nowhere to go. Please let us stay."

"I spoke to the earl about you," he replied. "In light of your recent rebellion, you won't be surprised to learn that he's declined to intervene in your case. He advises that I proceed with the eviction. He won't support a rabble-rouser."

Emeline shouldn't have been hurt, but she was. She'd convinced herself that Nicholas Price would show some compassion, that he wouldn't throw three vulnerable females out on the road. She had to stop imbuing him with traits he didn't possess. He didn't care about the estate. He'd admitted it, so why would she expect any sympathy?

Yet she couldn't keep herself from sneering, "The earl said that? Really?"

"Yes, sorry."

He didn't look *sorry*. He looked arrogantly satisfied with what he'd wrought.

"I don't believe you," Nan suddenly blurted out. "We met the earl. He was kind."

"He wouldn't make us leave," Nell declared.

"Hush," Emeline counseled, terrified as to how Mr. Mason might react.

"I want to talk to the earl myself," Nan demanded.

"What would you say to such an important man?" Mason snidely asked her. "Would you beg and plead like the common child you are?"

"Mr. Mason," Emeline scolded, "there's no need to be spiteful."

"No, there's not," he agreed. "My apology. Besides, the earl went back to London."

"He's gone?" Emeline foolishly pined. Apparently, a silly part of her feminine brain was living in a fantasy where he might canter up and rescue her.

"As he was getting on his horse," Mr. Mason said, "I explained your situation. He was unmoved. So you see, Missy"—he glared at Nan—"even if you had the courage to speak with him, you couldn't."

"Thank you for letting us know," Emeline tightly responded. "It's better to hear the truth than to hold out hope."

"Yes, it is."

The wagon had lumbered up, the men stoic but prepared to commence. They would chop down Emeline's house, then burn the rotted lumber, and she couldn't bear to watch. She urged the girls down the road.

They'd taken what they could carry, packing three pillowcases and an old satchel. The rest, they'd left behind. Her mother's embroidery. Her father's pipe. Their bedding and dishes and utensils. The last of her father's books.

It was the saddest day in a long string of sad days, and Emeline forced one foot in front of the other, determined that her sisters not realize the depth of her despair.

They reached the end of their narrow lane, and Nell asked, "Where shall we go, Emeline?"

"Let's try the village," she said. "It's market day, so it will be busy. We might stumble on a forgotten acquaintance who'll offer to assist us."

"I have the penny the earl gave me," Nan mentioned. "Maybe it will bring us some good luck."

"Maybe it will," Emeline concurred.

She was silent as they walked, listening to her sisters' chatter.

A farmer came by, and they caught a ride in his cart. He took them all the way to the village square where local craftsmen were doing a brisk trade.

They scrambled down and to Emeline's dismay, the first person they encountered was Vicar Blair.

In his view, people created their own difficulties, either from sloth or sin. Since her father's demise, she'd received numerous lectures where he considered her guilty of a combination of both.

"Miss Wilson," he snapped, cutting off any chance to evade him, "I would have a word with you."

He bellowed in his too-loud preacher's voice so that others would hear. To her chagrin, bystanders turned to witness her chastisement.

Behind him, his sister, Jo, ruefully shrugged her shoulders, wishing she could intervene but knowing she couldn't. During Emeline's tribulations, Jo had tried to be a friend, but she was allowed limited opportunities for socializing. Emeline couldn't figure out how such a sweet soul could be related to such a nasty boor.

"Hello, Vicar Blair."

"Mr. Mason informs me that you were cast out and your hovel razed."

"Yes, we were, and yes it was."

"Let this be a lesson to you."

It was pointless to argue with him, but she did it anyway. "What lesson would that be? That we're poor and could use some Christian charity?"

"By pestering Lord Stafford, you have meddled in the business affairs of men. I warned you to be humble and circumspect, but your vanity controlled you. As usual."

When the villagers had persuaded her to go to London, the vicar had vociferously counseled against it. He'd insisted she was on a fool's errand and shouldn't get involved. How she hated to admit that he'd been correct!

"I was just trying to help everyone."

"And look where it's landed you," he scornfully admonished.

"The earl should have behaved better toward all of us. I didn't mind begging him."

"Of course, you didn't. You're a woman. You would do any ridiculous thing."

"Is there any aid the church could give us?"

"You're not the only family that is struggling. We have no relief funds in our coffers. They've been long spent."

"With a reference from you, we could find a place to stay. We're not afraid to work for our bed and board."

"Who would take you in? You bothered and insulted the new earl. Who would be willing to incur his wrath if he learned they were sheltering you?"

He pushed by them, and Emeline was too beaten down to be angry. He was a pompous blowhard, and his comments had been no more than she'd expected.

Jo came up and hugged Emeline. Furtively, she slipped some coins into Emeline's hand.

"Talk to the blacksmith," she whispered. "He might let you sleep next to his forge for a few nights. At least you'd be warm."

"I will. Thank you."

"And there's a penury line forming on the other side of the square."

It was a spot where the most wretched citizens could wait, hoping for a job or scraps of food. Anyone with any skills already had a position. It was only those with no abilities—or renowned drunkards and lunatics—who embarrassed themselves in such a fashion.

"Are there any employers?"

"Some. There's a man who claims he's taking people to London, that he's sending them on to America for indenture."

Emeline shuddered. Was that to be their fate? The prospect of death and disease on the long sea voyage? Then auctioned off for a lifetime of servitude?

"There's always the poorhouse as a last resort," Jo said. "Don't be too proud to go there. Not if it means your sisters will have a roof over their heads."

"Oh, Jo..."

At the thought of winding up in the filthy, rat-infested place, Emeline's eyes filled with tears. How could this be her conclusion? She'd been so sure she could orchestrate a different ending.

Vicar Blair noticed that Jo wasn't following him. He spun around and called, "Josephine! Come!"

She hugged Emeline again and murmured, "Be strong."

"I will."

Emeline proceeded to the square, to the line for hungry beggars. She was now a beggar herself, so there was no reason *not* to stand with them. Perhaps she'd finally stumble on the luck that had proved so elusive.

She didn't dare imagine any other outcome.

"Where have you been?" Nicholas fumed. "I wanted to leave two hours ago."

"I have something to tell you," Stephen said.

"What is it?"

"I'm not going back to London with you."

"You're not what?"

"I'm not going. I'll join you in six weeks when our furlough is over."

Nicholas stared at his brother as if he were babbling in a foreign language.

"You're staying behind?"

"Yes."

"Why?"

"I like it here."

"Here?" Nicholas snorted with disgust, as if they were discussing Hades rather than a wealthy, beautiful estate in the heart of England.

"Yes, here."

"You're mad." Nicholas studied him, wondering if he was ill. "What is wrong with you?"

"There's nothing *wrong*. I just don't care for London; you know that. I hate your filthy house and the drinking and the parties and the women. I hate living like barbarians, and I detest all the miscreants who have glommed on to you merely because you're an earl."

"Lady Veronica's father is holding an engagement supper for us, and I want you there. Don't force me to socialize with them on my own."

"I hate Veronica and her father most of all. You're crazy, betrothing yourself to her."

"You're just jealous," Nicholas charged.

"Oh, spare me."

"I was able to pick the richest girl in the world to be my wife. You can't stand it."

"She's an immature, bitchy snob. I can't abide her, and you'll be sorry forever."

"I doubt it." Nicholas whipped away and mounted his horse. "Could you at least accompany me into the village? It's market day. I told Mason I'd show myself."

"If you're never coming back, what's the point?"

"People need to see that I'm real and not a phantom. They need to see my face and look me in the eye."

"So you can scare the hell out of them?"

"Yes. If another troublemaker like Miss Wilson steps forward, they have to know with whom they're dealing. I can't have them trying to thwart Mason."

"I suppose I can ride in with you, but it will be to meet the neighbors and merchants. I'm not about to help you frighten anyone."

"You're too, too good," Nicholas sarcastically cooed.

"Shut up."

Nicholas cooled his heels while Stephen's horse was saddled. They trotted off together, side by side, down the lane that led from the manor. It was a perfect spring morning, with summer just around the corner, and the estate could have been a fairyland.

If he'd been a more romantic sort of fellow, he might have paused to enjoy the bounty, might have counted his blessings and reveled in the fact that such a magical spot was his. But he wasn't a romantic fellow, and he refused to take any pleasure in his surroundings.

Let Stephen wallow in the boring, despised splendor. Nicholas was off to London where a rich bachelor could spend his time at more fruitful, satisfying endeavors.

The market was being held in the square, and he skirted the edge, not bothering to dismount. With how his tenants had treated Emeline Wilson, he had no desire to speak with any of them. Stephen could do it after Nicholas had departed. His brother was a much better ambassador.

They reached the rear of the assemblage, and Nicholas noticed that he'd slowed considerably. He and Stephen had rarely been separated, and he couldn't bear for them to split up. Clearly, he was making their final minutes last a little longer.

He might have uttered some ridiculous, maudlin comment, but the strangest sight caught his attention. He reined in so abruptly that his horse snorted in protest.

Miss Wilson and her sisters were leaned against the wall of a building in the company of what appeared to be a group of criminals and rag pickers. She had stuffed pillowcases setting at her feet, and she carried a tattered satchel that was so packed the buckles were straining.

A man circled her, assessing her as if she were a slave about to be purchased.

Was she selling herself? For what reason? Was the woman insane?

Yes, rang the reply in his head. She was insane. He knew that about her. She had a knack for getting herself into trouble like no other person he'd ever met.

"What in the hell are you up to now?" he blurted without thinking.

Miss Wilson flinched as if he'd struck her, and he leapt down and marched over.

"Did you hear me?" he seethed. "What are you up to?"

"Where did you come from?" she feebly said. "I thought you'd already left."

"*I* am asking the questions. Not you. Answer me."

"I'm...applying for a job."

"Really? It seems to me that you're being evaluated like a cow at auction. Exactly what kind of position are you hoping to find?"

The oaf who'd been evaluating her didn't realize who Nicholas was, and he blustered, "Listen to me, old chap, we were merely—"

Nicholas flashed a glare that could have melted lead. "I'm not old, and I'm not your *chap.* Get out of here before I rip you in half."

The man might have piped up again, but Stephen stepped beside Nicholas, and the fellow's bravado waned. He slithered away.

"Well, Miss Wilson?" Nicholas snarled. "I'm waiting for your explanation."

Nan and Nell burst into tears, and Miss Wilson held out her arms. They rushed into them, their cheeks pressed to her dress.

"Now see what you've done?" she frostily scolded.

"Me? What did I do?"

"This week has been so accursedly awful," she said. "Must it conclude with you yelling at me in front of the whole town?"

A large crowd had gathered, and Stephen bent nearer and whispered, "There are too many eavesdroppers. Perhaps we should take this someplace more private."

They were next to a barn, and Stephen gestured to it.

"Inside, Miss Wilson," Nicholas commanded, and when she didn't move, he added, "At once!"

Stephen pulled Nan and Nell away from their sister and escorted them in while Nicholas grabbed Miss Wilson and followed. As he tugged the heavy door closed, he graced her with his most ferocious scowl.

"What on earth is this about?" he demanded.

She didn't respond, but peered at him, appearing young and lost and so forlorn that it would have broken his heart—if he'd had a heart.

He turned to her sisters instead. "What's going on? Tell me."

They frowned at each other, then at Miss Wilson, as if trying to decide who should begin and what their story should be.

He focused on the girl to his right. "You're Nan?"

"Yes."

"Tell me!" he repeated in an imposing way she couldn't ignore.

She fiddled with her skirt, dithering, then admitted, "Today was the day we had to leave."

"Leave where?"

"Stafford."

"Why would you have to leave Stafford?"

"Because of the deadline."

"What deadline?"

"For the rent, silly. We couldn't pay the rent."

"Who said you had to go?"

"You did."

"*I* did."

"Yes. Don't you remember?"

Feeling sick, Nicholas glowered at his brother, and Stephen's expression was grim. He was sending a silent message. *Do something, you idiot!*

"There's been a mistake," Nicholas asserted. "Let's get you back to your cottage."

"We can't return to the cottage," Nell chimed in, gaping at him as if he were an imbecile.

"Why not?"

"You had Mr. Mason burn it down."

"What? When?"

"This morning. He came with some men. They chopped it down with axes and lit it on fire."

Stephen laid a hand on her shoulder. "How long have you known about this?"

"The past month."

Nicholas whipped his furious gaze to Miss Wilson. She'd known for a month! Why hadn't she apprised him? She'd certainly had plenty of chances!

While she'd been nagging and belittling him over his stewardship of Stafford, she'd never once hinted that *she* was the one in the most immediate jeopardy.

"You couldn't have told me?" he hissed.

"What would you have done about it?" she hissed back, finally finding her voice.

"I would have stopped it!"

"Why would you have? Mr. Mason was only obeying your orders."

There had been many occasions in Nicholas's life when he'd felt like a heel, but he'd never, ever, never felt lower or more despicable than he did at that moment.

He'd been to their cottage. Though decrepit and meager, the paltry abode had been a home, filled with furniture and personal items. Yet among the three of them, they had a few crammed pillowcases and a satchel.

The worst wave of dread swept over him.

"Where are the rest of your belongings?"

"We took what we could carry," Miss Wilson said. "Everything else was lost in the fire."

"Everything?" Nicholas gasped.

It was lucky he was tough and strong or his legs might have failed him.

The prior year, he'd set the estate on a course, recommended by Mason, but approved by himself, to get Stafford on a sound financial footing. The people affected hadn't seemed real, so the consequences that were implemented hadn't bothered him.

Mason had described a population of malingerers and sloths. He'd claimed the old countess had been too sentimental,

63

that she never fired anyone despite how frivolous or useless.

But Emeline and her sisters weren't lazy or indolent. They were simply three females who'd desperately needed his help, and he hadn't given it to them. It was a sobering insight, facing the human cost of his decisions.

What kind of man was he? What kind of lord and master? Who would let such a terrible incident occur? He wouldn't treat a dog as they'd been treated.

He and Stephen shared another visual exchange, then Nicholas walked to the barn door and yanked it open.

"What are you doing?" Miss Wilson asked.

"I'm going to Stafford Manor, and you're coming with me."

"We have no intention of—"

"Don't argue, Miss Wilson," he barked. "Don't complain and don't protest. For once, just be silent and do as you're told."

Chapter Six

"I repeat, What in the hell were you thinking?"

"Don't curse at me."

"If I thought you were listening, I'd speak in a respectful manner."

"I'll listen when you stop shouting."

Emeline glared at Lord Stafford, wishing she had his ability to intimidate. They were in his library, her sisters whisked off by Mr. Price to the kitchen for some breakfast.

When they'd still been present, the earl had been terse but courteous. After they'd departed, Emeline had been left to face him on her own, without the girls to serve as a buffer to his temper.

She didn't know how to deal with his volatile male personality. Her father, whom she'd adored, had been kind, educated, and humorous, of sound judgment and good cheer. There'd been no yelling or slamming of doors, no barked commands or furious verbal exchanges.

It had to be exhausting being Nicholas Price. How did he find the energy to maintain all that rage?

"You haven't answered my question," he said.

"That's because you've asked so many, I can't figure out where to start with replying."

"How about at the beginning?"

The beginning? Where would that be? On the day thirty years earlier when the old countess had hired her father as the town's teacher? On the day he married Emeline's mother? On the day her mother died birthing the twins when Emeline was only fourteen?

Emeline had been thrust into the role of mother, so there had been no opportunity to choose another path.

If she'd wed, as was expected of a young lady, she wouldn't currently be struggling. She'd have a home of her own, with a husband as breadwinner. She and her sisters would be safe instead of having been cast to the winds of fate by rich, capricious Nicholas Price.

He seemed to realize that she didn't respond to bellowing. He reined himself in, and she was grateful for his restraint. She was too beaten down for quarreling and in no condition to spar.

"Miss Wilson—Emeline—" he said more gently, "I'm trying to understand why you were selling yourself at the market."

"What was I supposed to do?"

"But to sell yourself to a stranger!" He shuddered at the prospect. "Have you any notion of the sorts of things that can happen to a woman under those circumstances?"

"Of course, I know. I'm not stupid."

"No, you're not, so why didn't you...you..." He threw up his hands, a man out of ideas. "Why didn't you go to your neighbors? Why not the church? Surely, the vicar could have provided some assistance."

"I went to him. There's no help to be had, and no one has an extra bread crumb or farthing to spare. I explained the situation to you when I came to London."

"And I have responded to your allegations." He shook a finger under her nose to emphasize his point. "Why can't I get through to you? This property is not a charity, and I can't afford to support malingerers."

"Such as me and my sisters? Yes, we've been such a *drain* on your coffers."

"When I gave the orders to Mason, I didn't mean people like you."

"Then who did you mean?"

"I meant people who were...were..." He halted, flummoxed again. "Why am I arguing with you? It's a waste of breath. You'll never comprehend my position."

Despite what he assumed, she comprehended his *position* all too well.

The estate, and his management of it, was beyond her realm of influence. She'd tried to make a difference but had been unable to affect any change. At the first sign of resistance from him, her neighbors had buckled to his authority. She wasn't convinced they truly wanted matters to improve. Perhaps they secretly enjoyed their misery, and they were welcome to it.

She had to cease worrying about everybody else and focus on her own troubles, her chief concern being—What now?

Yes, he'd rescued her from the market. Yes, he'd brought her to the manor, but so what? He'd offered to feed them, then...?

Once they were stabilized and walked out his door, they didn't even have a house to go back to. It was burned to the ground. Were they to live in a ditch out on the lane? Would he smile at them as he rode by on his expensive stallion? As he passed, would he toss them scraps from his dinner so they wouldn't starve?

Fatigue washed over her. She swayed to one side, then the other, and nearly collapsed. In a thrice, like the hero he was reputed to be, he swept her into his arms. Suddenly, she was cradled to his chest, but as swiftly as he'd picked her up, he deposited her in a chair.

He stood over her, frowning, his consternation clear.

"You don't seem the swooning type to me," he said.

"I'm not."

"Yet if I hadn't caught you, you'd be an unconscious heap on my rug."

She gazed at the floor and studied his boots. "I'm just a bit hungry."

"Hungry..."

"Yes."

A tense silence ensued, his anger wafting over her.

"How long has it been since you've eaten?"

"Yesterday morning."

"Let me guess, you had food, from the basket I sent you, but you gave it to your sisters."

The basket he'd promised hadn't been received. If he'd told Mr. Mason to have it delivered, Mason would never have followed through. She could have explained what occurred, but why bother? He refused to accept the truth about Mason, and he would simply discount her version of events.

"Yes," she murmured, "I gave them the last of the food."

"Do you ever put yourself first? Or can you only see that others need help but not you? If you become ill from self-neglect, who will care for Nan and Nell?"

"I can't bear for them to suffer because of me. It breaks my heart."

Tears surged and splashed down her cheeks, and she swiped at them with her hands. A deluge was coming on, and she felt as if she might weep for a week. She wanted to mourn what had been forfeit, her dead parents and lost home and lost life. There wasn't enough water in the world to supply the flood of grief pounding in her.

"Are you crying?" He was aghast.

"Yes," she admitted, too sad to claim otherwise.

"For pity's sake, you can't...*cry*. Stop it."

"We're not all as tough as you. I can't always control myself."

"But how are we to carry on a rational discussion when you're so emotional?"

"You're a smart fellow. I'm sure you'll figure it out."

"Emeline," he started, prepared to launch into another tirade.

"If you can't stand my upset, go away. I'll pull myself together in a few minutes, then you can shout at me again."

She kept staring at the floor, and she watched his feet as he dawdled, shifting his weight back and forth. She could sense his exasperation.

He was used to issuing orders and having them obeyed. He supposed he could command her to ignore her despair, like turning off a faucet, but he didn't realize the depth of her woe. She wasn't about to feign false cheer merely to accommodate him, not when her eviction had been commenced at his direction. If she wanted to cry, she would, and he couldn't prevent her.

He pondered and fumed, then growled with frustration. To her surprise, he lifted her up and scooted underneath her onto the chair. He settled her on his lap, her hip on his hard thigh, her face pressed to his nape. Her tears wet his shirt.

"You'd drive me to drink," he muttered, "if I didn't already imbibe."

"I'm sorry."

"Be silent, or I'll remember how much you annoy me."

Instantly, she forgot that she hated him, that he'd been the cause of her difficulties. He was offering comfort, and she was desperate to receive it.

"I've been alone and so afraid," she mumbled.

"I know."

"I haven't had anyone to advise or assist me. I haven't had anyone to take my side."

"Hush." He stroked her hair and back. "It will be all right now."

She didn't believe it could be all right ever again, but she was willing to pretend, willing to soak in the caress of his gentle hand, the whisper of his supportive words.

She might have sat there forever, wallowing in his solace, but she heard the door open. Someone hovered in the threshold, but didn't enter. Lord Stafford made a shooing motion, and as the door was quietly shut, Emeline was forced to recollect that the Earth was still spinning outside his library.

Who had peeked in? What would that person have thought? With reality quickly sinking in, embarrassment swept over her.

"It was my brother," he said as if he could read her mind. "Don't worry about him."

She drew away so she could peer into his blue eyes. She was so close to him, just inches apart, and her pulse pounded.

Though they were fully clothed and naught of import had occurred, she felt naked and exposed. He'd observed her at her weakest, at her most vulnerable, but she'd witnessed something of him, too. He had a capacity for empathy she was certain he'd later wish he hadn't revealed.

"I must look a fright." She chuckled, hoping to lighten the tension.

"Yes," he teasingly agreed, "you're a veritable drab. I've never seen such a hideous sight."

"Oh, you."

He produced a kerchief from his pocket and dabbed at her cheeks. As he dropped it, she assumed he would release her, but he didn't.

The most incredible moment developed, and her pulse raced at an even faster clip. She was perched on the edge of a miracle, as if any glorious deed could transpire.

He eased her nearer and touched his lips to hers. He was tentative, as if asking permission.

His advance rattled her, and she should have refused it, but she couldn't move beyond the fact that he was continuing to comfort her, and she hadn't yet had enough. She was an empty vessel of sorrow and remorse, and he could fill her to overflowing. She didn't have to *do* anything to make it happen. She merely had to accept what he was eager to give.

The kiss was chaste and dear, as if he were a young boy with his first sweetheart, as if she was a treasure he cherished. They both sighed, contentment surging between them.

They were such different people, with very different backgrounds, but they were so attuned. Almost as if...as if...their relationship was *meant* to be.

The notion was preposterous but blatantly apparent all the same. What could it portend? Had fate brought them together? If so, to what end? Where would it lead?

"What should I do with you, Miss Wilson?" he asked as he pulled away.

"Please don't kick us out on the road."

"As if I could. You seem to have the opinion that I'm an ogre."

"Well..."

"I'm trying to be kind and turn over a new leaf." He scowled ferociously. "I'd like to accomplish it without suffering any of your harangue."

"I wasn't going to harangue."

He snorted. "Don't ever lie to me. You're awfully bad at it."

He snuggled her down again, and she breathed slowly, inhaling his clean, masculine scents of leather and horses. He was contemplating, considering her future, and she held herself very still, not wanting to interrupt his musings.

Ultimately, he said, "When we're alone, I'm calling you Emeline."

She laughed and sat up. "You've been thinking and thinking, and that's all you could devise?"

"Yes. And you're to call me Nicholas."

"I never could."

"Why not?"

"It would indicate a heightened familiarity."

"Why would I care about that?"

"You're an earl. You're supposed to care."

"Let me clue you in on a little secret."

"What is it?"

"I hate being an earl, and I'm not concerned over how you address me."

"You should be concerned."

"I'm not, so Emeline and Nicholas it's to be from this point on. I'm afraid I have to insist."

He gripped her by the waist and set her on her feet. He stood, too.

"Come," he ordered.

"To where?"

"Why does a simple command always elicit a question from you? Why can't you just follow me without hesitating?"

"Because I don't trust you, and I naturally presume you're up to no good."

"Which is very wise. You should *never* trust me. But come with me anyway."

He clasped her wrist and dragged her toward the door.

Obviously, he'd reached a decision about her. What would it be? If he threw her out, this was the last time she'd ever see him. A day or two prior, she'd have been glad. Now, the prospect had her unaccountably sad.

"Where are we going?" she tried again.

"You need some breakfast. We'll get you fed."

"Then what?"

"Then...you should wash up. You're a mess."

She glowered at him. "Would you be serious?"

"Yes, I will be. I'm instructing the housekeeper to prepare a suite of rooms for the three of you. I want you here in the manor, where you're safe, while I make some plans for you."

"What sort of plans?"

"If I already knew, I wouldn't have to make them, now would I?"

"So...you're not kicking us out?"

"Gad, no."

"You mean it?"

"Emeline!" He frowned; she was trying his patience.

She flew into his arms and hugged him so tightly that she was surprised he could breathe.

"Thank you, thank you," she murmured over and over.

"You're welcome."

His voice was gruff, as if he was embarrassed by her gratitude. He kissed her hair, her temple, her neck, then eased her away and opened the door.

"She's gone?"

"Yes."

"Her cottage leveled?"

"Yes. Finally."

"I thought we'd never be shed of her."

Benedict Mason leaned across Vicar Blair's desk. They clinked their brandy glasses, toasting their success at ridding themselves of Emeline Wilson. Though it was midafternoon, and they shouldn't have been drinking, they had ample cause for celebration. And when good liquor was involved, Blair was always eager to participate.

Early on in his tenure at Stafford, Benedict had learned that Oscar Blair might preach fire and brimstone, but he wasn't adverse to privately partaking of alcohol. With Miss Wilson's downfall, a hearty tipple was definitely warranted.

In Benedict's world, people were either friends or enemies. Blair was an ally, their connection necessary so they could both get what they desired from the community. Blair demanded absolute spiritual authority, and Benedict demanded absolute fiscal authority. They understood their spheres of influence and didn't attempt to usurp the other's power. Their devious alliance was extremely rewarding, and Benedict worked to keep it functioning smoothly.

He liked Blair to be off guard, liked him to believe they were closer than they actually were. Whenever Benedict visited, he brought a gift, usually a pilfered bottle of the earl's best brandy. That way, Benedict had excellent liquor to swill when they congratulated themselves on some especially pernicious act.

Their latest project had been orchestrating the fate of Emeline Wilson. Benedict loathed her for refusing his courtship.

Blair loathed her simply for being a female, and he abhorred all women.

Benedict wouldn't allow her to remain in the area, both because she'd spurned him, but also because she'd been pestering Nicholas Price with her ridiculous ideas of equity and fairness.

Benedict enjoyed enormous autonomy. Often, he felt that Stafford belonged to him, rather than Nicholas Price, and he couldn't have Miss Wilson luring the earl to the estate. He'd wanted Emeline Wilson to go away, and he wanted the earl back with his army regiment so Benedict could carry on without interference.

"Are you aware of her plans?" Benedict asked.

"My sister mentioned that she was in the pauper's line at the market. There was a man from London offering to take our beggars to the city and beyond."

"Let's pray she went."

"Yes, let's do."

They clinked their glasses again, then Benedict finished his drink and departed. He mounted his horse—well, the earl's horse, but why quibble?—and headed to the manor. It was a beautiful spring day, the road busy with crowds coming to the market.

Those who recognized him glanced away, their fear obvious and gratifying. He couldn't foster a reputation for compassion or mercy. He had too many distasteful tasks to accomplish, and people needed to be wary so they wouldn't argue when he appeared on their stoops.

Only Emeline Wilson had been foolish enough to stand up to him, but look where her bravado had left her.

Ha! Out on her ear, with no friends and nowhere to go. Her plight would be a warning to others: Think twice before crossing him.

He trotted down the lane to the mansion, and he'd meant to ride past the main house and proceed to his own residence, but there were two horses tethered in the drive. He frowned, positive they were the animals the Price brothers had selected for their trip to town.

Benedict dismounted and bounded up the front stairs. As he rushed into the foyer, he nearly fainted as he saw the earl marching down the hall.

The knave was supposed to be gone! Why wasn't he?

Benedict gave an obsequious nod, and he smiled in welcome, concealing his exasperation and dislike.

"Lord Stafford, I thought you'd be halfway to the city by now."

"We've had a predicament arise."

"Nothing serious, I hope?"

"No, I just had to take care of a few minor details."

They were the worst words Benedict could ever hear.

"What were they? Was it a chore I could have handled for you? I hate to have you bothered by trifles."

"I stumbled on Emeline Wilson and her sisters at the market."

Benedict recognized a bog when he entered it, and he stepped cautiously.

"Oh...?"

"I didn't realize her cottage was on the list to be demolished."

Benedict studied Price, trying to glean his attitude, but Price was renowned as a great and unscrupulous card player. No emotion was visible.

"Yes," Benedict coolly admitted, "it has been scheduled for several months. The entire clearing has been leveled, and we're to plant wheat there instead."

"I'm vexed by her troubles. When I'd urged you to implement your suggestions toward solvency, I didn't understand that we would be uprooting *her* or that her ouster would be achieved in such a dastardly fashion."

"Miss Wilson's circumstance certainly engenders sympathy, but she exemplifies the problems here at the estate. She wasn't contributing, and you can't be expected to support her forever."

"I'm not sure my choices were the best ones."

"How so?"

"For the time being, I don't want any further evictions. Not until we've fully reviewed the matter."

"A wise idea. A man should be confident of the direction he's traveling."

"Miss Wilson and her sisters have been given rooms in the west wing."

"My, what an interesting turn of events!" he smoothly lied.

"How long will they be with us?"

"I don't know yet, but I need you to instruct the staff to show them every courtesy."

"I will."

"And I'd like to meet with you. In my library at four."

Price approached until they were toe to toe. He was a very intimidating fellow, larger than Benedict, taller and broader and definitely more handsome.

There were amazing stories about his conduct in battle, about his shrewd ability to lead men in perilous situations. He was a brawler who won the fights he started.

Benedict loathed him.

"May I inquire," Benedict politely said, "as to what we will be discussing? I should like to have the appropriate paperwork ready for you."

"We're going to discuss the estate," Price dangerously replied, rattling Benedict. "We'll be making some changes."

"In what area?"

"In every area."

Benedict bowed his head. "As always, I'm at your service."

Price walked on, and as Benedict breathed a sigh of relief, Price spun around.

"I'll be staying on for a few weeks," Price announced as if it was a threat. "I'm not leaving for London as I had planned."

"Marvelous," Benedict claimed.

"My brother is staying on, too."

"I look forward to a closer acquaintance with both of you."

"I'll see you at four."

Price continued on, and as soon as he vanished from view, Benedict plopped down on a nearby chair.

The earl! With his nosy, perceptive brother! Not leaving! Staying on!

Gad, what next!

Chapter Seven

Josephine Merrick watched the dancers moving through their steps. Their feet pounded down the grass in the center of the square. People were smiling and laughing. A trio of musicians stood on a dais, the fiddler playing a lively tune.

She tapped her foot, yearning to join in, but she never would. Her brother frowned on dancing, viewing it as the devil's mischief, but despite his admonitions, there were some enjoyments he couldn't halt.

It was after ten in the evening, market day drawing to a close. A whiskey keg had been opened, so the event had taken a more festive turn, and she couldn't stay any longer. Her presence would dampen spirits, with revelers afraid she might tattle to Oscar, and she didn't want to ruin the gaiety.

She'd been raising funds for the church, hawking pies and cakes, but the last item had been purchased, so there was no reason to linger. She said goodbye to her companions, and as she walked away, she could sense their whispering.

No one had ever mentioned it to her face, but she was aware that her brother was disliked. When he was such an ass, she couldn't *not* know he was detested.

Did they feel sorry for her? Did they deem her a fool for putting up with him?

She never let on that she was unhappy, and she never fretted over their opinions. Unless she married again—which she would never consider—she couldn't change her situation. Once had been more than enough, thank you very much.

She was twenty-five, but she lived like a nun and always had. Her father had been a vicar, too, and he'd been just as grim and stern as her brother. While growing up, there'd been no lighthearted moments or cheery encounters. It had all been prayer and sin and penance.

Her husband hadn't been quite so severe in his habits. She'd been allowed to shop and have friends and dress in clothes that weren't black. It was only in the bedroom that she'd been chastised. Yet often, she caught herself wishing she could return to those dreary days, days where she could sew a strip of lace on her collar without being called a harlot.

That's how pathetic her life had become! She occasionally missed her deceased husband simply because her world had been less bleak than it currently was.

Sometimes, she felt as if she was suffocating, as if she might start screaming and never stop. She ached to dance and carouse and sing without pausing to worry over how she might be punished later on. A desire burned in her, a hunger to possess more than she'd been given, to have things she couldn't name, and she constantly fought the potent urges.

Bonfires blazed at both ends of the square, fanning the flames of her cravings, and she hastened on. She reached the edge of the grass, ready to head down the street to the vicarage, and she took a final glance at the gathering.

As she did, the crowd split, and on the other side of the square, standing alone and gazing back at her was the earl's brother, Stephen Price. She hadn't realized he'd attended, and he certainly hadn't danced, or she'd have noticed.

Had he been looking for her? At the thought that he might have been, her pulse pounded with excitement.

In their odd meeting in the church, they'd shared secrets and sat in the pew holding hands. Nothing improper had occurred, but it had been very shocking and probably the most illicit deed she'd ever attempted.

She stared at him, mesmerized by how intently he was focused on her, and though it was strange, it seemed that time had ceased its ticking. The party faded away, and there was just him and her and no one else in the universe.

Then the horde closed in and she lost sight of him. In that wild instant, she suffered a frantic impulse to push into the throng in a frenzied bid to locate him, but she didn't.

What was wrong with her?

She blamed it on the full moon, on her advanced age and lengthy widowhood. An attractive man had merely smiled at her, and she was all aflutter!

She whipped away and rushed on, and the sounds of the merriment quickly waned. The village grew very quiet. To her dismay, she heard footsteps on the opposite side of the street, and she slowed and peeked over.

Stephen Price was there! He was shadowing her every stride! When she lagged, he lagged. When she hurried, he hurried, too.

What was he doing? What could he want?

A voice in her mind shouted warnings. She was overcome by the worst feeling that an amazing, terrible collision was about to transpire, and once it did, she would never be the same.

He took a step toward her, then another and another, and she almost ran in panic. What would happen when he arrived?

He approached until they were toe to toe, and he slipped his hand into hers and led her down an alley. She made a feeble effort to drag her feet, but she swiftly relented and eagerly went along. Apparently, whatever he was planning, she couldn't wait.

He halted at a small barn and entered, pulling her in after him. She nearly spoke, but he pressed a finger to her lips, urging silence. He searched for vagrants or a stable boy, and finding none, he proceeded to the rear and tumbled down into a mound of straw. He tugged her down with him.

For the briefest second, she resisted, but a moonbeam drifted in the window, shining on his raven-black hair, his muscular physique, and she ceded the battle.

She rolled onto her back, as he stretched out atop her, and embarrassing as it was to admit, she bit down a purr of delight. He was large and heavy, and she welcomed his weight, though she understood that she dare not show her enjoyment.

The sole part of her marriage that had been tolerable was the connubial acts her husband perpetrated in their marital bed. From the moment he'd first undressed her on their wedding night, she'd reveled in the decadency. But he'd been revolted by her wantonness.

Rapidly, she'd learned to be passive and still as he thrust away, but it had been so frustrating! She'd felt there should be more to it, and her body had agreed. Years had crawled by with her being raw and on edge. Her only respite had been the sporadic, furtive waves of pleasure that shot through her after their more vigorous couplings.

If her husband had ever discovered the peculiar episodes, his reprimands would have been even more harsh—perhaps even violent.

Surely, Mr. Price wouldn't be so cruel? During their short acquaintance, she'd deemed him to be kind and sympathetic. With a brother like Nicholas Price, he'd have to be!

If she exhibited an awkward physical thrill, he wouldn't be appalled. She couldn't bear it if he was.

He began kissing her and kissing her, and it was so stimulating, like nothing she'd encountered previously with her angry, tepid spouse. She couldn't decide what to make of it.

Did people actually carry on like this? Was such conduct common? She had no idea.

The way her pious brother told it, this was how the whole world behaved, but Jo had never seen any evidence. She'd always considered it a depraved myth, the sort schoolboys spewed to impress one another, yet Mr. Price was no fable. He was very, very real, and he was definitely adept at inciting a woman's passions.

His hands were in her hair, his tongue in her mouth, while down below, his loins were crushed to hers and flexing in a steady rhythm. His hard rod was positioned at the vee of her thighs, and she was stunned that he was so blatant in allowing her to feel it.

She was exhilarated, too. Imagine! She—plain, ordinary Jo Merrick—had aroused such an experienced, sophisticated fellow! While she wanted to respond, she didn't know how.

His busy fingers had moved to her breasts. He was massaging them, pinching and twisting the nipples, and she started to shake. Her entire torso was quivering with restraint.

What to do? What to do? The question raced in her head. She couldn't hide her titillation, but if she let go, how would he react?

He must have perceived her distress, for he drew away and frowned.

"What is it?" he asked. "What's wrong?"

To her horror, tears welled into her eyes.

"I'm ashamed," she admitted.

"Of what? Of being here with me?"

"No."

"Then what is it? Don't tell me you buy into that twaddle your brother spouts about the wages of sin and fornication."

"It's not that. I'm just...just..."

She'd had many frank sexual discussions in her life. Always with her husband and always with her being criticized for her failings. So it wasn't that she *couldn't* talk about the topic. She simply hadn't a clue how to explain her predicament.

"You desire me as much as I desire you." He appeared furious. "I didn't misread the signal you sent yesterday at the church."

"No, you didn't misread it."

"Since then, I've thought about you every second."

"You couldn't have."

"I did, so don't play the shy maiden. I've had several glasses of whiskey, and my circumspection has fled. Let's keep on, or let's go. Shall we leave? Shall I walk you to the vicarage? Is that what you want?"

"No!" she said more stridently.

He studied her, his gaze narrowing. He had a way of looking at a person, as if he could peer through her heart and straight to her soul. She squirmed with dismay, for apparently, he saw what she'd meant to conceal. His demeanor softened.

"What's wrong?" he asked again. "You can confide in me, remember? Do you loathe carnal activity? Is that it?"

"No, no, I...*love* it," she blurted out.

He grinned. "That's my girl."

"But you overwhelm me with your caresses. I don't know how to lie still."

"Why would you lie *still?*"

His perplexed expression confused her. Weren't women supposed to be submissive? If she'd heard it once, she'd heard it a thousand times: Sexual congress was for procreation and no other reason. A female shouldn't revel in it.

"My husband," she tentatively ventured, "informed me that I shouldn't...ah..."

"We've already established that he was an ass."

"Yes, yes he was."

"Why would you believe what he told you?"

"I don't necessarily believe it. I would just hate for you to think I'm...loose."

His grin widened. "Listen, if you want to be a tad *loose,* that's fine with me. In fact, I'd prefer it."

"You would?"

"Yes, so when we're alone like this, you're free to shout or scream or scratch or bite."

"You won't mind?"

"Why would I? Your squealing with pleasure is half the fun." He took her hands and placed them directly on his backside. "If you don't participate, I can't predict what I'll do."

It was all the permission she needed. They started in again and, letting him be her guide, she did whatever he did. If he stroked her arms, she stroked his. If he riffled her hair, she riffled his. She hugged and petted and licked and tasted.

Their ardor rose to a fevered pitch, and she didn't try to hide her enthusiasm. She couldn't hide it. She was writhing beneath him, struggling to get closer and closer but never getting near enough.

He opened the front of her dress and pushed at the fabric, baring her bosom. Then—to her astonished surprise—he dipped to her breast and sucked on her nipple.

She'd never felt so wicked, and she moaned and hissed, bucking with her hips, fighting to throw him off. She was mumbling under her breath, begging him to stop, begging him *not* to stop, but he ignored her pleas.

He yanked her skirt up her legs, then his fingers were in her drawers and sliding into her sheath. The instant he touched her, she exploded and cried out. Her voice was deep and low and needy—like that of an injured animal.

He merely chuckled and laid a palm over her mouth. His lips at her ear, he whispered, "You vixen! I said you could scream and shout, but I didn't mean you should wake the whole bloody neighborhood."

"Desist!" she whimpered from behind his hand. "I can't bear it."

"If you continue to raise a ruckus," he teased, "people will think we're...*fornicating* in here."

Somehow, without her noticing, he'd unbuttoned his trousers, and as he uttered the word *fornicating,* he rammed himself inside.

At feeling how big he was, how thoroughly he filled her, she was swept away by another wave of ecstasy. She wailed with relief, with a twisted combination of glee and shame, and he kissed her to swallow the clamor of her release.

"You're going to be the death of me," he said, laughing.

"Why?" she asked when she could speak again.

"Because you're wanton as hell, but you try so hard not to be."

He was braced on his elbows, working himself into her, and she was delighted that he would talk during the event. With her husband, it had always proceeded in an angry, tormented silence.

"How do you do that to me?" she inquired. "You make me so...so..."

"I'm a sorcerer."

"I believe it."

"Let me show you some other magic I know how to perform."

He began sucking on her nipple again, and she exulted in it, amazed and astounded as he kept on and on and on. Just when she assumed she could take no more, that he couldn't possibly hold back, he withdrew and spilled himself on her stomach.

Though flattered by his caution, he needn't have bothered. She'd had seven long years to conceive, and she'd accepted that she was barren. She wore her condition like a yoke of disgrace.

His hips ground to a halt, and with a grunt of satisfaction, he rolled off her. They stared at the roof, and he started to quietly chortle. She joined in, just as softly but just as heartily.

The silliness of what they'd done, the...*wildness* of it, was thrilling. What had come over them?

They were practically strangers. They'd been strolling down a dark street, then they'd peered at one another, and *voila!*, they'd raced into a barn and had rutted like animals.

"Gad," he mumbled, "I must be drunker than I thought."

"I've never had a drink in my life," she pointed out, "so what's my excuse?"

"You have none, you minx."

"I'm telling myself that I succumbed to your wily seduction."

"You loved every minute of it."

"Yes, I did."

He grabbed a handful of straw and swabbed his seed from her belly. Then he lowered her skirt and straightened her clothes. She watched him, mute and contemplative, as questions careened in her mind.

What would happen now? At any other time, with any other man, there would have been a hasty proposal, as well as a promise to confer with her brother in the morning. But the words weren't voiced, and she didn't expect them to be.

He was worldly and sophisticated, had traveled everywhere and seen everything. He was a soldier in the army! He probably tumbled trollops in barns every night. Their dalliance had been a whim for him, and if she alluded to any sort of extended bond, he'd likely scoff at her provincial notions.

Out in the alley, a pair of drunks staggered by. They were singing, their speech slurred. Mr. Price pulled her close, not breathing, until they'd passed on.

On hearing their noisy carousing, reality crashed down with a vengeance.

How long had she dawdled? What time was it? What if Oscar was awake when she entered the house? There'd be no way to conceal her transgression. Her hair was down, her cheeks reddened from the rub of Mr. Price's whiskers, and—she was certain—she'd be glowing.

Oscar wouldn't have to guess at her behavior. It would be obvious.

"I'd better go," she murmured.

"Will your brother be waiting up for you?"

"No, he went to bed ages ago."

She prayed it was true.

"Still, you'd best be careful."

"I will be."

His cool remark dashed any lingering hopes she might have had as to whether terms like *courtship* or *connection* would be mentioned. Their encounter had been an impetuous, immoral romp but naught more.

He rose and tugged her to her feet, then he crept to the door and peeked out. Seeing no one, he urged her through.

He was extremely composed, as if nothing extraordinary

had occurred, so she tried to match his aplomb, which was difficult. Her life had been turned upside down. She was reeling with elation, with worries over the present and the future, but then, she was a female, and she understood that men were rarely bothered by such concerns.

She scooted by him, and he clasped her wrist.

"We have to do this again," he vehemently whispered.

"You're mad. It's too dangerous."

"I'll only be at Stafford for six weeks. I'm not about to avoid you."

"I wouldn't want that."

"And if I bump into you, I know what will transpire." He pointed to the pile of straw where they'd frolicked. "I'll have to have you. We enjoy a strong attraction, and I'm not about to fight it."

"It would be impossible."

"We'll be discreet," he insisted. "We'll find a way to be together."

"Yes, we will," she agreed, even though it was insane. The village was too small, the chances for discovery too great. Yet at the moment, she didn't, didn't, didn't care. She yearned to twirl in circles and proclaim her happiness to the world.

He kissed her a final time, hard and fast then, with a hand on her rear, he pushed her out.

She tarried, gazing at him, anxious to speak but aware that she couldn't. She wanted to...*thank* him for choosing her, for singling her out, for showing her how it felt to truly be a woman. But she was quite sure he wouldn't wish to hear her gushing.

Boldly, she stepped to him and initiated a final kiss of her own, then she hurried away. She liked to imagine that he followed her to the vicarage, watching so that she arrived safely, but she didn't glance around to check.

She slipped into the vestibule and tiptoed to her room with no one being the wiser as to what she'd done.

Chapter Eight

Emeline walked down the hall to the earl's library. It was very late, and everyone abed—except for herself and, hopefully, Lord Stafford. She had to speak with him, and until she did, she'd never be able to sleep. Her thoughts were too scattered, her anxiety too extreme.

Since he'd brought her home earlier that morning, she hadn't seen him. He was supposedly still on the premises, but he'd been noticeably absent.

She was so insignificant that it would be easy for him to forget about her. If he departed for London before her situation was resolved, she couldn't predict what would happen. She would be at the mercy of Benedict Mason again, and the prospect was terrifying.

The earl had said he would make *plans* for her, but what kind? The answer was becoming more urgent.

She'd applied for numerous teaching positions in other areas of the country, but with scant success. Another rejection letter had arrived that afternoon, so there remained only two employers who hadn't replied. She wasn't optimistic.

Why not continue the school at Stafford? It was the obvious solution to her finding a job. She was determined to plead her case to Nicholas Price. She had a knack for persuading him. Could she work her magic once more?

She hurried to the library and peeked inside, but he wasn't there, so she returned to the stairs and climbed. On the landing, when she would have headed in one direction, she stared the other way. At the end of the long hall, a door was open, and a candle had been left burning. Should she blow it out?

It wasn't the earl's suite—that was up on the top floor—so she couldn't guess who would be there, and she didn't imagine anybody was. There were no other guests in the house.

She crept toward it, listening for sounds, but not hearing any. Suddenly, a glass shattered, and she jumped with alarm.

"Emeline?" a familiar male voice barked. When she didn't respond, he growled, "Miss Wilson! I'm talking to you. Get your ass in here."

She sidled over and peered in. "How did you know it was me?"

"I'd know that snotty stride anywhere."

He was in a sitting room, the bedchamber behind him, and slouched in a chair over by the hearth. A robe covered his shoulders, but the lapels drooped, his naked chest visible. He had on a pair of trousers, but they were made from a flowing fabric that draped across his thighs, the sort of garment a sultan might wear when entertaining his harem.

His feet were bare, his thick hair loose around his nape. He hadn't shaved, so his cheeks were darkened with stubble. He looked decadent and dangerous, and on seeing him, butterflies swarmed in her stomach.

He'd been drinking. There was a decanter of liquor on a table next to him. For some reason, he'd flung his glass at the fireplace. It had splintered, creating a mess that a servant would have to clean up. He was horridly spoiled; she couldn't envision him doing it himself.

"What is wrong with you?" she berated him.

"Close the door," was his reply.

"No."

"Close it!"

"No!"

She went over and picked up the larger chunks of broken glass, tossing them into the flames so that the idiot wouldn't cut his feet when he stumbled drunkenly to bed.

"Stop that," he ordered.

"Stop what?"

"You're not a maid, and you're not my wife. You don't have to tidy up after me."

"Why are you imbibing all alone and smashing the crystal?"

"None of your damn business."

He reached for the decanter, and she snatched it away and set it on the mantle.

"Give me that."

"You've had enough."

"You're not my mother, either. Don't lecture me."

"You're acting like a barbarian."

"I'm not acting. I *am* a barbarian."

"I believe you."

She stood in front of him, dithering over how to proceed. She didn't suppose she should leave him to his own devices, but she wasn't keen to dawdle while he grumbled and grouched.

"Don't scowl at me like that," he griped.

"Like what?"

"Like you're a cranky governess about to rap my knuckles."

"Somebody should tell you how to behave."

"Well, it's not going to be you, so don't try."

"You haven't answered my question," she reminded him.

"What was it?"

"Why are you in here? Why aren't you up in the earl's suite?"

"I let my brother have it."

"Why?"

"He enjoys the pomp and circumstance of this place, and he can have it. I wish to hell he'd been born first. Then I wouldn't have to bother with any of this nonsense."

She studied him, curious as to why he always seemed so unhappy. He'd grown up in an orphanage, but now, he was incredibly wealthy. Any sane man would celebrate such a turn of fortune, but not *him.*

"I see what's happening," she scolded. "You pity yourself."

"Why would I pity myself?"

"Because you're rich and powerful, and you don't think you deserve to have had so much affluence showered on you. You feel guilty."

"I didn't deserve it, but I don't feel guilty. This whole burden got dumped on me. I didn't ask for it. It just...*is.*"

"Quit moping. It's unbecoming."

He narrowed his gaze. "Was there something you needed?"

"Yes, actually. A favor."

"No."

"You didn't hear what it is."

"I don't care what it is. My answer is still *no.*"

She ignored him and forged ahead. "If you would—"

"Emeline, I said *no.*"

"You're being rude and ridiculous."

"And you're not?"

"I have a great idea," she insisted, "and we'll both benefit."

"I don't see how."

She threw up her arms in exasperation. "You don't even know what I'm going to say."

"I don't need to know. Since you're excited about it, I'm sure it will be absurd."

She pulled up a chair and seated herself. "I want you to start the school again, and I want you to hire me as the teacher."

"Do you ever stop?"

"No. This is the perfect plan. You wouldn't even have to pay me. You could remunerate me simply by letting me have another cottage."

"You'd toil away for no salary? Just for your lodging?"

"Yes."

"You wouldn't have any funds. How would you buy food for your sisters?"

"I'll find a way. I can take in laundry or raise chickens. I'm a hard worker."

"I've seen how you managed previously. You're completely incompetent."

"But I'm so good at teaching! I realize you hated the school, but—"

"I've never been asked about it."

She frowned. "Mr. Mason told me that you specifically ordered it shut down."

"I've never discussed it with him."

Emeline was puzzled. Mr. Mason had been very clear: He'd mentioned the subject to the earl, and the earl had said *absolutely not.* Yet now, the earl was claiming he and Mason had never conferred over it.

They were both liars, so who was she to believe?

She pressed on. "Let me tell you why it's important."

"No. Have you any clue as to how much money you've already cost me?"

She gaped at him. Was he grousing over the meals she and her sisters had eaten? Was he angry that they were sleeping in his beds and the sheets would have to be washed?

"How have I cost you anything?"

"I've halted the evictions."

"You have? Really?"

"Yes, but just for the time being. I may resume them in the future—after I've had more opportunity to reflect. Any losses I incur are all your fault."

"My fault?"

"You nagged until I couldn't bear your rants. I did it merely to silence you."

"I don't care what the reason. I'm just so glad."

"Mr. Mason is livid."

"I'll bet he is."

"He says you're a menace, and I shouldn't listen to you."

"Aren't you in charge?"

"Nominally."

"I'm proud of you. You did what was right for your tenants."

She was delighted to have goaded him to benevolence. What other boons might she be able to garner?

"So...about the school," she started again.

"Enough about your stupid school! Close the door."

He waved at it, expecting her to leap up and obey.

"I'm not about to be sequestered with you. People will talk."

"What people? In case you haven't noticed, everyone is asleep but us. We can do whatever we want."

He stood, suddenly seeming much more sober than she'd assumed. Before she grasped his intent, he marched over and shut the door himself. He leaned against the wood, arms crossed over his chest, blocking any egress.

"Open it!" she demanded. "At once."

"No."

She stomped over until they were toe to toe, and she shivered, but not with dread. A part of her—a very small part—was thrilled by his autocratic manner. She knew what it was like to be held by him, to be kissed by him, and she'd enjoy having either occur. Just so long as she kept her wits about her and didn't get carried away, which was definitely a problem.

Where he was concerned, it was entirely possible that she might misbehave.

"Mr. Mason informs me," he told her, "that your father was much too lenient in how he reared you."

"Mr. Mason hates me, and he has a few issues with the truth."

"He advises that you were educated far beyond what was required, and it's made you overly vain. If you ask me, a conceited female is an insufferable female."

"I didn't ask you."

"I cite your extensive learning so you can understand why this mission of yours, to revive the school, means naught to me." His lazy gaze meandered down her torso. "You have only one thing to offer that's of any value whatsoever."

"What would that be?"

Nervously, she bit her bottom lip, capturing his hot attention.

"I'm trapped at Stafford," he complained, "because of you."

"Because of me?"

"Yes, you've pestered me 'til I can't escape."

"You're not...*trapped*. You should welcome the chance to spend some time here."

"No, I'm trapped, and I can't predict when I'll be able to flee." He took a step toward her, and she took a step back. "I get bored easily, so I'll need to be entertained. You're responsible for my confinement, so I've decided that *you* will do the entertaining."

"What sort of entertaining did you have in mind?"

"You know what sort."

His focus dropped to her breasts and remained there, and though she was fully clothed, she felt naked and much too exposed.

"You're being absurd."

"No, I'm being perfectly rational."

"You must have...*women* for that type of endeavor."

"Not here."

"Find some. Import some."

"No, it has to be you, I'm afraid."

"I refuse."

"It's not up to you. It's up to me, and if you please me, Emeline, perhaps I'll reconsider your school."

"You liar. You never would. I'd sacrifice myself on the altar of your lust, and I'd have nothing to show for it but my total ruination."

"The altar of my lust?"

He laughed and laughed, and she couldn't help but note how handsome he was when he relaxed. He was always good looking, but in a stark, severe way. Merriment lightened his eyes and smoothed the worry lines around his mouth. He appeared younger, friendly, contented.

"You humor me beyond measure," he said.

"I'm glad to be of assistance."

"But I'm tired of this game I let you play."

"I haven't been playing any games."

"Yes, you have been, and you've distracted me so thoroughly, I forgot that *I* get to set the rules."

"What rules? How can you—"

"Emeline?"

"Yes?"

"You talk too much."

As if she were a bag of flour, he clasped her waist, tossed her over his shoulder, and marched to the bedchamber.

Nicholas wasn't sure what he was doing.

Emeline was hissing and kicking, her fists pounding his back, and the bed was approaching.

He threw her onto the mattress and fell on her before she could scramble away. Was he about to ravish her? Was that his plan?

He didn't think so, but he couldn't stop himself from careening down that road.

From the moment she'd stormed into his life, she'd been an enormous headache. If he wasn't fighting with her, he was dealing with the catastrophes she'd stirred. If they weren't bickering over his failings, he was putting out the rebellions she'd ignited.

He brooded over her constantly, as if she were a gnat lodged in his brain, or maybe a fatal disease that would eventually kill him. He ceaselessly obsessed: Where was she? What was she up to? What calamity would she next wreak?

She had an unlimited capacity for mischief, so she couldn't be left to flounder on her own. She needed watching, and he was disturbed to discover that he wanted to be the man who did the watching.

He'd had too much to drink, so it was likely that he was making bad decisions, but she was the cause of his inebriation.

By her flogging him with her penury, she'd harassed him until he was conflicted over his actions at Stafford. He didn't walk around second-guessing himself. He chose a course and moved forward. Yet what if he'd been wrong? What if he'd relied on Mason's advice when he shouldn't have?

When he thought of that quiet interlude in his library, as she'd wept on his shoulder...

He pushed the poignant vision out of his mind.

If he wanted anything from Emeline Wilson, it was what he wanted from all women—carnal relations. He didn't want to understand her or feel sorry for her or create a bond.

He was keen to have sex with her, but she was a maiden, living under his protection and control. Despite his low reputation, he wasn't such a brute that he would force her into an affair.

There was no benefit for her to participate. The estate was a small, close-knit community where marriage was the remedy for illicit conduct, but he would never wed her. Gad, he *couldn't* wed her. He was engaged to Lady Veronica, a union he would pursue at all costs.

So what was his intent?

He was too muddled to figure it out. He would dally and let what happened happen.

It was the cad's way out, but he didn't care. If he acted horridly, he'd get over it. He was always able to justify his reprehensible gaffes, and vaguely, he recalled telling her she should never trust him.

She'd been a fool to search him out in the middle of the night. If she started a fire and was burned by the flames, why was that his fault?

"Lord Stafford," she said, already complaining. Did the blasted woman ever cease?

"Nicholas, remember?"

"Would you release me?"

"No."

"Please?"

"No."

"What do you want from me?"

He frowned. "How old are you?"

"Twenty-four."

"At your advanced age, why would you have to ask?"

"Advanced!" she huffed, insulted.

"Haven't you ever been tumbled before? Or are you so prim and forbidding that no man has dared?"

"I'm not prim and forbidding."

Her face scrunched up like a prudish prune, and he laughed again.

He'd never met a female like her. She was such a rare creature—bright and beautiful and belligerent—and he was absolutely fascinated.

"Would you for once," he said, "be quiet and enjoy yourself?"

"I can't enjoy myself. I'm terrified over what you're about to do."

"What I'm about to *do* is what some fellow should have done years ago."

"What are you talking about?"

"You need a man in your bed like nobody's business. We'll work off some of that piss and vinegar that has you all bottled up."

He gazed at her, and their connection sparked. It had flared previously, so he recognized that they shared a physical attraction, but this seemed to be something more, something profound and deep that scared the hell out of him.

He didn't form attachments with women, and he most certainly didn't succumb to romantic inclinations. Was that what was blossoming? A romantic affection?

The notion didn't bear contemplating.

He had to focus on what mattered. Bed play was where he was most comfortable, where he knew how to behave and what to expect.

He leaned down and kissed her. For the briefest instant,

she stiffened in protest, then she relaxed and let him proceed.

His loins were pressed to hers and flexing in a slow rhythm, and very quickly, he'd traveled far past any safe point. He unbuttoned her gown and tugged at the fabric, exposing her to the waist, but she was so absorbed that she wasn't aware of what he'd done.

Though she didn't realize it, she had a very sexual nature, so it was easy to distract her. It was only as he caressed her bosom, bare skin to bare skin, that she gasped with surprise and tried to squirm away.

Her breasts were pert and round, the tips pink and inviting. He'd thought he preferred large-busted females, but apparently not. Her slim perfection aroused him in incalculable ways.

"You can't remove my clothes," she insisted.

"If I don't undress you, how will we have any fun?"

"Kissing I can do. Kissing I understand. Not the...other." She waved a hand over her torso, not possessing the vocabulary for salacious discussion.

She was yanking at her bodice, anxious to shield herself, but he wouldn't allow her to hide.

"Why are you always attired in gray and black?" he asked.

"Because I'm poor, you oaf, so I can't afford anything else. Besides, why would I need fancier garments? All I do is putter about the estate, trying to feed my sisters. That sort of existence doesn't exactly require frippery."

"How about wearing bright colors merely to look pretty?"

"Oh, yes," she sarcastically retorted, "personal grooming is my biggest worry."

"I think I'll buy you a new gown, just to see how fetching you can be. It might improve your mood."

"You're being ridiculous, and I wish you wouldn't—"

He bent down and sucked on her nipple.

"My goodness," she breathed.

"Hasn't any man ever touched you like this?"

"No, when would anyone have?"

"I'm the first?"

"Of course you're the first."

"Let me show you something."

"I'd rather you didn't."

"Let me show you anyway."

Working her skirt up her leg, his fingers were at her thigh, her hip, and he slipped them into her drawers. As he slid them into her sheath, he was delighted to find her wet and ready.

He smirked. The prospect of staying at Stafford was dreadful, but he'd stumbled on the ideal way to amuse himself. Emeline would provide hours of raucous, ribald diversion.

He stroked back and forth, back and forth, and she fought the deluge that was coming.

"What are you doing?" she asked.

"You don't know?"

"No, you lout! I don't know."

"Almost there," he coaxed.

He flicked with his thumb as he laved her nipple, and immediately, she was pitched into a potent orgasm. She shrieked with astonishment, making such a ruckus that he had to kiss her to swallow the sound. He held her as she spiraled up, then down, and as her ecstasy waned, he was on the verge of ravishment.

Typically, his base impulses were effortlessly controlled, yet with her, he was so titillated that he was about to violently take her against her will. He refused to hurt or scare her. She had to be eased into the notion of surrendering her virginity, so they could spend weeks satisfying their mutual passion.

If he acted like a bully, he would wreck their affair before it began.

Drawing away, he covered her with a blanket so he couldn't view what was driving him wild.

He rolled over and stared at the ceiling, struggling to calm the lust pounding through his veins. He had to get a grip on his riotous ardor, on his urge to have her at any cost. Then he would start in again.

"What was that?" she inquired.

"What was what?"

"What you did to me..." She looked very young, very innocent. "What was that?"

"It was sexual pleasure."

"Am I all right?"

"You're more than all right. In fact, you're magnificent."

"Am I still a...a...virgin?"

"Yes."

"Am I...pregnant now?"

Her naïveté was humorous, and he nearly chided her for it, but at realizing how inexperienced she was, he felt like the worst libertine. Why was he taking advantage of her?

He'd never lain with a female who was so clueless about carnal matters. He dabbled with whores and doxies who knew what he wanted and how to accomplish it without any fuss. He'd forgotten that there were women like Emeline, women who were chaste and virtuous and uncorrupted.

The poor thing! Having to endure his callous seduction! He was a ruthless, unprincipled bounder, and she'd rue the day they'd crossed paths.

He shifted onto his side, and she shifted, too, so they were facing each other. She peered at him, wide-eyed with shock.

"No, you're not pregnant," he said.

"How does it happen?"

"It begins with what we just did, but there's quite a bit more to it. Perhaps I'll show you some time"—he grinned—"if you're very, very nice to me."

"As if I'd let you do that to me again!"

"You liked it. Don't deny it."

"You overwhelm my better sense. If I'm not careful, there's no telling what I might allow."

"Lucky me," he murmured, and a wave of tenderness swept over him. His heart made the oddest flip-flopping motion, as if it had grown too large and didn't fit under his ribs.

"I should leave," she said.

"In a minute."

He pulled her to him, his arm holding her close, her cheek pressed to his chest.

He was comforted by the scent of her, by the warmth of her skin nestled to his. Before he knew it, inebriation took its toll, and he dozed.

When he woke, it was morning, and she was gone, with not so much as a hint in the room that she'd been there at all.

Chapter Nine

"I have a letter from your father."

"Really?"

Annie Price jumped up and down and clapped her hands, then she remembered herself. They were seated in Mother Superior's office, a small room where the elderly nun conducted business. It wasn't the sort of spot to encourage displays of enthusiasm.

The convent was a very quiet place, and the Sisters of Mercy a very quiet group. None had taken a vow of silence, but they didn't laugh with joy or shout with anger.

Annie was never scolded for her outbursts, but her emotions often flared in ways that startled everyone.

She struggled to contain her excitement. "A letter! How wonderful."

"He and your uncle have traveled to Stafford."

"Finally!"

She and the nun smiled. Her father had regaled her with stories of her Uncle Nicholas's good fortune. It was like a fairytale—the poor orphan boy picked from the crowd and raised up to live with kings.

Annie and the nuns had avidly followed the proceedings as if they were part of it, and they were—after a fashion. As her father grew richer, he would pay more money for Annie's expenses, so the Stafford earldom represented a huge benefit for all concerned.

Her father kept insisting that he was about to send for her, so that they could be together, but that day never arrived. When he'd first suggested it, she'd assumed he meant immediately, but as month had turned to year, she'd realized a hard truth—

the chances were great that it would never transpire.

Now, whenever he talked about how he was making *plans*, she would nod and reply with all the appropriate remarks, but she no longer expected any changes.

At age ten, she wasn't a little girl anymore, and she didn't believe in happy endings. If she ultimately wound up with her father, she would be glad, but she wouldn't pin any hopes on him.

"Does he describe the estate?" she asked.

"He says it's very beautiful and even more grand than he'd envisioned it would be."

"And my uncle, since he's gone to Stafford, is he pleased with it?"

"Your father doesn't reveal the earl's opinion, but I'm sure he's delighted. Who wouldn't be?"

Annie smiled again. Her father claimed she'd known her uncle when she was a baby, that she'd briefly resided with both men after her mother had died, but Annie didn't recollect. She'd been too tiny. Her father came to Belgium twice a year for a short visit, but her uncle never accompanied him. In the sheltered world of the convent, he didn't seem like a real person.

"What about me?" she tentatively ventured. "Has Father mentioned my joining him at Stafford?"

"Of course."

"What does he say?"

"A very interesting comment, I think. He's investigating the neighbors at Stafford. He's searching for a family who would be willing to take you in until he can muster out of the army."

"You're joking."

"No. He informs me that someone will come from London, before the summer is through, to escort you to England."

Annie had been standing, and at the amazing news, she eased down into the chair behind her.

"Do you suppose he means it?"

"He's your father, Annie, and he loves you. I'm certain he always means it."

"But this time..."

Mother Superior was aware of how frequently Annie's dreams had been dashed by her father, and she always soothed

Annie's disappointment over his failed promises. She leaned across her desk and patted Annie's hand.

"I'm very confident," Mother Superior said. "Your father has established himself at Stafford, so there's no reason why you can't be brought to live there."

"By August, would you imagine? Could it happen that soon?"

"Perhaps even sooner. Maybe you'll be leaving us by July."

"July," Annie murmured, as if the word were magic.

The nun held out the letter. "Go ahead. Take it and read it for yourself."

Annie grabbed it and bowed out. She climbed the stairs to her room in the attic. Though her father was wealthy, she received no special treatment, so it was simply furnished.

She flopped onto her bed, and she studied her father's message over and over until she'd memorized it. At the bottom of the page, she traced her finger over the last sentence: *I will be sending someone to fetch you to England.*

Giggling with glee, she pressed the paper to her chest, directly over her heart. She gazed at her meager belongings, wondering if she should begin packing.

When her escort appeared, she wanted to depart without delay.

"I have the most wicked idea."

Lady Veronica Stewart glanced over at her best friend, Portia.

"Tell me," Veronica insisted.

"If you're so worried about Lord Stafford, why don't you pay him a surprise visit?"

"I couldn't."

"Why couldn't you?"

"What would my father say?"

"What the duke doesn't know won't hurt him. Don't ask his permission; just go."

"Just...*go*? How scandalous."

She and Portia were in her father's most luxurious coach, out for an afternoon of shopping. Her wedding wasn't until the end of August, but she was filling her trousseau with the calculated strategy of a war general. There were so many boxes and bags, they scarcely had any space to sit on the seats.

Nicholas hadn't yet told her the spot he'd chosen for their honeymoon, but she demanded that it be Italy. If he selected anywhere else, she'd just die!

Portia had loaned her a novel where the heroine had been kidnapped and held hostage by the hero in a villa overlooking the Mediterranean. It had been the most romantic tale ever, and Veronica wouldn't settle for any other locale, for she was convinced that Italy would render the conclusion she sought. While they were there, Nicholas would fall madly in love with her.

"We're scheduled to attend the Fitzroys' house party," Portia was saying.

"So?"

"On the way, we'll pass within twenty miles of Stafford Manor. Why not take a detour and call on your betrothed?"

Veronica's pulse pounded with excitement. "I could, couldn't I?"

"It's not as if he can complain. You're about to be his countess. It's only natural that you'd want to see your new home."

"Stafford will never be my *home*."

Veronica gave a mock shudder, and Portia laughed.

Veronica's father had kept her imprisoned in the country until she was sixteen. After he'd finally allowed her to escape to town, she'd been able to breathe for the first time ever. She thrived on the social whirl in the city, and she wouldn't ever again wilt away in some quaint, rustic village.

"Will you have his townhouse open year 'round?" Portia asked.

"Yes, except for two weeks in the fall. He has to host an annual hunt at Stafford."

"With the best guest list, of course."

"Oh, of course." She intended to become the *ton's* premiere hostess. "I may agree to Christmas, too, but I haven't decided. We have to distribute gifts to the staff, but the housekeeper could do it for us. We wouldn't have to actually be there in person."

"The servants ought to be glad you notice them at all. They

can hardly blame you if you don't wish to travel in the winter."

Veronica's mind was awhirl with possibilities, and she frowned at Portia.

"If we stop at Stafford, we'll add a day onto the trip. How would I explain it?"

"Honestly, Veronica, how did you ever manage without me? You simply tell your father you're leaving on Monday and arriving at Fitzroys' on Wednesday. Then you write to Mrs. Fitzroy and tell her you'll be there on Thursday. She doesn't correspond with your father. He'll never know you were late."

"And if I'm caught?"

"You lie to the duke and claim you spent a few hours having an innocent tour. Where's the harm?"

"It could work," Veronica mused.

"Yes, it could. Stick with me, Veronica, and I'll get you where you need to go."

Veronica snorted at that.

She was desperate to see Stafford, but it wasn't due to any interest in the estate. It was because of Nicholas and the terrible rumors that were circulating.

From the instant news had spread about Nicholas inheriting his title, every girl in the kingdom had set her sights on him. He was reputed to be handsome and brave and mysterious, and in their vivid imaginations, no other man could compare.

With her white-blond hair, blue eyes, and plump figure, she was the prettiest, richest debutante to come out in ages. She hadn't been surprised when Nicholas had met her at a ball, then spoke to her father the next morning.

The duke had had qualms about Nicholas's low antecedents, but in light of the property he'd bring to the family, her father had gotten over his reservations quickly enough. He'd asked Veronica her opinion, and she hadn't hesitated to accept Nicholas's proposal.

Except that her engagement wasn't turning out as she'd anticipated. It had her speculating over what her life would be like once she married him. She wouldn't let him ignore her as he'd been doing.

Since their betrothal, he hadn't danced attendance on her a single time, so she hadn't had a chance to flaunt him at any high-profile occasions. Everyone noted his absences, and awful stories had been disseminated as to why he was so *busy.* Veronica was anxious to learn if they were true or not.

The gossips maintained that he'd fled to the country with his mistress in tow, that he'd deliberately insulted Veronica by taking his harlot to the estate. Supposedly, his doxy would be his hostess when Veronica wasn't in residence.

Veronica couldn't help but be concerned.

Hadn't she ought to check? Was it wrong to ease her mind? If word filtered to London that she'd called on him, it would quell the hideous reports. After all, Nicholas wouldn't permit a visit if his mistress was ensconced on the premises.

Still, she couldn't keep from asking, "What if she's really there? What shall I do?"

"First of all, if she's there—and I think we agree that it's a big *if*—you'll never see her. Lord Stafford will shuttle her out the back so fast her head will be spinning."

"She'll be gone; that's what I want."

"She won't dare to return, either."

"No, she won't."

"And with your brazen appearance, he'll understand that he can't trifle with your affections."

"He's behaved horridly to me."

"Yes, he has, but we'll bring him up to snuff."

The two friends grinned, complicit and positive they'd have the matter resolved in a thrice.

Stephen started down the hall when the unexpected sound of girlish laughter had him stumbling to a halt. The mansion was so large and so empty of human habitation that it was odd to hear children's voices.

He neared the foyer and peeked around the corner to find Miss Wilson's sisters playing on the stairs. They were involved in a complicated game, and though he spied on them for several minutes, he couldn't figure out the rules.

It was a heartening sign that they'd adapted so swiftly to new circumstances. Once Annie was at Stafford, he hoped she would acclimate just as rapidly. The twins were Annie's same age. Perhaps they could be her companions.

He'd done his best by his daughter, and he intended to make up for his failings by building a life with her at Stafford. His plan was all mapped out.

Nicholas had so much land, and he didn't care about any of it. He could be persuaded to grant some to Stephen, then instantly, Stephen would become a marvelous catch.

He'd marry a mature, sensible woman, which would provide Annie with the mother she'd never had. Then he'd have more children. He would farm and watch over his family, and he would grow old with a smile on his face.

Nicholas could waste away in the army, could wed his snotty, adolescent bride, could live in misery and gloom. Stephen was determined to be happy.

Someone knocked on the door, and he'd moved to answer it when the twins beat him to it.

He huddled in the shadows, praying it wasn't the vicar seeking an audience with Nicholas. His brother was still in bed and extremely hungover. Stephen didn't relish the notion of explaining to the rude minister why the earl was unavailable— and always would be!

He was delighted to discover instead that it was Josephine Merrick. Elation pounded through him, but an enormous amount of lust pounded, too.

She was pretty as ever, vibrant and vigorous, and she aroused him beyond his limits. Their tryst had been stunning. He'd never participated in anything similar, and he was eager to do it again and already calculating how he could get her alone.

"Mrs. Merrick!" the twins cried together, and they leapt forward to hug her.

"There you are! I was in the village, and I heard you were here. I had to check for myself."

"The earl saved us!" they exclaimed in unison.

"He rode into the market," Nan told her, "and when he learned what had happened, he put us right up on his horse and fetched us home."

Nell added, "He was so angry with Mr. Mason."

"The earl was angry? You must be joking."

"It's true, it's true," they crowed as if Nicholas's kindness was too extraordinary to be believed.

"I'm so glad," Mrs. Merrick said. "I was very angry myself."

Stephen imagined many derogatory comments about his brother might follow, so he made his presence known. Briskly, he stepped toward them as if he'd been marching down the hall all along.

"Mrs. Merrick, welcome."

At his greeting, she beamed with pleasure.

"Mr. Price, how lovely to see you again."

He supposed she actually had come to inquire as to Miss Wilson and her sisters, but he was vain enough to suppose that she'd come to visit him, too. He was impressed by her daring.

The entire morning, he'd struggled to devise a reason to stop by the vicarage, but he couldn't without calling on the vicar, too, so he hadn't gone.

"I was hoping to speak with Emeline," she mentioned.

"I don't have any idea where she is," Stephen replied, and he looked at the girls. "Do you know?"

"She went to the village to run some errands for the housekeeper," Nan said.

"Oh, drat," Mrs. Merrick responded, "I was just there. I must have missed her."

"She's trying to be useful, so the earl doesn't change his mind and decide we're a burden."

"You're not a burden," Stephen insisted.

"Of course, they're not," Mrs. Merrick agreed.

"Would you like to wait for her?" Stephen offered.

"I probably shouldn't. Oscar is expecting me by noon."

But she didn't leave.

"How about if I walk you?" he suggested. "It's beautiful weather outside, and I've been cooped up with the account ledgers."

"That would be wonderful."

She said goodbye to the girls, and they hurried off, which gave him the opportunity he'd been seeking. He grabbed her wrist and dragged her down the deserted corridor to an empty salon at the end.

The drapes were shut and the furniture covered with sheets. There was no fire, so it was cold as ice, but they would generate their own heat.

He pushed her against the wood of the door, and he fell on her like a ravenous beast. This had to be why she'd come to the manor, but if it wasn't, he cared not. He couldn't see her and not desire her.

His tongue was in her mouth, his hands on her hips, her breasts. As he pinched her nipples, she moaned in delicious agony. He clasped her thighs and wrapped her legs around his waist.

In a matter of seconds, his loins were crushed to hers, the fabric of trousers and drawers all that kept them from coupling.

"What are we doing?" she asked, gasping for air.

"We're racing down the road to perdition. How do you like the view?"

He fumbled with his trousers and impaled himself, filling her in one, smooth thrust. She wailed—loudly—and he slapped a palm across her lips to stifle the sound.

She straddled his hips, with him standing, so they were off balance and giggling like halfwits. The naughtiness of their actions, the recklessness, was incomprehensible.

He flexed once, twice, and they both came in a fiery rush. He was too disordered to remember to pull out, and he spilled himself into her womb. His knees were quaking, his face buried at her nape as his pulse slowed.

Finally, he drew away, and she slid down his torso until her feet touched the floor.

"My, my!" She was patting her hair, straightening her clothes. "Do all adults behave like this?"

"Only the ones who are mad."

"I was perfectly sane before you arrived at Stafford."

"So was I."

"In a few short days, you've turned me into a lunatic."

She snorted with mirth, smothering her hilarity against his shirt. He nestled her close, liking how her smaller body fit his much larger frame.

"What is happening to me?" she queried.

"You've missed having a man in your bed, and I'm happy to oblige."

"You are going to get me in so much trouble." She clutched the lapels of his coat and shook him. "And I'm not even worried about it."

"Neither am I."

She rose on tiptoe and kissed him.

"Thank you for helping Emeline," she said. "She's needed a lucky break."

"I had nothing to do with it. It was all my brother's idea."

"There have been too many horror stories about him, so I won't give him the credit." She took a deep breath and let it out. Composing herself, she was once again the vicar's quiet, unassuming sister.

"I really must be off," she told him. "Oscar won't sit down to his meal without me. If I'm late, I'll never hear the end of it."

"I could pound him bloody for you. Would you like me to?"

"Don't tempt me." She held her wrist to her nose and sniffed. "Ah, I can smell you on my skin! How will I endure a boring dinner with my brother? I can't pretend everything is the same."

"Don't ponder sin or fornication or how much you enjoy the size of my—"

She wagged a scolding finger. "You! Be silent."

"I can't. Not when I'm around you."

"Try a bit harder, would you?"

She opened the door a crack and peeked out. The hall was empty, and she hurried out. He followed.

"I'm walking you home," he said.

"Only if you promise to keep your hands to yourself." She frowned. "And you can't keep looking at me like that."

"Like what?"

"Like you want to eat me alive."

"I *do* want to eat you alive."

She gazed upward and murmured, "Lord, give me the strength to control myself."

"I don't think He intervenes in this sort of thing."

"It can't hurt to try."

Oscar was in his study, staring out the window as the clock rang with a single chime, indicating that it was one o'clock.

Josephine was an hour late.

In the mornings, she made charity calls for him so that he didn't have to bother. He hated visiting the sick, the poor, or the dying. People brought on their own troubles, and he had no sympathy for them, but *she* oozed compassion.

Until he was wed—a future event he viewed with extreme distaste—she would serve as his hostess, so it was her duty to minister to his flock, much as it would be his wife's after he chose a bride. But she was aware of the requirements when she left the house.

She had to be back by noon so she could freshen up. Then they would dine promptly at twelve-thirty. He was a fastidious man, and he liked his routines. When his schedule was interrupted, it soured the remainder of his day.

Her tardiness was disrespectful, but then, she had always been much too independent. She presumed she could act in any brazen fashion and there would be no consequences.

Their father's strict rules had not tamed her. Her husband's severe criticisms—criticisms leveled for her own good—had not tamed her. Oscar's firm guidance and moral instruction had not tamed her.

She would blithely make note of his concerns, then carry on however she pleased.

None of them had ever taken a belt to her, but maybe it was time. If she could be taught to fear the lash, she might temper her defiance.

Down the lane, he observed her sauntering along, and as she neared, he realized she wasn't alone. The earl's brother was with her. They weren't behaving improperly, but still, Josephine was grinning at him like a flirtatious trollop.

They stopped at the gate, and Mr. Price bowed courteously. She uttered a remark that had him laughing, and he continued on.

Oscar's fury simmered to a boil. While he'd grown hungry and his meal cold, she'd been throwing herself at the earl's brother! Had she no shame? No sense of status or class? How could she humiliate herself over the likes of Stephen Price?

Mr. Price was an ungodly heathen who, with the elevation of his impious brother, had been raised up above everyone. He could now pick any woman in the world to be his bride, so he'd deem a female of Josephine's humble position to be a trifle, a plaything for his manly lusts. Didn't Josephine know any better?

Or perhaps she welcomed his attention. Her husband had never discussed the sordid details of their marriage, but he'd often hinted at her having disgusting tendencies. Was Stephen

Price drawing his sister's base inclinations to the fore?

Oscar would kill her before he'd let it happen.

He shifted away from the window, and he waited silently, listening as she entered the house, as she hung her cloak and apologized to the maid for being late.

He poked his head into the hall, his face blank.

"Josephine, would you come here? I must speak with you."

"Yes, Oscar, certainly." Hustling toward him, she smiled and stepped into the room. "I'm sorry I was delayed. There appears to be an influenza circulating the neighborhood. I couldn't finish as quickly as I'd hoped."

He closed the door, and as he spun the key in the lock, he hissed, "Where have you been?"

"What? I went visiting."

"Don't lie to me!"

"I'm not lying!"

"You were with that blackguard, Stephen Price."

"Mr. Price? Yes, I ran into him on the way home. He accompanied me. There was no harm done."

He loomed up over her, liking how she shrank away, as if afraid he would strike her, and he had to admit the notion was tempting. However, the maid and cook were on the premises, so he couldn't administer the punishment she deserved.

"So long as you are living under my roof," he snarled, "you will not prostitute yourself."

"You're being ridiculous."

"Am I? I saw him looking at you."

"You're mad. He was being friendly."

"I saw you looking back." He grabbed her by the scruff of her neck, and he squeezed tight, shaking her as if she were a bad dog.

"Get down on your knees! Get down and beg the Lord for forgiveness."

Mute and aggrieved, she gaped at him but didn't move, so he forced her down. Recalcitrant whore that she was, she resisted with all her might, so he pushed and pushed until he had her on the floor. He held her there, as she cried and prayed, and he kept on and on until his back and arms ached, and he grew too weary to persist.

He tossed her away, and she stumbled to the side.

"Go to your room," he spat, "and reflect on your sins. And if I catch you talking to Mr. Price again, I will beat you within an inch of your life."

She scurried out and scrambled to the vestibule on her hands and knees. As she reached the stairs, she used the banister to pull herself up. Then she climbed to her bedchamber and shut herself in to repent in private where he wouldn't have to watch.

Chapter Ten

"You're to do what?"

"Measure you."

"Why?"

Emeline scowled at Widow Brookhurst. Though most wives did their own sewing, she was the premier seamstress in the area. People sought her out for special garments like wedding dresses or baptismal gowns. They were in her shop in the village where Emeline had stopped to pick up supplies for the housekeeper at Stafford Manor.

"My instructions," the widow explained, "were from the earl's brother. The earl is buying you clothes."

"The earl is buying me...*clothes*?"

"Yes. Your sisters, too. Bring them by tomorrow so I can check how tall they are."

"When were you informed of this?"

"Earlier this morning. Mr. Price came by personally." The woman raised a brow. "You're to have whatever you need. I'm to spare no expense."

Emeline shook her head. "There must be some mistake."

"I received an order," the widow huffed, "and I intend to fill it. It's worth a fortune to me—both now and in the future."

"But why would the earl buy me clothes? I don't understand."

"I'm supposing it's because he let Mr. Mason burn your house down—with all your possessions inside."

"Mr. Mason has burned many houses. The earl hasn't replaced anyone else's belongings."

"No, he hasn't."

Mrs. Brookhurst studied Emeline, and a warning bell began to chime. The widow was obviously speculating that Nicholas Price wouldn't purchase expensive gifts for Emeline unless she'd done something to deserve them. What was he thinking by encouraging such gossip? Didn't he realize the stories that would spread?

"I'd better return to the estate," Emeline said. "I have to ask what this is about."

"Oh, I *know* what it's about," Mrs. Brookhurst baldly retorted.

"I have no idea what you mean."

"You're very pretty, Emeline, and he's a rich, handsome bachelor. You watch yourself."

"Mrs. Brookhurst! Honestly! I hardly require a lecture on morals."

"Well, someone should speak up. Your mother isn't around to counsel you. A girl could easily get herself into trouble with a fellow like him."

Dazed, Emeline had spun to go when Mrs. Brookhurst called, "Wait! I have a package for you."

"What's in it?"

"I had a few items that I'd prepared for other customers, but they'll fit you. The earl insists you have them. I'll send on the other pieces once they arrive."

"What *pieces*?"

"He had me write to a shop in London where they have a selection of ready-made garments. He wants you fancied up faster than I can accomplish it."

"That is ridiculous."

"It's interesting, how fond he's grown. And so quickly, too."

"He's not...*fond*," Emeline seethed. "He's insane."

"What about these?" Mrs. Brookhurst held up a neatly wrapped parcel. "If you'd rather not fuss with them, I can carry them to the manor for you."

"Please don't."

"They're paid for." The widow shrugged. "You might as well have them."

Her temper spiking, Emeline whipped away and stomped out.

If the entire neighborhood didn't yet know about the gift,

they'd soon learn of it.

What a disaster! Nicholas—yes, Nicholas was how she now thought of him; he was no longer *the earl*—had left her in a dangerous position.

The previous night, she'd lain in his bed and had gleefully allowed him to do delicious, amazing things to her. Pathetically, she was keen to misbehave again, the moment a clandestine tryst could be arranged.

She'd told Mrs. Brookhurst that he was insane, but Emeline was the one who was mad.

When they'd been snuggled together, he'd mentioned buying her a dress, but she hadn't imagined he was serious. She'd naively deemed their encounter to be a spontaneous episode of mutual passion, but he seemed to have had a different opinion.

Apparently, he presumed her favors could be purchased, and she was to be paid for her participation. If the price was high enough, what else might he expect her to try?

Offended and furious, she marched on, when another notion occurred to her.

He was a male, and an especially obtuse one at that. Perhaps he'd intended no insult. Perhaps he simply hadn't been informed that a man of his station couldn't give a gift to a woman in hers, that the gesture would be misconstrued.

While she was aware that she constantly imbued him with traits he didn't possess, she was eager to have the second possibility—that he was a clueless idiot—be the actual fact.

The mansion came into view, and she entered the house and proceeded to the kitchen to deliver the provisions she'd retrieved in the village. She lingered, eavesdropping on the servants. She was anxious to ask where Nicholas was, but she couldn't pose a question without generating unwanted attention.

Eventually, she found out he was in the small dining salon, awaiting his breakfast. It was twelve-thirty in the afternoon, and the cook and her helpers were scurrying around, cracking eggs and slicing bread.

She slipped out, wondering if she dared barge in on his meal without invitation, but she swiftly persuaded herself that she could. For goodness sake, she'd completely disgraced herself with him, and he'd touched her in her most private places. If that didn't confer some sort of status, she didn't know what did.

She approached the doorway and peeked in. He was alone, his head in his hands, and he cut such a solitary figure that her heart ached. He looked so forlorn and dejected, his typical proud bearing tucked away.

What must it be like to be him? She'd heard the most tragic stories about his childhood, yet he'd built a life for himself in the army where he was reputed to be a man of great courage and fidelity.

He'd overcome so many obstacles. Who could blame him for being arrogant? After starting at the lowest point, he'd been elevated to one of the highest spots in the land. Wasn't he entitled to his conceit?

He appeared to have just staggered out of bed. He hadn't washed or shaved. His hair was down and uncombed, the tangled strands brushing his shoulders. He'd put on a coat and trousers, but he hadn't donned a shirt so his chest was bare.

With what had transpired between them, how would they interact? Would he be flirtatious and fawning? Or would he be his usual abrupt self?

If she'd been hoping for a tender welcome, he quashed any foolishness.

"Emeline," he snapped without glancing up, "stop lurking and get your ass in here."

"How did you know it was me?"

"I told you last night, I'd recognize that snotty stride anywhere."

"I can't begin to guess what that means."

"It *means* you walk like a scolding shrew. When I hear you coming, I brace myself for a reprimand."

She pulled out a chair, and as she seated herself, he frowned and winced.

"Would you close the curtains?"

"No. It's almost one o'clock. It's about time you roused yourself."

"My head is pounding like there's an anvil inside it. The sunlight only makes it worse."

"You'll survive."

"You're too cruel, Miss Wilson. Why do I tolerate you?"

"I force you to behave. You secretly enjoy it."

Suddenly, her sisters raced by out in the hall. They were shrieking like wild monkeys swinging through the trees.

"Ah!" he groaned, rubbing his temples. "What's that noise?"

She laughed. "It's the sound of children playing."

"Children? In *this* house?"

"My sisters are here, remember?"

"Oh..."

"I'm sorry. I didn't realize they were raising such a ruckus. I'll tell them to pipe down."

She started to rise, but he reached over and furtively squeezed her hand.

"No, don't. They can be as loud as they like. I don't mind."

The butler traipsed in, two footmen trailing after him, carrying trays laden with food.

It had been over a year since they'd served their master, so they'd made a huge fuss. Platter after platter was arranged before him, eggs and toast and fruit and ham. The choices went on and on until it became embarrassing. It was enough for an army, but he scarcely noticed.

The butler hovered, waiting for a word, a command, but Nicholas remained slumped in his chair.

"Shall I prepare a plate for you, my Lord Stafford?" the butler said.

"I can do it myself."

"How about Miss Wilson? We weren't aware she was joining you."

Nicholas glared at her, mutely asking if she was hungry, and she smiled at the butler. "I don't need anything, Mr. Jenkins. I rose at a normal hour and ate at a normal hour. Unlike *some* people I could name."

"Has she always been this sassy?" Nicholas inquired of Mr. Jenkins.

"Ah...ah..." The elderly gentleman was too polite to answer honestly.

"Should I have her whipped for insubordination? Or should I simply dunk her in the horse trough until she cools off?"

The butler's eyes were round as saucers, and the footmen gaped with alarm.

"Quit being obnoxious," she admonished. "They assume

you're serious."

"I *am* serious."

"He is not," she scoffed to the three men.

"If you keep jabbering so I can't eat, you'll discover how serious I am." He waved the servants away, and as they hurried out, he called to Mr. Jenkins, "If she continues to pester me, I'll have you bring me a whip."

The poor fellow stiffened with affront but trudged on.

"You are horrid," she said as their strides faded. "They'll spread tales that you're a brute."

"I am a brute, now be silent and let me dine in peace."

He filled his plate to overflowing and wolfed it down. He filled it again and wolfed that, too. She poured his tea, watching as he ate and ate and ate.

Finally, he shoved the food away, and he slouched, scowling.

"All right." He sighed. "I'm ready."

"Ready for what?"

"What have I done this time? You only seek me out to chastise me."

"I do not."

"You do, too. I feel as if I've hired a nanny. What crisis has arisen? Let's see if I can fix it."

He gazed at her, his hot attention sending shivers down her spine. He was dangerous and delectable, and she yearned to reach out and touch him. It was so difficult to pretend they were barely acquainted.

"You bought me clothes."

"That's your problem?"

"Yes. I didn't ask for them."

"No, you didn't, but you need a new dress more than any woman I've ever met."

"You're missing the point."

"What is it? Would you please get to it? I've slept late, and I have a thousand chores to finish."

"People will talk."

"I don't care."

"They'll think that I...*earned* them in an indecent way."

"You did earn them in an indecent way." She sucked in a shocked breath, and he squeezed her hand again. "I'm joking,

Em."

"My neighbors won't know that. I have to live here after you go back to London. I can't have my reputation ruined."

"I had Mr. Mason burn all your possessions. I owe you."

"I still have a gown or two. I stuffed a pillowcase with the last of my things. I'm fine."

"I can't stand to have you walking around like a frump. You're too pretty."

"Thank you for the lovely compliment"—she blushed to high heaven—"but I can't accept any gifts."

"Not even for your sisters? You'd rather have them attired in rags?"

He studied her, his focus warm and inviting, then he jumped up and went to the door. He opened it and hollered as he yanked and yanked on the bell pull.

"Mr. Jenkins, I need you!"

The beleaguered man thundered up the stairs, obviously worried there was a calamity brewing.

"Yes, yes, milord, what is it?"

"I had Miss Wilson's cottage destroyed."

"I am aware of that fact, sir."

"She and her sisters have nothing left—because of me."

Jenkins made a feeble gesture, and he peered over at Emeline for assistance. She shrugged.

"In order to redeem myself," Nicholas said, "I have bought them some clothes. I realize it's odd for me to lavish her with such an extravagance, but I'm very sorry for my behavior. It's my penance."

Jenkins gawked at Emeline, then Nicholas, then Emeline, and he nodded. "Very good, sir."

"While I'm in residence, she'll be busy attending me."

"I see."

"There should be no concern over it."

"I'm certain there won't be, milord."

"I've hired her as my...my...secretary."

"Your...secretary?"

Emeline gasped. Women didn't serve as secretaries. It was unheard of. Only men were deemed intelligent enough to handle such complicated tasks.

"Mr. Mason has informed me," Nicholas kept on, "that she

was overly educated by her father."

"Too true, sir."

"I decided to put all that schooling to work for me."

"A wise idea, I'm sure."

"This is another reason she needs clothes. She can't be employed by me in such an important capacity while looking like a pauper."

"Definitely not."

"Tell everyone what I've told you," he said. "I'll have no disrespectful gossip about her. She's living in the manor because of her job. She has to have a wardrobe commensurate with her position. Anyone who spreads rumors will answer to me."

"Yes, my lord Stafford."

Nicholas eased him out. "That will be all. You're excused."

He shut the door in Jenkins's stunned face, and he paused, listening until the man's steps faded, then he turned to her. He was grinning like an idiot.

"You are crazy," she fumed.

"Crazy like a fox." He tapped a finger on his temple. "Now I can spend as much time with you as I like, and it won't be considered unusual. And if I want to buy you a new dress, I damn well will, and I won't have to hear you complain."

"Would you open the door?"

"No. You're my secretary. I can be in a closed room with you. No one will think twice about it."

"*I* will think twice."

"You don't get to have an opinion."

He came back to his chair and seated himself. He clasped hold of her hand and traced circles on her wrist. When he stared at her as he was, her thoughts became jumbled. He seemed to want something from her that she couldn't give. Or perhaps he didn't know what he sought, and he hoped she'd enlighten him.

Around him, she felt special, as if he valued her above all women, which was ridiculous in the extreme. But she couldn't stop the race of pleasure she suffered when she wondered if she might be beginning to matter to him.

How could he peer at her so ardently without there being a deeper meaning attached?

"You sneaked out of my bed," he said. "I awoke and you weren't there."

"You assumed I'd stay the night?"

"Yes."

"You're insane. I can't figure out why I visited you in the first place."

"I missed you," he absurdly declared.

"You did not."

"I did. Isn't that bizarre?"

Without warning, he grabbed her and dragged her to him. Her bottom was balanced on his thigh, her breasts crushed to his chest.

He kissed her slowly and mercilessly, his tongue in her mouth, his fingers roaming over her torso. Her muscles relaxed, her bones relaxed, her pores relaxed until she worried she might melt into a puddle on the rug.

She hadn't the fortitude to deflect his delicious onslaught. She wished she could confess her predicament to an older, more experienced woman who could counsel her on how to resist him. Because what female would *want* to resist him?

It seemed as if she were perched on the edge of a cliff, that she'd jumped off and was falling and falling and falling. Where would she be when she landed?

"Good morning," he said as he drew away.

"Good morning. How is your hangover?"

"I'm feeling better by the moment."

"Do you drink excessive amounts so that you have an excuse for your bad behavior?"

"No, I drink because I like it. And I misbehave because I'm a rogue and a scapegrace."

"I don't believe that about you."

"What don't you believe?"

"You enjoy acting the scoundrel, and you like pretending that you're a lout, but you're not. Not deep down."

"You're wrong. I'm as awful as everyone claims. You shouldn't forget it."

"Why have people thinking the worst of you? Under all the bluster, you're actually a fine person."

"My little champion," he murmured, and he kissed her again.

This time, as he pulled away, she extricated herself and moved to put the table between them as a barrier. If he touched her, she couldn't concentrate, and she definitely needed to focus.

She was tumbling down a slippery slope. He insisted on being kind to her, but she misconstrued his generosity, imbuing it with a significance she was positive he didn't intend.

In her mind, she'd built up fantasies where he was helping her because he was smitten, which had to be nonsense. He wasn't the type to bond in any abiding way, and she wasn't worldly enough to separate their physical attraction from the emotional one she was developing for him.

"Why are you bothering with me?" she queried.

"What do you mean?"

"I can't be alone with you for two seconds without you making advances."

"Are you complaining?"

"No, I'm just puzzled. I don't understand why you'd involve yourself."

"You amuse me. You're so entertaining."

"That's it?"

"If you consider how easily I'm bored, I'd say it's quite a lot."

"You don't envision anything...*more* happening, do you?"

"What more could there be?"

"Do you fancy me?" she humiliated herself by asking.

"Yes."

His torrid gaze took a leisurely trip down her body, stopping at all the pertinent spots.

"But...it's not *me* precisely, is it?" she pressed. "You could dally with me or it could be any woman."

He snorted. "I'm a bit choosey. I wouldn't take up with any old shrew."

"I see." Feeling like a fool, she started for the door.

"Where are you going?" he inquired.

"I can't continue on with you. I don't know how."

"What's to know?"

"How long are you planning to be here?"

He shrugged. "A week? Maybe two?"

"You'd never make...a...commitment to me, would you?"

"No."

He said it gently, but still, it hurt.

"We'd flirt and play and then you'd leave for London without looking back?"

"You've pretty much covered it."

"Will you ever visit Stafford again?"

"Not if I don't have to."

She reached for the knob.

"It's just kissing, Em."

"It's more than that, and you know it."

"I agree." He grinned his devil's grin. "It's a tad more than that."

"You're very experienced at amour, aren't you?"

"Not at amour. At lust. You shouldn't confuse the two. Lust is what's flaring between us, and I'm very adept at satisfying it."

"I'm not experienced, and I don't care to be."

"I've told you not to lie to me. You're so bad at it. You like what we do together. You're simply too prim to admit it."

"You're correct: I'm much too prim, and you're much too sophisticated."

She walked out, and he snarled, "Emeline!"

"What?"

He was irked that she'd depart, and she wasn't surprised by his spurt of temper. He liked having his own way too much.

"Were you expecting something else from me?" he asked.

Yes, yes! "No. I merely like to be clear so that I remember my place."

"I don't grow fond of women. I don't bond with them. Not even when it's one whose company I enjoy. I don't have that type of stable character."

"I understand." She nodded. "You mentioned to Mr. Jenkins that you'd hired me as your secretary."

He made a waffling motion with his hand. "I don't need a secretary. I have an office full of clerks in London to chase after my paperwork."

"I'm happy to help you. I'm skilled at writing and factoring."

"I'll keep that in mind."

"Otherwise, I won't be able to attend you anymore."

"There are plenty of single females in the area. I'm sure I

can find someone to divert me for the remainder of my stay."

Turning to the pot of tea, he poured a cup, then heaped another plate of food. He began eating. He ignored her completely, as if he'd forgotten she existed, as if she'd become invisible.

She panicked. Did she really intend not to see him again? It was too sad to imagine.

Frantically, stupidly, she was ready to rush back in, to snuggle herself on his lap and tell him she hadn't meant any of it. But she couldn't. By its very nature, an illicit liaison was a recipe for disaster, and she hadn't the detachment required to pull it off.

She would hope for his continued kindness and compassion. She would pray that she hadn't misjudged him and that he would assist her in the end, but she couldn't seek more.

She trudged down the hall, all the while wishing that he would call to her, that they might have a different conclusion, but silence dogged her every step.

Benedict Mason rode up the lane toward the manor. After meeting with Nicholas Price the previous afternoon, he'd been in a foul mood so he'd fled for a few hours. He couldn't have gossip spreading that he was no longer in charge or that his prior actions were being reversed, but he wasn't certain how to regain his advantage.

Emeline Wilson and her sisters had been moved into the mansion. Evictions and other cost-saving measures were on hold. Nicholas and Stephen Price hadn't left.

It was annoying, having them underfoot and undermining his decisions. And he was most especially unnerved by their examining the account ledgers. Not that he thought either brother was particularly literate. They'd been raised in an orphanage, so he doubted they could add and subtract.

Yet it couldn't hurt to be cautious, and Benedict was nothing if not wary.

Up ahead, he saw Widow Brookhurst. She was carrying a large package. He approached, hailed her and reined in.

"Good day, Mrs. Brookhurst," he greeted.

"Mr. Mason."

"What have you there? Is it a parcel for the housekeeper? I'm happy to take it the rest of the way for you."

Benedict had assumed it was mended tablecloths or some such, so he was stunned when she replied, "It's not for the housekeeper. It's for Emeline Wilson."

Miss Wilson was destitute. How had she bought anything?

"Really? What has she purchased?"

"*She* hasn't. It's a gift from the earl."

"What did you say?"

"He sent his brother to my shop early this morning with an order for a wardrobe of clothes." She hefted the bundle. "This is the first installment."

"An entire wardrobe?"

"Yes."

"What have you provided?"

"Three dresses and some undergarments."

"Undergarments!"

"There's more coming from London, too. For her *and* her sisters."

Benedict kept his expression blank, but his mind raced with speculation. As for the widow, she looked eager to spill all, and Benedict wasn't about to discourage her.

"Why would the earl buy her clothes?" he queried. "Did his brother divulge the reason?"

"No, and it's not my place to comment, but..."

"Comment away. Your opinion is safe with me."

She frowned. "I wouldn't want my remarks getting back to the earl. I'd hate to upset him or to have him presuming I'm not grateful for his favor."

"You have my word: I won't tell a soul."

She studied him, her distrust obvious, but she was too keen to tattle. "I can't fathom why Miss Wilson would receive such a boon."

"Neither can I."

"It's not any of my business how the earl chooses to spend his fortune. I recognize that. Still, I'm asking myself *why* he'd spend some of it in this fashion."

"It's a valid question."

"It couldn't have been free, with no strings attached. What

did she do for him? Or what did she agree to do in the future? I can't come to a good answer. Can you?"

"No, I can't." Benedict reached out a hand. "Give me the package. I'll have it delivered for you."

She lifted it up. "Thank you. Saves me the trouble."

"You're welcome." She started off, and he called, "Widow Brookhurst?"

"Yes?"

"I'd appreciate it if you didn't mention this conversation to anyone."

"Believe me, I won't. I'd rather not know about any of this. I always liked her parents. Her mother must be rolling in her grave."

"I wouldn't be surprised," he murmured as she continued on.

He proceeded to the manor, the illicit parcel balanced on his saddle, as he methodically reviewed the situation.

Had Emeline played the whore for Captain Price? Was she that low of character? Would she abandon her morals for a handsome face and a fat purse?

Benedict had proposed an honorable courtship to Emeline, with marriage as the goal at the end, but she'd spurned him.

Had she now surrendered her virginity for a few paltry trifles?

If so, she wouldn't be the first female in history to trade chastity for security. At the notion that she might have—that she had indecently granted to Nicholas Price what Benedict had decently sought—he rippled with outrage.

He would watch and listen. He would spy and investigate. If he ultimately learned that Mrs. Brookhurst's suspicions were true, he didn't know what he might do.

But Emeline would be very, very sorry.

Chapter Eleven

"I don't know what will happen now."

"What would you like to have happen?"

Josephine glanced over at Emeline. They had finally crossed paths in the village, and Jo was walking her to the manor. She should have been returning home, but after Oscar's recent outburst, she was extremely distraught and in no hurry.

Emeline looked healthier than she had in ages. Her cheeks were rosy with color, her hair clean and shiny. She was wearing a new dress, sewn from a flowery print that brought out the emerald in her eyes.

It was a beautiful afternoon. The sky was so blue, the woods so green, the birds singing in the trees. She was happy to be chatting with a friend, but wished she had more opportunity to become better acquainted. Oscar kept her so confined, and she was never allowed to socialize.

She'd like to unburden herself to a confidante, would like to seek advice about her affair with Mr. Price, about her problems with her brother. But she never would. Some things were meant to be private, and certainly an illicit liaison and an abusive brother had to be at the top of the list.

"I want to stay at Stafford," Emeline said, answering Jo's question. "I want to start the school again."

"It was such a marvelous benefit to the neighborhood."

"I always thought so. If only I could convince the earl."

"You've discussed it with him?"

"On numerous occasions."

"Really?"

"He's not the ogre he's reputed to be."

"Which indicates you've spent enough time with him to have formed an opinion."

"He's actually quite an interesting person."

"I'm surprised you'd say so. Considering how he treated you the day he arrived at the estate, I'm amazed you have a civil word to offer."

"He enjoys being difficult, and he goes out of his way to be obnoxious. He thrives on it."

"Are you sure it's deliberate behavior? In light of the troubles he's caused, I'm more inclined to believe that cruelty is his genuine nature and not an act."

"He has a compassionate streak a mile long, but he hides it."

"I've met his brother." Jo was careful not to reveal the merest hint of the conflicted feelings roiling through her.

"Have you? What do you think of him?"

"He's very cordial, compared to his older sibling. He, too, claims the earl is wonderful—once you get to know him."

"That's the tricky part, I suppose," Emeline said, "getting to truly *know* him. He doesn't let anyone close except Mr. Price. Have you heard what he did for me?"

"No, what?"

"He bought me this dress."

"He what?" Jo stopped and pulled Emeline around to face her.

"He bought me this dress and several others. He purchased clothes for Nan and Nell, too."

"Why?"

"When he found out that he'd had our cottage burned, he felt awful."

"You're joking."

"He insisted on replacing what was destroyed in the fire. We're so desperate; I couldn't refuse."

"It's peculiar that he would bother himself over it."

"Isn't it, though? This is what I mean about his being kind. Who would have expected such generosity from him?"

"Not me," Jo said.

"Not me, either," Emeline agreed. She hesitantly ventured, "Should I keep the clothes? Especially the ones for Nan and Nell. I realize it looks bad, and I can't have people gossiping."

125

"Absolutely, you should keep the clothes." Jo clucked her tongue with disgust. "The man is a menace, and after all the aggravation he's inflicted on you, a new wardrobe is the least of what you deserve."

"Are you sure?"

"I'm very sure, and if I hear anybody grousing, I'll punch them in the nose."

They laughed, and Jo took her arm and continued on again. They strolled silently, with Jo lost in contemplation.

She wished she believed in magic. She wished she could cast a spell and become a different sort of woman with a different sort of life. She'd always been a decent person. Why was there no reward for her efforts?

Down the road, horses' hooves sounded. As they rounded the bend, they saw Lord Stafford and Mr. Price riding toward them.

Jo stifled a smile, but Emeline stiffened with affront.

"I don't want to talk to him," she said.

"To whom? The earl?"

"Yes."

"Why not?"

"He exhausts me."

"They're heading directly for us, so we can't avoid a conversation. Have you thanked him for the dress? It seems a safe enough subject."

"He'll have to brag about giving it to me. He's insufferable."

"Every man I've ever met has been insufferable. I imagine I'll survive one more display of it."

She patted Emeline's hand as she braced herself, waiting for them to near. They were so magnificent, mounted on the earl's finest horses and attired in their uniforms, red coats, white trousers, black boots polished to a dazzling shine.

"They're so handsome," Jo said.

"But they know they are, and I can't abide such arrogance."

"All men are arrogant, too. It's embedded in their character at birth."

Emeline chuckled. "With that attitude, you'll never find another husband."

"Why would I want another one?"

"Good afternoon, ladies," Mr. Price called as they

approached.

"Hello," Jo and Emeline replied together.

The earl was silent, appearing irked that they'd delayed his passing.

"Lord Stafford"—Jo forced herself to be affable—"thank you for bringing Emeline and her sisters to the manor. Thank you for helping them. I'm very grateful."

He frowned. "Why would you be grateful?"

"She's my friend. I hated to see her in dire straits."

He regarded Emeline with extreme disdain.

"She has friends?" he asked. "I'm surprised. How do you put up with her?"

"Very funny," Emeline fumed, and she peered over at Jo. "I told you he'd be obnoxious. He assumes you'll be impressed by discourtesy."

"I'm an earl now, remember?" Lord Stafford sneered at Emeline. "I don't have to be courteous. I can act however I please."

The air was charged with an undercurrent Jo didn't understand. The earl was scowling at Emeline, and she was scowling right back. Obviously, they were quarreling, but Jo couldn't figure out why. They weren't sufficiently acquainted for fighting, and Emeline possessed no status that would allow for her to chastise him.

He seemed as if he might offer another rude remark, then thought better of it. He urged his horse forward and circled by them.

Mr. Price hadn't budged, and when the earl noticed his brother hadn't followed, he glanced over his shoulder.

"Are you coming or not?" the earl inquired.

Mr. Price gazed at Jo. "Are you on your way home?"

"Yes."

"I'll walk you."

"You don't need to trouble yourself."

"It's no trouble." He waved his brother on. "I'm going to accompany Mrs. Merrick to the village."

"Suit yourself," the earl said. Then he quipped to Emeline, "What about you, Miss Wilson?"

"What about me?"

"Are you capable of proceeding to the manor on your own?

Or do you require an escort?"

"I can get there on my own. I'm used to taking care of myself."

"Yes, you are, and we've already established what a bang-up job you've been doing."

"Nicholas!" Mr. Price scolded, but the earl ignored him and kicked his horse into a trot. He kept on without looking back.

"Ooh, that man!" Emeline grumbled, but she watched him go, unable to wrench herself away.

For an instant, her mask slipped, and Jo witnessed a disturbing amount of unveiled longing.

Was Emeline infatuated? Was the earl? Perhaps there was more to his rescuing her from the market and buying her clothes than she'd admitted.

Jo knew a few things about amour that Emeline hadn't had the chance to learn. If she'd involved herself with Nicholas Price, only heartache would result.

What was Emeline thinking? She *wasn't* thinking; that was the problem. Jo's reasoning had become muddled, too. They were two ordinary females whose lives had been turned upside down by two extraordinary males. She and Emeline resided in a small town in the country, and their backgrounds and experiences were no match for those of the Price brothers.

The pair would be at Stafford for such a short time. What havoc would they wreak before they moved on?

"How can you tolerate him?" Jo asked Mr. Price as he dismounted.

"He grows on you."

"You got the charm in the family. What did he get?"

"The title and the money."

Jo laughed as Emeline made her goodbyes and left. Then Jo and Mr. Price started for the village. They were side by side, strolling companionably, her skirt occasionally brushing his trousers.

She was cataloguing every moment of the encounter so she would never forget a single detail. She wanted to always remember the way he looked, the way he smelled, the way his boots crunched on the gravel.

All the while, she was calculating the distance remaining, trying to decide when they had arrived at the final safe point.

Oscar had been very clear in his warning about Mr. Price, and she wouldn't tempt fate.

If he discovered that she'd defied him, there was no predicting what he might do, and while Jo had flirted with the idea of carrying on their torrid liaison, she simply couldn't. The risk was too great.

"Would you call me Stephen?" he asked.

"When we're alone, and if you promise to call me Jo."

"I will—when we're alone."

It was a sweet gesture, and over the next several minutes before they parted forever, she would say his name as many times as she could.

"Stephen, why is your brother being so kind to Emeline?"

"Guilty conscience. He has a conscience. He just doesn't heed it very often."

"Does he fancy her?"

"In a manly fashion?"

"Yes."

He scoffed. "His taste in women runs in quite a different direction."

"What direction is that?"

"Not one I can describe for your virtuous ears."

"Would he take advantage of her?"

"No. Why are you worried about him?"

"She's not very sophisticated, and she doesn't have her father to protect her. He bought her clothes, and she's living at the manor. I'm a tad anxious about his intentions."

"Don't be. He doesn't chase after innocents. He doesn't need to. Women throw themselves at his feet. They always have."

"What about you? Do women throw themselves at your feet?"

"Not usually, but lately, I've been luckier."

He leaned in and stole a kiss before she could ask him not to. For the briefest second, she dawdled, relishing the warmth of his lips, then she sighed with regret and eased away.

He frowned. "What's wrong?"

"I have to tell you something."

She gazed into his handsome face, memorizing the color of his eyes, the slant of his nose and cleft of his chin.

"About...?"

"I can't continue our affair, Stephen."

"Why not?"

"The better question is, why did I participate in the first place?"

"Because we enjoy a potent attraction, that's why."

"We're not animals. We have to control our worst impulses."

"Speak for yourself." He grinned, but she didn't grin back, and his smile faded.

"What's happened?" he inquired.

"My brother saw us the other afternoon, out in front of the vicarage."

"So?"

"He's very strict, and he doesn't feel it's appropriate for us to fraternize."

"You agree with him?"

"It's not up to me."

"For pity's sake, I'm not some beggar in a ditch. I'm the earl's brother. We were merely walking down the lane."

"Appearances matter to him. I reside under his roof, and I have to abide by his rules."

"Why?"

"I don't have anywhere else to go. You know that."

"You're twenty-five years old, Jo. You're a widow. It's not as if you're some green girl I seduced off a street corner. Show some backbone. Tell him we're friends and he has to deal with it."

She sighed again. It was so easy to be a man, to be independent and in charge of your own life, to have your own money so you could do whatever you wanted.

Stephen Price could never understand what it was like to be her, to be without options, without hope, and at the mercy of someone like Oscar.

She constantly straddled a tightrope, eager to evade his wrath while managing some semblance of a normal existence. She would give anything to escape, but to where? How?

"It's not possible for me to defy him," she solemnly said.

"I'll talk to him for you."

"No, you won't. I can't have you interfering."

"He serves at Nicholas's pleasure. I'll remind him of that fact. You'll be amazed at the change in behavior that will follow."

"You don't know my brother."

"And *you* don't know mine."

"It wouldn't help to speak with Oscar. It would just stir more trouble for me."

"*More* trouble? What's he done?"

He tensed, as if he might march to the vicarage and pound Oscar into the ground. The notion was tremendously satisfying, and she was thrilled that he could be so incensed on her behalf, but she would never encourage him to reckless conduct.

What if Stephen learned how Oscar truly treated her? What if he had Oscar dismissed from his post? Then what? She and Oscar would both be tossed out with no income and no shelter.

"Oscar has done nothing to me," she calmly lied, "except to request that I remember my position in the community."

His temper flared. "Bugger your position. Bugger this community."

"Stephen, please. There's no need to be crude."

He reined himself in. "No, there's not. I apologize."

Suddenly, his demeanor altered. His fondness was carefully concealed, and he could have been a stranger. She couldn't bear to see him upset—when she'd been the cause of his distress.

"Don't be angry," she pleaded. She wrapped her arms around his waist, but it was like hugging a log.

"I'm not angry." His own arms were locked at his sides as he restrained himself from hugging her back.

"What else can I do, Stephen? This is a small town, and I live with my brother. I'm not some doxy from the city who has no ties."

"Are you sure we should end it?"

"Yes. The chance of discovery is simply too great and the ramifications too dire."

"What about me? What about what I want?"

"What about you?" she gently replied. "You'll be here for a few weeks, then you're leaving. When you go, I can't have my world in tatters."

"I would never hurt you."

131

"I realize that, but if we were found out—which we eventually would be—catastrophe would rain down on me whether you intended it or not."

They stood together, silent, miserable, and she held her breath in anticipation. If he really desired her, they were at the spot where he could fix their predicament. The remedy for carnal activity was matrimony. It was the usual solution. It was the perfect and quick answer to their sizzling attraction.

He wasn't a fool. He was aware of how to rectify their situation, and while she'd resolved to never wed again, she wouldn't mind wedding *him*. Oscar would never consent to a match, but if Stephen was willing to support her, Oscar's opinion was irrelevant.

She was an adult. Stephen could propose, and she could accept. They could obtain a Special License, and in a few days, they could be legitimately snuggled in his bed as husband and wife. They could stay there forever if he wished.

But apparently, he didn't wish it. Or perhaps, he wasn't in the mood to be shackled. Why would he be? As he kept pointing out, he was an earl's brother. He could pick any rich girl in the kingdom for his bride. He dabbled with women of Jo's class for a different sort of role entirely.

Plus, she always conveniently forgot that she was barren, and a man of Stephen's status would want a dozen children. Even if he'd consider choosing a common wife, he would never choose *her*.

"Well then"—he stepped away from her—"I guess this is good-bye."

"I guess it is."

"I'm glad I met you," he said.

"I'm glad, too."

"If you ever need anything, let me know. I'll assist you if I can."

"You're a decent man, Stephen Price."

"I try to be. I have to work doubly hard to make up for my brother's failings."

Without another word, he yanked away. He jumped on his horse and trotted off.

Jo tarried, her heart breaking, until he was swallowed up by the trees.

She nearly screamed for him to come back, but she didn't. It was wrong to lust after him. She'd been chasing a dream. A pretty dream, but a dangerous one all the same.

She headed for home, her legs weak, her bones rubbery, and there was a ringing in her ears, as if she'd been struck deaf. In a fog, she moved through the village, mumbling greetings to people she passed, but not recognizing any of them.

Finally, she staggered to the vicarage. There was a horse tethered out front, so they had a guest, but she couldn't bear the notion of serving tea and playing hostess. She almost spun and ran, but if Oscar was watching out the window, she didn't dare. Where could she hide anyway?

She went inside and hung her cloak on the hook. Very quietly, she tiptoed by the parlor, praying she was invisible and could scurry past without being summoned. But her luck was all bad.

"Josephine," her brother said, "there you are. Please join us."

She forced herself to enter the room. "Hello, Oscar."

"Mr. Mason has paid us a visit."

Jo turned to the man she loathed so deeply, the man who had caused so much misery for so many.

He and Oscar were fast friends, always huddling behind closed doors, but Jo was furious whenever Oscar let him in the house. It was a slap in the face to all those whom Mason had harmed.

"Hello, Mr. Mason." She seated herself in the chair across. "How kind of you to stop by."

"Mrs. Merrick, I insist you call me Benedict."

Unnerved, she glanced at her brother.

"I have great news," Oscar gushed.

"What is it?"

"Mr. Mason and I have discussed the possibility of his courting you, and I've given my permission."

"Court me?"

"Yes."

She felt as if she'd fallen into an abandoned mine pit, that she was tumbling down and down, and when she landed at the bottom, she would be crushed to death.

Courted by Benedict Mason? Was Oscar mad? Why hadn't

he asked her opinion before springing the decision on her? How was she to respond? *No, thank you?*

Both men were grinning, and Mason was puffed up like a rooster, so she had to maneuver very, very carefully.

"I'm honored," she murmured.

"I knew you would be," Oscar said. "That's why I spoke to him about you."

"I appreciate your thinking of me."

"He'll come by on Sunday and escort you to church. The two of you can sit together. Afterward, he's accepted my invitation to Sunday dinner."

"How...lovely."

"Now then"—Oscar pointed to the tea tray—"would you pour for us?"

Jo managed to stand, but she was off balance and dizzy, and she clasped her chair to steady herself.

"Actually, Oscar," she said, "I'm not feeling very well. Would you mind terribly if I retired?"

Oscar scowled. "It's nothing dire, I hope."

"No. I just have the worst headache. I need to lie down."

Oscar might have refused, but Mason intervened. "Certainly, we excuse you."

Jo nodded. "I'm grateful."

She started out as he added, "I'll see you Sunday morning."

"I can't wait."

She climbed the stairs to her room as a wave of nausea swept over her. She grabbed the chamber pot under the bed and vomited up the contents of her stomach.

Chapter Twelve

Nicholas stood by the window, staring out at the park. The moon was up, so he had a good view of his property that stretched to the horizon, but the sight brought him no satisfaction. He could have been gazing at any piece of land.

It was very late, the house silent, and he might have been the last man on Earth.

He'd spent his life, caring for Stephen, but now, Stephen was pulling away. He would forge a new path that didn't include Nicholas. Stephen had always been the driving force that kept Nicholas focused on his goals. If he didn't have to worry about his younger brother, where did that leave him?

Would he stay in the army? For how long? To what end? Would he fight senseless wars until he was crippled or killed?

In a few months, he'd be married to Veronica, and he tried to picture how matrimony would alter him, but he couldn't see what differences it would render. He didn't plan to live with Veronica, and they'd never discussed domestic issues—they'd hardly ever spoken—so he wasn't sure what she was expecting.

She was a spoiled, rich girl, who thrived on clothes and parties, so he doubted matrimony would change *her*, either.

He wanted to fill his nursery with a dozen boys, but only so he'd have plenty of heirs to prevent his relatives from ever inheriting. For that reason alone, he should have been anticipating his wedding night, but he couldn't generate any enthusiasm for the event. Veronica was very beautiful, but in an icy manner that didn't ignite his masculine passions.

Why are you marrying her? a voice shouted in his head. *Why go through with it?*

The question occasionally plagued him, usually on quiet

evenings when he was being maudlin, but he ignored it.

"You know why you're doing it," he muttered to himself.

He was doing it to show the *ton* that he could. He was doing it to enrage the people who'd shunned his parents. There were several lofty pricks who would never get over the infamy, and the notion always made him smile.

A noise sounded out in the hall, and he braced, hoping it was Emeline, but he swiftly realized it wasn't her. It was just the old mansion creaking, and disappointment washed over him.

What was wrong with him? He never moped, but since his arrival at the estate, he was brooding incessantly.

A decanter of brandy was set on the mantle over the hearth, and he grabbed it and poured himself a drink. He sipped it slowly, but it wasn't the cure for what ailed him.

Not counting their brief quarrel out on the lane, he hadn't talked to Emeline in three days. He'd assumed their flirtation was proceeding in a fine fashion, so he'd been surprised at her abruptly informing him that it was over.

After she'd enlightened him, he'd presumed he didn't mind, but his world was incredibly empty without her in it. She'd inserted herself in a flagrant way, and he'd grown used to having her around.

Apparently, he'd developed a fondness for her, one he didn't like and wasn't interested in pursuing, yet he seemed intent on pursuing it anyway.

She didn't want to continue their dalliance? Well, to hell with her! Why should her wishes be paramount? It was his damn house, and she resided in it at his pleasure.

At the moment, his *pleasure* was that she entertain him.

He poured another drink, downed it in a quick gulp, then exited his room and went to the stairs.

Lust and liquor were driving him. It was a deadly combination that often goaded him into trouble, but he couldn't tamp down his need to be with her. He felt as if a magnet were dragging him to her, and he couldn't avoid its strong pull.

He marched to her door and raised a hand to knock, then thought better of it. He wasn't about to give her a chance to refuse him entrance, so he spun the knob and strolled in.

The sitting room was dark, the last embers of a fire glowing in the fireplace. In the bedchamber beyond, a candle burned. He could see her bed, but she wasn't in it.

"Emeline," he snapped, "where are you?"

Bare feet padded across the floor, and she appeared in the doorway. As she espied him, she gasped and lurched back into the bedroom. She raced around the bed, but it was an ineffective shield against him.

He advanced toward her, delighted to note that she was attired only in a robe, with nothing on underneath. Her hair was down and brushed out, the curly locks falling to her waist, and he could smell warm water and soap as if she'd been bathing.

She looked fresh-scrubbed, innocent and decadent all at once, and a flood of lust shot through him.

He desired her as he'd never desired another woman, and he couldn't figure out why. Perhaps there was no answer. Perhaps it was simply a mystery of the universe that wasn't meant to be solved.

"Hold it right there, you bounder."

"No."

"You can't just...just...come in here in the middle of the night."

"Why not? It's my house, and I'm the earl. How many times must I tell you I can do whatever I like?"

He reached for her, and she tried to run, but there was nowhere to go. He grabbed her, and together, they tumbled onto the mattress. He hugged her to his side, a leg draped over her thighs.

"Oh, you are the worst bully," she fumed.

"I know."

"And you're not sorry."

"No, I'm not."

He grinned, but she scowled, and he was determined to wipe it away.

It was the oddest thing, but when he was with her, he felt so much better. The demons plaguing him had vanished, and he couldn't remember why he'd been unhappy.

"Why are you up so late?" she asked.

"I couldn't sleep."

"So you decided to harass me, instead?"

"Yes."

He leaned down and kissed her, and he was annoyed to find himself sighing with contentment.

"I thought we weren't doing this anymore," she complained as he drew away.

"I thought we weren't either, but you're being ridiculous."

"*I* am being ridiculous? You're a cad, who is bent on ruining me and destroying my reputation. I'm trying to save myself."

"We enjoy a potent attraction. Why ignore it?"

"Have you a single honorable intention toward me?"

"No."

She huffed out a disgusted breath, and he was irked by her reaction.

Women adored him. From lowest doxy to highest aristocratic lady, they all assumed they could win, then tame him. They fought to be the one he fancied. Only Emeline Wilson was immune to his charms.

He'd shown how he could change her world. She was living in his mansion, sleeping in his bed, and eating his food. She didn't have to worry about anything.

If ever there was a female who could benefit from an alliance with a rich, powerful male, it was she. But she didn't understand the advantages, and it aggravated him that he had to point them out.

"Have you ever stopped to think," he said, "how you could profit by a liaison with me?"

"I'm not a harlot, and I won't accept compensation."

"That's not what I mean. If you would agree to please me while I'm at Stafford, I would—"

"How long will that be? A few more hours? A day or two?"

"I might be here a whole 'nother week."

"I rest my case. Why should I surrender my virginity merely to satisfy your base urges?"

"Miss Wilson, you love my *base* urges. Admit it."

"Don't twist my words. You're much too sophisticated at these sorts of games, and I refuse to play them with you."

He wasn't playing a game. He was suffering from a terrible attraction, and he wanted to act on it. Her life was all misery and gloom. Wouldn't a torrid affair be just the ticket to improve her mood?

"Will you tell me something?" she asked. "Be serious for once."

"I'll be serious as a rabid dog."

"Lord Stafford..."

"Call me Nicholas."

"No."

"Then I won't listen to your question."

She hemmed and hawed, then said, "Nicholas—"

He laughed and laughed. "You are so easy to manipulate." He swooped in and stole a kiss. "What is it?"

"What is to happen to me and my sisters? It was very kind of you to move us into the manor, but what are we to do next?"

He hadn't considered it. He liked knowing that she was on the premises, that he might round a corner and see her down the hall. He'd even come to like the sound of her sisters careening down the grand staircase.

Though he had to return to London, he felt trapped in a magical spot where he could split into two pieces. One part of him would continue to dawdle at Stafford with Emeline while the other part—his *real* self—would go back to the city, to his marriage and his career in the army.

What should happen to her? He had no idea.

"You'll stay here," he said.

"For how long?"

"For as long as you want."

"People would be shocked."

"So?"

"I care what they think of me."

"You shouldn't. I saw how you were treated that day I arrived. They don't deserve your esteem, and you shouldn't fret over their opinion. It seems to already be awfully low. I can't imagine how you could push it any lower."

"I'm respected in the community," she insisted.

"If you say so."

"I am!"

"Fine. You're respected." He shrugged, giving ground. "I noticed you've been wearing the dresses I bought you."

"Yes, I have been."

"Weren't you adamantly opposed to accepting any gifts?"

"I changed my mind."

"What about your lofty principles?"

"Evidently, I have none whatsoever."

"You haven't said *thank you*."

"I won't, either. You're too vain by half. Any expression of gratitude would make your head swell even further."

He laughed again. He didn't know why he put up with her or why she humored him so completely. He wouldn't have tolerated churlishness in another, but with her, he was fascinated by how she viewed him.

When every other woman loved him, why didn't she? The more she proclaimed her dislike, the more intent he was on reversing her attitude.

"You're been looking very fetching," he told her.

"Don't you dare compliment me."

What female didn't like flattery? What was her problem? As opposed to some of the praise he'd spewed in his life, with her he actually *meant* it.

"Why shouldn't I compliment you?"

"Because—when you're charming—you confuse me. I forget that I hate you."

"We've been through this. You don't hate me. You simply need to recollect how good we are together."

He was tired of talking to her. If he wasn't careful, she'd gab all night, and he'd never have the chance to do what he'd come to do.

He bent down and nuzzled her nape, gratified when goose bumps cascaded down her arms.

"Of all the clothes I purchased for you," he said, "guess which item is my favorite."

"Which one?"

"This robe you have on. It's practically indecent how it hugs your curves."

His fingers were busy, loosening the belt so he could nibble a trail to her cleavage. He dipped under the fabric and sucked a nipple into his mouth.

She hissed and arched up, and he was thrilled by her reaction. She was full of passion, but it was all misdirected. Her energy was never expended on tasks that mattered, on tasks that would bring her pleasure. If she became more selfish and less altruistic, she'd be happier for it; she'd be better off.

"Nicholas," she murmured, and on hearing his name, his idiotic pulse galloped with delight.

"What?"

"Don't hurt me. Swear that you won't."

"Hurt you?" he muttered. "Gad, I'd rather cut off my arm."

"I'm so afraid of where this is leading."

"There's no need to be afraid."

"You demand so many things from me, but I don't know how to give them to you."

"I'll show you how."

"Don't break my heart. Promise me."

"Of course, I won't. I promise."

It was a dishonest reply, but he offered it anyway. On the battlefield, where death was always a possibility, his word was his bond. In all other endeavors, he was a deceitful scoundrel. In his sexual quests, he was no different than any other man. He would take what he wanted and damn the consequences.

He would persist in his relationship with her, but he still planned to leave Stafford at the earliest opportunity. If rumors spread after he was gone, he wouldn't be around to defend her, and he wouldn't come back to fix any damage he'd caused.

Marriage was the sole remedy that would make her whole, but it wasn't one he could provide. He was engaged to another, and even if he wasn't, she would never be the bride he would choose.

She wasn't a wealthy daughter of the *ton*, so as a wife, she held no appeal. But she held a vast amount of appeal in other, more corporeal ways that he was eager to exploit.

Except that, when she gazed at him as she was, he caught himself hesitating. Perish the thought! He—who never hesitated—suddenly felt guilty.

He'd visited her room to press his advantage, to take whatever she could be coerced into surrendering, but now, he was second-guessing. He had to behave more honorably than he'd envisioned he would. Not that he had to be a saint, but he couldn't act like the most despicable sinner.

"It will be all right, Em," he vowed. "Trust me."

"I absolutely don't."

He chuckled, wishing he could be the man she needed.

"We'll be cautious," he insisted.

"Even if we're cautious, you can't predict what might occur."

"Yes, I can. I'm the master of my universe. If I decree that nothing bad will transpire, then nothing bad will."

She sighed. "Vain beast. How can I resist you?"

It was precisely the sort of capitulation he'd been anxious to attain.

He began kissing her, going slow, reveling in the moment, and he was astonished at how much he enjoyed it. Usually, he didn't waste any effort on kissing. Since he fornicated mostly with whores, he never delayed. Carnal release was the goal, so there was no point in dawdling.

Yet with Emeline, he was content to tarry, and he was learning that the real pleasure was in the journey, not in the abrupt ending.

He dropped to her nipples, laving them as her hips flexed with his own. Her robe was open, her loins crushed to his. The fabric of his trousers was all that kept him from racing to ecstasy, and it took every ounce of fortitude he possessed to ignore his raging anatomy.

He touched her between her legs, his fingers sliding into her sheath. She was wet and ready, and instantly, he pushed her into a potent orgasm.

This time, she knew what was coming and what her body was doing. She soared to the heavens, *oohing* and *aahing* in a fashion that thrilled and sobered him.

She was so naïve, so unschooled in the wicked ways of the world. It was rare when he crossed paths with a person who was so...*normal*. He always forgot that she was unsullied and free from the depravity upon which he thrived.

Her excitement waned while his ardor remained unassuaged. He shifted off her and spooned himself to her back. They were quiet, pensive, as he stroked a hand up and down her arm and hip.

"You're smiling," she eventually said. "Why?"

"I seduced you so quickly that I didn't bother to remove any of my clothes. My shirt is still buttoned, and my boots are still on."

"Should I worry about your lusty appetites? Are you in the

habit of disrobing around women?"

He swatted her rump. "None of your business, my little scamp."

She purred and stretched, her curvaceous bottom snuggled to his inflamed cockstand. He moaned in agony and pulled her nearer so he could relish a long thrust that was completely unsatisfying.

"You've made me a wanton," she admitted.

"Good."

"Next time, I want you to undress. I want to see you."

"I'll think about it."

He was having enough trouble restraining himself with his trousers on. If he was naked, there was no telling what he might do.

"You never told me why you couldn't sleep," she drowsily mumbled.

"I have a lot on my mind."

"Such as...?" When he didn't respond, she rose up on an elbow and peered back at him. "Share a secret with me."

He stared into her big green eyes and was amazed to hear himself confess, "It's so strange to be here at Stafford."

"Why?"

"It's supposed to be my home now, but I never had a *home*. I can't fathom how to embrace it."

"You'll figure out how."

"Yes, I imagine I will."

He settled her down so she wasn't looking at him.

He never talked about his feelings with anyone, and he didn't like that he'd discussed his conflicted sentiments regarding Stafford. With how attracted he was to her, she had an enormous physical hold over him. He couldn't have her garnering an emotional one, too.

"What will become of me and my sisters?" She yawned through her query. "You never answered that question, either."

"What would you like to occur?"

"I'd like to suddenly discover that I'm heir to a great fortune. I'd like to be incredibly rich, where I never again have to fret over how to support myself. Sort of like what happened to *you*, for instance."

"Very funny."

"Your life isn't so bad, you know."

"I know."

"You merely like to complain."

He snorted. "You could be right about that."

She reached over her shoulder and laid her palm on his cheek. It was a simple gesture, but it rocked him to his core. He shut his eyes and reveled in an onslaught of affection.

"Seriously, Em," he said when he could speak again, "if you could have anything you wanted, what would it be?"

"I can't think of a single thing. It's been so long since I've had a wish come true that I've forgotten how to dream."

Her reply was too sad, and he was on the verge of offering her gifts he was certain she'd never cherish.

It was the first time he'd genuinely appreciated his money and position. He'd like to spoil her—if she'd allow him to. The problem was that he couldn't so much as buy her a damn dress without her spitting in outrage.

Wasn't that just his luck? He'd finally found a female upon whom he'd like to lavish some of his largesse, but she refused his generosity.

"Let me reopen the school," she begged.

"You and your blasted school," he scoffed, though kindly.

"I want to be useful to you."

"You are useful to me." He caressed a naughty hand down her flank.

"Why do you hate Stafford so much?"

"Ancient history, Em. It's not important."

"It is to me."

"Give it a rest."

"I will—for now. But I'll ask you again tomorrow."

"I *might* tell you. If I'm feeling charitable."

She grew quiet, and he thought she'd dozed off when she said, "I'd like to show you around the estate. If you could meet some of your tenants and learn of their tribulations, I know you'd be happier."

"We'll see." He toyed with her hair, riffling through the lush strands. "Go to sleep."

"I will, but don't you fall asleep, too."

"I'll try not to."

"I mean it. You can't be caught in here."

"I won't be."

He nestled with her, listening as her breathing slowed, as her body relaxed. It was a magical moment, the likes of which he'd never previously experienced with a woman, and he didn't want to leave.

His erection hadn't waned in the slightest, and he wondered how he would bear up with being so constantly aroused.

Had he decided not to deflower her? It wasn't healthy to be so titillated, and if he wouldn't push her into copulation, he had to get himself to London and find someone to tend his needs.

To his amazement, he wasn't in any hurry to return to the city. Would he stay on at Stafford? Was that his plan?

There were only five weeks left of his furlough from the army. Five weeks to remain at Stafford and dally with Emeline. Or five weeks to spend in London where every conceivable vice and vixen was available.

The very idea—that he would choose Emeline and Stafford over the thrills to be had in town—was terrifying. What was happening to him?

He slipped out of her bed, grabbed a quilt, and tucked it around her. For an eternity, he gazed at her, reflecting on how small she looked, how content.

She'd suffered no qualms over slumbering in his presence, and she was a fool to trust him. She supposed—wrongly—that he had her best interests at heart, but he was stupidly, pathetically glad that she did.

He went to the door, peeked out, and tiptoed away.

Chapter Thirteen

Oscar Blair marched down the aisle of the church, his robes billowing out, a Bible clutched to his chest. Organ music rattled the rafters, reminding everyone of God's power over them.

The Sunday service was concluded, and he exited onto the front steps. The congregation followed him out. It was the part of ministering he hated most, the socializing demanded of him as their leader.

He was much happier when he was alone, filling his hours by reading Scripture and writing sermons.

"May the Lord be with you," he murmured, shaking hands over and over.

Not inclined to linger, he hurried people along. He kept glancing inside where Josephine was chatting with Emeline Wilson rather than Benedict Mason, who was bringing up the rear of the crowd.

Finally, Emeline strolled out.

"Where are your sisters, Miss Wilson?" he asked. "You know I don't allow children to miss services. It sets them on a bad path."

"They've come down with colds, Vicar Blair. I had them stay away so you weren't interrupted by their sniffling."

A likely story, he fumed. Her father had been a recalcitrant churchgoer. Oscar had battled with him constantly over his sporadic attendance.

"I'll expect to see them next Sunday."

"I'm sure they'll be better by then."

"They certainly should be, considering your sudden stroke

of good fortune."

Her smile faltered. "What do you mean?"

"You always manage to land on your feet, Emeline. It stokes your vanity."

She frowned. "What is stoking my vanity?"

"You're living at the manor and prevailing on the earl's generosity. As usual, you've inserted yourself where you don't belong and raised yourself above your class. There will be consequences. I suggest you be ready for them."

"I'm not *prevailing* on the earl," she dared to argue. "He's simply provided some Christian charity to me."

"You didn't deserve any."

"And as to my residing in the manor, he's hired me to work for him. I'm earning my keep."

"You are unwed," he hissed, "but brazenly ensconced in the home of a known fornicator. A bachelor, no less. Your morals have flown out the window."

"Honestly, Vicar Blair, you shouldn't—"

"Don't defend yourself to me. The Lord sees all, Emeline Wilson. You've been judged and found lacking."

"Yes, I suppose you're correct," she blithely agreed. She gestured to the lane where a carriage was approaching. "If you'll excuse me? I must be going."

She scurried away, and Oscar watched—aghast—as Lord Stafford arrived to pick her up. His vehicle was built for two, with just the narrow seat where they would sit very close together. It was scandalous!

"Emeline," he called, "what are you thinking?"

"I told you, I'm working for the earl. I'm giving him a tour of the area."

"A tour? You and the earl—alone?"

"We'll be visiting some people in the neighborhood who are struggling."

Oscar wondered if he might faint. He'd practically begged for a meeting with Nicholas Price, but couldn't wrangle one. Yet apparently, every miscreant in a five-mile radius would be blessed with an appointment.

Emeline rubbed salt in his wound by saying, "I thought it might paint a better picture of what's been happening."

It was so inappropriate for her to inject herself into men's business. Why couldn't she understand? As a female, she wasn't intelligent enough to comprehend issues of significance, but she insinuated herself anyway.

"I've counseled you and counseled you, Emeline, not to involve yourself in matters that don't concern you."

"How can conditions at the estate not *concern* me? If the earl hadn't taken pity on me, I'd be living in a ditch."

"His patronage has swelled your pride. For shame, Emeline! For shame!"

"Sorry." She shrugged as if the damage to her reputation—and eventually her soul—was of no import.

Without so much as a wave of acknowledgment to Oscar, the earl jumped down to help Emeline climb in his gig.

Oscar's outrage increased. Emeline appeared to be bosom buddies with the earl, while he—Oscar—hadn't met the man. Oscar had once been the old countess's favorite, but now, he was being treated no differently than the lowest beggar.

He stomped down the stairs and approached the couple.

"Lord Stafford"—he extended his hand in welcome—"I am Vicar Blair."

It was extremely improper for Oscar to introduce himself, but what else could he do?

"Hello, Blair."

The earl didn't shake his outstretched hand. It dangled between them, and finally, Oscar dropped it.

"You missed Sunday services," Oscar complained.

"You shouldn't count on my attendance."

"But you must set an example for the community."

"I'm not interested in being an *example*." The earl looked at the church, and he smirked. "Besides, if I walked through the doors, I might get struck by lightning."

He spun away, and Oscar bristled with indignation. He wouldn't be dismissed as if he were of no consequence.

"Lord Stafford!" he said more sharply than he'd intended.

The earl whipped around. "What?"

"I must know when you'll come by the vicarage. We need to discuss the congregation and my future plans for it."

"I don't care about your plans. Whatever you choose is fine with me. Just stop being such a sanctimonious busybody."

Oscar's cheeks flamed red. His fury sparked. "I'm an expert

at guiding my flock to the ways of the Lord. The old countess never had a word of criticism in how I conducted myself."

"Well, she's no longer here, is she? I'm in charge, and I can't abide your religious posturing."

"Lord Stafford," Emeline interrupted, "if you were to—"

"Emeline!" Oscar barked. "How many times must I remind you? You are a woman, and thus, you have no place in this conversation. Be silent."

The earl turned to her. "You were saying, Miss Wilson?"

"We're keeping the vicar from his Sunday dinner. Perhaps we should be going."

"Yes, perhaps we should."

Oscar was so angry, he was trembling.

He glared, mute and aggrieved, as the earl lifted her into the gig. He released her, then whirled to face Oscar, and Oscar humiliated himself by asking, "When will you be available for an appointment?"

"I won't ever be." The earl leaned nearer and whispered, "Miss Wilson is an employee of mine. I don't take kindly to her being disrespected. Not by anyone."

"Emeline requires regular male guidance. I shall render it whenever necessary."

"Insult her again, and I'll pound you into the ground."

"You would threaten a man of the cloth?"

"Push me, and I'll do more than threaten. Don't forget: You serve at my pleasure. How much do you value your job? Don't annoy me or you'll wish you hadn't."

The arrogant brute sauntered away, went 'round the carriage, and climbed in. As if he hadn't a care in the world, as if he hadn't just offended a minister of the Church, he clicked the reins and they were off.

Oscar understood that he possessed a sizeable temper, so he strove to present a calm front to others. Yet at that moment, if he'd been holding a gun, he'd have shot Nicholas Price right between his swiftly retreating shoulder blades.

He tugged on his robe, patted his burning cheeks, then headed for the vicarage and the hot meal that awaited.

Stephen dawdled in the cemetery, watching as Sunday

services ended. He was eager to waylay Josephine so they could sneak away and talk.

He thought she would agree to a rendezvous. She had to be as miserable as he was over their separation, and he was determined to convince her to reverse her course.

Initially, when she'd broken off their affair, he hadn't been bothered by her decision. While he enjoyed their physical attraction, he'd never been at a loss for sexual partners, particularly now with his brother's prominence.

Women chased after him, just as they chased after Nicholas, and he'd assumed he would select a bride from the crop of aristocratic girls as Nicholas had.

Then it had dawned on him—why should he?

He'd met plenty of the daughters of the *ton*, and nary a one was mature enough to marry, let alone take on the chore of raising Annie. For that important task, he needed a person who was sensible and pragmatic, who could ignore Annie's illegitimate status and love her anyway.

Why not ask Jo to be his bride?

She was pretty, friendly, and compassionate, and she had the character of a saint. She was living in the worst of circumstances, yet she always had a smile on her face, and if she could put up with her priggish brother, she could put up with anything.

He smugly supposed that she'd be flattered by a proposal. He would rescue her from dire straits, would give her her own home, but this time, with a husband who cherished her.

She'd have a daughter right away, and if they were lucky, they'd have more children. She claimed she was barren, and it was accepted fact that—when a marriage produced no offspring—it was the woman's fault. But he'd seen several instances where barren women had become pregnant with new spouses after their husbands had died.

He was an optimist and believed that they'd have more children. And if they didn't? He'd be happy with Jo and Annie.

The church doors opened, and he was almost giddy with anticipation. Vicar Blair emerged, and he stood on the steps, chatting with his parishioners as they exited.

Very quickly, the crowd emptied out, until Emeline Wilson was the last to appear. The vicar had some sharp words for her, and she stoically endured her scolding, then she sidled away.

She waved toward the lane, and Stephen peered over to see his brother approaching in a carriage. Nicholas leapt down and was helping Miss Wilson into the vehicle, when the vicar accosted him.

Stephen considered leaving his hiding spot among the tombstones in order to save the poor minister, but before he could, Nicholas said something that made the vicar blanch with dismay. Had Nicholas fired the pious dunce? Had he cursed at him? Had he blasphemed?

With Nicholas, there was no telling.

Nicholas spun away and climbed into the gig. He grabbed the reins, and as he did, he flashed a look at Miss Wilson that had Stephen wincing with alarm. If he hadn't been observing so closely, he'd have missed it.

He knew that look. He'd witnessed it dozens, if not hundreds of times in his life. Gad, his brother was seducing Emeline Wilson! Was he insane?

Nicholas had mentioned that he'd put Miss Wilson to work, but obviously, Stephen hadn't comprehended the exact sort of job his brother had in mind.

This wasn't the city where Nicholas could act however he pleased. This was a rural village, in conservative, traditional England. A man didn't trifle with a maiden unless matrimony was his objective, and for Nicholas, it certainly wasn't.

He was betrothed! Even if he wasn't, he'd never pick Miss Wilson as his bride. She was about to end up ruined and disgraced, and what would happen to her then?

She'd be expecting a different conclusion, but Nicholas would never ride to her rescue. Even if he *promised* her a commitment, he wouldn't keep it.

"Oh, for pity's sake," Stephen grumbled. "What next?"

He foresaw a lengthy line of trouble, of scandal and recrimination and debts that would have to be paid, but he didn't want any of it to flare up. Nor did he want to be the one forced to deal with the situation, and Stephen *always* had to sweep up Nicholas's messes.

His brother needed a stern talking to. He had to remember who he was and who Miss Wilson was, and Stephen was the only person who could make him listen.

He had to return to the manor with all due haste, and he'd mounted his horse when Jo strolled out of the church with

Benedict Mason. She was holding his arm, grinning as if he was humorous and witty. For his part, Mason seemed completely altered from the man he actually was.

The gruff, stern land agent had become the doting swain.

Were they courting? They had to be. How long had they been attached? How deep was Jo's affection?

She'd never mentioned the relationship. Why not? What kind of woman was she? If she could tumble into a barn with Stephen while being wooed by another, she had to have no integrity, at all.

A surge of fury rushed through him. He kicked his horse into a gallop and raced from the cemetery. He flew by the cooing couple, his horse's hooves spraying them with rocks and dirt, but he didn't care and he didn't glance back.

"We need to talk."

Nicholas stared down the hall to where his brother was standing in the doorway to the library. Obviously, Stephen was peeved over some budding disaster, but Nicholas was in no mood to hear about it.

He started off, prepared to ignore his brother's summons, and Stephen added, "Now, Nicholas."

"Later. I'm busy at the moment."

He'd spent a near-perfect afternoon with Emeline, chatting with tenants who'd fallen on hard times. Her view of the estate had given him an entirely new perspective, and he wasn't ready for the encounter to end.

It had been a delicious torment, sitting with her, pretending no heightened acquaintance, and he was weary of the distance she'd imposed.

She'd gone to her room, to wash and rest before tea, and he planned to join her there for a bit of naughty dallying. His brother could wait.

"Get your ass in here," Stephen snapped, "or I will grab you and drag you in."

"Have you finally decided you're man enough?"

It was an old taunt, frequently hurled.

He and Stephen had often quarreled in their lives, but they rarely engaged in fisticuffs because Stephen knew better than to brawl. Nicholas was the elder brother but also the tougher, stronger brother. He fought dirty. He delivered low blows. Stephen was too honorable, and he could never win against such an unprincipled opponent.

Yet to Nicholas's surprise, Stephen loomed toward him, as if he was eager to give it another shot. Nicholas couldn't fathom what was needling him, and he raised his hands in mock surrender.

"All right, all right. Have it your way."

Stephen returned to the library, and Nicholas followed. He was crossing the foyer when the front door opened. Benedict Mason entered.

Nicholas nodded in greeting and said, "I need to speak with you in the morning."

"As always, Lord Stafford, I am at your service. May I ask the topic?"

"I'm lifting the restrictions as to hunting and fishing in the park."

"I don't believe that's wise, milord."

"I'm not concerned as to whether it's *wise*, Mr. Mason. It's what I want."

"People will come to expect such a benefit. They'll grow accustomed. If circumstances change in the future, you'll never be able to rescind it."

"Why would I ever rescind it? I have more than enough. I can share; it won't kill me." Mason looked as if he might argue, and Nicholas decreed, "Spread the word. Make sure everyone knows."

"If I may, milord, I should like to review the financial ramifications, so I can present a more complete case for my position at our morning meeting."

"No."

Nicholas walked on, and though he caught a glimpse of Mason's dour expression, he wasn't worried by Mason's reluctance.

Mason might disagree with Nicholas's decision, but he'd implement it. He was aware of who paid his salary, who provided him with his fine house behind the manor, and he wouldn't jeopardize it over an issue as silly as fishing.

Over the prior year, Nicholas had let Mason convince him

that harsh austerity measures were warranted. But Emeline had persuaded him to try a different path.

He didn't have to be cruel or ruthless. Prosperity could be achieved as quickly with mercy and compassion as it could be with spite and malice.

Just that easily, Mason was forgotten. Nicholas burst into the library and kicked the door shut with his boot. It banged hard enough to rattle the windows. He stomped to the sideboard and poured himself a whiskey. Then, fortified for battle, he seated himself at the large oak desk.

He hated the ostentatious room, with its expensive chandeliers, soft carpets, and bookshelves that rose to the ceiling. It stoked a pretentiousness he didn't feel, as if the space was grander than he was and he didn't fit in it.

He swiveled and gazed out at the park. From his vantage point, he could see the gate at the end of the driveway. On that horrid long-ago day, when he and Stephen had stood there like beggars, had the old earl sat in the same chair, callously observing as they'd been turned away?

Disturbed by the image, he whipped around to face his brother.

"What is it?" he demanded. "Please get on with it. I'm in a hurry."

Stephen poured his own whiskey, then plopped into the chair opposite.

"What has you so preoccupied?" Stephen asked.

"None of your business."

"I saw you this morning with Miss Wilson."

"So?"

Nicholas glared, and Stephen glared back, the seconds ticking by. The silence stretched to infinity. Stephen acted as Nicholas's conscience, and Nicholas usually heeded him, but not always. Not when he desperately craved what he wasn't supposed to have.

"You might as well confess," Stephen ultimately said, "and don't lie to me."

"I wouldn't dream of it," Nicholas sarcastically replied.

"What have you done?"

"I've started an affair."

Stephen nodded, as if Nicholas had confirmed his every low

opinion.

"Have you deflowered her, you wretch?"

"A gentleman should never kiss and tell."

"A *gentleman* shouldn't, so you don't qualify." Nicholas raised an arrogant brow, and Stephen bellowed, "Have you forged ahead?"

"Not yet."

"But you plan on it?"

Nicholas shrugged.

He wasn't sure what he wanted. He was roiling with lust, but couldn't seem to alleviate it. For some idiotic reason, he'd decided to behave honorably toward her, but he couldn't figure out how to accomplish chivalry while naked.

Stephen slapped a hand on the desk, a loud *crack* echoing off the high ceiling.

"Do you plan to ruin her?"

"Perhaps."

"What will become of her after you're through?"

"Why would anything happen? We've been extremely discreet."

"This is a very small place. Everyone will eventually learn of it."

"They will not," he declared with an annoying confidence.

"What if she winds up pregnant?"

"She won't."

"Are you God now?" Stephen taunted. "Can you commence and halt procreation?"

"Shut up."

"When your liaison is discovered—as it will be—how will you proceed? Will you marry her?"

"You know I can't."

"So what is your option? Will you leave her at the mercy of Oscar Blair? Would you like me to predict how he'll deal with her?"

"She'll be fine; you're making too much of this."

"She was never taught about men like you," Stephen said. "She doesn't realize the cold heart that beats in your chest. She believes your affection is genuine and that you have matrimony in mind."

"She's wrong."

"Have you told her about Veronica?"

At the question, Nicholas's pulse fluttered. He hadn't mentioned his engagement and didn't see why he should. London seemed far away, Veronica a figment of his imagination.

"No, I haven't told her. Why would I? She'd be crushed."

"Oh Nick..." Stephen sighed with disgust. He downed his drink, then went over and poured a second. He downed that, too. "Here is what you're going to do."

"You're issuing ultimatums? To me?"

"No, I'm saving that girl's life. She's endured plenty, and I won't let you wreck what little remains for her."

"Maybe it's not up to you," Nicholas snidely goaded. "Maybe for once, I'll act however the hell I want, your fussy morals be damned."

Stephen shocked them both by pitching his glass at the fireplace. It shattered into dozens of pieces, shards flying everywhere.

"Are you insane?" Nicholas seethed as Stephen marched to the desk. He leaned over, his palms braced on the polished wood.

"Here is what you are going to do," he nagged again. "You will get up in the morning. You'll eat breakfast, saddle your horse, then ride to London. You will not say goodbye to her. You will not give her any hint of your intentions. You will simply sneak away, then you will *never* come back until you hear—in the distant future—that she is happily married to some local boy who loves her as you never could."

Nicholas's thoughts reeled, the notion of *his* Em wed to another making him ill. He absolutely could not envision such a thing.

"I'm not ready to return to London," he protested.

"If you don't do as I've bid you, I will tell her about Veronica. I'll tell her you're betrothed and have been for months." Stephen leaned even nearer and hissed, "I'll tell her that your wedding is at the end of August! How would you guess she'll take the news?"

"You wouldn't dare."

"Wouldn't I? I'm not bluffing. Don't force my hand."

Stephen eased away and sank into his chair. They were silent again, glowering.

A thousand words were on the tip of Nicholas's tongue. He yearned to explain his strange infatuation, to justify his conduct, even though there was no excuse for it.

Still, he felt compelled to plead, "She'd never understand about Veronica."

"No, she wouldn't."

"Why would you deliberately hurt her?"

Stephen scoffed. "Why would *I* hurt her? Oh, that's rich."

"She'll hate me."

"She should hate you. You're contemptible."

"She doesn't think I am. She thinks I'm wonderful."

"Then someone should tell her the truth. It might as well be me."

Stephen's derision was clear, but then, he'd known Nicholas for a long time. Stephen had no illusions about Nicholas's character, and Nicholas couldn't abide his condemning stare. He shifted to gaze out the window again, surveying his property, all the way to the gate that held such a lonely, awful memory.

Was it so wrong to dally with Emeline? He'd never really had anything that mattered. *She* mattered. Stephen was asking him to let her go, and Nicholas couldn't bear the idea. Part of it was general stubbornness. If he was ordered to behave in a certain manner, he'd do the opposite merely to be contrary.

Yet he *wanted* Emeline—both for the moment and into the future. Whether that would be weeks or months, he couldn't say. But the prospect of splitting with her was galling.

"What if I..."—he paused, formulating nonsensical plans— "what if I took her to London with me? I could set her up in a house, and she could be my—"

"No."

"Why not? There are worse fates than being mistress to an earl."

"You expect she'd agree to such an immoral situation? That she'd subject her young sisters to it?"

"She might," Nicholas persisted, even though he knew she never would.

"She's in love with you! She's convinced you're about to propose marriage. You mentioned that she thinks you're wonderful. What will her opinion be after you make another sort of proposal entirely?"

"It could happen. You'd be surprised how easily I can persuade a woman."

"No I wouldn't. I know you, remember? What about Veronica? You're about to marry her. If you hook up with a mistress right before the wedding, she'll find out. Wives always do. What would you guess *her* opinion will be?"

"My personal life will never be any of her business."

Stephen barked out a laugh. "If that's what you assume, then you're an idiot." He stood and went to the door.

"Where are you going?"

"I'm sick of you. I want to be out of your sight."

"Well, I'm not too thrilled with you, either. Get out before I throw you out."

"I'm not returning to London with you."

"You've already told me so a dozen times."

"And I'm not returning to the army."

"What?"

"I've written some letters. I'm trying to muster out early, so Annie can come to England later in the summer."

Nicholas had constantly been vexed by Stephen's attachment to his daughter. He barely knew the girl and hadn't lived with her but for a few months when she was a baby. What had caused such a strong bond?

Nor could he fathom Stephen's desire to settle at Stafford. Why would he?

"You're bringing Annie here?" Nicholas sneered, terribly hurt by Stephen's decision and covering it with spite. "It will finally be just the two of you, the happy little family you've always craved."

"Yes, my happy little family." Stephen opened the door. "I'll give you 'til nine o'clock tomorrow morning. If you haven't departed by then, Miss Wilson and I will have a long, interesting chat."

Stephen walked out, and Nicholas tarried in the quiet, pondering, reviewing his options, finishing his drink. Then he stormed to the barn, saddled his fastest horse, and rode off into the waning afternoon.

Benedict dawdled in the foyer, observing as the earl

slammed the library door, then he tiptoed down the hall and pressed his ear to the wood.

He'd had it with the Price brothers and wanted them gone. They couldn't head for London quick enough to suit him.

He'd made the tough choices on Lord Stafford's behalf. He'd done all the dirty work, and now—thanks to Emeline's interference—the earl was unraveling many of Benedict's best ideas.

He was in a temper and had to figure out how to wean the earl away from Emeline's destructive influence. Hopefully, a bit of eavesdropping would provide some clues as to how Benedict should proceed.

The two brothers were silent, one of them stomping around then, to Benedict's eternal astonishment, the conversation began and the immediate topic was Emeline.

You might as well confess, Mr. Price demanded, *and don't lie to me.*

I wouldn't dream of it, the earl snidely replied.

What have you done?

I've started an affair.

Have you deflowered her, you wretch?

A gentleman should never kiss and tell.

Benedict staggered away, hurrying down the deserted corridors until he lurched into an empty parlor. Panting with shock, he leaned against the wall to steady himself.

Widow Brookhurst's suspicions had been correct: Emeline was a whore, swayed to harlotry by the worst scoundrel in England!

Benedict had previously tendered a decent, honest marriage proposal to Emeline, but for the price of a few dresses, she'd rather prostitute herself to Nicholas Price.

The news was murderously offensive and beyond his comprehension.

He didn't know how he would use the information—the vicar certainly had to be apprised—but he would exploit it to her detriment. He would bide his time, he would watch and wait.

Nicholas Price wouldn't be at Stafford forever. He would leave very soon. Perhaps by tomorrow or the next day. Once he was gone, Emeline's fate would be sealed.

Chapter Fourteen

"What will happen to us?"

"I have no idea, but I'm sure it will be something grand."

Emeline tucked the blanket over Nan, then turned to the other bed and did the same for Nell.

"You received a letter today," Nell said.

"How would you know that, you little scamp?"

"We were spying on Mr. Jenkins," she admitted, unabashed. "Who was it from? Was it from another school?"

"Yes."

"Was it good news?"

"Not this time. They've hired someone else, but I'm certain a positive response will arrive very soon."

She kept her smile firmly fixed so the twins wouldn't note her anxiety. She'd applied for dozens of jobs, but she had no experience *and* two sisters to bring along to any situation. Employers weren't eager to retain people with such large burdens.

She was waiting for one last reply, but she wasn't optimistic.

"What about Lord Stafford?" Nan asked. "Why won't he let you start the school here? He seems so nice. I don't understand why he won't agree."

"He's still considering it," Emeline lied.

"Guess what we think," Nell said, and they both giggled.

"What?" Emeline inquired.

"You and the earl should get married."

"Get married!"

"If you were his wife, it would solve all our problems,

wouldn't it?"

"We're not marrying, so you can shove that silly notion out of your busy heads."

"You like him," Nan pointed out, "and we like him, too."

"And we can tell he likes you," Nell added.

"We're friends," Emeline sternly insisted, "and I work for him. There's no more to it than that, and you shouldn't expect there might be."

"If you say so." Nan's comment set off a second round of giggles.

"I *do* say so, and I won't have the two of you talking about this. If any of the servants heard you, I'd be extremely embarrassed."

The last thing she needed was her sisters constructing a fairytale. She'd given Nicholas plenty of chances to answer Nan's original question—*What will happen to us?*—but he wasn't inclined to make a decision. Then again, he hadn't tossed them out, either.

It was a frustrating limbo, and she'd been annoyingly timid about pushing him for a resolution. Life in the manor was so easy, and she'd quickly acclimated. She didn't *want* her circumstances to change, for it would mean he was tired of her. If she lost his favor, he would put her aside and move on, and she'd never be with him again.

"Sleep now," she murmured.

She blew out the candle and proceeded to her room. She walked slowly, wondering if she might bump into him on the stairs, but she didn't.

Since their afternoon visiting, she hadn't seen him. A servant had mentioned that he'd ridden off on his horse, but Emeline couldn't pry as to why he'd left or where he'd gone. She could only wait for him to return.

Dawdling, she prepared for bed, washing up, brushing her hair, dressing in the robe he'd bought her. She went to the window seat and snuggled on the cushion. She stared out across the park, praying the roads would convey him home safely.

An eternity passed before boot steps sounded off in the distance. She sagged with relief and pressed her fingers to the cool glass of the window. Peering out at the stars, she whispered frantic wishes: that he was hale and unharmed, that he wouldn't hurt her when their affair was concluded, that she would survive in the world as it would be after he departed forever.

He came closer and closer, and with each stride, her fears lessened. Why had she so calmly accepted that there was no future for them?

She was an optimist who tackled problems and vowed to fix them. Why was she so willing to concede a bad end? Why should she automatically assume that they would separate?

Yes, he was an earl and far above her in station, but he hadn't always been. Until the prior year, he'd been an orphan whose sole prospect was his rank in the army. A stroke of fate had elevated him, but deep inside, he was an ordinary man.

They could wed. They could build a life together at Stafford.

Suddenly, her pulse was racing with excitement, and she told herself that she would do whatever he asked to bring about the finale she craved.

He stopped at her door but didn't enter. For the longest while, he hovered in the hall, as if debating whether to come in. He tarried until she grew afraid that he'd keep on, so she clambered to the floor, hurried over, and spun the knob herself.

They gazed at each other, not speaking, a thousand words swirling between them that couldn't be voiced aloud. His color was high, his hair tousled by the wind. Masculine smells of horses and cold night air wafted from his clothes.

There was a bleakness in his eyes that made them especially blue. The cocky, conceited soldier had vanished, replaced by a troubled, weary soul.

"Are you all right?" she queried.

Nodding, he stepped into the room and enfolded her in his arms. He crushed her to his chest, holding her as if he might never release her.

"I missed you," she said.

"You shouldn't have."

"When I learned that you'd left the estate, that you were riding around in the dark, I was so worried."

"You should never fret about me. I'm always fine. I always land on my feet."

He drew away and took her hands in his. They stood, swaying, like besotted adolescents.

"Where did you go?" she asked.

"Nowhere in particular."

"What's wrong?"

"I just have a lot on my mind. I had to clear it."

"Have you cleared it?"

"More or less."

"Tell me what vexes you. Maybe I can help."

"*You* vex me."

"I hope in a good way?"

"Yes, in a very good way."

He shrugged out of his coat and dropped it on a nearby chair, then he walked to her bedchamber, leading her behind him. He lay down on the bed and stretched out, and he pulled her down with him. She nestled at his side as he studied the ceiling, lost in thought.

His distress was palpable, but he didn't seem able to discuss what was bothering him. Apparently, she would have to begin any conversation.

"What are you thinking about?" she inquired.

"You."

She propped herself up on an elbow. "What about me?"

He traced a finger across her bottom lip. "I'm glad we met."

"So am I."

"I'll always be glad."

"I will be, too."

His tone had her heart racing again, but not with elation. He was assessing her as if memorizing her features, as if cataloguing them for later reflection.

"I have to return to London soon," he told her.

"Why?"

"I never intended to be here this long. I'm due back with my regiment."

"Will you travel to Stafford occasionally in the future?"

There was a lengthy pause, then he said, "I will as often as I can."

"Will we still be"—she struggled to find the correct word— "friends?"

"Absolutely."

"What about me and my sisters? What will become of us?"

Another protracted pause ensued, and ultimately, he asked, "Would you ever consider coming to London with me?"

"To London?" She laughed and shook her head. "No. Why couldn't you stay at Stafford with *me*?"

"It's complicated."

"No, it's not. It's very, very simple." She rested a hand on his cheek. "When you first arrived at the estate, you had misgivings, but they're fading. You're changing; you're starting to enjoy your ownership."

"I suppose I am."

"I don't want you to go away." She tossed the dice, risking all. "I want you to remain here. With me."

"You'd like that, would you?"

"You would, too. Please don't deny it. You've never had a home of your own. This could be your home. We could marry, we could be so happy."

He chuckled but sadly. "You have such a high opinion of me."

"You deserve it! You're wonderful, but you spend all your time trying to be awful. I see the special man hiding beneath all the bluster. You could be that man for me. I know you could."

"You make it sound so easy."

"It *is* easy. You could muster out of the army. You could come home. To Stafford. To *me*."

"What would I do with you?" He smiled. "I'm not used to living around a female. You'd drive me insane with all your chatter."

"You like me a tad more than you care to admit."

He took a deep breath, let it out slowly. "You could be right about that."

"Is it because you're an earl now? Is that it? You're too far above me?"

"Gad, no. You're very fine, *too* fine for the likes of me."

She received some solace from the compliment. "Then what is it? Why are you so disconcerted?"

"I shouldn't have visited you tonight, but I couldn't keep myself away."

"Of course, you should have visited. If you don't belong here with me, where do you belong?"

He stared and stared, and she thought he might confide in

her, but instead, he kissed her. He rolled her onto her back, his heavy body pressing her into the mattress. She pulled him closer, but she couldn't get him near enough.

She wanted to be so securely connected that there would be no distance between them, that they would be one person rather than two, but she had no idea how to accomplish it.

He seemed to be on a frantic quest, as well. There was an air of desperation about him, as if he were drowning and in need of her rescue. She would gladly save him; she just didn't understand the dangers so she couldn't devise the best method.

He fumbled with the belt on her robe, and very quickly, she was naked. She didn't try to stop him, didn't complain or demur. There was such joy in pleasing him.

His fingers were busy, and swiftly, she was titillated to the point of madness. But this time, she yearned for more from him than he'd given her previously.

"I love you." She hadn't meant for the declaration to slip out, but she couldn't hold it in.

"You shouldn't tell me that."

"Why not? It's true. You know it is." He was nibbling at her breast, and she dragged him to her so that he had to look her in the eye. "Have you ever been loved, Nicholas?"

"No, never."

"Then let me be the one."

He sighed. "You shouldn't have these strong feelings. Believe me. I'm not worth it."

"Yes, you are! How can I convince you?"

"I'm not who you presume I am."

"Says who?"

"Says me."

"What do you know about anything? You're a man, so you're a fool."

He snorted. "I'm sure you're correct."

"Shower me with your affection. Let it all rain down on me. Whatever you ask, whatever you need, I'll give it to you."

He studied her, his torment clear. It was obvious that a huge debate was raging in his mind. Finally, he nodded, as if he'd reached a decision.

"I want to be happy, Em," he said. "I want *you* to make me happy."

"I will, you silly oaf."

"For once, I'll forge ahead and damn the consequences."

Nicholas gazed at Emeline. Had those words actually come out of his mouth? Would he proceed to the worst conclusion of all?

Apparently, he would.

After his quarrel with Stephen, he'd spent hours riding the back roads, pushing his horse to the limit. He'd rein in at roadside inns, to drink and brood, then canter on. He'd been in a fine state, pining for things he couldn't name, things he couldn't have.

Emeline had wormed herself into his life, to a spot where he couldn't imagine her gone from it. She belonged to him and with him, and the notion of fleeing and leaving her behind as Stephen had demanded, was too bizarre to consider.

Yet Stephen was right, she deserved more than a sordid alliance. Any relationship was idiotic and impossible, and he should never have permitted his fondness to simmer to a boil. He'd known better, but he'd selfishly done it anyway.

He'd allowed Emeline to become important to him, and he couldn't comprehend why. Lust was spurring his fascination, and if they copulated a time or two, he was positive his infatuation would sizzle out. In his sexual affairs, it was always the same story. Like a dog at the hunt, he chased his prey until he caught it, but the moment the pursuit was ended, he lost interest.

He would cede to Stephen's blackmail and return to London in the morning. But he couldn't go without learning what it was like to have her in the only way that mattered.

He began kissing her and kissing her, driving her up the spiral of desire. He toyed with her breasts, with her nipples, as his naughty fingers slithered into her sheath.

It was an easy task, bringing her to orgasm. She soared to the heavens, then floated back down, and she was chuckling, sputtering with delight.

Her joy was infectious. He was laughing, too, reveling in her pleasure, and for once, he would join her in it. He'd denied himself, and his restraint had put him on an odd path of regret and reflection that he hated.

As she calmed and stilled, he was unbuttoning his

trousers.

"I can't believe I keep letting you do that to me," she said.

"Deep down, you're a wanton. You love it when I arouse you, and carnal play is like an addictive drug. The more we indulge, the more you'll crave."

"Are you saying you're irresistible?"

"That's precisely what I'm saying."

"Is that why you're grinning like the cat that ate the canary?"

"Yes. I'm thrilled to have uncovered your true nature."

"Vain beast."

"Yes, I am. I definitely am."

They quieted, his features sobering, and she cocked her head, evaluating him as if she could see all the way to his black heart.

"You look so sad," she said. "Tell me what you're thinking."

"I'm not sad. I just need something from you."

"What is it?"

"Remember when we first started all this?"

"As if I could forget."

"I told you there was more to it."

"Yes, you did."

"I want to show you the rest."

"I'm not sure what you're asking of me."

"I want to join my body to yours, as a husband does with his wife."

He touched her between her legs, indicating his goal, but short of actually proceeding, she could never understand.

"Explain to me what will occur."

"It's simpler if I demonstrate."

"You said it's what a husband 'does with his wife'. How can we if we're not married?"

"It's merely physical conduct. You don't have to be wed."

"It's wrong if we're not."

He shrugged. "Some people insist that it is."

"Not you?"

"No, not me." He kissed her, sweetly, tenderly. "I want this, Em. So much. I'm desperate to know you like this."

"You make it so hard to say *no.*"

"Then don't."

"I want you to be happy. I'm just afraid."

"Of what?"

"If I agree, it will mean everything to me, but it should mean something to you, too. I'm afraid that it won't."

"Oh, Em, it's the greatest gift you could ever bestow."

She hesitated, and he could see that he was wearing her down, that she was anxious to relent.

Ultimately, she nodded. "Yes, Nicholas, whatever you need, I'm glad to give it to you."

At her capitulation, he should have been elated, but he wasn't. His conscience was railing at him, shouting that he was a scoundrel, but he couldn't listen. He felt as if he were in a runaway carriage, that he couldn't slow it down or alter its course. He could only hold on through the wild ride.

"Promise me," he pleaded, "that you'll never be sorry."

"I never will be. I promise."

"Promise me that—no matter what happens in the future—you'll always cherish this memory."

"I always will."

Sentiment swept over him, and suddenly, he was terribly conflicted. Though he owed her no fidelity, it seemed as if he was cheating on her, being disloyal for hiding his situation with Veronica.

He was on the verge of changing his mind, but she must have sensed his anguish.

"It will be all right, Nicholas," she gently soothed.

"I couldn't bear to hurt you."

"You never will."

She pulled him to her, and *she* started their next race to ecstasy by initiating a stirring kiss in which he gleefully participated. He used her fervor to her detriment, persuading himself that she was eager for what was coming. They were both keen to proceed. They would both be better off after they were through.

He aroused her, his hands roaming, his mouth nibbling, until she was once more on the brink of bliss. Baring his flanks, he tugged down his trousers, his torso dropping between her thighs. He took his cock and wedged the tip into her sheath.

At the peculiar positioning, she tensed and frowned.

"What are you doing?" she asked.

"I'm going to join my body to yours, remember?"

"Are you sure this is the correct way?"

Her innocent question underscored the depravity of his conduct, but he ignored his reservations.

"Yes, I'm sure this is correct." He wedged in a tad farther. "It will hurt—just for a moment. Then it will feel grand."

"It doesn't *feel* grand now."

"It will. Trust me."

"You know I don't."

She smiled a smile that was old and wise, as if she knew something he didn't. He glanced away and dipped to her breasts, laving them, nursing at them until her pleasure rose and crested.

As her orgasm commenced, as she cried out, he clutched her hips and thrust once and again, and burst through her maidenhead.

"Oh..." she breathed, and she hugged him very tight.

He drew away slightly, and he was aghast to see tears in her eyes.

"I'm...I'm sorry, Em. I didn't—"

"I'm fine, I'm fine."

"Are you certain?"

"The pain is waning—as you told me it would."

"It will be over in a minute."

"It already is."

He'd never lain with a virgin before, so he hadn't understood how monumental the episode would be. Mustering all his fortitude, he held himself very still, waiting while she acclimated.

Her hot maiden's blood was urging him to finish, and as she relaxed the tiniest bit, he began to flex. He was much too rough, pushing in all the way, then retreating to the tip, and the encounter escalated much too quickly. He couldn't slow the approaching rush.

The most alarming explosion of passion flooded his loins, and he couldn't tamp it down. He'd planned to do the sane thing, the rational thing, and withdraw at the last second, but he'd never been so titillated, and he recklessly emptied himself against her womb.

Cheryl Holt

With a shudder, he ground to a halt and slid away. He snuggled her onto her side, and he spooned himself to her back.

They were silent, with him running a hand up and down her arm and thigh. He was very attuned to her, and he could sense her roiling emotions. He might have probed her thoughts, but he'd rutted like a beast, and he was afraid of what she might say.

Eventually, she murmured, "It was different than I imagined it would be."

"In what way?"

"I didn't realize it was so...physical. I assumed it would be...I don't know...more romantic, I guess."

He winced. "It can be very romantic. I simply didn't do it very well. You entice me beyond my limit. I couldn't control myself."

"I didn't want you to control yourself."

"It gets better with repetition."

They were quiet for another lengthy interval, then she asked, "I'm not a virgin anymore, am I?"

"No."

"Could I be pregnant?"

"It can't happen from just one time," he claimed, not having any idea why he'd lie.

For an insane instant, he almost wished she was pregnant. He could picture the little girl they'd create. She'd have Emeline's big green eyes and pretty blond hair. Or perhaps it would be a boy with his handsome looks, attitude, and swagger. But he shoved the poignant vision aside.

He was betrothed and would be married very soon, and while he didn't care about Veronica, he wasn't such a tactless brute that he'd sire an illegitimate child shortly before the ceremony. In wedding him, Veronica would have to put up with a great deal, but he wouldn't make her put up with *that*. It wouldn't be fair to her or Emeline.

So Emeline couldn't be pregnant. He was the master of his world. He would command it away, and it would never transpire.

His hand rested on her waist. She clasped hold and linked their fingers, giving his a squeeze.

"This was for the best, wasn't it?" she queried.

170

"Of course it was."

"It changed everything. We can be together now."

"Yes, we can," he agreed. He was too drowsy to decipher what she meant. Carnal lethargy was sweeping him away, so he was in no mood to chat.

"We'll go forward, as I'd hoped we would." She paused, and with a hitch in her voice—was she crying?—she said, "Are you happy?"

"Yes, Em, I'm very happy."

"I'm so glad I'm yours. Yours forever."

"Mine forever," he concurred.

Her breathing lagged, her body relaxing, as slumber approached.

"You can't stay in here," she mumbled.

"I won't. I'll wait 'til you doze off, then I'll leave."

She gave his fingers a final squeeze, but no more words were spoken.

The quiet settled in, the air cooling, and he tugged a blanket over them. He tarried, listening, watching her. He wanted to remember her as she was at that moment—warm and sleepy and sexy and beautiful. And too, too trusting.

The first crack of dawn appeared on the horizon, and he slipped from the bed.

He stood, straightening his clothes, gazing down at her. There was the strangest pressure in the center of his chest, as if his heart was...was...breaking.

Goodbye, he whispered, and he turned and tiptoed away.

Chapter Fifteen

"There it is! Look!"

Veronica pointed out the carriage window, and her friend, Portia, leaned across the seat to peer out at Stafford Manor.

Veronica was terribly nervous, but trying not to show it. She'd been on pins and needles, watching for her initial glimpse of the mansion. If it wasn't incredibly imposing, Portia would tell everyone that Veronica was taking a step down.

Veronica was very spoiled—there was no use denying it—and she insisted on having the best of everything. She couldn't have her reputation tarnished by a plain, modest residence. It had to be absolutely grand or she'd just die!

"It's fine," Portia said. "Not as big as your father's—"

"Father is a duke," Veronica snapped. "Nicholas can hardly be blamed for his home being less impressive than ours."

"But it has its own charm."

"Yes, it does," Veronica agreed.

It was set on the side of a hill, with orchards of fruit trees leading up to it. The stone was a pretty tan color that glowed in the morning sunlight. It appeared to be a magical spot where a princess, which she deemed herself to be, could live happily ever after with her prince.

Not that she intended to *live* at Stafford, but the house would suffice for her infrequent forays to the country.

Her visit to Nicholas, unexpected and uninvited, was thrilling and reckless. Since she'd be alone with him for the first time ever, she'd built up numerous scenarios in her head as to what might occur without a chaperone dogging her every stride.

He was reputed to be vastly skilled with the ladies. Would

he, by chance, shower her with some of his extensive experience? If she could wrangle a few delicious kisses, she would consider the trip an enormous success.

"I can't wait," Portia said, "to see Lord Stafford's face when you climb out of the carriage."

"Neither can I. He'll probably faint with shock."

"Wouldn't that be hilarious? It would provide us with stories for months."

At the notion of Nicholas suffering a fit of the vapors, they both laughed.

"What if *she* is here when we arrive?" Portia asked, *she* being the brazen hussy who was supposedly ensconced on the premises.

Rumors of a mistress were still rampant, and Veronica hadn't made any progress in learning if they were true or not.

Well, she'd soon discover the actual state of affairs. If there was a doxy, the trollop would definitely know her place when Veronica was finished with her.

"If she is here," Veronica mused, "she won't be staying for long."

"What will you do to be rid of her?"

"I haven't decided, but I wouldn't be beyond taking a stick to her backside. She'll be sorry to have crossed me."

"Oh, you're too, too horrid." Portia chortled with glee. "What about Lord Stafford? What if we find out that he's betrayed you—as everyone claims?"

"I'm not ready to believe the worst of him. Yet. He is to be my husband, after all. He deserves my respect."

"If he's squandered it, though," Portia pressed, "what then?"

"He'll be very sorry, too."

Emeline walked down the grand staircase. She could barely contain her joy and was fighting the urge to grin.

While she was usually an early riser, the prior night's activity with Nicholas had kept her occupied much too late. It was nearly nine o'clock, and she was finally traipsing down to breakfast.

Sexual dalliance it seemed, with the most marvelous man

in the world, could generate a huge appetite.

She was anxious to eat, then locate him. He'd made some promises, and she'd given herself to him to seal those promises, so they had many topics to discuss. He planned to return to the army, but she wanted him to retire and come home to Stafford as fast as he could.

They could marry before he left. That way, when he was far away, he would know she was impatiently waiting for him and thinking about him all the time.

As she reached the foyer, she glanced out the front window. She stopped and stared.

Nicholas was there, arguing with his brother. He was dressed in his uniform, his horse saddled, a pack tied on the back.

Her heart pounded. Was he leaving? He couldn't be! Not before they'd talked!

She hurried to the door and rushed outside.

"Lord Stafford!" she called, scarcely able to recollect that she shouldn't refer to him as Nicholas.

Both brothers whipped around, and they glared at her as if she'd done something wrong.

Mr. Price muttered, "Damn it."

"Lord Stafford," she said again, "what's happening?"

Nicholas frowned at Emeline, at his brother, at Emeline, then he told Mr. Price, "Give me a minute alone with her."

"No," Mr. Price maddeningly replied. "This needs to end. Right here, right now."

She stumbled to a halt. They were big and brawny, and they towered over her, making her feel small and insignificant.

"I thought you'd sleep in this morning," Nicholas said.

"I was just coming down to breakfast." She studied his clothes, his horse, and she asked, "What are you doing?"

Nicholas didn't answer, and his brother explained, "He's departing for London. Immediately."

"But...why?"

"You know why," Mr. Price scathingly retorted.

Emeline blanched, her cheeks reddening with shame and fury.

"Tell me why," she demanded of Nicholas. "Not your brother. *You.* Tell me."

He shrugged. "I have to go."

"For how long? Forever?"

He hesitated, then admitted, "Yes."

His cheeks reddened, too, but likely from chagrin at being caught.

"You were sneaking away? Without a goodbye?"

"Miss Wilson," Mr. Price counseled, "remember yourself. Remember where you are and who might be listening. Why would the earl need to say goodbye to you?"

Humiliation swept over her, and she wondered if she might faint.

While she'd assumed her remarkable connection with Nicholas would bring about a wedding, he'd used their bond as bait he could dangle to convince her to raise her skirt.

"You didn't mean any of it, did you?" she charged. "It was all a lie."

He glowered at his brother. "Go away. Now. I must speak with her."

"No."

Nicholas took a menacing step toward Mr. Price. He leaned in and quietly threatened, "If you don't give me some privacy, I will beat you to a bloody pulp."

The brothers shared a heated visual exchange, then Mr. Price moved away.

Nicholas turned to her, and he looked altered from how he'd previously been. Any prior fondness had vanished, and she tried to figure out what she was witnessing instead. It wasn't boredom so much as irritation that she was creating a scene, and he would have to deal with it before he could be on his way.

"Well...?" she asked.

"I have to go, Em."

"Why?"

"I never should have started in with you, and there's no appropriate conclusion except for me to separate myself."

"It's awfully convenient that you didn't arrive at this decision until *after* last night."

"Trust me, this is for the best."

"I don't trust you, so you'll never get me to agree."

"I'm more experienced in these affairs than you."

"Are you?" she derisively scoffed.

"We couldn't keep on as we had been. I'm doing this for you, Em. You have to continue living here. You can't have your reputation sullied because of me.

"When was I supposed to learn that you'd left? *How* was I supposed to learn of it? Or were you hoping I'd hear the servants gossiping in the halls?"

"My brother was to confer with you this afternoon."

"How kind of him," she sneered, and she began to cry. She didn't mean to, but she couldn't hold her tears at bay. There were too many.

"I loved you," she pathetically said.

At her repeating the foolish declaration, he winced as if she'd struck him.

"I told you not to," he gently replied. "I told you I wasn't worth it."

"I thought you would marry me. I gave myself to you—because I believed you would."

"It was the lust talking, Em. I'm a scoundrel. I always have been."

If he'd taken out a gun and shot her, he couldn't have been any more cruel. She moaned with dismay and swiped at her tears.

"Em," he murmured, "don't be sad. I can't bear it when you are."

He reached out as if he might touch her, and his brother snapped, "Nicholas!"

The earl dropped his hand. The most awkward silence descended, and she wished the ground would open and swallow her whole.

She felt silly and ridiculous; she'd been tricked and deceived. It was an old story: the handsome, charming aristocrat seducing the unsuspecting, naïve girl. On a daily basis, it played out all over the kingdom.

"What have you determined about my situation?" she inquired. "Are my sisters and I moving out of the manor?"

Mr. Price came forward. "We'll discuss it after my brother is gone."

Gad, was she to be thrown out on the road? Could Lord Stafford really be that malicious? She'd imprudently consorted with him. Was eviction to be the price for her misbehavior?

Mr. Price gestured to the earl's horse. "This attempt at farewell is horrid and pointless. Let's get you out of here."

Lord Stafford looked pained, as if he might try to defend himself or justify his actions, but she couldn't listen.

She might have turned and run into the house, but she was distracted by the realization that there was a coach coming up the lane. Their conversation had been so gripping that they hadn't noticed its approach. The three of them spun to gape.

It was a fancy vehicle, pulled by six white horses that trotted with matching strides. The outriders wore green livery, decorated with gold braid and buttons. There was an ornate crest on the door.

"For pity's sake," Mr. Price growled as it rumbled to a halt.

The two brothers shared another caustic visual exchange, then Mr. Price pushed the earl toward the conveyance.

"Go over and say hello," Mr. Price instructed. "It's not as if you can ignore her."

"Who is it?" Emeline asked, but neither man answered.

"I'll explain later," the earl told her.

"No, you won't," Mr. Price huffed. "Your *chats* with Miss Wilson are over. I insist on it."

"I hate that you had to find out like this," the earl said to Emeline.

As if she'd become invisible, he whipped away and went to the carriage. Like an imbecile, she dawdled, watching him.

A young woman poked her head out the window. She waved and called, "Nicholas! Nicholas! Surprise!"

The earl was very formal. He stood straight and nodded. "Hello, Veronica."

"I'll bet you didn't expect to see me."

"No, I didn't."

"We were passing by, on our way to the Fitzroys' house party. Portia—you remember my friend, Portia, don't you?"

"No."

"You met her at my father's supper? Anyway, she mentioned that we were in the neighborhood, and I decided we simply had to stop."

"Welcome to Stafford."

Covetously, she assessed the mansion. "It's lovely. I'm sure I'll be very comfortable here."

"I'm sure you will be, too," he agreed.

A footman opened the door and lowered the step. The earl extended his hand, and the woman, Veronica, took it and climbed out. With her white-blond hair, big blue eyes, and Cupid's mouth, she was the most beautiful, exotic creature Emeline had ever seen.

She was petite but voluptuous, with a slender waist, impressive bosom, and numerous curves in all the right spots. From the extravagant cut of her expensive gown and the sparkling jewels on her neck, wrists, and shoes, it was obvious she was very rich.

Though she appeared to be seventeen or eighteen, she exuded a sophistication and aplomb that Emeline could never have matched. The earl was charmed, his attention fully riveted, and Emeline felt ill with alarm.

She glanced up at Mr. Price and nervously asked, "Who is she?"

"*She* is Lady Veronica Stewart. *She* is my brother's fiancée."

Mr. Price—bless him—had very quick reflexes. He caught Emeline around the waist so she didn't embarrass herself by falling to the ground in a stunned heap.

"Steady, Miss Wilson, steady," Stephen whispered, her entire weight balanced on his arm. If he hadn't reacted, she'd have been unconscious at his feet.

"Let me go," she begged.

"Just a moment more," he advised, "then it will all be over."

"Please?" she begged again.

"Veronica has the instincts of a shark. Don't encourage her to turn them on you. You'll always regret it."

The warning centered her, and she pulled herself together as much as she could. Her legs gained strength, and she was able to stand on her own, but she was weaving, as if the slightest breeze would knock her down.

Nicholas was being the perfect gentleman for Veronica, pretending naught was amiss, and Stephen had to give him credit. What man would know how to behave when confronted by his fiancée while saying an emotional goodbye to his latest paramour?

The episode might have been humorous—if it wasn't so

thoroughly distasteful. Miss Wilson was crushed, which was why Stephen had demanded Nicholas leave for London. Too bad they'd been delayed by five minutes.

Veronica flashed a flirtatious grin at Nicholas, and she tipped her cheek toward him. He grinned, too, like the besotted swain he definitely wasn't. He bent down and supplied the kiss that Veronica was seeking.

Beside him, Miss Wilson began to quake quite visibly.

"How long have they been engaged?" she murmured.

"A few months."

"Have they set the wedding date?"

"The end of August. It's to be the highlight of the London season and the grandest fete in decades. Royalty from all over Europe are invited." Brutally, he added, "Her father's a duke. She's his only daughter."

Miss Wilson sucked in a shocked breath, her legs giving out a second time, and he slipped a supportive arm around her waist again.

He was being deliberately cruel, but she should have no illusions about Nicholas. She couldn't be allowed to harbor any insane fantasies that she could change him or mold him into a better man.

He was the person she was viewing that very instant, a person of no morals or scruples, who was lacking in loyalty and fidelity. He never made commitments, and he was incapable of forming bonds or keeping promises.

Their childhood experiences had warped him, had left him too tough, too ready to do whatever was necessary to protect himself. He had no conscience. He would always choose the route that suited his own purposes, and he'd destroy anyone who got in his way.

Veronica grabbed Nicholas's arm in a proprietary manner. They approached, Portia trailing behind.

"Hello, Mr. Price," Veronica simpered.

"Hello, milady." Nicholas had told Stephen that he could call her Veronica, but Stephen couldn't abide her and had no desire to be on familiar terms.

"You've met Portia." Veronica didn't glance back at her companion.

"I have." Stephen bowed to her friend.

"Who is this?" She glared at Miss Wilson, studying her simple dress in a derogatory fashion. "Is she a servant? Could she take my bags up to my room?"

"She's a guest," Nicholas managed to choke out.

"A guest!" Veronica tsked. "You're a bachelor, Nicholas. How very odd. She's been crying. Why? Have you awful men hurt her feelings?"

"I'm Emeline Wilson," Miss Wilson had the backbone to say, when neither Stephen nor Nicholas was courteous enough to introduce her.

"How nice." Veronica rudely turned away so Miss Wilson would understand that Veronica couldn't care less, that she deemed Miss Wilson to be of no consequence. She smiled at Nicholas. "Let's go inside. I'm dying to explore the house. Give me a tour. I especially wish to see the countess's suite."

Nicholas hesitated, the moment awkward, but there was no reason *not* to show her.

They would have to play the part of polite hosts, but with any luck, the encounter wouldn't last long. Veronica was spoiled and easily bored. She appeared to have brought only her friend and her maid, so she couldn't spend the night. Hopefully, she'd snoop for a bit, then travel on.

"Yes, Nick," Stephen urged, "show her the house."

Stephen was desperate to get Veronica out of sight before poor Miss Wilson collapsed.

"Come," Nicholas said to Veronica, but he paused again.

He stared at Miss Wilson, yearning to offer a pertinent remark, but what could it possibly be? He sighed, then spun away and guided Veronica up the stairs. Portia trotted after them.

Stephen and Miss Wilson tarried until they vanished, then he led her off in the opposite direction. She was in a state of shock, so she put up no resistance.

He went in the rear of the manor, to an area Veronica would never visit. He escorted her into a deserted parlor and closed the door. He steered her over to a chair and sat her down.

There was a sideboard along the wall. He walked over and poured her a brandy. He held it out, but she didn't reach for it. She seemed paralyzed, so he lifted the glass to her lips.

"Take a drink," he commanded. She shook her head, but he pressed, "Drink up. You'll feel better."

With a trembling hand, she clasped it and downed a hefty swallow. The potent liquor had her eyes watering, and she coughed once, but she was made of stern stuff. She gulped another swallow, then another and another, 'til the glass was empty.

"Thank you," she said as she set it on a nearby table.

"You're welcome."

"I wasn't aware that he was betrothed."

"I realize that."

"I thought he was..." She broke off. "Never mind. It doesn't matter what I thought."

"Do you know very much about my brother, Miss Wilson?"

"I assumed I did, but I'm now sure I know nothing about him, at all."

"He never told you about our parents?"

"No, and really, Mr. Price, why would he have? We're just acquaintances. I'm hardly a confidante."

As she voiced the bald-faced lie, he didn't contradict her. Her cheeks flushed, providing ample evidence of her mortification. And perhaps it wasn't a lie. In light of Nicholas's preferences, it might have been a strictly physical relationship. They might never have talked.

Whatever the situation, Stephen would let her pretend there had been no affair, but he *wouldn't* let her wallow in some mental folly where she believed she might have meant something to Nicholas.

She would be hurt by Stephen's bluntness, and he hated to wound her, but there was no other way to proceed.

"My father grew up at this estate," he informed her.

"I had heard that."

"He was raised as if he were the earl's son, with all the wealth and trappings that could be bestowed on such a fortunate fellow."

"Why are you telling me this?"

"I need you to comprehend why my brother behaves as he does. I need you to understand what he's truly like and why the two of you could never have ended up together."

"You're being ridiculous," she said. "Such a preposterous

conclusion has never occurred to me."

"Hasn't it?"

"No." She peered down at the rug, unable to meet his gaze.

"One year, when my father was in London, he fell in love with the most flamboyant—but very common—actress. He wed her shortly after. For this monumental affront to the Price family, he was disowned and disavowed."

"What has that to do with me or your brother?"

"I'm getting to that. My parents were killed in a carriage accident when Nicholas was six and I was four. We were orphans, but our relatives viewed us as the sinful stain of our parents' illicit affiliation."

"It wasn't illicit. They were married!"

"Quite so, Miss Wilson. A minister from my father's church wrote to the old earl, notifying him that he was bringing us back to Stafford."

Suddenly, Stephen was having trouble continuing. When the trip to Stafford had transpired, he'd been so young. He had one tiny memory of that vile day, but it still had the power to cripple him with unwanted emotion.

Anxious to compose himself, he whirled away and went to the sideboard to pour his own brandy. As he sipped it, Miss Wilson asked, "What happened when you arrived at the estate?"

"The earl had men at the gate with orders to prevent us from entering. We were turned away—two little boys with nowhere to go."

"My goodness. I wasn't aware..."

"Few people are." He pushed down the well of grief that always bubbled up when he recounted the experience. "Over the ensuing months, the minister contacted other of our kin— cousins and aunts and the like—but no one would help us. So...we were raised in an orphanage, the lost children of this incredibly wealthy, aristocratic family."

"And your brother?"

"Vowed vengeance against all of them. He intends to wed as high as he can to rub their noses in his rise to eminence. He wants to show them that they can't keep him out, that he can waltz into their midst and behave however he wishes."

"I see."

"Once he was installed as earl, his first act was to find the prettiest, richest girl of the *ton* and propose to her."

"Lady Veronica."

"Yes." He fussed over his brandy, letting the silence play out, letting reality sink in. "He'll marry her no matter what. While he's been here at Stafford, he's never for a single second considered doing anything else—and he never will."

"Well, of course, he won't." She tried for a smile but failed. "Lady Veronica is very beautiful. What man wouldn't want her for a bride?"

"What man, indeed?"

They were quiet for an eternity, with Miss Wilson studying the floor and Stephen studying her.

"I should go," she finally said, but she didn't move.

"I've known my brother a long time, Miss Wilson."

"I know you have."

"He can be very charming—when he chooses to be. An unsuspecting female might be taken off guard. An unsuspecting female might involve herself in ways she hadn't planned."

"That woman would be very, very foolish."

"Yes, she would be, because my brother will always do what will benefit him the most. He will never care who he harms in the process."

Pensive and morose, she nodded. "Why would you suppose he didn't mention that he was betrothed?"

"He wouldn't think it was any of your business."

She sighed with regret. "He was leaving today without a goodbye."

"I ordered him away, Miss Wilson. It had come to my attention that he might have been inappropriately dallying with someone. I insisted he depart before he caused any trouble for her."

"He wanted to go? He was amenable?"

"He never voiced a word of argument," he lied, "for he recognized that there was no reason for him to stay. Was there?"

"No, no reason occurs to me. Has he ever divulged what is to happen to me and my sisters? We've been living at the manor, but it's time we left. I've asked him what we are to do, but he's never had an answer."

"For now, you're to settle in the village. There is a room for rent above the blacksmith's barn. But eventually, you must select a new location far away from Stafford. I'll help you with accommodations."

"In a different town?"

"Yes. There's nothing for you here."

"Is this what your brother requested of me?"

"Yes," he lied again.

She fiddled with her skirt, dawdling, prolonging the moment, then she pushed herself to her feet. "You've been very kind. I appreciate it."

"I'm sorry to have been so blunt."

"It's all right. I was wondering if I could impose on you for a few hours."

"I'll assist you in any way I can."

"I was to have a picnic with my sisters, but I'm feeling a bit low. I'd like to rest until I'm more myself."

"I'd be happy to entertain them for you."

"You don't need to. If you could escort them into the village, Mrs. Merrick would watch them."

At hearing Jo's name, he covered a wince. "I'll take them to her."

She went to the door and opened it, and as she stepped into the hall, she glanced back. She was a tragic figure, so lovely, so forlorn, and Stephen could see why his brother had been smitten.

"I never meant to hurt anyone," she said. "I wasn't told about Lady Veronica or I would never have—"

"I know." He interrupted her so she wouldn't have to embarrass herself with a humiliating admission. "Nicholas never means to hurt anyone, either. It's just his habit to be callous."

She walked on, her strides fading, and he slid into the chair she'd vacated.

It was another mess Nicholas had made, another calamity Stephen had had to fix for him, and Stephen was so weary. He was sick at heart, furious with himself, with his brother, with Miss Wilson for being so trusting and gullible.

He staggered off to find his brother, hopefully to extinguish any other fires before Nicholas could fan the flames.

Chapter Sixteen

A knock sounded on Emeline's door, but she didn't rise to answer it. She couldn't. She was too numb and unable to move.

She felt old and worn out, a woman past her prime, who had no one to help her, no one upon whom she could rely. Every endeavor she'd attempted had failed, every dream had been dashed.

The knock rapped again. The knob turned, and a housemaid poked her nose in.

"Miss Wilson?"

"Yes?"

"A letter came for you."

When Emeline simply stared, unspeaking, the girl walked over and handed it to her. Emeline didn't reach for it, and the girl glanced about and laid it on a table.

"Are you ill, Miss Wilson? May I bring you something?"

"I'm a bit under the weather, but I don't need anything. Thank you for asking."

"Perhaps a pot of tea? Cook has a blended remedy that would settle your stomach."

"My stomach's fine. I'm just weary."

The girl left, and Emeline was cynical enough to wonder if she'd been fishing for gossip. Was she, at that very moment, racing down to the kitchen to tattle over Emeline's reduced condition?

Emeline had thought herself so smart, so furtive in her affair with the earl, but if Mr. Price had been aware of it, the entire staff had probably known. There was no more vicious group than servants who'd had a colleague raised above them.

Had they all been informed of the earl's engagement—with Emeline the sole person who hadn't been apprised? Had they watched her make a fool of herself while gleefully waiting for her folly to crash down around her?

Emeline glared at the letter. She couldn't imagine who had written, and she couldn't bear to pick it up. It would only contain more bad news.

Finally, she rose, and she trudged over to see that it was from a school in Cornwall. It was the last one to which she'd applied, and she'd been expecting to hear that she was too inexperienced or too old or that they'd hired somebody else.

She tugged at the flap and was stunned to find that it was the exact opposite of what she'd anticipated.

They wanted her! The position started at the end of the summer, and the major benefit was a two-room cottage. They were hoping she could come right away so she could acclimate before classes commenced. If she replied in the affirmative, they would send coach fare.

She pressed the letter over her heart and held it there, as if the words could imbue her with the vigor she needed to accept and comply. Leave Stafford forever. Travel across the country with her sisters in tow. Build a life for herself among strangers. Yet what other option was there?

Lord Stafford was tossing her out of the manor, and he had suggested temporary lodging over the blacksmith's barn. Mr. Price would move her there, but she would soon be relocated to another village.

Considering what she'd given to the earl, the proposed resolution was paltry compensation and much less than what she deserved, but who was she to argue?

She had no one to blame but herself for her current predicament, and she ought to be grateful that the earl had tendered any reparation, at all. He could have just had the maids pack her bags and put them out on the road.

What reason was there to stay at Stafford? Aside from Josephine with whom she was only casually acquainted, she had no real friends. Her neighbors feigned cordiality, but when push had come to shove, they'd abandoned her in the earl's driveway for a bag of seed and a jug of ale.

Why would she remain?

She wouldn't, but her decision had naught to do with her

neighbors or their opinions.

In the future, Lord Stafford would occasionally visit the estate. He'd bring his bride. Emeline might bump into him as he rode by on the lane. She might have to observe as he lorded himself over a crowd during the harvest festival.

She couldn't abide the notion of seeing him with his simpering wife on his arm. According to his brother, the earl wanted the whole world to take note of his winning Lady Veronica.

Well, the *world* could notice and laud him, but Emeline didn't have to. She—who had convinced herself that he was perfect—knew his true character. She recognized the cruel monster behind the handsome façade.

As she pondered his despicable treatment, she grew angry.

Why was she being such a meek lamb? She'd never been timid or shy, and she'd done nothing wrong—except fall in love with a libertine who didn't reciprocate her intense sentiment.

Was she to suffer his awful behavior without complaint? Was she to slither out the rear door as if she was ashamed?

She wasn't ashamed! And she wouldn't hang her head and mope as if *she* was the miscreant in the sordid affair. Lord Stafford was a scoundrel, and Emeline wouldn't pretend any differently.

She had many comments to share with the exalted Earl of Stafford, and he was going to listen to every one of them. She had no brother or father to stand up for her, so she had to stand up for herself.

After he left for London, she'd have no chance to speak with him ever again. If she didn't tell him what she thought, she'd regret it forever.

She hurried to her writing desk and penned a reply to the school in Cornwall. She accepted the post and agreed to travel upon receipt of the coach fare. Then she stormed into the hall, eager to hunt down the earl.

There were few servants about, and those she encountered didn't know where he was. She started searching floor by floor.

Wherever he'd gone, she'd find him, and when she was finished, his ears would be on fire!

She walked for ages, checking various places, and gradually, her rage began to wane. It was difficult to sustain such virulent fury, and with each stride, she reassessed.

Why chastise him? Why scold? What was the point? She didn't matter to him in the slightest. Why waste the energy? He'd simply scoff at her criticism.

She slowed, her livid promenade lagging, then halting. To her dismay, she'd ended up outside his bedchamber, the smaller one he'd picked for himself upon his arrival.

The door was open, and she peered in like a beggar on the street.

She remembered the special evening she'd spent in his bed. They had talked and dallied and shared, and the memory pressed down on her like a heavy weight under which she couldn't keep her balance.

Sadness swept over her. She didn't hate him. She *loved* him, and she always would. It was killing her to know that she'd been so insignificant.

Suddenly, she heard his voice. He was in the dressing room behind his bedchamber.

Her stupid pulse raced with grief, but with joy, too. He was exiting his suite, coming toward her. Perhaps if they could have a moment to chat, he would explain why he'd used her so horridly. If he could just make her understand, she wouldn't be quite so bereft.

He stepped into view, and Emeline was about to call out his name, when she realized that Lady Veronica was still with him. The exquisite blond girl rose on tiptoe, and the earl kissed her full on the mouth. The embrace was chaste and quick, but it was an embrace nonetheless.

Emeline felt as if all the blood had been drained from her body, all the air sucked from the sky, and she was suffocating. She gasped with shock.

He spun, smiling, until he saw who was loitering and gaping. For a long, torturous interval, his gaze locked with hers, then she whirled away and ran.

In her frenzied retreat, she thought he shouted, "Em!", but she was sure it was her fevered imagination.

"It's a beautiful house, Nicholas."

"I'm glad you approve."

Veronica looked up at him.

An hour earlier, she'd managed to lose Portia. Her friend had been hungry, and she'd wandered into a dining room where a buffet had been laid out. Veronica had left her there and sneaked off with her fiancé. It was the first time they'd ever been alone.

During the three months of their engagement, they'd rarely interacted, so she'd forgotten how manly he was. At being so vividly reminded, she was thrilled.

With him so tall and dark, and her so shapely and fair, they would cast a dashing shadow across the social world of aristocratic London. She would have the most handsome husband in the kingdom, and heads would turn wherever they went. Every female of her acquaintance would be green with envy.

"Mother requires your presence in town," she advised him, "for some wedding preparations."

"I don't need to come," he said. "Whatever you decide is fine with me."

"But you and your brother must visit our tailor. I've chosen the fabric for your wedding clothes, and they're eager to get sewing. The date is approaching so rapidly."

"My brother and I will wear our uniforms. You don't have to make a fuss."

"I don't wish you to wear your uniforms. I wish you to wear what *I* have selected." To lessen the sting of her remark, she flashed a flirtatious grin. "I'm afraid I have to insist."

He didn't reply, and she frowned, trying to interpret what his silence indicated. Was he amenable? Would he come to London as she'd demanded? Or was he merely being courteous when he had no intention of doing as she'd asked?

She wasn't accustomed to being ignored, and she refused to have her plans thwarted. Her wedding would be fabulous, and he couldn't be permitted to spoil it.

They trudged along, not speaking, and she was growing irked by his mulish contemplation.

She'd finally escaped her chaperones, but he hardly seemed to care. She was a chatterbox, but he was barely listening. He kept peeking out the windows, as if worried over what was occurring outside.

Apparently, every detail about the estate was more important than her.

"You'll allow me to remodel the manor, won't you?" she inquired.

"Remodel? Why would you? This mansion is the gaudiest place I've ever seen. The furniture is in excellent shape, and it's of the highest quality. It would be a waste of money."

"It would make me happy—buying things for my new home. You want to make me happy, don't you?"

She had a very clear image of herself totting about London to the merchants from whom she'd purchase the latest styles and colors. She could envision just how she'd dress for her appointments, just how she'd barter and haggle and shop. He couldn't ruin her fun, couldn't prevent her from doing what all brides did after their weddings.

He was quiet again, and she wondered if he'd agreed or not, but she couldn't figure out how to press him for answers.

For the prior three years, she'd been courted and wooed, but her suitors had all been near her own age. They were malleable and easily coerced. Nicholas was nothing like any of those boys. He wasn't concerned over how she viewed him, and he'd expended no effort to learn what she wanted or to ensure that she received it.

"Where is our honeymoon to be?" she queried. "I'm dying to know, and you haven't breathed a word."

He scowled. "I'm coming to London for the wedding, then I'm returning immediately to my post."

"Don't be ridiculous. Of course, you're not. I think we should go to Italy. Wouldn't it be exciting to rent a villa on the Mediterranean? How long could we stay? Would six months be all right?"

If she couldn't finish off her glorious wedding with a glorious wedding trip, what was the use of getting married?

He halted at a door and gestured inside.

"You asked to see where I sleep," he said. "This is it."

She glanced into a very plain salon, one that was no different from a dozen others he'd shown her. He'd given the earl's grand quarters to his brother, and he, Nicholas, had taken lesser lodgings. What sort of man would relinquish the earl's suite for this paltry set of rooms?

"I want to look." She grabbed his arm, hoping to pull him in after her, but he wouldn't budge.

"Your father wouldn't like you to be alone with me in my bedchamber."

"My father isn't here, is he? What he doesn't know won't hurt him."

She marched in, leaving him to skulk in the hall like an imbecile.

There was very little evidence of him in the sitting room, no trinkets tossed on a table, no coat thrown over a chair, so she brazenly proceeded to the bedroom and the dressing room beyond.

In it, she found the type of items for which she'd been searching: his razor and shaving cup, a pair of muddy riding boots in the corner, and—scandalously—a bath robe hanging from a hook.

She imagined herself wed to him, having the right to simply waltz in whenever she chose. Several of her friends had already married, and they whispered shocking tales of their husbands prancing about naked, of frightening physical acts carried out in the dark of night. She was anxious to learn what they were, but no one would explain.

She tried to picture him without his clothes, and she supposed he'd resemble a Greek statue, all smooth skin and sculpted muscle. The very idea made her cheeks heat, and she could barely keep from picking up a towel and fanning herself.

She spun around, and he was dawdling in the doorway, leaned against the frame. He appeared bored, and she was aggravated in the extreme. When he gazed at her, he ought to be overcome by desire.

Sauntering over, she approached until her skirt brushed his legs. She was being very forward, but what else was she to do? So far, he'd been tediously polite, and she was determined to elicit a reaction.

She was skilled at flirting, and she could drive a man wild with passion. He didn't stand a chance at resisting her.

She toyed with a button on his shirt, tracing her finger round and round in circles. He didn't move away, but he didn't move any nearer, either. He simply stared, evincing no heightened interest and no curiosity as to her advance.

"I've heard the worst stories about you," she said.

"Have you?"

"Yes. That's why I came to Stafford. I had to find out if they were true."

He didn't remark on her brash statement, didn't probe as to what the stories might be or if they had altered her opinion of his character.

"Would you like me to tell you what some of them are?"

"Not really."

"Everyone in London swears you have a mistress, that she's living here openly with you. Is she?"

He stepped away. "Let's get you downstairs. You need to be going or you'll never make Fitzroys by nightfall."

"I'm staying at Stafford tonight, and you haven't answered my question. Is your mistress in residence? If she is, I insist on being introduced to her so that I may punch her in the nose."

She cocked her head and grinned, a playful pose that was very fetching. She constantly practiced it in front of the mirror. He'd wonder if she was jesting or serious. After all, what gently-bred young lady would mention such a disgraceful person?

She hadn't seen any indication of a woman's touch in the house, and the only female she'd run across was the odious Miss Wilson who'd been weeping down in the driveway. Miss Wilson was pretty enough, but she'd been attired in an unadorned day dress, her hair in a ponytail, so she was much too plain to be the doxy Veronica was seeking.

Or was she?

Having never previously met a trollop, Veronica had no idea what to look for.

"You're not spending the night," he said.

"Why can't I? No one knows I'm here, and I won't tell anyone I visited."

"If no one knows you're here, then it's all the more reason you should go. These sorts of juvenile antics have a way of leaking out."

"Juvenile!" she huffed.

"If word of your jaunt drifted back to your father, I'd have to explain why I allowed you to behave so outrageously. It's not a conversation I ever intend to have."

He walked off, which irked her beyond her limit.

"Nicholas!" She stomped her foot to get his attention.

"What?" He whipped around. "Before you say anything, I should like to inform you that you have prevailed on my hospitality, delayed me in the implementation of my own journey, and insulted my character. I'm a tad exasperated."

"You've been an absolute grouch from the second I arrived. You could at least pretend to be glad to see me."

"I don't care for theatrics, and I must ask that you not engage in them, or you will soon learn that my patience is short and my temper hot."

He was glaring as if he didn't...*like* her, and the notion that he might not was unnerving. Had she been too bold? He was so worldly; she'd assumed he would be thrilled to discover that she was no simpering miss.

What if she'd wrecked everything? Gad, what if he decided she was loose and called off their betrothal?

In a panic, she smiled and sashayed over, offering him a good view of her shapely, swaying hips. He definitely noticed, and she gained some satisfaction from proving that he wasn't made of stone.

She peered up at him, getting lost in the blue of his eyes.

"Don't be such a grump."

"I'm sorry. I just have a lot on my mind today."

"Do you know what I think?"

"What?"

"I think we're very much alone, and you haven't tried to kiss me. Not a single time."

His gaze dropped to her mouth and lingered there. She held her breath, certain he would proceed.

But instead, he said, "It's not wise for us to travel down that road."

"Spoilsport."

"I guess I am."

"Admit it," she taunted, "you dream about kissing me."

"You're awfully set on yourself."

He spun away and strolled off. In a few steps, he'd be out of the bedchamber. A few steps after that, they'd be in the hall.

How could she steal a kiss in the hall?

She started after him, fighting the urge the stamp her foot again, and as she hurried out, she happened to glance in the mirror. The angle was just right for her to see Miss Wilson lurking in the outer doorway and debating whether to enter the suite. She looked forlorn and miserable.

Why would the woman seek out Nicholas? In his private chamber no less! There was no proper purpose. She had to be the strumpet over whom Veronica had been relentlessly mocked.

Her temper boiled over.

"Nicholas!" Her tone was coaxing.

He hadn't observed Miss Wilson yet, and he turned back to Veronica.

"What now?"

"I came all this way, and I only wanted one thing. You haven't given it to me."

"What is it?"

"I already told you."

She marched over and snuggled herself to him, being intimate and familiar as if she was in the habit of hugging him.

Before he had a clue of what she planned, she rose on tiptoe, and *she* kissed him. For the briefest second, he permitted the embrace then, as if he were a fond cousin rather than her fiancé, he eased her away.

As he did, Miss Wilson gasped. He whirled to ascertain who was watching, and Veronica's worst fears were confirmed. He appeared to have been punched in the stomach.

Miss Wilson slapped a hand over her mouth, then she ran off, vanishing in an instant.

"Dammit!" he muttered, and he shouted, "Em!"

But she continued on. He might have chased after her, but Veronica slipped her arm into his, halting any escape.

"What do you suppose she wanted?" Veronica asked, all innocence.

"I...I...don't know," he stammered, his distress obvious.

"Would you escort me downstairs? You mentioned I should probably get going, and I must find Portia so we can be off."

"I need to...to..."

He was extremely befuddled—the first time she'd ever seen him at a loss—and she seized the advantage. She led him to the hall and walked in the direction opposite from Miss Wilson.

"This house is so big," she pouted. "I'll never locate the front foyer on my own."

Her expression demanded his assistance, and there was no reason for him *not* to accompany her.

"It's this way," he mumbled, Miss Wilson forgotten entirely in his desire to placate his dearest betrothed.

Chapter Seventeen

Josephine hid in the shadows, the wet evening grass soaking her shoes. She was behind Stafford Manor, lurking underneath the balustrade and hoping Stephen came outside.

Earlier in the morning, he'd brought the twins to the vicarage. He'd been kind to the two girls and courteous to her brother, but he'd been extremely rude to Jo.

She'd thought she wanted to end their affair. She'd thought she was strong enough to never see him again, but she'd been wrong. As he'd sauntered into her front parlor, she had nearly fainted with surprise. The pleasure had been that intense.

She'd spent the afternoon with Nan and Nell, and she'd slyly peppered them with questions about routines in the mansion. They'd shared many interesting tidbits, including the fact that Stephen often enjoyed a cheroot on the verandah after supper.

When he'd returned to fetch the girls home, she'd tried to catch his eye, to indicate that they should meet, but he'd studiously ignored her blatant hints. So she had risked life and limb—and reputation—to seek him out.

The furtive trek to the manor had been dark and frightening, and she'd forced herself to make it, but it had probably been for naught. Stephen had never appeared, and she was about to give up, when above her, a door opened.

Booted strides marched across the stone patio, and suddenly, there he was, his shape outlined by a lamp glowing in a parlor. He put a cigar to his mouth, the tip glowing as he inhaled, smoke circling up above his head.

"Stephen," she murmured. He froze but didn't reply, so more loudly, she repeated, "Stephen!"

Frowning, he leaned over the rail.

"Jo? Is that you?"

"Yes."

"Are you all right? Is something amiss?"

"No, no. Could I talk to you?"

"I don't think that's a good idea."

"Please? I've walked all this way."

"Why didn't you just knock on the front door?"

"You know why."

"Heaven forbid that you be seen speaking with the earl's brother."

She refused to argue in a whisper, from ten feet away. If she could touch him, she was sure his resentment would fade and they could start over.

"Please, Stephen," she said again.

His irritation great, he went to the steps and stomped down. Without a word, he clasped her hand and took off at a brisk pace. She stumbled after him, trying to keep up.

He guided her along the foundation of the house, ducking under windows, until they halted at a rear entrance. They descended a short set of stairs into the wine cellar.

She held very still, trembling, as he located a candle and used the tip of his cheroot to light the wick. He tossed the cigar under his heel and stamped it out, and as the flame grew, she could see rows and rows of bottles neatly stacked.

"Is this secretive enough for you?" he sneered.

"Don't be angry."

"I'm not angry. I'd have to care about you to be angry."

"I need your advice. I don't have anyone else to ask."

"So you came to me? Why would you? A few days ago, you were very clear that you don't wish to pursue an acquaintance. Am I deaf? Did I misunderstand?"

To her horror, her eyes filled with tears. She was sad and despairing and desperate for his counsel and friendship, but the conversation wasn't proceeding at all as she'd planned.

She was anxious to chat with the funny, sexy, charming man who had led her off to dally in deserted barns, not this cold, furious stranger.

"If you suppose," he griped, "that a flood of tears will have any effect on me, you're gravely mistaken."

"Stop acting like this."

"Like what?"

"Like you're someone I don't know."

"You *don't* know me, and this is not an act. You broke off our affair, and I acceded to your demand. What more is there to say? Were you expecting me to chase after you like a besotted boy?"

Yes! No! I'm so confused!

He'd erected a hard shell to keep her out, and she had to pierce through it. As he'd mentioned, it had only been a few days. How could his affection have vanished so rapidly?

It couldn't have.

She closed the distance that separated them, and he watched her come. He was wary, unyielding, but she was determined to evoke a response.

She wrapped her arms around him and pressed her body to his. Though he pretended apathy, his cock stirred, and at feeling it, she could have wept with joy.

"How long have you been courting?" he asked.

"What?"

"Benedict Mason. How long? Were you fornicating with me while playing the shy maiden for him?"

She pulled away and scowled. "*He* is courting. *I* am not."

"You could have fooled me."

"It was my brother's idea. Not mine. I haven't a clue why Oscar proposed it or why Mr. Mason agreed. We have nothing in common, and I loathe him."

"I saw you after church on Sunday. You didn't look as if you loathe him."

"I can't be uncivil. Oscar has decreed that I submit to his attentions, so I must comply."

"You're such a mouse, Mrs. Merrick. How do you live with yourself?"

His disdain exhausted her. What did he know about her tribulations? What did he know about anything?

He could never imagine how difficult it was to placate Oscar or how feverishly she worked to keep him happy.

Her existence had constantly been the same, and she couldn't envision any other life. Oscar was a bitter, cruel man, but she'd always been ruled by bitter, cruel men. The home she shared with him was no different from the one she'd shared with her father, then her husband. It was no different from the one she'd share with Mr. Mason if Oscar forced her to marry.

It was dangerous and impossible to stand up to her brother, to speak out or defend herself. She could only plod forward, praying that she would survive with her sanity intact.

Stephen Price, with his stellar career, steady income, male independence, and rich brother was in no position to chastise.

How dare he judge her!

She was sick of his contempt and resolved to push and push until he behaved in a manner more to her liking. There was a way they connected, a way he couldn't resist.

She rose on tiptoe and touched her mouth to his. For an eternity, he was stiff as a board, fighting his attraction. She stroked her hands down his back, across his buttocks, to his loins. By the time she reached between his legs and stroked his balls, he relented in a hot torrent of need.

He grabbed her and braced her against a post, her legs around his waist. His lips never parting from hers, he managed to unbutton his trousers and raise her skirt. In a thrice, he was impaled, and she cried out in pain and relief.

He thrust like a wild bull, his cock ramming into her over and over. He opened her dress and shoved at the fabric, baring her breast. As he fell to her nipple, as he sucked hard, he came in a fiery rush, his seed flooding her womb.

Then, with a furious jerk, he drew away and stood her on her feet. Their frenzied coupling had left her off balance, and she stumbled over and collapsed onto the bottom stair. He moved to the opposite wall, a palm on the rough brick, as he struggled to mediate his breathing.

Finally, he calmed and straightened. With clumsy fingers, he repaired his clothes, then spun toward her.

"What do you want from me?" He looked tormented. "You ask me to go away, so I oblige you. You start courting someone else, yet you show up here and practically ravish me. What do you want!"

"I can't marry Mr. Mason, but Oscar is determined."

"How is that my problem? I'm not your father. I'm not your kin. Why would you presume on me?"

"Aren't you my friend?"

"I could have been—once—but you weren't interested. I'm not a fool, and I won't waste my energy on a lost cause."

"I didn't want you to leave me alone!" she wailed.

"You couldn't prove it by me."

A dozen pleas raced through her mind: *Save me! Wed me yourself! Don't let Mr. Mason have me! Fight for me! Make me your own!*

But she didn't utter any of them aloud.

"Mr. Mason doesn't love me," she complained.

"So? What has love to do with matrimony?"

"I was wed previously to a brute I detested. I won't endure such agony ever again. If I have to marry, then I insist it be to a husband who is glad to have me."

It was the perfect overture for him to propose, and she gazed at him with beseeching eyes, but the thick oaf didn't grasp what she was requesting. How could she get him to figure it out? Would she have to hit him alongside the head with a club?

"A few weeks ago," he said, "when my brother initially traveled to Stafford, do you know why I came with him?"

"I assumed you were eager to see the estate."

"No. It's because I plan to settle at Stafford after I retire from the army."

"Well...good."

"I'm bringing my family here."

"Your what?"

Gad! Was he married? If he was, she'd kill him, and she'd never suffer an ounce of remorse. She'd go to the gallows with a smile on her face!

"My *family*," he continued, "with the exception of my brother whom I can barely abide, consists of my very illegitimate daughter."

"You have a daughter?"

"Yes. Born out of wedlock."

He stated the fact like a boast, as if he imagined she might swoon over the shocking news, and she had to admit that she was unnerved.

Illicit fornication was a terrible sin, but when it resulted in a baby, it was even more egregious.

"What's her name?" Jo inquired.

"Annie."

"Who is her mother?"

"A camp follower I scarcely knew. When I was younger, I used to rut like a dog with any trollop who would spread her legs. I like to believe that I've changed since then, but I guess I haven't."

He glared as if she belonged in the same category as his camp follower, and his derision made her feel ashamed.

"There's no need to be crude," she told him.

"If you don't want to listen to my risqué stories, go home. I didn't ask you here."

"Where is she now?"

"Mother or daughter?"

"Both."

"Mother died in childbirth. Daughter lives in a convent, run by the Sisters of Mercy in Antwerp, Belgium. She's ten."

"Do you ever see her?"

"Once or twice a year—when I can get away from my regiment."

"What does she think of your being gone so much? Does she miss you?"

"She hardly knows me. I doubt she misses me at all."

The cold confession wounded Jo. She stared at the floor, her fingers laced together as if in prayer.

Why was the world so unfair?

She'd been married for most of a decade. She'd spent all of that time either flat on her back as her husband pumped away between her thighs or on her knees, begging God to grant her a simple wish of one, tiny baby. Every female in the kingdom seemed able to conceive. Why not her?

She'd never gotten pregnant, and she'd grown to believe that she didn't deserve to be a mother, that God had abandoned her.

Yet Stephen Price had been given a precious gift he neither wanted nor cherished. He had a child he never saw and had made no effort to raise. He paid others to do it for him.

What type of man didn't want his daughter? What did such conduct indicate about his true character?

"You're lucky," she said.

"Am I? You know, Mrs. Merrick—"

"Don't call me Mrs. Merrick."

"I'd rather not be on familiar terms."

She sighed. "Fine. Have it your way."

"When I first visited your brother at the rectory, I had a reason."

"What was it?"

"I'm bringing Annie here later in the summer. I've already written to the Mother Superior, instructing her that I'll be sending someone to fetch her as soon as I can arrange it."

"How will you orchestrate her entrée into Stafford society?" She posed the question more harshly than she'd intended. "Will you simply show up with her, then command that she be accepted?"

"I don't give a damn about these rural villagers. They'll welcome her and be gracious about it, or they'll move on."

"This is a very conservative place, and Oscar a very conservative preacher. It might not be as easy as you're expecting. I'm just warning you."

"Warning received."

"Why did you meet with my brother?"

"I was hoping he could refer me to a kindly widow who would take her in until I can muster out of the army. After I spoke with him, I decided not to discuss it. But how about you, Josephine? Are you acquainted with any *kindly* widows in Stafford?"

The dig was sharp and, in a temper, she leapt to her feet. She wished she was a man, that she was strong enough to pound him into the ground.

"What are you saying? Are you asking me if I'd watch over her until you come back?"

"No."

"Then what is your point?"

"I mention it merely because I want you to understand how disillusioned I've been in the sorts of people I've encountered here."

"Meaning *me.*"

"Yes, meaning you."

"I could do it for you," she seethed.

"Really, Jo? You could? How? Will you march to your brother and tell him there's a sinful little girl who would like to live in his house? Or perhaps you could take on the chore after you've wed Mr. Mason." Sarcastically, he added, "I'm sure he'll be amenable."

"I could make them agree," she insisted, but her fury was waning.

He nodded to the door. "Go ahead. Scurry to your brother. Inform him you can't marry Mason because you'll be too busy helping me with Annie."

She tried to picture the conversation with Oscar, but couldn't. To her great shame, she was as meek and obedient as Stephen had accused her of being. She had no notion of how to issue demands to a man, how to garner what she craved.

Oscar would never allow her to assist Annie Price. If Jo went behind his back and proceeded anyway, where would she be when Stephen returned from the army? Her job as Annie's guardian would end, and Jo would have nowhere to go. If she defied Oscar over Annie, he would never let her come home.

At that moment, she hated herself. She felt lower than she ever had when her husband railed at her, lower than when Oscar charged her with vanity or sloth.

"You're correct," she submissively concurred. "I couldn't speak to Oscar about it."

"Precisely."

"I'm sorry."

"I'm not. My daughter has been hiding in the shadows all her life. She's never belonged anywhere—just as I have never belonged. I'm bringing her to Stafford, and when I do, I intend to find her a mother."

"You're going to wed?"

"Yes, and it will be someone with a spine, someone who will be proud to be Annie's parent. I need a woman who's tough, who isn't afraid of a few small-town snobs who see scandal behind every bush. My daughter deserves nothing less."

"Too true."

She gazed at the floor again, feeling petty and small.

Apparently, during their brief, torrid affair, he'd been judging her, but she'd failed miserably. It was humbling to realize that he might have wed *her*—if she'd been a different kind of person. Had she evinced the slightest hint of staunch character, he'd have proposed in an instant.

He was studying her, as if waiting for her to defend her cowardice, but she had no comment. His derogatory opinion was valid, and it was silly to argue about it.

"Will there be anything else?" he finally asked.

"No."

"Goodbye then. I hope you'll wish me well in my travels."

She frowned. "Are you leaving?"

"With my brother in the morning."

"I thought you were staying for the next month, until your furlough was ended."

"I've decided there's no reason to stay." He paused, watching her. "Is there?"

"No, I don't suppose there is."

He sighed, as if she'd supplied the wrong answer. What did the blasted man want? What did he expect from her? He'd been very clear: He was looking for an Amazon warrior and she was a timid mouse.

"Goodbye," he said again.

"Goodbye."

She started up the stairs so he wouldn't see the tears dripping down her cheeks. She refused to give him further cause to bark and chastise.

"Would you like me to have a carriage prepared?" he called. "I could drive you home."

"There's no need. I can find my own way."

She hurried out and ran to the lane. She was so distraught that she'd lost the impulse for stealth. She didn't care if she was observed, didn't care if she had to explain where she'd been.

Her heart broken, her humiliation vast, she kept going as fast as she was able. She didn't stop until she was locked in her empty bedroom in Oscar's quiet house. Her lonely future stretched before her like the road to Hades.

Chapter Eighteen

"Have you seen your sister?"

The twins were sitting on the stairs, looking as glum as Nicholas felt.

"I think she's up in her bedchamber," Nan said.

Nicholas had just been there but hadn't stumbled on her. He'd been searching for her since the previous day, since she'd witnessed Veronica kissing him. He hadn't located her, and no one else had, either. Veronica had continued on to her house party, but Emeline remained in hiding.

She hadn't come down for tea or supper. She hadn't slept in her bed. Breakfast was over, but she hadn't eaten.

In a few minutes, he and his brother were heading for London, but he couldn't go until he'd spoken to her.

Over the weeks that he'd dallied with Emeline, it had been easy to pretend that Veronica and his betrothal weren't real. But in a fleet moment, her arrival had shattered the fantasy.

He'd tried to warn Emeline that she shouldn't grow fond of him, but he hadn't tried very hard. He'd relished her affection, and he'd encouraged her when he shouldn't have.

At being confronted with how he'd deceived her, he was mortified by his contemptible conduct. He had to fix what he'd done, but he wasn't sure how.

He wasn't an erudite man. What words could possibly smooth over his horrid betrayal? And it *was* a betrayal; he couldn't persuade himself that it wasn't.

"Would you girls check her room for me?" he asked. "I stopped by a bit ago, but she wasn't there. Maybe she's returned by now."

They stared at him but didn't move.

"Are you two fighting?" Nell inquired.

"No," he scoffed. "Why would you think that?"

"Emeline is very sad, and we don't know why."

"You've talked to her this morning?"

"Yes."

He was so relieved! He'd been afraid that something might have happened to her. Yet he couldn't run around, demanding information as to her whereabouts. He was supposed to simply be her boss, with no deeper connection.

"I'm glad you've seen her," he said. "I was getting worried."

"She told us that we're leaving Stafford, but we don't want to go."

"You're not leaving," he insisted. "You're staying right here. She's being silly."

They kept staring at him, and their big green eyes—Em's green eyes—made him fidget with guilt. He nodded toward the upper floors. "Find her for me. I haven't had any luck. Tell her I'll be in the library."

They trudged off, and he watched them climb the stairs, then he spun and went to the library to wait for her.

It was only nine o'clock but, needing to quell the shaking of his hands, he poured himself a brandy and downed it in a quick gulp.

He never examined his behavior or fretted over his motives. He barged through the world, positive of his goals and confident of his place in it, but now, he was questioning everything.

Why had he forged ahead with her? Why had he proceeded when he'd known that there would be a bad end? Why had he hurt her?

He was so fond of Emeline, and he felt so close to her. He liked that they were friends, that they had bonded in a fashion he never had with another. For once, he was ashamed of himself, and remorse was eating him alive.

Boot steps sounded in the hall, and his brother peeked in.

Stephen had abruptly decided to return to London, and Nicholas had no idea why. In light of Nicholas's maudlin mood, he was eager for the company.

"The horses are ready," Stephen said. "Let's go."

"I still have to talk to Miss Wilson."

"You haven't yet?"

"No."

"Oh, for pity's sake," Stephen grumbled. "Make it fast. Make it blunt. I don't want her languishing, assuming you'll change your mind. She's a romantic at heart. She has to understand that you're a complete ass and will never renege on your engagement."

"Don't tell me how to handle this."

"Someone should."

"And that would be you?" Nicholas snidely retorted.

"Yes. So far, you've done nothing but spread chaos and confusion. Clean up after yourself. Have mercy on her. Cut your ties. Be brutal if you have to, but finish it."

"I will, I will."

Stephen scowled, convinced that Nicholas wasn't wise enough to say what needed to be said, and Nicholas himself wasn't certain if he was up to the task. He'd harmed Emeline in so many ways, and there was no recompense that could repair the damage he'd inflicted.

Ultimately, Stephen shrugged. "I'll check the horses. Don't dawdle. I want to get out of here."

He stomped off, and Nicholas sat, brooding and alone. He gazed out the window, at the manicured park stretching to infinity, the woods and rolling hills off in the distance.

There was a peaceful ambiance to the estate that he enjoyed, and he had to admit that—when he was mired in the hectic city, then his hectic army camp—he would miss the slow serenity.

Out in the hall, strides echoed again. They were a female's softer tread, and he would recognize them anywhere.

Suddenly panicked, he rushed to the sideboard for a second shot of liquid courage. Then he seated himself behind the large desk.

She entered, looking beleaguered, as if she'd fought a battle and lost. She was very pale, and she appeared smaller, as if his duplicity had shrunk her. Or perhaps—on learning of what a treacherous bastard he was—some of her vitality had drifted away.

They stared and stared, and obviously, she expected him to begin. He'd planned out exactly what he'd tell her, but with her arrival, his speech seemed frivolous and wrong. He couldn't start.

"You asked to speak with me, Lord Stafford?" she finally inquired.

"Please come in."

He pointed to the chair across, and she walked over and sat.

As he studied her, it occurred to him that this might be the last time he ever saw her. There was a sharp pain in the center of his chest, but he ignored it.

"We don't have to be so formal, do we?" he said. "Call me Nicholas."

"What did you want?" she coldly replied, and he sighed with regret.

The distance she was determined to impose was probably for the best, but it didn't mean he had to like it.

"Are you all right?" he queried.

"Of course. Why wouldn't I be?"

"I just want you to know how sorry I am that I—"

She cut him off. "I'm very busy today. Was there something you needed?"

"Let me apologize."

"I'd rather you didn't."

He fumbled with the ink jar, tapped his fingers on the desktop, then pathetically mumbled, "I should have told you about her, but I couldn't figure out how."

"I can't imagine to whom you're referring."

"I hurt you when I was—"

"Are we finished?"

She stood, too incensed to listen, but he was desperate for her to understand the fiasco from his perspective.

He was perplexed over Veronica, why she'd grabbed him, why she'd kissed him. They were scarcely acquainted, and he'd been stunned by her bold conduct.

Where once he might have welcomed what she was offering and taken more than he should, he hadn't been interested. Stupid though it was, he'd felt as if he was...*cheating* on Emeline.

The entire morning as he and Veronica had strolled through the house, she'd chattered away, but Nicholas hadn't a clue as to her topics of conversation. He'd been too preoccupied over what Stephen might be saying to Emeline.

Stephen had hustled her away to explain the situation, and he hadn't sugarcoated it. Any affection she'd possessed had been drummed out of her by a harsh application of the truth.

But what had Nicholas expected?

Emeline was an idealist and optimist, who saw the best in everyone and who worked to make the world a better place. She asked him for boons—but for the benefit of others. She presumed on his generosity—but for the sake of those less fortunate than her.

She was decent and honorable, and he'd been redeemed by their relationship. How typical that he would wreck it.

He gestured to her chair again. "Sit down."

"I must be going."

"Emeline—"

"I would appreciate it if you'd call me Miss Wilson."

She was prepared to storm out, but he couldn't let her before he imparted the news he was so eager to share.

There was one thing she wanted more than anything, one gift he could bestow that would solve all her problems. By his doing so, perhaps—just perhaps—she would eventually realize that he'd cared about her, despite how badly he'd behaved.

He tried to smile, hoping to alleviate some of the tension between them, but cordiality was impossible, and he gave up.

"I've made some arrangements for you," he said.

She eased herself down. "Your brother already informed me. We're to be hidden away in a room over the blacksmith's barn." She flashed a glare so full of loathing that she could have stabbed him with it.

"He told you that?"

"Yes."

"It's not what I requested."

"Shortly after, we're to leave Stafford—as soon as he can find us somewhere else to live. Heaven forbid that we remain here where our presence might upset the earl's bride."

His temper flared. "Those were never my instructions."

"Weren't they? What did you expect then? Were we to continue on at the manor until you came back a married man?"

"I hadn't planned that far ahead."

"Maybe your wife and I could become friends, although we don't have much in common. I'd have to develop an interest in baubles and frippery before we could communicate."

His cheeks flamed with chagrin. "I guess I deserved that."

"Do you imagine you'll be happy with her?"

"Happy enough, I suppose. I hadn't actually thought about it."

"You've probably been too busy, learning about the *estate* and all."

"Em, I wish you would—"

She held up a hand, as if fending him off. "I'm sorry, but I don't know how to have this discussion, and I refuse to bicker. Is there a point you're trying to make?"

"Yes, there is. You've been anxious to restart your father's school, and I've decided to let you."

He'd been on pins and needles, assuming the announcement would please her, that she might even thank him, but she evinced no reaction, at all. He stumbled to regroup.

"I own a house in the village," he said, "and the tenants will be out on the fifteenth." When she didn't comment, he added, "That's in two weeks."

"So it is."

"It's a fine residence, in solid condition. It's furnished, too. You and the twins will live in the main section, and you'll use the extra parlor for your schoolroom." He paused. Still no reaction. "I've spoken to Mr. Mason about it. He'll order any supplies, and you're to have an unlimited budget. Whatever you need, I intend for you to have it."

She assessed him as if he was babbling in a foreign language. "You mentioned," she said, "that we'd move in two weeks. Where would we stay in the meantime?"

"Here at the manor."

A fleeting smile crossed her lips, then vanished. He frowned, struggling to deduce what it indicated.

Was she glad? Was she excited? Why wasn't she oozing with enthusiasm?

Why didn't she *say* something?

"You won't pay any rent," he advised, "in case you were wondering."

"I wasn't wondering."

"Part of your salary will be your lodgings—that being the house. I'll grant you a monthly stipend, too, enough to hire a cook and a servant. Mr. Mason will deliver your wages on the first of each month."

"Mr. Mason will?"

"Yes."

That mysterious smile flitted by again.

"He'll do it, Em," he insisted. "I realize you've had some issues with him in the past, but he understands that this project is important to me. You'll have his full cooperation."

"Then I'm certain it will be a huge success."

"I'm certain it will be, too." He scowled. "So...are you happy about this? I thought you would be."

"I'm absolutely ecstatic." She was so indifferent that she might have been a marble statue.

"Well...I'm...ah...relieved to hear it."

Their discussion was concluded, and he knew he should get up and leave, but he couldn't. Something was wrong. He had the distinct impression that he hadn't communicated his objectives very clearly, and he was baffled by her apathy.

He was making amends. She comprehended that fact, didn't she? This was his penance, his atonement. She wasn't being cast out on the road, and he wasn't abandoning her. He was providing for her financially so she would never again have to fret over money or shelter. She'd be able to support her sisters. She'd be employed at a job she loved.

Yet she gave no sign that she viewed any of it as a benefit.

Blasted woman!

"I have to go," he said.

"Yes, you do." She rose. "Thank you for conferring with me."

"I'll miss you," he poignantly told her.

"I doubt it."

"I will. I'm glad we met."

"Your brother is waiting."

He nodded, his pulse pounding with distress. "Goodbye."

"Goodbye to you, and good luck with your marriage. I hope matrimony brings you exactly what you deserve."

At the sly insult, he snorted. "I'm sure it will."

She started out, and he suffered the worst moment of panic.

When she filled him with such joy and contentment, why would he split with her? Why would he choose London and a life that offered no satisfaction at all?

The questions roiled through him, but he shook them off. He *knew* why he was headed for London. He was off to wed Veronica, and he had no desire to change his path. Not for anyone.

Still, as she stepped into the hall, he frantically called, "Em?"

She whipped around and retorted, "It's Miss Wilson to you."

Then she was gone, and it was over.

Emeline hovered in the window seat in her bedchamber. If she wedged herself into the corner, she could see the stable. Two horses were saddled, ready for a journey. Mr. Price was mounted on one of them, which meant the earl was about to appear.

She was determined to watch him leave. It seemed necessary, like lancing a boil or cauterizing a wound.

She supposed she should be weeping, but she was too numb for sentiment. Her heart was broken, and she couldn't catch her breath. Her bones ached, and she was terribly feverish, as if coming down with a fatal ague.

How much misery could a human being endure? How much despair could be heaped on a person before she simply collapsed under the weight?

A vision flashed, of him sitting at his fancy desk, tossing her a few crumbs of remuneration, and her blood boiled with fury.

It had been pointless to meet with him, but curiosity had goaded her into it. She hadn't felt strong enough to face him, but she'd convinced herself there was no way he could injure her further.

She'd been wrong.

He'd wanted to *explain* himself. He wanted her to...*understand.*

She shuddered with disgust.

The man was insane, and she was just as mad for having involved herself with him. He'd warned her of his low character, but she'd refused to believe him.

Well, she definitely believed him now.

After surrendering her chastity, her payment was to be the reopening of her father's school. At any other time during the prior year, she'd have been elated, but no longer.

The earl thought she'd agreed to be his teacher, and she hadn't dissuaded him.

She smirked. As if Mr. Mason would help her! Nicholas Price was an idiot if he assumed so.

She'd written to the school in Cornwall, accepting the post there. For the next few weeks, she and her sisters would stay at the manor, as the earl had insisted they should. But once she received the coach fare, they'd move to Cornwall. And they'd never return.

Although there were many things she didn't understand about Nicholas Price, there were many other things she understood all too clearly.

He had cared for Emeline—much more than he'd ever admitted to himself. The depth of his affection would dawn on him when he was all alone, when the nights were long and quiet.

He would marry his beautiful, rich Veronica, but he would never be happy with her. In the not too distant future, he would visit the estate, looking for Emeline and the solace she'd provided.

Only she would be gone, and no one would be able to tell him where she was.

She wouldn't share her destination with anybody, not even Josephine, for if word leaked out, there would be people at Stafford who could inform him of her location. She'd spend the rest of her life, peering over her shoulder, hoping he was on his way to bring her home.

Every time a carriage was spotted on the road, every time she learned there was a stranger in town, she would wonder if he'd finally found her.

She wouldn't live like that. She wouldn't give him that much power over her.

On the day he showed up at Stafford, eager to be with her again, he deserved to discover that she had left and was never coming back. She wanted him to feel as she did at that very moment: friendless, unloved, lost, and bereft.

Outside, Mr. Price straightened, and shortly, Lord Stafford strolled into view. He checked the straps on his saddle, as he and his brother chatted, but they were too far away for Emeline to hear what they were saying.

Her sisters ran up, and Lord Stafford smiled at them. He knelt down, and Nan gave him a flower. He tucked it into his coat.

To Emeline's great surprise, he wrapped his arms around both girls and pulled them into a tight hug. For an eternity, the three of them hovered there, until he drew away and stood. He appeared very sad, and Emeline garnered some satisfaction from the realization that he would probably return sooner rather than later.

"But I won't be here," she murmured.

He mounted slowly, as if he'd aged, and he shifted about forever, getting comfortable in the saddle. He spoke to the girls, and they replied, then he waved, and he and his brother started off.

Their horses walked, then trotted, then cantered. She watched as they grew smaller and smaller, until they were just a speck on the horizon.

They arrived at the end of the driveway and rode onto the lane that would lead them through Stafford village, then to London and the wide world beyond.

He was leaving very much behind—herself and his home—and she was certain he would at least peek around as the manor vanished from sight, but he never glanced back a single time.

Chapter Nineteen

"Has the earl left?"

"Yes."

"And his brother?"

"Departed, too."

"Good riddance."

Benedict Mason couldn't agree more. He raised his brandy glass and clinked it to Oscar Blair's. They were in the vicarage, in Blair's study.

They had a mutual interest in having the Price brothers gone from Stafford.

The earl was a heathen and blasphemer, so Blair wouldn't ever want him looking too closely at some of the methods he employed to keep his congregation in line. A sinner like Price might not deem some transgressions to be worth the punishment Blair liked to extract.

As to Benedict, he was especially glad to see Stephen Price ride away.

When the brothers had initially arrived, Benedict was convinced that they were barely literate and wouldn't know an account ledger from a hedgerow. But the prior evening, he'd been walking after dark, and he'd passed the estate office at the rear of the manor. Mr. Price had been there, sitting at Benedict's desk and snooping through the books.

He'd been taking notes, adding and subtracting long columns of numbers, and Benedict was unsettled by his heightened attention. He'd yearned to march in and demand answers, but he could hardly complain that the Price brothers were reviewing their finances. Yet the discovery had had him pacing the floor most of the night.

With the brothers having trotted off, his first order of business would be to check his math for any incriminating errors. His second order of business was to deal with Emeline Wilson once and for all.

Lord Stafford's parting instructions had been that Emeline was to have her accursed school. The decision had Benedict too incensed to think straight.

The truth had finally been told. The earl was paying her for services rendered. And a fine remuneration it was, too. A cozy house in the village. A classroom with the most modern books and amenities. A salary. Servants.

He would not stand for it and—he was certain—neither would the vicar.

"There is another topic we must address," he informed Blair. "It's rather unpleasant."

"What is it?"

"I should have come to you sooner, but with the earl still in residence, I didn't dare."

"Tell me."

"It's Emeline Wilson."

Blair sighed. "Isn't it always? What's she done now?"

"I doubt you'll believe me. When I stumbled on the news myself, I was stunned."

"Where she is concerned, nothing would surprise me."

Benedict was silent, his rage bubbling up, and he found himself too embarrassed to describe what he'd learned.

He didn't speak, and the vicar pressed, "Well? Let's have it. My curiosity is begging to be assuaged."

"I apologize for being blunt, but there's no gracious way to begin."

"Candor is welcome."

"Yes, but this is quite a bit beyond candor."

"Just spit it out. I'm sure I'll survive."

"She...she...while living at the manor, she's been engaged in a sexual affair with Nicholas Price."

Blair squinted as if confused. "What?"

"They've been having a sexual affair. She shared his bed."

"They fornicated? Without benefit of marriage?"

"Yes."

"The man is the very devil. I'm convinced of it."

"He is very wicked," Benedict agreed.

"Did he seduce her or was she forced?"

"There was no force involved. She might be highly educated, but she's a fool who swallowed his lies. He probably promised he'd marry her."

"He never would," Blair scoffed.

"You and I know that, but she's a sheltered female. She wouldn't understand the physical...*urges* of a cad like Nicholas Price."

"No, she wouldn't," Blair concurred. "You're positive of this?"

"Absolutely."

"How dare she!" Blair hissed. "For shame!"

Blair cheeks heated with fury, and Benedict almost felt sorry for Emeline. Almost.

Benedict had seen how Blair punished another girl who'd had the nerve to immorally copulate. His reaction had been ugly and vicious, but it certainly kept other illicit couplings to a minimum.

"What shall we do with her?" Blair asked.

"I have a few suggestions."

"First and foremost, she will be accused of harlotry and brought up on charges."

"Of course," Benedict said, "but we must proceed cautiously."

"Why? We must make an example of her." Blair appeared gleeful at the prospect. "The whole town must hear how she's sinned. I insist on it."

"The earl was fond of her."

"So? What bearing has his sentiment on her crime?"

"If he came back and discovered that we'd moved against her, he might be angry."

Blair pondered, then nodded. "That could pose some difficulties."

"I thought we could use that sheriff you know, the fellow we used before."

Blair had an old acquaintance, Sheriff Pratt, who was more than happy to take care of neighborhood *situations*—if the price was right. They had called on him previously, when they'd been plagued by troublemakers who needed to vanish.

The prior four miscreants had all been men, and Benedict had no inkling of what became of them. They hadn't returned to Stafford, and it was rumored that they'd been transported to Australia.

Emeline could be spirited away, and there'd be no trace of where she'd gone. After her antics with the earl over her purported strike, she was generally disliked, so there would be no inquiries about her.

However, if questions were ever raised, Blair and Benedict were good liars. They could easily say they had no idea what had happened to her. They were pillars of the community. Who would contradict their story?

"What about her sisters?" Blair asked. "In light of this scandal, she's hardly a fit guardian."

"We could have them placed in the poorhouse, but it might be better to send them on to an orphanage in London. If they disappear, too, everyone will simply assume they went somewhere with their sister."

"I would prefer the orphanage," Blair mused.

"Will you write to Sheriff Pratt or shall I?"

"I will," Blair said.

"I'd like to have this handled in the next few weeks. The earl ordered me to move her into a house in the village—"

"A house!" Blair gasped. "Of her own?"

"Yes. She's to live there as long as she likes."

"Is he mad? We're a pious town. He must know we'd never tolerate such indecency."

"She must have been quite adept at earning her keep," Benedict caustically asserted. "She must have learned just how to please him."

"The filthy slut," Blair muttered, surprising Benedict with his voicing the crude term. "To think that I've had her in my home, that she's friends with my sister."

"It boggles the mind, doesn't it?"

"Yes, it does, but we'll have the problem fixed in no time."

Blair's eyes were burning with the religious fervor that came over him whenever he was gearing up to root out evil, and he'd found an easy mark in Emeline. She didn't stand a chance against him.

She had no one to help her, no one who'd be concerned

over her plight, except perhaps Mrs. Merrick. But Emeline would be long gone before Mrs. Merrick realized she was missing.

His business finished, Benedict stood.

"Contact me when you hear from the sheriff," he said.

"I'll let you know immediately."

They shook hands, and Benedict left. He whistled all the way to the manor.

"Miss Wilson?"

"Yes?"

A maid peeked in Emeline's bedroom door.

"Mr. Mason asked me to fetch you to his office. He needs to speak with you."

Emeline huffed out an irritated breath.

Wasn't it just her luck? The irksome man was supposed to be at her beck and call as they reopened the school, but since the earl's departure, he'd avoided her like the plague.

Now, when there was no reason to chat with him ever again, he'd suddenly reared his pompous head.

The coach fare from Cornwall had been received, and she was furtively packing their meager possessions. She planned for them to leave the manor casually, as if they were simply taking a stroll, but they weren't coming back.

At the end of the driveway, they wouldn't go to Stafford village, but to a town in the opposite direction. They would spend the night at an inn, then travel on the public coach the following morning.

She couldn't arrive at her post looking like paupers, so they would each wear one of the dresses Lord Stafford had purchased for them. The rest of his gifts would be left behind.

In her new life, she wanted no mementoes of Nicholas Price to weigh her down, so she would take only what she'd had when they initially moved into the manor. Later on, once they were settled in Cornwall, she would buy her sisters clothes with her own money.

"I'm very busy," she told the maid. "Could you advise Mr. Mason that I'll meet with him tomorrow?"

Ha! Tomorrow she'd be gone.

"He says it's very important. You must come down."

Emeline gnawed on her cheek, wanting to decline but knowing she couldn't. Benedict Mason was so arrogant. If she refused to attend him, she'd draw notice to herself at the very moment she yearned to be invisible.

"All right," she grumbled. "He's in his office?"

"Yes, miss."

She started out and as she passed the girl, she asked, "Have you seen my sisters?"

"Not all morning."

"If you stumble on them, would you inform them that I need them to be up here in my room when I return?"

"I will."

Emeline hurried down the stairs, proceeding through the deserted halls that led to Mason's office at the rear of the mansion.

She was curious as to why she'd been summoned, and she figured he was prepared to discuss the school. She had to make the appropriate responses, so she rehearsed several possible conversations in her head, but none of it mattered.

In her mind, she was already far away from Stafford.

She approached the door and knocked. As he bade her enter, she spun the knob and walked in. To her consternation, Mr. Mason wasn't alone. Vicar Blair was with him, and she nearly snarled with disgust.

If he'd visited the manor, he was intent on scolding her over some perceived misdeed, but she was in no mood to listen.

They were glaring as if she were the worst felon in history, and they'd positioned the space for an inquisition. There was a single chair against the wall, where it was obvious they expected her to sit. Two other, bigger chairs faced it.

"You wanted to see me, Mr. Mason?" she said.

"Be seated, Miss Wilson," he replied.

"I'll stand, thank you."

Behind her, the door closed, and the key grated in the lock. She glanced over to observe a third man loitering in the corner. She didn't know him, but his presence intimated trouble.

He was a hulking, portly fellow, probably Vicar Blair's age of forty, but he looked older, as if he'd had a harder life.

"Who are you?" she demanded, her manners having fled.

She was too irritated for games or mysteries.

"I am Sheriff Pratt. I'm a friend of the vicar's." He nodded to the chair. "Sit down, miss. Don't let's argue about it."

"I'd rather not."

To her astonishment, the oaf grabbed her by the arm and pushed her down into it. When she tried to rise, he put a beefy hand on her shoulder to hold her in place.

Emeline shrugged him off and warned, "Don't touch me."

He ignored her and peered over at Vicar Blair. "Let's get on with it. I want to sleep in my own bed tonight, so we'll need to be on the road in the next hour."

"You can go now if you wish." Emeline smiled sweetly at him. "We don't mind."

"Emeline!" Vicar Blair snapped, and she focused her scowl on him.

"What? I have no idea why you brought me here, and I won't stay to be manhandled or browbeaten."

"Fine," the vicar said. "I'll come straight to the point. You're being charged with illicit fornication and harlotry. How do you plead?"

"I'm...I'm...what?"

"You're charged with fornication and harlotry. Will you admit or deny your crimes?"

"My...crimes? You're being ridiculous, and I'm leaving."

"Oh, no you're not," the sheriff barked. He shifted in a menacing way, as if he might physically restrain her.

Were they insane?

"What are you talking about?" she asked of Vicar Blair. "I am a respectable gentlewoman, from a good family. My father was school teacher at this estate for three decades—as you're well aware."

"Yes, he was," the vicar haughtily intoned, "and if he could see you now, what would he think?"

"My father loved me," she fumed, "and he was proud of me. What would he think if he could see *you* now?"

Mr. Mason butted in. "You haven't answered Vicar Blair. Will you admit or deny?"

"I vehemently deny, and I won't sit here and be slandered by either of you."

She leapt to her feet, and while Sheriff Pratt reached for

her, she was too quick. She raced to the door and rattled the knob, having forgotten that the sheriff locked it. Though she yanked and yanked, it wouldn't open.

She whipped around.

"Let me out! I insist!"

"You'll go when I say you can." The sheriff gestured to her chair. "Return to your seat and behave yourself. I'm not above wrestling with a recalcitrant woman, but I'd just as soon not."

He grabbed her again, but she jerked away and went to the other side of the room. She stood, glowering.

"You have insulted and offended me," she furiously said, "and I demand to know what this is about."

"We have ample evidence of your perfidy," Vicar Blair declared. "We only allowed this meeting as a courtesy. We're giving you a chance to defend yourself."

"Against what?" she scoffed. "I told you, I haven't the vaguest notion of what you're claiming."

"Don't you?" The vicar was very smug. "Tell us about your affair with Lord Stafford."

"Lord...Stafford?"

Her pulse pounded with dread.

As they'd tossed out words like *harlotry* and *fornication*, it had never occurred to her that they were referring to her trysts with Nicholas Price.

Her relationship with him had been fueled by love and affection. At least on her end. She shouldn't have dallied with him, but she'd done it with the best of intentions. She'd thought he would marry her. She'd thought her esteem was fully reciprocated.

She'd been dead wrong, but she'd proceeded with high hopes and big dreams.

The vicar's allegation made their association sound sordid and obscene. He made it sound...criminal.

A woman couldn't blithely consort with a man. There were laws banning it. There were morals to prohibit it. There were community standards of decency and decorum to follow. There were church teachings as to sin and damnation.

Still, she blustered, "Lord Stafford and I are friends. He helped me financially when my sisters and I were in dire straits. He let us live here at the manor, and he gave me a job as his secretary. I worked for him."

"Flat on your back, it would seem," Vicar Blair vulgarly retorted.

His cold certainty rattled her.

"Name one witness who can speak against me! Name one witness who ever observed so much as a glance between us that was inappropriate!"

"Actually," Benedict Mason said, "*I* am that witness. I was happy to impart all that I discovered about the two of you."

"You!" she huffed. "I scarcely know you. What basis could you have to accuse me of anything?"

The vicar picked up a stack of papers and waved them at Emeline.

"Mr. Mason has penned an extensive deposition. Shall I read some of it to you?"

Emeline panicked. She was cornered and couldn't decide her course of action.

She understood that she had to deny and deny and deny any affair, but at what cost? If she asked him *not* to read from the deposition, was she implicating herself? If she brazened it out and urged him to go ahead, he might spew embarrassing personal details. She'd likely faint.

She could think of nothing worse than to stand before the three of them while Oscar Blair recited a list of her transgressions. What could Mr. Mason possibly have told him? It had to be very, very bad.

She thought of Nicholas Price, the man she'd cherished, the man she'd presumed would be her husband. He was in London, leading his rich, indolent bachelor's life while she'd been left behind to face disgrace and humiliation all alone.

Was he aware of what they were doing? If he wasn't, and he ever learned of it, would he even care?

She didn't suppose he would. He'd be wed soon, and once he was, she'd be a distant memory, just one gullible woman in a long line of gullible women who'd crawled in and out of his bed over the years.

"You don't have to read it," she said.

"Why is that?" the vicar queried. "Is it because you know what it contains?"

"No, I just rather you didn't."

He started anyway. "'On Tuesday last, I, Benedict Mason, land agent for Nicholas Price, Lord Stafford, was in the hall outside the earl's library. The door was ajar, and I could hear him talking to his brother, Mr. Stephen Price. To my extreme surprise, they were discussing the earl's tenant, Miss Emeline Wilson, a single, unmarried lady whom the earl had brought to reside in the manor with him.'"

The vicar paused. "Shall I continue?"

"There's no need," Emeline pleaded.

Vicar Blair kept on. "'Mr. Stephen Price asked the earl about a sexual liaison he was pursuing with Miss Wilson. The earl boasted about the relationship and shared numerous salacious descriptions of Miss Wilson's anatomy. He also provided several vivid accounts of the carnal acts in which the pair had regularly engaged.'"

Emeline gasped. She hadn't meant to; the sound emerged before she could hold it in.

"He was boasting, Miss Wilson," Mr. Mason said, "and he was quite pleased with himself. He was eager for his brother to know all."

"I don't believe you."

"The earl is a hardened soldier," Mr. Mason pointed out. "What on earth were you thinking, involving yourself with someone like him? Did you imagine yourself clever? Did you imagine yourself discreet? How could you presume you would never be found out?"

Emeline began to shake. Her legs felt rubbery, as if they might give way, and she stumbled over to the chair she hadn't wanted to use. She eased herself down.

What to do? What to do?

Vicar Blair riffled the papers again. "Apparently, you've been well paid for your whoring. So far, you've received a new wardrobe, both for yourself and your sisters. Next, you're to receive a house and a stipend and a—"

"Stop it!" she cried. "It wasn't like that!"

"Wasn't it? When a female spreads her legs for a man, then is paid for her efforts, it is prostitution, Emeline. It's no different than if you'd been lurking in the shadows at Covent Garden, and he'd tossed you a few pennies when he was through."

The sheriff added, "Whores are hanged for less."

Ashamed and mortified, she stared at the floor. She realized that she ought to be refuting the allegations, but Vicar Blair was so *sure*. She couldn't guess how to temper his opinion. In his view, she'd already been tried and convicted.

And what purpose was to be gained by contradicting Mr. Mason's version of events? Emeline *had* sinned with Nicholas Price. She *had* lain with him outside marriage. She *had* dishonored herself with immoral behavior. All of their claims were true, so how could she insist otherwise? It seemed futile.

"I would like to contact Lord Stafford," she said. "I ask that I be allowed to write to him."

The vicar scowled. "Write to him? What for?"

"He would tell you how it actually was between us."

"We know how it *was*," Vicar Blair sneered.

Mr. Mason inquired, "Have you seen the London paper?"

"No, when would I have?" she replied.

He had a copy of it, and he whipped through the pages, searching for the one he wanted. As he located it, he shoved it in her face.

She tried to skim the article he indicated, but as she noted the subject, her vision blurred, and she couldn't make out the words.

"The earl has been called back to active duty," Mr. Mason explained. "He won't be able to return to London in August for his wedding as he'd planned."

"So?" she mumbled. "How would that concern me?"

"He has moved up the date. It's to be held this Friday."

Vicar Blair snickered. "Do you really suppose, Emeline, that he'd care to hear from you just now?"

He'd moved up the date? He'd be wed on Friday?

After Lady Veronica visited Stafford, Emeline had understood that he was destined to marry the beautiful, rich girl, but she hadn't truly believed it would ever transpire. In some silly feminine part of her brain, she'd assumed he wouldn't proceed, that he would recognize his mistake and come back to her.

Instead, he'd flitted off to London and decided to wed earlier than previously scheduled. *Much* earlier than scheduled.

Her shaking increased, and she was trembling so violently that she could barely remain in her chair.

"I should like to see my sisters," she said.

"That won't be possible," Vicar Blair responded. "Considering the gravity of your conduct, I have determined you to be an unfit guardian. They have been taken from you."

"What? No!"

"Such young, impressionable children have no business being raised by you."

"I want to see them! Where are they?"

"Currently, they've been conveyed to the poorhouse. Ultimately, they will be remanded to an orphanage in London."

Emeline was so enraged that she jumped up and lunged at Blair, but this time, Sheriff Pratt was prepared for an outburst. For such a large man, he reacted very quickly. He grabbed her arms and forced her to her knees so she was prostrate in front of the vicar, as if begging his forgiveness.

"Harlot!" Vicar Blair charged. "Harlot be damned!"

Exuding wrath, he rose and loomed over her as Emeline hissed and wrestled against Sheriff Pratt's tight grip.

"I demand to speak with my sisters!" she shouted. "I demand to contact Lord Stafford."

"I am disgusted to the marrow of my bones," the vicar shouted back. "Get her out of my sight."

He stormed from the room as Emeline struggled to break free and chase after him, but the sheriff was much too strong.

Though she scratched and fought, he bound her wrists with a rope, then he wrapped a bandana over her mouth to stifle any cries for help.

He hustled her out the rear door to a waiting carriage. He picked her up and tossed her into it, then he climbed in after her.

The driver had anticipated their arrival, and he cracked the whip, the horses lurching away at a fast clip.

In an instant, Emeline vanished from Stafford, and it just so happened that the stable yard and park were empty of onlookers so there were no witnesses to what had occurred. She might have been a ghost, disappeared into thin air.

Chapter Twenty

Jo trudged to the vicarage, wishing she had somewhere else to go. She was so miserably unhappy, and in light of some of the awful moments she'd experienced in her life, she hadn't imagined she could ever again be so dejected. Yet apparently, there was no end to the low points that could arrive.

Stephen Price had been gone for two weeks. He'd burst across the sky like a comet, and in the process, he'd wrecked everything.

After her husband's death, when she'd moved to Stafford, she'd carefully constructed a world for herself so she could survive the humdrum years. That world was painted in boring shades of tan and gray. Nothing exciting was supposed to occur.

She was a woman who'd lusted after much, but who had never been able to grab hold of what she truly wanted. She'd learned to settle; she'd learned to do without.

Stephen had shaken up her staid existence, and she felt as if she'd been scraped raw, her yearnings exposed. She'd become a roiling torrent of dissatisfaction.

She approached the house, and there was a carriage parked at the gate. Her brother climbed out and motioned to the driver who clicked the reins. The vehicle started toward her.

As it rattled by, one of the Wilson twins popped up in the window.

"Mrs. Merrick!" she cried, appearing terrified. "Mrs. Merrick, we don't know what's—"

An older matron lunged up and yanked her inside. The curtain was jerked shut, and the carriage kept on.

Jo turned and glared at her brother. He was watching it

rumble off, a grim smile on his arrogant face. Unease swept over her.

There had always been rumors of his autocratic behavior, of his stepping beyond the bounds of conduct permitted a preacher, but no lapses had ever been proven. It was all gossip, allegedly stirred by the less-pious members of the community who didn't like him.

With no earl in residence, he'd seized an enormous amount of authority, and he wielded his power without supervision or restraint. What sort of trouble could such a despot instigate? The possibilities were frightening.

"Where are the twins going?" she asked, hurrying to him. "Who was that woman?"

"Leave it be, Josephine. It's none of your affair."

"Tell me."

"You will not question me! You know better."

He marched into the vicarage, and she followed, running to keep up.

Ignoring her, he hung his coat on a hook, then went into his study. He poured himself a brandy and sat at his desk. To her assessing eye, it looked as if he was celebrating.

What on earth had he done?

"Is Emeline all right?" She pestered him even though he'd insisted she not. "Has something happened?"

"Josephine!" he snapped. "Be silent."

"I demand to know what is occurring."

"If I thought this was any of your business, I would confide in you."

With her mood being so sour, she was too annoyed to be circumspect. They might have had their first quarrel ever, but any bickering was forestalled by a knock at the door.

The maid answered it, and shortly, Mr. Mason was shown in. He was as smug as her brother.

"Hello, Mrs. Merrick," he said.

"Mr. Mason."

She tried to smile but couldn't manage it. She wasn't glad to see him and couldn't pretend.

Over the past few weeks, he'd invited her on numerous outings, but she'd deftly devised pretexts to avoid him. She hadn't had to be alone with him a single time, but she couldn't demur forever. If she wasn't more sociable, Oscar would order her to fraternize.

"You're particularly fetching this afternoon," he told her.

"Thank you."

He was always unfailingly polite, and it was disconcerting to have compliments spew from his cold, cruel mouth.

"If you'll excuse us, Josephine?" her brother interrupted. "Mr. Mason and I have important matters to discuss."

"Certainly." She was relieved to have a reason to flee the room.

She walked into the hall and pulled the door closed, and as she was moving away, she noted that the latch hadn't caught. As she reached to shut it again, she realized that it was ajar and their conversation audible. They were chatting quietly, and when they mentioned Emeline, she couldn't help but listen.

"Is she gone?" her brother asked.

"Vanished like smoke."

"Any problems? Any witnesses?"

"No. Sheriff Pratt whisked her away so fast that my head is still spinning."

A sheriff? A sheriff took Emeline away?

"I only deal with professionals," Oscar bragged.

"Pratt is very good. Emeline kicked and fussed, but she was too small to put up much of a fight."

"I'm delighted to be shed of her—and so easily, too. I should have taken action months ago."

"What about the twins?" Mr. Mason inquired.

"They've been seized, and I've arranged transport to the London orphanage tomorrow morning."

"So...all three have disappeared, and it will be ages before anyone notices they're missing. This has been a fine day's work."

"I agree."

"If any curious busybodies ever come sniffing, we'll simply shrug. Why would we know anything about Emeline Wilson? I heard she has family in Sussex. Perhaps she went to stay there."

"I heard the very same," Oscar said.

They chuckled, and there was a clinking sound as if they were enjoying a toast.

Jo began to shake with fury. Emeline had been arrested? She'd been physically overpowered? The twins were being shipped to a London orphanage?

Decades of repressed rage bubbled up inside her. Every slight, every insult, every abuse surged to the surface, and she was hopping mad.

She laid a palm on the wood of the door and shoved it open with such force that it whipped around and smacked into the wall behind. Both men jumped, but their guilty expressions were quickly masked.

"What have you two done?" Jo seethed.

"Go to your room, Josephine," her brother commanded.

She focused her livid attention on Mr. Mason. "I will not leave until you confess your behavior."

"Go!" her brother hissed.

"What if I don't? Will you call in your sheriff and have him wrestle *me* to the ground?"

Mr. Mason frowned at Oscar. "Maybe I should explain it to her."

"No, it would be better if you left. I'll handle it."

"If you're sure?"

"I'm sure."

"She's in a temper," Mason pointed out, "so she isn't thinking clearly. We can't have her blabbing to the whole town."

"She won't," Oscar replied, and it sounded like a threat.

"I saw the twins in the carriage," Jo said. "I'll never be silent about it."

"Dammit, Blair!" Mr. Mason muttered. "You only had to rid us of two young girls. You couldn't do it without being observed?"

"I won't be lectured by you," Oscar huffed. "Now leave us so that I may deal with my sister."

Mr. Mason turned to Jo. "We'll talk later."

"I'd rather have the barber yank out all my teeth," she retorted.

He clicked his heels together and bowed, but didn't offer a goodbye. She stood, facing her brother, until the front door closed.

A deadly pause descended, then her brother rose, wrath wafting off him.

"Get down on your knees!" he roared. "Get down and beg the Lord God to forgive your vanity! How dare you sass me! How dare you shame me while we have company!"

He started toward her, looking dangerous, as if he might strike her.

At every other occasion in her life, Jo had folded before him, but not this time. She ran to the fireplace and grabbed the iron poker. As he lunged for her, she swung it at him.

"If you touch me," she warned, "I will beat you bloody."

"You haven't the temerity for violence," he blustered, but to her stunned surprise, he took a step back—as if he was afraid of her. His tepid reaction bolstered her courage.

"Where is Emeline?"

He smirked, refusing to say, and she swiped the poker across his desk. Ink pots, brandy glasses, and a tea tray went flying.

The maid rushed in. "Mrs. Merrick? What is it? What's happened?"

"Get out!" Oscar yelled, and the girl blanched.

"Don't move," Jo told her. "Stand here and listen to what your *vicar* has done to Emeline Wilson and her sisters. He was just about to boast of it."

"You will not ever," he raged, "mention that harlot's name in my home again."

On hearing the obscene term, Jo and the maid gasped.

"What do you mean?"

"She has disgraced herself with the earl of Stafford. She has played the whore for him. The entire time he was visiting the estate, she played the whore!"

He shouted the accusation at the top of his lungs. His face was red, the veins in his neck bulging. He could have been the devil rising up from Hell.

"And the twins?" Jo demanded. "They're children. What sins have they committed?"

"They have committed no sin. Their sister is a harlot, and thus, an unfit guardian. They have been separated from her custody and control."

"I don't believe you about Emeline," Jo scoffed. "You're lying, and I'll see that you pay for it. If it's the last thing I do, I'll see that you pay."

"With what currency?"

"You'll be damned for this," Jo hurled.

"Not by my God," he proudly claimed. "I have carried out His work this day. He is pleased with me—His humble servant."

"You. Are. Mad."

Pushing by the maid, she stormed out and raced up the stairs. She locked her door, then she paced and paced, trying to devise a plan, to figure out how she could learn Emeline's whereabouts, how she could muster some help.

The men in the neighborhood were too timid to assist her. They'd been beaten down by events and were too cowardly to rise against Oscar or Benedict Mason. Nor would they participate in any enterprise that might anger the earl. They wouldn't act without knowing where he stood in the matter.

She thought about Lord Stafford, and she remembered that afternoon out on the lane when she and Emeline had been walking. The Price brothers had ridden up, and sparks ignited between Emeline and the earl.

Jo had been concerned enough to question Stephen, to wonder if she should have a *talk* with Emeline.

If the earl had ruined Emeline, then he owed her some support as remuneration. He certainly owed her his protection—whether they had dallied or not. She was one of his tenants, and she'd grown up on his estate. He had to be apprised of the harm his vicar and land agent were perpetrating in his name.

She calmed, realizing that she had to get to London as fast as she could. Stephen would know how to find his brother. Stephen would tell her what to do.

Downstairs, a door slammed. She peered out the window to see that her brother had left the house. He had on his hat and coat, and he was heading to the barn to saddle his horse, which meant he'd be gone for hours.

She crawled under her bed and pulled out her portmanteau. Swiftly, she filled it with the bare essentials, then she gazed around, convinced she would never return. It would be awful to forget any significant items, but she owned so little.

Save for a tiny miniature of her exhausted, beleaguered mother, there was nothing she wanted.

She buckled the straps on her bag, then tiptoed down to the front parlor. Oscar kept the Sunday collection money behind a loose brick next to the hearth. He was a lax bookkeeper, and often, months passed without his balancing accounts, without his sending cash on to the bank as was required.

With nary a ripple in her conscience, she removed the brick and took every penny.

She stared up to Heaven and murmured, "Forgive me, Lord, but it's for a good cause. I'll pay it back. I promise!"

She spun and hastened away without a word to anyone.

"How about this?"

"No. How many times must I tell you? My brother and I are wearing our uniforms."

Stephen glared at the fussy, effeminate tailor hired by Lady Veronica's mother. They were in Nicholas's London house, in an upstairs salon. The tailor had an armload of formal coats that he wanted Stephen to try on, but Stephen had no intention of consenting.

The ceremony was in three days, so everyone was in a dither. Craftspeople—chefs and the like—had assumed they had the rest of the summer to prepare, but the schedule had been shredded, and Stephen refused to be dragged into the chaos.

He didn't care about Lady Veronica or the wedding. He most especially didn't care about the frantic, last-minute arrangements. Nicholas was making the biggest mistake of his life, and he'd regret it forever. Stephen couldn't persuade him to cry off, and the notion of having Veronica Stewart as his sister-in-law was revolting.

"Your uniforms are inappropriate for the event," the tailor declared. "They'll set the wrong tone and interfere with the bride's coloring."

"Oh dear," Stephen sarcastically retorted, "how will she survive it?"

"This one is very stylish." The man held out a coat and flashed a simpering smile. "Let's see how it looks on you, shall we?"

"Let's not and say we did."

"It's important to Lady Veronica."

Cheryl Holt

"I don't give a rat's ass about her."

The man huffed with indignation but, undaunted, he approached as if he might wrestle Stephen into it. Stephen wasn't about to have the gay blade put his hands on Stephen's body, for he was certain the fellow would enjoy it too much.

"Touch me," Stephen threatened, "and I'll break your arm."

The tailor pursed his lips. "I'll have to report back to Lady Veronica's mother. I'll have to inform her that you're being totally uncooperative."

"You do that."

"I can't predict what the consequences will be."

"I'll risk it."

The man trembled with affront and began gathering up his supplies. As he stomped away, a maid peeked in.

When he and Nicholas had first arrived in England, they'd hired no staff, but on their return from Stafford, Stephen had sought out an employment agency and had brought in several people to cook and clean.

Gad, Lady Veronica was about to be living in the accursed residence! While the condition of the place had improved, Stephen doubted she'd deem it acceptable.

"Mr. Price?" the girl said.

"Yes?"

"You have a visitor."

Stephen frowned, unable to fathom who it might be. They had occasional callers—*female* callers—but they all came to see Nicholas.

"Who is it?"

"A Mrs. Josephine Merrick."

Stephen cocked his head as if he hadn't heard correctly. "Who?"

"It's Mrs. Josephine Merrick, from Stafford village. Are you at home?"

Jo had traveled all the way from Stafford? Why would she have?

They'd said all there was to say, and he couldn't imagine what remained.

Though his brother had temporarily delayed him in his plan to bring Annie to Stafford, by summer's end she would be at the estate.

234

In the meantime, Stephen would find himself a wife, and she wouldn't be any of the silly London debutantes who were suddenly throwing themselves at him simply because he was now an earl's brother.

He'd select the first decent woman he encountered, marry her, and settle at Stafford. He'd grow old there, surrounded by his family.

Jo would suffocate in the vicarage, being denigrated and harassed by her brother.

A vision flitted by, of the two of them elderly and wizened. He'd bump into her out on the lane. She'd be hunched over and worn out while he'd be vital and thriving.

Which of us made the right choice? he'd ask her. *Don't you wish you'd picked a life with me, instead of with your pious, ridiculous brother?*

"What should I tell her, Mr. Price?" the maid inquired. "She mentioned that she's come a long distance and that it's urgent."

"Urgent?" he scoffed.

There was no subject *urgent*, except the possibility that she was increasing. But it wasn't soon enough for her to discover that she was pregnant, and besides, she insisted she was barren. She'd nearly been divorced over it.

What else could she want?

The only other likely topic was a rehashing of their abbreviated affair, but he'd slit his wrists before he'd discuss it again. Couldn't she just let the past lie? Must they argue over it like a pair of angry washerwomen?

"I won't speak with her," he decided.

"She was afraid you might refuse, so she wrote you this letter."

The girl held it out, and he walked over and took it.

He studied it, tapping the corner on his palm. Without a doubt, if he opened it, he'd be sucked into her pathetic world. He'd always regret it.

"It doesn't matter what she's written," he said. "Whatever her problems, I don't care to hear about them." At his heartless statement, the girl couldn't hide a scowl, and he added, "I'm scarcely acquainted with her, and I have no idea why she'd seek me out."

"Very good, sir."

"Please advise her that I am *not* at home."

"What if she asks when you'll return?"

"Inform her that I've already gone back to the army, and you don't know when I'll be in England again."

The maid nodded and left, and he went to the hearth and pitched the letter into the fire. In a few seconds, it was consumed by the flames and reduced to a pile of ash.

"I'm sorry, Mrs. Merrick, but Mr. Price isn't here."

"Where is he?" Jo queried. "Could I track him down somewhere, or should I wait until he comes back?"

"He's not in London. He's been recalled to his regiment."

"Really."

"Yes."

Silent and incredulous, she stared with exasperation. The girl was a bad liar, and her cheeks flushed bright red.

A servant always knew if the master was in residence or not. And a servant especially knew if the master was in *England* or not. If Stephen was on his way to Europe, why had the maid bothered to ask if he would see Jo?

"May I have my letter?" Jo inquired.

"Ah..." The maid flushed an even deeper shade of red, and she shuffled her feet. "It's upstairs. I'll keep it for him."

"How long will that be?" Jo snidely said. "Two years? Five years? My news will be a bit dated by then."

"Probably, Mrs. Merrick."

Jo grumbled with frustration. "Did he even read it?"

"I don't believe so."

"Why wouldn't he talk to me? Have you a message?"

She shook her head. "No."

Jo sighed. What had she expected? Where Stephen Price was concerned, she'd made her mistakes, and obviously, he was more rigid than she'd assumed. She'd hurt him, and he didn't easily forgive.

Previously, Jo would have slithered away, defeated, but the little mouse he loathed had vanished. It had been replaced by a lioness who was roaring with aggravation.

She was ready to push her way inside, being perfectly amenable to storming through the house until she located him, but she was distracted by a horse leaving from the rear stable. She glanced over to find Stephen cantering off down the street.

"Coward!" she shouted, and her word seemed to strike him. He stiffened as if she'd hit him with a rock, but he kept going.

She peered at the maid.

"I apologize, ma'am," the girl said.

"Do you suppose he'll return?"

"I don't have any idea. He's very rarely here."

"Is his brother at home? Could I speak with him instead? It's dreadfully important."

"We haven't seen the earl in days. It's been awfully hectic, what with the wedding and all."

"What wedding? Who is getting married?"

"The earl."

"When?"

"This Friday. It was to be held at the end of August, but they've moved up the date."

The earl was engaged? He was about to be married?

According to Oscar, the earl had conducted an illicit affair with Emeline. Had he been betrothed the whole time?

What a cad! What a scoundrel!

If he was occupied with wedding preparations, what chance had Jo of convincing him to aid her? He had so many other irons in the fire. Why would he expend an ounce of effort on Emeline?

Still, she had to try.

"Listen," she said to the maid, "I need you to talk to Mr. Price for me. I need you to be sure he reads my letter."

"I wouldn't have the authority to make him, ma'am."

"Better yet, if you see the earl, tell him to read it."

"I don't know how I would."

"My friend, Emeline, is in terrible trouble. Repeat her name for me: Emeline Wilson."

"Emeline Wilson, yes, ma'am."

"Can you remember it?"

"Yes."

"She is one of the earl's tenants, and he's very fond of her. His land agent has had her arrested on false charges. Her and her sisters."

"Arrested! My goodness!"

"Her sisters are only ten years old. The earl must hurry to Stafford immediately."

"But he's marrying in three days! He might not be able."

Jo opened her purse and retrieved a coin. She slipped it into the maid's hand. "Speak to him for me. Swear that you will."

The girl studied the money, then Jo, then the money again.

"I will, ma'am—if I see him—but you hadn't ought to count on it."

"Thank you so much."

The maid went inside and shut the door, and Jo dawdled on the stoop, wondering what to do. She plopped down and waited for Stephen, but to no avail. The earl didn't arrive, either. Neither did anyone else. For a household that was having a society wedding, the place seemed deserted.

She tarried until the sun dropped in the western sky, until the temperature grew so cool that she was shivering.

She didn't dare be caught out on the streets after dark, so she walked to a busy thoroughfare and hired a hackney to take her to the coaching inn where she was staying.

As she bumped along, her temper ignited, and by the time she was in her room, it was a full-on boil.

Stephen was letting his wounded pride rule him. The stupid oaf! His departure from Stafford had generated a moment of exceptional clarity, and she wouldn't ignore it. She loved him and wanted to marry him so she could be with him forever.

Evening waned and night fell, and as she pondered, the wildest idea began to form.

Stephen was bringing his daughter to Stafford, and he would eventually bring a wife there, too. He was seeking a no-nonsense female who wasn't afraid to stare down the village gossips.

He thought Jo was a scared rabbit, but she'd changed. He'd never believe her, though, so she'd have to prove it. She'd have to show him that she could cherish his daughter as no other woman ever would.

By dawn, she was feverish with the urge to be on the road.

She sat at the desk in the corner, and she penned three

identical letters to the earl. Then, as the first coach rolled into the yard, she grabbed her bag and rushed downstairs.

She handed the letters to the proprietor. "I need these delivered to the same address, at different hours, over the next two days."

"To the same address?"

"Yes. I'm desperate to have them read, so I'm sending extra copies."

The man noticed the name on the front. "The Earl of Stafford? My!"

"There's been a death in the family," she lied. "His favorite nephew drowned. We're trying to notify him so he won't miss the funeral, but we haven't had any luck."

She passed on a note with directions to the earl's London mansion, and she gave him some money for his trouble.

"You'll see to it?" she asked. "You'll have them delivered?"

"Yes, ma'am. I'll get them there. How about one this morning? Another this afternoon? And the third tomorrow?"

"That's perfect."

She sighed with relief. She didn't know how else to contact the earl. It hardly seemed productive to camp out on his stoop, and she couldn't guess his habits or routines. How would she ever locate him among the London hoards? Hopefully, the word *URGENT* scrawled in large bold print would capture someone's attention. Surely, a servant would track him down.

"Now then," she said, "I'm interested in booking passage to Antwerp, Belgium. I have to visit a convent there, and I need advice as to ships and schedules."

"Belgium? Why that's any easy trip. Let me explain how you go about it."

Chapter Twenty-One

"If we aid wounded veterans, we'll simply be encouraging them in their poverty."

Several men muttered, "Here, here!"

Nicholas grabbed his whiskey and took a slow drink, drowning all the derogatory replies that were dying to spill out.

He was at his prenuptial supper, being hosted by Veronica's godparents. Very soon, the butler would announce the meal—if Veronica would ever deign to arrive—and they'd all traipse in to eat.

He gazed around the ornate salon. There were probably eighty guests present: dukes and earls and barons, leaders of government and industry. They'd come to toast Nicholas for his having snagged Veronica as his bride.

It should have been the greatest night of his life, but he was so miserable!

Stephen had refused to attend, so he was alone, surrounded by people he didn't know and didn't like.

When Veronica was present at a fete—he'd discovered that she was habitually late—he was able to distract himself by counting how many of her character traits annoyed him. It was a game he'd learned to play: List the reasons that prove you're insane.

Pride was driving him; he realized that it was. He was extremely vain, and he'd never been good at admitting his mistakes. Forging ahead was idiotic, but he'd been on the same path for too long, and it seemed impossible to shuck off his engagement and walk away.

He was loitering like a dunce, fuming as those around him expounded on the issues of the day. He'd been too busy serving his country so he hadn't yet attended to his duties in Parliament, and he wasn't cognizant of the subjects being debated. Apparently, a bill was pending that would help crippled soldiers by providing them with pensions and jobs.

The maimed invalids, missing arms and legs, were becoming a nuisance in the city. They were everywhere, begging for coins and scraps of food, and the rich were discomfited by having to view their condition.

The remarks being bandied were crude and stupid, and Nicholas was at the limit of what he'd listen to without responding. Didn't the bloody snobs remember who he was? For pity's sake, he was a captain in the army! He was wearing his uniform! Could they be any more condescending?

They had to assume he was deaf. Or perhaps they thought, once he'd accepted the title of *earl,* he'd lost his compassion for ordinary citizens.

He hadn't.

Behind him, a man claimed, "I've heard some of them do it intentionally."

"Do what?" someone asked.

"They allow themselves to be injured so that they may return home and not have to work again. They enjoy being on the public dole."

"I've heard the very same," another agreed, and there was a second murmuring of, "Here, here!"

"They're general rabble who have some nerve, demanding that we—"

"That's it," Nicholas grumbled.

He threw his glass on the floor and whipped around. Three men gaped at him. Not certain which one had been the most insulting, he honed in on the fellow in the middle. He was short, fat, and ugly and he had a vapid expression.

"Enough!" Nicholas bellowed.

"Really, Lord Stafford," the imprudent oaf contended, "I haven't said what we don't all know."

Quick as a snake, Nicholas seized him by the throat and lifted him up so that they were nose to nose.

"Shut your rude mouth," Nicholas ordered, "or I'll shut it for you." He squeezed his fingers, cutting off air.

"I...I...argh..."

"If you utter one more disparaging word, I'll beat you to a pulp—right now with all your snooty friends watching."

"Nicholas!" Veronica's father scolded. "Honestly! Let him go! Let him go!"

Numerous hands reached out to pry them apart, and Nicholas was yanked away. His victim staggered and was caught by his companions.

The room had grown deathly still. Everyone was gawking, as if a barbarian had been loosed in their midst. It was the exact type of reaction he'd always dreamed of wringing from them, but as he faced them down, their collective disdain was infuriating.

He felt young and foolish and out of his element, as if he'd entered the wrong party by mistake.

Veronica's father was hissing in his ear. "Your behavior is most inappropriate. Step outside and compose yourself. Do not return until you are able to conduct yourself in a suitable manner."

He shoved Nicholas away and, like a chastened boy, Nicholas left without argument. He went into the hall, then headed to the foyer and out the door, curious as to whether he might keep on going. What was preventing him? He didn't want to speak to any of them ever again, didn't want to pretend they were cordial or that they had anything in common.

Why was he hanging on through such a nightmare? The only logical decision was to cry off. *Why couldn't he? Why? Why?*

The questions nagged at him, but he had no answers.

He stood on the stoop, gulping in fresh air, and he stared out at the dark sky, hating that he couldn't see the stars.

His thoughts wandered to Emeline, and he wondered how she was faring. Was she gazing up at the same sky? Could she see the stars that were hidden from him in town?

That last morning, when he'd talked to her in his library, she'd been so quiet. He'd done what he could for her, his every choice designed to make her happy, but she hadn't seemed to be.

He knew he'd hurt her, and he hoped his parting gifts—the house, school, and stipend—would show her how sorry he was.

He liked to imagine her at Stafford, ensconced in her new home, sitting in the schoolroom and preparing her lessons. It was a pretty picture, one that soothed him enormously. Someday, he would visit the estate, and he'd find her settled and content. She wouldn't be angry anymore; she'd thank him for the life he'd given her.

He peered down the drive, and out on the street, there were hoards of people huddled by the gate. They were gaping up at the mansion, eager to catch a glimpse of London's famous and infamous. He walked over and strolled among them, and they removed their hats and curtsied as if he should be exalted and admired.

Money could do that for a person, he'd found. Money could make a man into someone he wasn't.

When he might have continued on, a coach swept into view, halting any escape. An old-fashioned pair of trumpets blared to announce its approach. On noting that it was his betrothed, having orchestrated a flashy entrance, he rolled his eyes.

Why didn't he slip into the crowd and disappear? He was naught but an emasculated eunuch, good for nothing but obsequious bowing to the wishes of others.

If Emeline could see me now, he glumly pondered, *what would she think?*

He pushed her out of his mind. He'd made his choice, he'd picked his path, and it didn't include Emeline Wilson. He could have stayed at Stafford, could have married her and built a family with her and her sisters, but he hadn't. It was no use regretting.

The coach stopped next to him, and he waited forever, gnashing his teeth, as the step was lowered and the door opened. Finally, she emerged to the *oohs* and *aahs* of the assembled throng—many applauded—and Nicholas couldn't blame them for being agog.

She looked like a fairy princess, attired in a gown so shimmery that the fabric might have been spun from gold. Perhaps it had been. The skirt had a long train, and four maids alighted behind her to carry it as she promenaded into the mansion.

She knew how to amaze and dazzle, how to get others to worship her. Too bad they were the sorts of characteristics he loathed in a female.

"Nicholas"—her smile was tight—"you've worn your uniform. How...nice."

"Yes, isn't it?"

There had been an enormous fight over his and Stephen's clothes for the wedding. Harsh words had also been hurled over the fact that the ceremony was rushed and there would be no honeymoon.

However, the squabbling had occurred between Veronica and her mother, with Veronica demanding that her mother *do* something. Nicholas had had no part in the quarrel and wouldn't have heeded either woman if they'd had the temerity to confront him, which they hadn't. Lucky for them.

"Let's go in, shall we?" She extended her arm for him to take.

"Yes, let's."

They started off together, as if they were marching down the aisle at the cathedral, and the notion was terrifying. His throat was closing, and he couldn't breathe.

The prospect of returning to the party was unbearable, and he was so lost in his pitiful reverie, that he scarcely realized someone was calling, "Captain Price! Captain Price!"

He frowned as a beggar stumbled toward him. Dressed in rags, he was filthy and decrepit. His left arm was missing, the empty sleeve of his shirt tucked in the waist of his trousers.

"It's me, Captain," the fellow said. "It's me, Ted Smith. Don't you remember?"

"Teddy?" Nicholas asked. "Is it really you?"

"Yes, Captain. Aren't you a sight for sore eyes!"

Ted had served under him for three years until he'd been maimed and sent home. Nicholas had never heard from him again, and though he'd posted several letters to England, inquiring after his health, he'd never received a reply. Ultimately, he'd wondered if the young man hadn't perished from his injuries.

"What happened to you, Ted?" Nicholas queried, appalled by his condition.

"I've had a spot of trouble, Captain. I admit it."

"But...I thought you went to live with your parents. I thought they were going to take care of you."

"Both passed away, sir, with the influenza. I didn't find out 'til I arrived and there was a new family settled in our house."

Veronica tried to tug Nicholas away. "Nicholas, come on!

Mother and Father are expecting me, and I'm horridly late."

Nicholas ignored her.

"Wasn't your father the village minister?"

Ted had grown up in church, listening to his father's sermons, so he'd been the regiment's makeshift preacher. Whenever they'd needed prayers or a quick funeral, he'd volunteered.

"Yes, my father was a vicar," Ted explained, "so the house wasn't really ours. It belonged to the church."

"Why didn't anyone help you? How did you end up in London?"

"I had a job offer, so I moved to the city, but it didn't work out, and I didn't have any money to return to the country. With the folks being deceased, there wasn't anything to return to anyway."

Veronica fumed and tugged harder. "Nicholas!"

"Could you spare a bit of change, Captain? I promise to pay you back when I can."

The spectators were intrigued by the conversation, and they were pressing in while Veronica's outriders were pushing and shoving, clearing a path for her.

Someone tripped and someone staggered, and suddenly, Ted—in his grimy, tattered clothes—was knocked into Veronica. Their contact was brief and minimal, but she shrieked with outrage.

"Get him off me! Get him off!" she screamed, even though he wasn't touching her.

Her outriders withdrew clubs and started swinging them. Innocent bystanders cursed and jumped out of range, which had others reeling and falling. A full-on riot seemed likely, and he and Veronica were pulled forward by her servants.

Nicholas hurried where he was led, wanting Veronica inside before a melee ensued. The butler held the door, and as they swept into the foyer, he slammed and locked it behind them.

After the noisy chaos of the street, it was very quiet. Veronica trembled with fury.

"Filthy beggar!" She was wiping at her skirt as if it was dirty, but it wasn't.

"Filthy, disgusting beggar!"

"I know him," Nicholas said. "He served with me."

"Soliciting you for money," she scathingly continued. "Accosting us as if we were a pair of...missionaries. How dare he!"

"He's poor. He's hungry."

"He didn't have an arm, the revolting swine! He deigned to touch me and he didn't have an arm!"

Her mother appeared down the hall, coming to check on the commotion.

"Mother!" Veronica's voice was shrill with offense. "Mother, you won't believe what he let happen to me!"

She stormed off, spewing a flood of vitriol, as her mother guided her into a nearby parlor and shut the door. In a matter of seconds, Nicholas was alone with the butler. The man stared implacably, not a hint showing as to his opinion of Veronica's display, of the fact that her footmen had been beating people with sticks out in the driveway.

"Lord Stafford," the man said, "I have a letter for you."

"A letter?" Nicholas scowled, unable to imagine who might have written or why it would have arrived at the supper party.

"Yes, it came a bit ago. I was searching for you, but you'd stepped out."

He retrieved it from a drawer in a table. As Nicholas reached for it, he saw the word, *URGENT!*, penned on the front, but he didn't recognize the handwriting.

"Do you know who it's from? Or who delivered it?"

"It was brought from your residence by a servant. Your staff has been trying to track you down all afternoon. I'm told it's imperative that you read it immediately."

"Thank you."

He stuffed it in his coat.

He needed to find Ted and learn where he was staying, but he wouldn't exit into the unrest. An angry mob had formed, and he had no desire to brawl. Not without a weapon or Stephen guarding his back.

Instead, he dawdled, wishing he could simply vanish. He was weary and dismayed and...sad. Yes, he was very sad; he couldn't deny it.

Veronica emerged from the room where she'd been whining to her mother. She stomped over, her fury still not quelled, but he was in no mood for a tantrum.

"Let's go in." She grabbed his arm. "Father has waited too long. His patience is waning."

"He'll get over it."

"You spoiled everything!"

"It was your outriders inciting the crowd. I was just standing there minding my own business."

"You, and your...*soldier.* I'm insulted to the marrow of my bones."

"He's an old friend, down on his luck. What was I supposed to do? Ignore him?"

"Yes, that's precisely what you were supposed to do! You permitted him to speak to me! He ruined my entrance and soiled my gown!"

"Your gown is fine," he tersely said.

She peered over her shoulder, to where her mother was lurking. "See what I mean, Mother? See how he treats me?"

He raised a brow, daring the woman to comment, and she wisely kept silent.

The butler went on ahead, and Nicholas could hear them being announced to the supper guests. As if a magic wand had been waved, Veronica's rage evaporated. Suddenly, she was all grace and smiles, and he trudged along at her side like a lapdog.

He should have walked the other way, out of his engagement and out of her life, but his predicament was his own fault.

He had deliberately sought her out to be his bride. *He* had proposed. *He* could have picked any girl in the world, but he'd picked her. Stephen had vociferously counseled against it, but Nicholas never listened to anyone, and his chickens were coming home to roost.

He was fool. He was an idiot. He was getting exactly what he deserved.

They entered the salon, and there was a smattering of applause, but apparently, it was much less than she'd anticipated. She frowned, irked that more people weren't gushing. Obviously, her mother hadn't informed her that he'd been tossed out prior to her arrival. He was nobody's favorite.

Her father was at the front, offering a toast, and Veronica dropped away and went forward without him. She was in her element, preening, and so absorbed in the moment that she didn't realize he'd moved away.

He slipped to a rear corner, observing the proceedings as if he had no connection to them. The letter in his coat crinkled, reminding him that it was there, and he pulled it out and flicked at the seal.

The news was so peculiar—and so unexpected—that he had to read it three times before it made any sense. Emeline had been...arrested? Over her illicit affair with Nicholas? The twins had been sent to an orphanage?

It didn't seem possible, yet the plea for assistance had come from Josephine Merrick. Nicholas didn't know her well, but she wasn't the type prone to fantasy or exaggeration.

What the bloody hell had happened? Were Blair and Mason insane? Did they actually imagine that Nicholas wouldn't care? That he wouldn't react?

"Nicholas!"

He shook his head, as if the sharp sound of his name had yanked him from a deep sleep.

"Nicholas!"

He glanced up. Veronica was standing with her father. Everyone was gaping at him.

"What?" he asked.

"Father made his toast," she hissed like a petulant toddler, "and now, you have to make yours."

He stared at her, at her father, at the portly, stuffy men surrounding him. He stared at her mother, at the festooned, arrogant matrons surrounding her. He assessed their clothes and their jewels and their expensive wine glasses and fussy hors d'oeuvre plates.

Melancholy swept over him. He missed Emeline, and he wanted to be at Stafford. Why was he here when he could be *there*? If he'd stayed where he belonged—with Emeline—she'd be safe and he'd be happy.

"What am I doing?" he muttered to himself.

"Nicholas!" Veronica nagged again. "Why must you constantly embarrass me?"

"Look, a situation has come up." He crumpled the letter and pitched it into the fire. "I have to go."

"You have to what?" Veronica gasped.

"I have to go."

"You can't leave. I won't allow it."

"Now see here, Captain Price," her father blustered.

"No, *you* see here."

Veronica gave an ear-splitting shriek. "Mother!"

"The wedding is off," Nicholas told her father. "I'll contact you in a few days, after I've dealt with this emergency. We'll work something out."

"Work something *out?*" her father railed. The veins in his neck were bulging, as if he was about to suffer an apoplexy. "Listen to me you cur, you beast, you...you...interloper."

"I'll contact you," Nicholas repeated.

He spun and dashed out, and behind him, he could hear shouting and incensed exclamations, but he didn't slow down. The stupid dullards had never deemed him worthy of their darling Veronica, and after they calmed, they'd all be relieved that she'd escaped his dastardly clutches.

He raced outside, glad to note that the mob had dispersed. There was no riot occurring. He ran into the street and peered around, searching for Ted and finding him down on the corner.

"Ted!" he called and he hastened over.

"Captain!" Ted extended his hand in welcome, and Nicholas clasped hold.

"Sorry for the trouble. I didn't mean to bother the lady."

"Don't worry about her. She's nothing to me." He started them toward his carriage that was parked down the block.

"Where are we going?" Ted asked.

"To my house. You'll remain there while I sort out a problem at my estate."

"Really, Captain? Are you sure?"

"I'm absolutely sure." Nicholas patted Ted's shoulder. "My servants will feed you and get you back on your feet. Then once I return to town, we'll figure out what's to be done with you."

"Thank you, Captain," Ted murmured. "It seems as if all my prayers have suddenly been answered."

They neared the carriage, the lamp giving off a soft glow, and Nicholas saw tears in Ted's eyes, but he pretended not to notice.

He helped Ted climb in, then climbed in himself. The door was slammed, and they rushed for home so Nicholas could locate Stephen, saddle their horses, and depart for Stafford right away.

Chapter Twenty-Two

"Let us pray."

Oscar whirled away from the altar to face the congregation, although *congregation* was now an incorrect description for the handful of worshipers scattered in the pews.

Six people! Six people had deigned to attend Sunday service. In the past, the church would have been filled to capacity. On special occasions, such as Christmas or Easter, there often wasn't enough space to accommodate the large crowd.

In a form of protest, everyone had stayed away. The community was flaunting its displeasure over his actions toward Emeline and her sisters, and he couldn't believe they would question his motives. He was an ordained minister with the highest credentials and stellar reputation.

How dare they snub him! How dare they rebel!

From the moment Emeline had disappeared, there had been grumbling and complaints. His very own maid, who'd witnessed his quarrel with Josephine, had blabbed hither and yon about what she'd heard. He'd fired her for insubordination, but it had only fueled the flames of rumor and innuendo.

It was another sin to lay at Emeline's feet, and the next time he saw Josephine, he'd tell her so—in no uncertain terms.

Where was his sister anyway? Without a hint as to her intentions, she'd packed a bag and left. When she came crawling back, begging for shelter, she'd learn her lesson once and for all.

He snapped his Bible closed, and the sound echoed off the empty seats, underscoring how ridiculously people were behaving. Would they risk their immortal souls over the likes of

Emeline? He thought not.

"Let us pray!" he repeated more petulantly, but not a single head bowed in deference. He glowered, but they refused to be cowed.

"As you decline to join in," he fumed, "I shall skip forward to deliver my sermon. Obviously, all of you could benefit from a stern administration of the truth."

Silence and sneers greeted him. One man yawned.

"Today, I will address several topics, including respect for authority, respect for the church, respect for—"

"Where is Emeline Wilson?"

The interruption was the last straw. They weren't in a tavern where patrons could shout and bicker.

"Who said that?" he bellowed.

Old Mr. Templeton stood. "What have you and Mason done with her?"

"We are in God's house"—Oscar pounded his fist on the podium—"and you will not utter that harlot's name under His roof!"

At his spewing the horrid term, there were gasps, and Templeton was undaunted.

"I know Emeline was many things, but she wasn't that. I don't care what lies you tell."

"We are not in a collegiate debating society," Oscar haughtily scolded. "This is a religious service. If you can't listen and absorb the Holy Word, then I insist you leave."

"While we're at it," another oaf butted in, "where's your sister? Ain't nobody seen her since your maid stumbled on you beating her bloody in the vicarage."

"Beating her?" Oscar's voice was shrill.

Was that the story that had spread? How was he to counter it? They might well have asked when he'd quit beating his dog. He couldn't mount a defense.

"I've not laid a hand on my sister," he declared, "despite how thoroughly she deserved a good whipping."

"Where is she then?" Mr. Templeton demanded. "What are you hiding?"

"You doubt me?" Oscar thundered. "Me? I am your moral compass. You will not impugn my integrity."

"If you don't start giving me some straight answers,"

Templeton retorted, "I'm going to London to fetch the earl to Stafford. He'll be extremely interested in your activities."

On his mentioning of Lord Stafford, Oscar blanched. He and Mason couldn't have the disreputable scoundrel apprised of their exploits. Nicholas Price was volatile and dangerous, and Mason had maintained that he was fond of Emeline. If she'd been harmed, there was no predicting how he might retaliate.

The doors at the rear of the church slammed open, sunlight streaming in, and a large man was silhouetted in the threshold. Oscar squinted, trying to see who it was. He couldn't abide tardiness, and his parishioners knew better than to arrive late.

"You there!" Oscar called. "The service is already in progress. Come in or depart."

There was a long, tense pause, then the fellow said, "I believe I'll come in."

He marched through the vestibule, a second man tromping in behind him. They entered the church proper, and as they materialized out of the shadows—gad, Nicholas and Stephen Price!—Oscar gulped with dismay.

"Lord Stafford," he weakly rasped, "I thought you were in London."

"It seems I've returned."

"How kind of you to grace us with your presence."

"Isn't it, though?"

The blackguard studied the rows of vacant seats.

"It's a bit quiet this morning, vicar," he pointed out.

"There's an influenza going around," Oscar fibbed. "People are ill."

"Are they?"

The earl snorted, then arrogantly strode down the aisle. He sat in the front pew to Oscar's right. His brother sat in the pew to Oscar's left. They both slouched, their legs stretched out, ankles crossed.

Their disrespect was infuriating, and Oscar was about to remark when Mr. Templeton asked, "Lord Stafford, may I speak?"

"In a moment, Mr. Templeton. Your esteemed vicar is in the middle of his sermon. I'd like to hear the topic."

Oscar gnawed on his cheek. He'd been discussing Emeline Wilson. Since the earl had been complicit in her ruin, he was equally guilty of moral turpitude. Whatever castigation was flung at Emeline, the earl warranted the same rebuke.

Didn't he?

To Oscar's great shame, he hesitated.

Nicholas Price wouldn't appreciate being scolded. Yet Oscar was the earl's spiritual leader. If he didn't urge the earl onto a virtuous path, who would?

Still, there was Oscar's job to consider. And the vicarage, and his salary, and his fine clothes, and his delicious dinners. Only a fool would risk so much.

"Well, vicar," the earl taunted, "I'm waiting. Get on with it before I fall asleep."

Lord Stafford stared up at him, his blue eyes filled with contempt for all that Oscar was and all that he represented. There was a challenge in his gaze, and Oscar was determined to quash it.

"I was preaching of harlots," Oscar intoned, not flinching.

"Were you?"

"I was explaining the damage a corrupt woman can inflict on a man's soul. The siren's song can lure a man to his doom."

"Those sirens don't have to do much *luring*," the earl smirked. "Most men walk to their doom without any coaxing at all."

His levity was maddening, and Oscar would not be mocked. His temper soared.

"Will you confess your sins, Lord Stafford?" Oscar roared. "Will you admit your depravity and seek the Lord's forgiveness?"

"I'd rather not," he snidely replied. "Let's talk about Emeline Wilson instead."

"You will not speak of that whore in my church!"

Quick as lightning, the earl was on his feet. In two leaps, he was behind the podium, and he had Oscar by the throat.

"I've made inquiries about your Sheriff Pratt," the earl warned, "so I know where he lives. Tell me where he's taken her and save me the trouble of tracking him down."

"I will tell you nothing," Oscar hissed. "If punishment is imposed on the petty harlot, it is no more than she deserves."

Lord Stafford was very strong. With one arm, he threw Oscar away, and Oscar crashed into a table covered with vases of flowers and burning candles. A mix of hot wax and fetid water dripped onto his vestments. He tried to stand but his limbs wouldn't obey.

The earl loomed into view. "Emeline Wilson is my—"

"She is a whore!" Oscar insisted.

If he hadn't been so flustered, he might have seen the blow coming, but he didn't. Nicholas Price punched him in the face. Oscar embarrassed himself by whimpering and slumping to the floor.

"Emeline is my tenant," the earl started again, "and my dear friend, and my affianced bride."

"She is not."

"She is, you pathetic swine. How dare you insult her with your slurs and lies."

Lord Stafford grabbed Oscar by his clothes, pulling him up 'til they were nose to nose. "Did you think I wouldn't find out what you'd done? Did you think I wouldn't care?"

Suddenly, Mr. Price was there, saying, "Let him go, Nicholas. Let him go."

"No, I intend to kill him."

"We have to get her home," Mr. Price said. "Focus on that. We'll locate this sheriff, and once she's safe, we'll deal with Blair."

Mr. Price pushed his brother away, as Mr. Templeton piped up from out in the pews. "May I speak now, milord?"

"What is it?" the earl queried. "Please make it fast. I'm in a bit of a hurry."

"While you're questioning this sheriff about Miss Wilson, could you also ask him about the vicar's sister?"

"Mrs. Merrick? What about her?"

"She's disappeared."

"Disappeared?"

"Yes. On the day that Blair and Mason took Emeline and the twins, Mrs. Merrick learned of it. She confronted the vicar, and they had a dreadful quarrel. No one's seen her since."

"What do you suspect happened to her?" the earl inquired.

"He was always awful to the poor woman. His maid and cook have described how he browbeat her, locked her in her room, and the like. Folks are wondering if he hasn't finally killed her."

Mr. Price grabbed Oscar—just as his brother had a minute

earlier—and yanked him to his feet.

"What have you done to her?" Mr. Price shouted.

"Me? I've done nothing!" Oscar asserted.

"Where is she?" Mr. Price bellowed so loudly that Oscar's ears rang.

The earl approached Oscar and seethed, "You have one chance to tell me the truth. Admit your crime, and it will go easier on you."

"My crime!" Oscar huffed. "Don't be ridiculous."

The earl peered out at Mr. Templeton. "You're sure she's missing?"

"Vanished without a trace, milord. We've been pestering the vicar as to her whereabouts, but he won't say."

"Then there's no hope for it, Blair." The earl sighed. "I'm placing you under arrest for the murder of your sister."

"Of all the ludicrous, insane, fantastical—" Oscar began to protest, but Mr. Price cut him off.

"Shut up," Mr. Price threatened, "or I will rip your head from your shoulders."

"Mr. Templeton," the earl called, "could you escort the vicar to the jail for me?"

"I'd be delighted, Lord Stafford."

"Release me!" Oscar snarled. "I am a servant of the Lord. I am the vicar of your church. I will not be treated like a common—"

Mr. Price clasped Oscar's wrists and pinned his arms, as the earl retrieved a kerchief from his coat and stuffed it in Oscar's mouth.

"I believe," the earl snapped, "that my brother told you to shut the hell up."

"Mmm...mmm..." Oscar was unable to talk, but the two brothers perceived his message: *I'll kill you for this, I'll kill you for this.* Under the circumstances, it probably wasn't the best of sentiments.

"Until I return," the earl ordered, "I want him held on bread and water rations."

"I'll see to it," Mr. Templeton offered, appearing gleeful at the prospect.

"Now, I have to go," the earl said. "Save me some time, Blair. Where has Sheriff Pratt taken Emeline?"

Oscar glared, his loathing clear, but the earl simply grinned.

"If we can't convince an executioner to hang you," the earl boasted, "I'll be happy to pull the rope myself."

"You'll have to get in line ahead of me," Mr. Price retorted.

"As to you, *Vicar* Blair," the earl sneered, "you've preached your last sermon in my church. And if Emeline or her sisters has been harmed, you've drawn your last breath, too."

The earl and his brother raced out.

"Sheriff Pratt!"

Emeline used her breakfast plate to bang on the bars of her cell, but she wasn't sure why she bothered. He hadn't responded to any of her summons.

She hated the uncertainty over her future. Throughout her days in his jail, Pratt was the only person she saw. Despite how she questioned him, he wouldn't provide the tiniest detail of what was to occur. Nor would he divulge any information about Nan and Nell.

Emeline had no idea where they were, so even if she managed to escape Pratt's clutches, she hadn't a clue where to search. It wasn't as if she could rush to Stafford and ask Mr. Mason or Oscar Blair.

"Oh, Nicholas," she murmured, "do you know what happened? Do you care?"

She was positive he didn't. He was married and off on his honeymoon. Emeline was at the bottom of a very long list of topics that would never cross his mind, and it bordered on insanity that she would even wonder about him.

Since he'd left, so much had transpired that she didn't feel they'd actually met. He could have been a character in a novel or a warrior in a poem. He didn't seem real anymore.

Pratt's footsteps sounded, and she struggled to remain calm. She was terrified that—on one of his visits—he would escort her to the gallows.

He lumbered to the door, and to her surprise, he unlocked it and gestured for her to exit. She wanted to comply, but fear had her frozen in place.

"Where am I going?"

"To London."

"Why London?"

"You'll find out when you get there."

"Please, I need to know. Why can't you say?"

He shrugged. "I suppose it can't hurt to tell you. You're being transported."

Her heart sank. "To where?"

"Australia."

"I don't wish to travel to Australia."

"Did you hear me ask your opinion?"

"And my sisters. Will they be joining me?"

"You hadn't ought to worry about them. It will only make things more difficult for you."

"Why? Have they been harmed?"

"No, but you're better off letting go of the past. It will be easier for you."

"I raised my sisters from the time they were babies. They're as dear to me as if they were my own daughters. Surely, you can see why I'm afraid for them. I can't just let them *go*."

He didn't reply but waved toward the street.

"Daylight's wasting," he said. "We must be off."

"On whose authority am I being sent to London? Have I been convicted? Of what charge?"

"It doesn't matter."

"It does to me."

"It's irrelevant. Don't work yourself into a dither."

He'd brought a rope, and he stomped over, grabbed her arms and forced them behind her back. He tied her wrists tightly enough to cut the skin and hinder circulation.

"There's no need to be such a brute," she complained.

"I intend that you aren't able to flee."

"I won't try. I promise."

"You wouldn't be the first whore who ran on me."

"I wouldn't dream of running."

He snorted. "Wouldn't you? Trust me, little lady, I can see it in your eyes. You're determined to thwart me, but I mean to deliver you as contracted."

"To whom am I being delivered?"

"Never you mind, but be aware that you'll fetch me a pretty

penny."

Had she been sold like an African slave? How could such a despicable deed be permitted in a civilized society? She had to prevent him from proceeding, but she couldn't figure out how.

He marched her outside, and though she kicked and protested, her paltry efforts had no effect. A cart awaited them, an enclosed box on the back that had a sturdy lock on the door. Panic swept over her. She was certain that—if she climbed in— she'd vanish and no one would ever know what became of her.

Her resistance increased, but she couldn't stop him. He tossed her in, and she huddled on the floor as he jumped onto the front seat and whipped the horses into a trot.

The cart had no springs, and with her limbs bound, she couldn't brace herself as they flew over holes and bumps. She was jostled incessantly, her head aching, her body bruised.

After an eternity had passed, they slowed and turned off the road, the vehicle bouncing to a halt. Pratt hauled her out, and she glanced around to discover that they were in a secluded woods, standing next to a hunter's cottage.

"What's happening?" she asked. "Why are we here?"

Pratt pushed her toward the door. "Go on in."

She dug in her heels. "Not until you tell me who's in there."

"Why are you so contrary? Why can't you simply do as you're told?"

"I was born contrary."

"That I can believe."

He pushed her again, but she wouldn't budge, so he dragged her over.

"The man paid me good money," Pratt explained, "and I've promised him an hour with you."

"What?"

"Don't fight him. There's no use getting yourself hurt."

"What do you mean?"

"I'll be timing him, so bear up. It will be over before you know it."

She started to brawl in earnest, and Pratt cuffed her alongside the head, hard enough that she saw stars.

"You hit me!"

"Well, don't be stupid, and I won't have to resort to violence."

"Whatever you've planned, I won't meekly consent like a lamb to the slaughter."

"You'll obey me, or I'll tie you down. Don't make me. I suspect he'd enjoy it too much."

He knocked once, and a man bid them enter. Pratt carried her in.

The shutters were closed, the room dimly lit, the man hidden in the shadows, and Emeline gasped as Pratt said, "Here she is, Mr. Mason. Do what you will with her, but when you're finished, she needs to be in sound enough condition to travel."

"She'll be able to travel."

"One hour."

"One hour," Mason concurred, "but don't be in any hurry."

"One hour," Pratt repeated, "and that's it."

He tugged at her bindings, releasing her, then he turned to go.

"Don't leave me with him," Emeline begged, and she ran over and pulled Pratt to a halt.

"Don't resist," Pratt counseled. "Just get through it, and we'll continue on."

"Please!" she implored, but Pratt shoved her at Mason, and Mason caught her.

"Hello, Emeline," Mason crooned. "Fancy meeting you here."

Emeline tried to lunge away, to chase after Pratt, but Mason trapped her against his body. His private parts were pressed to her thigh, and she could feel his erect phallus.

Ravishment? Was that his ploy? He'd paid for the privilege?

"Sheriff!" Emeline called, and Pratt whipped around.

"What?"

"Lord Stafford will kill you when he finds out."

"How will he learn of it, Miss Wilson? Who will tell him? You? You'll never have the chance."

"He'll find out. I'll make sure of it."

Pratt smirked. "I'm shaking in my boots."

He left as Mason snickered, "Dearest Emeline, it seems we're alone."

"Don't touch me."

She elbowed him in the ribs, hoping the blow would loosen his grip, but he clamped hold tighter than ever.

"I'd offer you wine," he said, "but we don't have time for socializing. Let's get down to business."

There was a bed along the wall, and he tried to wrestle her onto it, but if he thought she'd blithely comply, he was gravely mistaken. Her arms were free, and she would utilize every ounce of her strength, would die in the effort, before she'd submit.

She was kicking with her feet, clawing with her nails, but wherever she attacked, he merely yanked her fingers away.

"You shouldn't have spurned me, Emeline," he complained, out of breath from their grappling.

"If you'd been the last man on Earth, I wouldn't have accepted your proposal."

"A foolish decision—as you can now see. Imagine how different things would be if you'd agreed to have me. You'd be safe at home in Stafford, instead of here in a deserted cabin and about to be raped."

"I would never have married you. You're a bully, and I hate you too much."

"I realize that. You were too eager to play the whore for Captain Price."

"I loved him."

"Love, bah! Fat lot of good it's done you."

"He loved me too," she lied. "He'll retaliate against you."

"No, he won't. He's too stupid to figure out that you're missing."

"Someone will tell him."

"Who will notice that you've vanished? Not your paltry earl. You're so vain that you assume others care about you."

"Nicholas Price is ten times the man you'll ever be."

"Be silent!" Mason hissed.

"He is! That's what galls you, isn't it? You could never match up to him. You'll spend the remainder of your days working for him, following his orders, obeying his commands."

"Shut up!"

"In your entire pathetic life, you'll never be anything but a servant to your betters."

"Whore! Whore!"

She twisted away and scratched at his face, slashing his skin. He wailed with outrage, as he wrapped his hands around her neck and started to squeeze.

With her comments, she'd simply meant to distract him, using diversion to foster escape, but she'd been too successful at antagonizing him. He was angered to the point of madness, and in seconds, she was in desperate trouble.

He pushed her onto the bed, and he was leaning over her, his wrath and larger size an unbearable force. She pried at his fingers, but she was off balance and had no leverage. Swiftly, she was discombobulated. Her torso grew limp, her vision failing. Her world was reduced to only Benedict Mason, his evil eyes and the onslaught of pressure on her throat.

Some odd banging noises wafted by, but they were far off in the distance and irrelevant to her dire situation. She was losing consciousness, fading away. Was she hallucinating, too?

A door crashed open and footsteps tromped across the floor.

"Unhand her," a voice shouted, "or I will kill you where you stand."

Mason frowned, confused, but he didn't ease his grip. He was too intent on strangling her.

"Unhand her, you dog!"

There was another bang, this one very loud and very real. Mason fell away. He glanced over his shoulder, a palm on his chest. Blood oozed into the fabric of his shirt.

"You shot me," Mason muttered, peering down at his wound in disbelief.

A man approached, and he seized Mason by his coat and flung him away.

Emeline couldn't think straight, couldn't see straight. It seemed as if Lord Stafford had arrived, as if he'd come to save her. But that couldn't be. He'd just gotten married. He was on his honeymoon.

She shook her head, struggling to focus, but he was still there.

"Em, Em," he breathlessly said, "are you all right?"

She tried to answer him, but speech was impossible.

He reached for her and pulled her into a tight embrace. Instantly, she was soothed by the familiar odors of leather, horses, and tobacco that always hung to his clothes.

"Oh, my Lord," he murmured, "say something. Tell me he didn't hurt you."

Anxious to reply, she gazed up at him and collapsed in a stunned heap.

Chapter Twenty-Three

"What have you to say in your defense?"

"Nothing."

Benedict Mason glared at Nicholas Price, visually sending all his malice and ill will, but the exalted Lord Stafford hardly noticed.

"Humor me," the earl coaxed. "I'm fascinated by your behavior. What were you thinking?"

"I have no comment," Benedict responded.

"When I first hired you, you seemed like such a rational, stable fellow. Look at you now."

They were in the library at the manor, with the earl seated behind his desk and Benedict facing him. Luckily, he'd been permitted to sit in a chair. If he'd been ordered to stand, he couldn't have. His wound had left him that weak.

After he'd been shot, the Price brothers had tossed him in Pratt's wagon and returned him to the estate. Through the entire trip, he'd been bumped and jostled, and though he'd been seriously injured, they'd offered him no medical treatment.

Upon arriving at Stafford, he'd been locked in a room in the cellar. A footman had brought wine, bread, and bandages. He'd wrapped Benedict's chest as best he could, but he was no physician.

The bleeding had stopped, but no other care had been rendered. Benedict thought the ball might still be lodged under the skin, that it needed to be dug out. The wound was festering, and he felt feverish and confused.

"May I see a doctor?" Benedict inquired.

"No. Why would you assume you could harm Emeline

Wilson and her sisters?"

"I demand to speak with an attorney."

"That won't be possible."

"I demand it!" Benedict decreed, but he wheezed out the words, so they lost their impetus.

"All the attorneys in the neighborhood are busy."

"Then take me before a judge. I insist on posting bail."

"There's a magistrate assigned to this area, but he's not due to visit for several weeks." The earl flashed an evil smile. "In his absence, it's up to me to mete out any punishment."

"I refuse to be judged by you," Benedict sneered.

"You act as if you have a say in the matter."

"Where is Sheriff Pratt?"

"Pratt is dead. I killed him myself."

"Dead! You can't murder an officer of the law."

"Really?" the earl sarcastically replied. "No one told me it wasn't allowed. Besides, let's not refer to him as an officer of the *law*. I think we can agree that he forfeited any respectable title."

"Where is his body?"

"I buried him in the forest."

Benedict gaped with dismay. The earl was completely calm, not concerned in the least that he'd committed cold-blooded murder. If he would blithely kill a sheriff, what might he do to a mere land agent?

"I'll see that you hang for it," Benedict stupidly threatened.

"Will you?" The earl's lazy gaze meandered down Benedict's torso, assessing his deteriorated condition. "Can you actually suppose anyone would believe you over me? I'm a peer of the realm and a decorated war hero. What are you?"

What, indeed? Benedict mused, and he mumbled, "Cocky bastard."

"Now, now, let's don't bring my poor mother into it. I have it on good authority that my father married her. I couldn't possibly be a bastard."

"Let me talk to the vicar." He and Blair had to get their stories straight, and Blair might be able to spread the word about Nicholas Price slaying Sheriff Pratt.

"Haven't you heard?" the earl asked. "Blair is under arrest, too."

Benedict gasped. "For what?"

"For murdering his sister."

"Josephine? You're claiming he murdered Josephine?"

"I'm not *claiming*. I'm flat-out saying it's true."

"That's insane."

"Yes, it is, but then, in my opinion, the vicar was never playing with a full deck."

Benedict was perplexed by the news. Blair wasn't a killer. He was too much of a coward. He hired others to do his dirty work.

"You'll never make me believe it," Benedict scoffed.

"Believe it or no, I don't care. He's been a sorry prisoner, and unfortunately for you, an even worse conspirator."

"What do you mean?"

"As far as allies go, you picked a bad one. He's spilled his guts about you and your crimes."

"He couldn't have told you anything," Benedict blustered, "for there's nothing to tell."

"I have men riding to London to fetch the twins home from that orphanage."

"Dammit!"

"And once Emeline is feeling better, we'll have much more evidence against you. Are you aware of the penalty for kidnapping, attempted rape, and attempted murder?"

Emeline, Emeline, Emeline... If Benedict never heard her name again, it would be too soon!

He remembered how his fingers had circled her throat, the way her face had reddened as he'd strangled her. If he had any regrets, it was that he hadn't had time to finish what he'd started.

"She's a whore!" Benedict blurted like a fool. "She was asking for it."

In an instant, Lord Stafford leapt around the desk and loomed over Benedict. He grabbed Benedict by the shoulder, pushing a thumb into Benedict's wound.

Benedict howled in agony as the earl leaned down and hissed, "If you ever speak of her again, if she ever so much as crosses your filthy little mind, I will kill you."

The earl stepped away, and he sat, unruffled and composed, while Benedict tried to focus, tried to stay conscious through the pain.

Vaguely, he realized that the library door had opened, and the earl's brother was standing with the earl. He had a stack of papers that he arranged on the desktop.

The earl perused them, then he glanced at Benedict, his loathing so blatant that Benedict blanched.

"Tell me how much money you stole from me," the earl commanded.

"I stole nothing," Benedict contended.

"I'm guessing it's thousands of pounds," his brother posited. "He took money, but he also quietly sold your possessions and crops."

"Mr. Mason," the earl snidely mocked, "you always pretended to be so ethical."

"I found his bank books," Mr. Price said, "so we'll be able to recover most of it."

"Lucky for him," the earl retorted, "or I might have had to shoot him again to gain some satisfaction."

Benedict squirmed in his chair. He wanted to lie down and sleep for a week. He wanted to see a doctor. He wanted a kind nurse to hold his hand, dab a cool cloth on his brow, and murmur to him that he'd be all right.

"How should we deal with you, Mason?" the earl asked. "I'm curious as to your opinion."

"Everything I did," Benedict argued, "I did for you. To save your estate. To make you richer."

"You committed fraud, you embezzled and swindled and deceived, and you did it for *me*?"

When the earl put it that way, it didn't sound quite so marvelous. Benedict studied him, wondering—as he often had in the prior year—how such a low-born scoundrel could rise so high, how he could be hailed as Benedict's lord and master.

"I didn't know you could read," Benedict complained, "let alone add."

"It's the curse of modern-day England," the earl said. "Even orphans can be taught a thing or two."

"What will happen to me?" Benedict inquired, terrified over his fate. If Pratt was dead and Blair under arrest, what hope had Benedict of an equitable outcome?

"I'm giving you two choices," the earl responded. "I don't care which you pick."

"What are they?"

"Choice number one: you may remain here, and I hang you at dawn."

"I haven't had a trial!"

"So? Who will stop me? Sheriff Pratt?"

They engaged in a staring match that Benedict couldn't win.

"Or?" he queried. "I have two choices. What is the other?"

"You can be transported to Australia on the ship that was meant for Emeline Wilson. Her spot has suddenly become available."

"But I'm not feeling well! My wound is infected. I'll die on the trip!"

"Perhaps, but you'll die here for sure. At dawn."

Benedict slumped in his seat, his mind awhirl with fury and regret.

It had been such a simple plan: be shed of Emeline once and for all. Bring calm and sanity to the estate. How had it all gone so wrong?

"Don't make me leave," he begged. "Stafford is my home now."

Mr. Price glanced at his brother. "Those are probably the very words Miss Wilson used when she pleaded with Mason not to be sent away."

"I'm certain they are," the earl agreed. "What's it to be, Mason. Will I hang you in the morning? Or will you scurry away like the rat you are?"

Benedict fumed and fretted, anxious to ease the earl's wrath, but it seemed impossible. Ultimately, he moaned, "I'll take my chances on the high seas."

"A wise decision." The earl stood, as if passing sentence. "Don't ever return. If I learn you've somehow slithered back to England, I'll hunt you down and rid the kingdom of your vile presence." He peered at his brother. "Get him out of my sight."

Mr. Price grabbed Benedict by the arm and yanked him to his feet. The abrupt motion wrenched at his wound, and he shrieked in anguish. The earl watched—stoic and indifferent—as Benedict was dragged from the room.

Nicholas knocked on the door to Emeline's bedchamber. He was extremely nervous but trying not to show it.

Since he'd rescued her a week earlier, he'd rarely seen her. He'd been too busy, tamping out the fires Blair and Mason had ignited.

She'd been in no condition to receive him anyway, and he'd hired a team of nurses to tend her 'round the clock. They'd given him hourly reports as to her recuperation, and she was much better. He was so excited to be with her, to tell her what he'd been thinking.

He knocked again, and footsteps approached.

She opened the door herself but offered no greeting. Though it was a warm afternoon, she had a scarf covering her neck. For a moment, he was puzzled, then he realized she was hiding the bruises inflicted by Mason.

Eager to assess the damage, he reached out to tug the scarf away, but she leaned back so he couldn't touch her. He managed to view just of trace of discoloration, but nothing more.

They stared and stared.

He'd planned to take her into his arms, to hold her to his chest as he apologized and beseeched her to forgive him. But he was forestalled by her demeanor.

She might have been a stranger to whom he'd never been introduced, and she didn't look happy to see him.

She was clutching a notepad, and she extended it so he could read what she'd written. *My throat is still very sore. The doctor advises that I shouldn't talk for a while.*

He stepped as if to enter her sitting room, but she didn't move to let him.

Obviously, he'd forfeited any right to be in her bedchamber. He might have argued with her or arrogantly mentioned that it was his damn house and she couldn't keep him out, but he didn't have the heart to be brusque with her.

"May I come in?" he asked like a supplicant.

She wrote on her pad, *Why?*

"I need to speak with you."

She pointed down, indicating that she would meet him downstairs.

"My library?" he inquired. "In five minutes?"

She nodded, and he left, his euphoria fading.

With her health improved, he'd assumed they would start over, but evidently, she had a different opinion. While he'd been overcome by sentiment, it was clear that love, romance, and marriage were the last topics that vexed her.

All of his recent actions had been taken for her. To make her happy. To make her feel safe. Yet she didn't seem grateful. Or perhaps she wasn't aware of what he'd done on her behalf.

Mason had been spirited away, and he'd never darken their lives again. His wound was grave and infected, and he'd likely drop dead in London before his ship could sail.

In the morning, Oscar Blair would be tried by a jury and convicted of the murder of his sister. His sentence would be carried out shortly after the hearing was concluded.

Prior to his being hanged, Nicholas hoped Blair would confess where he'd stashed Mrs. Merrick's body. Nicholas would like to give the poor woman a proper burial in the church cemetery, but without some hint from Blair as to her location, the chances of finding her were remote.

He went to the sideboard and downed a brandy, then he sat behind his desk, anxious to look relaxed and in control.

In reality, he was a wreck. Nightmares plagued him where Em was in danger and he couldn't reach her in time. His choices and behavior had him ruing and regretting. He was contrite and ashamed, and he couldn't continue on in such a state of emotional upheaval.

He had to earn her pardon, then wed her as rapidly as the deed could be accomplished. He wanted her bound to him forever, and until he was certain that she was his—with a marriage license to prove it—he wouldn't rest easy.

She came in slowly, appearing fragile and vulnerable. As she seated herself across from him, she was so altered from the quirky, animated woman he'd initially met that it didn't seem possible she was the same person.

"I just received a message from London," he told her. "My men have the twins in their custody, and they're fine. They're on their way home. They should be here before the day is out."

He'd thought the news might enliven her, but she simply mouthed, *Thank you.*

"Mason is gone, and he'll never return."

She scowled and shook her head. Then, with a furious

pencil, she scrawled, *Don't ever mention him to me again.*

"I won't. I apologize. I hadn't understood how much it would upset you."

He studied her, at a loss over how to proceed. He was searching for an opportunity to pour his heart out, to confess how he'd changed, but she evinced no interest in what he might wish to confide.

"Were you informed about...Mrs. Merrick?"

Yes.

"Blair's trial is tomorrow."

Jo was my only friend, she wrote. *I hope he hangs.*

"That's my intent." He paused, feeling tongue-tied and awkward. "Ah...I've already found a minister to replace him."

She raised a brow in question.

"He served in my regiment, and I ran into him in the city. His name is Ted Smith." No reaction. "He was maimed—he lost an arm—so he's had a rough patch. He's a decent fellow and exactly the sort to rebuild the community after Blair."

He hurried on, worried that she wasn't listening, that she didn't care.

"In fact, I'm sending Ted out with a team. He'll hunt for some other of my injured veterans and bring them to the estate. To live. To work. I'm sorry I never appreciated my new position and wealth. You tried to convince me to cherish what I have, to help people who are struggling, but I refused to—"

She held up a hand, cutting him off. *Why are you here?*

"I had a frantic letter from Mrs. Merrick. It may have been her final act before her brother murdered her. She said you were in trouble, so I came at once."

Why? she wrote again.

"Because I love you."

At his declaration, she gasped and penned, *Don't lie to me.*

"I'm not lying. I couldn't bear to learn that you needed me, but I wasn't here."

Where is your wife? Why isn't she with you?

"I didn't marry her." She frowned, and he added, "I *couldn't* marry her."

Why? Apparently, it was the only word she knew.

"I want to marry *you,* instead. I want to marry you right away. Will you have me?"

In huge, angry letters, she printed, *NEVER IN A THOUSAND YEARS!!!*

Chaos erupted in the foyer, as the front door was slammed open. There was girlish babbling, stomping of feet, his brother calling for Nicholas.

"Nan...Nell..." Emeline breathed, her voice sounding rusty and ruined.

She hastened out without a goodbye.

"Was that the last time you saw her?"

"Yes, milord."

The housemaid from the vicarage simpered at the earl, trying to impress him with her testimony, and Oscar yearned to march over and throttle her.

They were in the local tavern, the tables removed and the chairs arranged into a makeshift courtroom. People were jammed to the rafters, the entire citizenry keen to have him brought low.

He was shackled to a bench, and because he kept interrupting, the earl had had him gagged. He could only intimidate with his eyes, which had no effect. The jurors assessed him with disdain.

If the consequences hadn't been so dire, he might have laughed at the absurdity. It seemed like a bad dream, as if the debacle was happening to some other poor sot.

"Why did you leave Mrs. Merrick alone?" the earl asked the maid. "If you were afraid for her, why leave the parlor?"

"She ran up to her bedchamber," the girl said, "and locked her door. Then I went to the kitchen, to discuss matters with the cook. We had a lengthy conversation, and when I resumed my duties, the vicar and Mrs. Merrick were both gone."

"Did you see the vicar again that day?"

"No, and I stayed 'til after dark. He missed his supper."

The crowd murmured with excitement. Oscar was renowned as a persnickety and punctual eater, and the fact that he'd skipped a meal sealed the general opinion that he was guilty. Their collective scowls inquired: Where had he been? Out in the woods, digging an unmarked grave?

Lord Stafford peered out at the gathering. "Is there anyone

else who saw Mrs. Merrick after the quarrel with her brother? Anyone? If you're here, speak up."

There was grumbling and shuffling as the spectators glanced around, but Oscar hadn't expected a response. Josephine had fled, but to where? Oscar had absolutely no clue, and no one would listen to him.

The earl nodded to his brother, who stood behind Oscar, and Mr. Price removed Oscar's gag.

"Well, Blair," the earl said, "I'll give you a final chance to come clean."

"I have no idea what's become of Josephine." He was innocent of malfeasance and wouldn't exhibit any remorse to a roomful of fools.

"If you didn't kill her," the earl pressed, "where is she? How would she have gotten there? Your maid testified that her belongings were all accounted for."

"She vanished," Oscar tightly replied, "but it was none of my doing. When I returned home that evening, I'd been robbed, the collection money taken. I assume she stole it and used it to finance her departure." He glowered at the earl. "If you're so intent on pursuing a criminal, I suggest you find her and restore the church's funds to me."

At Oscar's comment, the observers gasped.

From the jury box, Mr. Templeton chided, "You're blaming a dead woman for the missing money?"

"For shame," several others muttered.

Mr. Price was particularly incensed. "Don't you dare besmirch her memory." He seized Oscar by his coat. "If you insult her again, you won't have to wait for the hangman's noose. I'll kill you right here, right now."

"That's enough." The earl interceded, and Mr. Price released his grip. The earl spun to the jury. "You've heard the evidence. What say all of you?"

To a man, the puppets he'd assembled shouted, "Guilty!"

"Thank you, gentleman." The earl's stony gaze fell on Oscar. "Tell me where you buried her."

"I *didn't*," Oscar insisted.

"You've been judged by your peers," the earl spat. "Don't make a mockery of their verdict."

"Their decision means naught to me."

"I'm sick of his whining," Mr. Price told his brother. "Should I gag him again?"

"Not just yet," the earl replied. "Mr. Blair, will you—"

"I am a man of God," Oscar huffed, "and you will address me accordingly. It's *Vicar* Blair to you."

"In your dreams maybe," the earl retorted as the crowd snickered, "but not in reality. I've already given your job to someone else."

"What? No! I forbid it!"

"He's promised to say a nice prayer at your funeral. Now let's get back to your sister. Where is her body?"

"I don't know!"

"I want to bury her in the church cemetery. If you confess her whereabouts, I'll show some respect for you after your demise—not that you deserve it."

"What will you do?"

"I'll cut you down the moment we hang you, and I'll bury you directly after."

"And if I don't provide her location?" Oscar sneered, realizing too late that his question sounded like an admission.

"You'll dangle for weeks, so that the crows can peck out your eyes and eat at your flesh. It's what I'd pick for you, but I can't imagine it's what you'd prefer."

"You're a monster!"

"I definitely can be. What is your choice? Where is your sister?"

Oscar's mind raced as he tried to formulate a plan to delay any action. Fleetingly, he considered lying, supplying a fake spot as to Josephine's corpse. They'd all run off to check, and he'd buy himself some time. But when they found they'd been duped, they'd be even more eager for blood.

"I wish to meet with an attorney," Oscar declared.

"Why would you need an attorney? You've had your trial. How could an attorney help you?"

"Then I must speak with Benedict Mason."

"He's on his way to the penal colonies in Australia."

"On what grounds?"

"Kidnapping, attempted rape, and attempted murder."

Oscar blanched. "I demand to...to...confer with Sheriff Pratt."

Pratt was supposed to be a professional, but he'd mucked up the entire operation. He was responsible for the whole mess, so it was only fitting that he rescue Oscar.

"Who is Sheriff Pratt?" the earl inquired.

"Sheriff Pratt! Sheriff Pratt!"

"Never heard of him." The earl gestured to his brother. "*Now*, you may gag him."

Mr. Price stuck the kerchief into Oscar's mouth and untied his bindings. The earl rose, appearing regal and lethal. The courtroom rose with him. Oscar refused to join in. He glared mulishly, and Mr. Price jerked him to his feet.

"Oscar Blair," the earl solemnly proclaimed, "you stand convicted of the murder of your sister, Mrs. Josephine Merrick. The penalty for murder is death by hanging. I have given you a chance for mercy, a chance to admit where you've hidden her body, but you declined to take it, and I see no reason to delay sentence."

The earl motioned to his brother again. "Escort him out to the village green. To the oak tree on the south end." He stared at the crowd. "Men, you may accompany me. Ladies, though your interest in justice is laudable, I will not let you attend. Please return to your homes and remain there until this sad business is over."

The men dawdled as the women trudged out. Mr. Price bound Oscar's wrists and led him to the door. Oscar was bleating with fury, protesting his innocence, but he was muted by the gag. He struggled against Mr. Price's firm grip but couldn't pry himself loose. Even if he could manage it, what was the point?

He could never escape the Price brothers. They were like a force of nature, a gale that had blown into town and swept away all that was decent and good.

They marched out of the tavern and across the grass, and Oscar's legs failed him. Mr. Price hauled him along as if he were an invalid. They approached the tree and, the verdict having been a foregone conclusion, the noose was already in place, as was the chair where he would perch until it was kicked out from under him.

Though the female residents had been ordered away, Emeline Wilson watched him come.

Emeline! Emeline! he shrieked with his eyes. *You know me!*

You know I wouldn't kill Josephine! Stop them! Stop this!

Mr. Price pulled Oscar forward until he was directly in front of her.

"I am here to bear witness for Josephine." Emeline's voice was odd—as if she had a bad sore throat. "She was beautiful and kind. She was my friend. You didn't deserve to have her as your sister."

Emeline moved away, and Mr. Price shoved him at the chair.

"Climb up, Blair," Mr. Price commanded.

No, no! Oscar couldn't comply, so the earl and his brother lifted him onto it. Mr. Price yanked away the kerchief as Oscar wet himself, urine flooding his trousers.

"Have you any last words?" the earl asked.

"I didn't do it!"

"You still deny your perfidy?" the earl scoffed. "You're about to meet your Maker, Blair. This might be the time to exhibit some humility."

A thin, maimed young man stepped forward, a Bible clutched to his chest.

"I'm Ted Smith, Mr. Blair," the man said. "I'd like to pray with you. Is there a certain passage you prefer?"

"Get away from me!" Oscar kicked at the Holy Book, sending it flying to the ground, and he didn't suffer an ounce of remorse.

What benefit had the stupid text ever provided? His entire life, he'd abided by its teachings, yet in the end, he was being wrongfully hanged by a felonious scoundrel.

Mr. Smith picked up the Bible and dusted it off. "You're a tad distraught, which is understandable. I'll select a psalm for you."

He chose the Twenty-Third and began to read, but his speed was much too fast for Oscar's liking. All too soon, he finished and snapped the book closed. The earl slipped the noose over Oscar's head, and Oscar quivered with terror.

"I won't ask again, Blair," the earl warned. "Any final words?"

"Yes! Yes! I've always been a righteous person, a pious person. I worked hard and tried my best. I guided my congregation from sin to virtue, and I—"

"Must we listen to this?" Mr. Price complained.

"No." The earl tugged on the rope, tightening it so that it cut into Oscar's neck.

Oscar gazed out at the men of the village. They had been his flock, and he searched for a friendly face but couldn't find one. Was there no compassion in their hearts? Was there no sympathy? How could the world be so cruel?

He was about to beg, to weep, when suddenly, a coach rounded the corner and rumbled into the square.

A little girl popped up in the window, and everyone gawked as she called, "Papa! Papa! It's me, Annie! I've come all the way from Belgium."

Mr. Price's jaw dropped with surprise, and he rushed away from Oscar and hurried to the carriage.

"Annie?" Mr. Price murmured, amazed. "Is it really you?"

He reached for the door and pulled it open. The girl leapt out and into his arms.

A woman emerged behind her, and there was a communal gasp of shock.

"Hello, Stephen," Josephine said. "I have a confession to make. I hope you're not angry." She frowned, taking in the peculiar scene, the enraged citizens of the town, her brother on a chair with a noose circling his neck. "Have I missed something important?"

"I'll be damned," the earl muttered. He looked over at Oscar. "I guess you were telling the truth."

Oscar fainted dead away.

Chapter Twenty-Four

"Good night, my little darling."

"Good night, Papa." Annie paused, then asked, "I surprised you, didn't I?"

"Yes, you did."

"Are you happy I came?"

"I am *so* happy. I can't tell you how much."

Stephen pulled up her covers, tucking her in as he hadn't since she was a tiny baby. He leaned down and kissed the top of her head.

"Mrs. Merrick said you'd be glad."

"She was correct."

"I like her; she's funny." Annie's eyes were drooping. She was yawning, nodding off. "I was afraid on the ship, but she told the best stories. It made me forget the rocking of the waves."

Since she'd arrived, she hadn't stopped chattering. The words of a lifetime had been bottled inside her, and they were tumbling out. He hadn't known that one small girl could be such a whirlwind.

She was in her own room, but the Wilson twins were across the hall. The three were the same age, and they'd quickly bonded. Very soon, he suspected they would be sharing quarters rather than occupying two separate chambers.

In the morning, there would be children's laughter in the mansion, singing and skipping and merry games on the stairs. He liked to think that the house was being reborn, welcoming family, resonating with the sounds of new joy. The prospect was enormously comforting.

"You get to sleep now," he murmured.

"You'll be here in the morning, won't you?"

"I'll be right here. We won't ever be parted again."

He prayed that was true, but it wasn't the moment to mention it. He had to finish with the army, so there'd be some wrangling over his discharge. Hopefully, it could be handled with a bunch of paperwork so he wouldn't have to leave Stafford.

With Mason banished to Australia, and the estate suffering from a myriad of problems, Nicholas had urged Stephen to serve as land agent in Mason's stead. Stephen had jumped at the chance. He intended to plant roots at Stafford, roots so deep that he could never be forced away.

"Good night," he repeated, but she didn't reply.

She'd finally run out of steam, and he stood, watching her, mesmerized by the rise and fall of the blankets as she inhaled and exhaled.

Ultimately, exhaustion took its toll, and he tiptoed out. The past few days had been filled with drama and chaos, and he was relieved to have it over. Nicholas still had to deal with Oscar Blair, but with Josephine having reappeared, Nicholas's choices weren't so dire.

However he punished Blair, Stephen didn't care. Blair was complicit in the crimes committed against Emeline Wilson, and so long as Nicholas dispatched him far away, Stephen wasn't concerned if Blair was dead or alive, imprisoned or free.

He proceeded to his room, passing down the quiet corridors. He wasn't staying in the earl's grand suite as he had earlier in the summer. Then, Nicholas hadn't been interested in the trappings of his title, and he'd refused the more ostentatious accommodations.

However, upon their recent return, he'd claimed the space as his own on the assumption that he was about to marry Emeline. He'd built up an entire fantasy where he would rescue her and she'd be so grateful that she'd wed him immediately.

He'd even applied for a Special License. It was sitting on his desk down in the library—unused and unnecessary.

Ha! Stephen hooted with glee whenever he thought of how Emeline had rejected his brother. The supreme marital catch in England, the consummate lady's man, the notorious lover and exploiter of women, had met his match.

Emeline Wilson didn't want him, and Nicholas was in a state of shock. It was such a rich, hilarious ending that Stephen couldn't stop laughing, and he liked Emeline more and more because of it.

She was tough. She had grit. She had pride and sense. Eventually, she'd relent—Nicholas was a master at cunning and he'd wear her down—and Stephen would be delighted to have her as his sister-in-law.

He approached his door, and he paused to wonder where Jo's room was located. He needed to ask her some questions, but events had been too hectic, and they hadn't had a chance to speak about what she'd done.

She'd traipsed off to Belgium, pretending she had the authority to fetch Annie to England. Her plan had been devised in secret and carried out with no assistance. How had she mustered the courage? It contradicted everything he knew about her, and he didn't understand her behavior.

He wanted to thank her for bringing Annie to Stafford. If left to his own devices, he might never have accomplished the deed. Though his intentions had been honorable, he'd always found reasons to delay.

Jo had taken matters into her own hands, had forged ahead where Stephen hadn't dared. Annie was home, where she belonged. Because of Jo. Not because of Stephen. Stephen had proved himself a great talker, a great dreamer, but Jo had turned out to be the great *doer*.

With her incredible adventure completed, she was sending him a message, but he couldn't figure out what it was. He was dying to inquire, but not in the middle of the night when he was drained and feeling a tad low. He was still physically attracted to her, and in his current condition, any contact might conclude in a manner best avoided.

He spun the knob and entered, expecting the place to be dark, but to his surprise, there was a cheery fire in the hearth. A small table was in front of it, pillows scattered about for lounging and staring into the flames. There was a bottle of wine, a decanter of brandy, and two glasses on the floor. Someone had been drinking the wine.

"What the devil...?" he muttered.

He went to the bedchamber, seeing a brace of candles, another warm fire. In the dressing room beyond, there were more candles, yet another fire.

In the air, he could smell heated water and scented bath salts.

Was someone taking a bath? At midnight? In his dressing room?

He glanced around, worried that he'd walked into the wrong suite by mistake, but no, there were his riding boots in the corner, his pistols on a chair, his coat thrown across the foot of the bed.

Unsettled to the point of alarm, he crept over and peeked in. The sight that greeted him was so astounding that he had to blink and blink to clear his vision.

"Mrs. Merrick?" he said.

"It's *Jo* to you, and don't argue about it."

She was reclined in his bathing tub. Naked. Her glorious brunette hair was piled on her head, damp tendrils curling on her shoulders. She was wet and delectable, and though he hadn't meant to react, his cock was hard as stone.

She noticed instantly and flashed a sultry smile. Then she stood, water sluicing down her curvaceous body as she stepped out and grabbed a towel.

As if they'd shared the suite forever, as if they were an old married couple, she dried herself as he watched. He was flabbergasted by her audacity, aroused by her nudity, and perplexed in the extreme.

What had happened to her?

The last time they'd spoken, she'd been a quivering, apologetic rabbit who was frightened of her own shadow. Now she was...was...

He didn't know what she was, but the trip to Belgium had changed her. This Josephine Merrick was bold and blunt and shameless, and he was too stunned to comment for he had no idea what to say.

"Is Annie asleep?" she asked.

"Yes, finally."

"That girl can talk! After the excitement over our arrival, I doubted she'd ever be able to rest."

"I didn't think she would, either."

"She'll calm down once she's been at Stafford awhile, once she accepts that she won't have to ever leave. She was so nervous about seeing you again."

"She needn't have been."

"I told her that, but she's a child. *Telling* her and having you prove it are two different animals."

She expounded as if she were an expert on parenting, as if she were a nanny or governess or had birthed a dozen babies herself. She was a mystery beyond his comprehension.

"Why are you here?" he asked.

"In your room, do you mean?"

"Yes—here in my bedchamber. Why are you?"

"You don't know?"

"No."

Galvanizing his attention, she ran the towel 'round and 'round her breasts, then tossed it away. She marched over to a hook on the wall, pulled down his robe, and put it on. The sleeves were too long, so she rolled them up, but she didn't cinch the belt, so the center of her lush torso was on display.

She sauntered toward him, the hem of the garment wafting behind her. He had a perfect view of bosom, belly, mons and thighs, and he shouldn't have stared, but he couldn't help it. When desire sizzled so fiercely between them, it was impossible not to want her.

She snuggled herself to him. On the way over, she'd grabbed a glass off the dresser—whiskey from the smell of it—and she downed the contents in a single swallow.

"You're drinking...liquor?" he stammered.

"I've discovered that I enjoy it. It relaxes me."

"Who are you?" he teased. "Have we met?"

"I don't believe so."

"I could swear you're Josephine Merrick, the vicar's widowed sister."

"Didn't you hear? Vicar Blair killed Josephine. Someone came back in her place and is hiding in her body."

"Who came back?"

"A new sort of woman, one who will engage in any wild behavior, one who is madly, passionately in love with you."

"What?" He shook his head. "I don't understand you at all."

"What's to understand? I suddenly find myself eager to wed a sexy, hardened soldier."

"That would be me?"

"Yes, that would be you."

"What about your brother?"

"I don't care about Oscar. Lord Stafford can do whatever he wants to him."

"And Annie?"

"I love her, and I will be her mother. You're *not* marrying anyone else. You're *not* letting anyone else raise her."

"But people might gossip. People might complain about her being here, that she's my natural daughter."

"Then they'll have to deal with me."

He studied her ferocious gaze, her firm expression. Josephine Merrick had gone to Belgium, and yes, someone else had definitely returned.

"You want to marry me?" he said.

"Yes, and you haven't proposed. I suggest you get on with it—before I change my mind." She kissed him slowly, seductively, her tongue in his mouth, her hands on his ass. "There are two things you should probably know first."

"Uh-oh. What are they?"

"For my wedding gift, I need you to give me some money."

"What for?"

"I stole the collection money from Oscar—to fund my trip to Belgium."

"*You* stole it?"

"Yes."

He laughed and laughed. "Your brother was almost hanged over it. We thought he was lying, besmirching your deceased memory."

"No, it was me, but I can't start our life together on such a wicked note. I promised the Lord I'd pay it back. So...will you help me?"

"Of course, I will. What is the second thing?"

"You and I, Mr. Price, are going to have a baby."

His breath hitched in his lungs. "We're...what?"

"We're having a baby." She shrugged out of his robe and it slid to the floor. "It seems I'm not barren, after all. Now let's go to bed. I'm exhausted."

She clasped his wrist and led him over to it. He followed like a puppet on a string.

"No peeking."

"I wouldn't dream of it."

"I'm serious. Don't look until we tell you."

"I won't, I won't!"

Emeline kept her eyes tightly closed. Nan and Nell were guiding her. Annie Price, their best friend in the entire world, tagged along behind. Emeline had to trust that, between the three of them, they wouldn't let her trip over a stump or fall in a hole.

They had coaxed her into the village, claiming Mr. Price had given them pennies to buy ribbons for their hair. Yet once they'd arrived, another plan had presented itself.

They were escorting her somewhere, and Emeline was glad to have their secret revealed. For some time, it had been obvious they had a scheme brewing. There'd been giggles and whispers and conversations that halted when she entered a room.

Whatever mischief they'd hatched, she hoped it wasn't awful, that she could smile through the unveiling.

"Are your eyes still closed?" Nan inquired.

"Yes."

"No peeking!" she warned again.

"I'm not."

They were next to a building, and inside, Emeline could hear people frantically murmuring, "She's here! She's here! Ssh!"

It wasn't her birthday, so what could it be?

A door creaked, and Emeline was pulled across the threshold. Nell and Nan cried, "Open up. Look!"

Emeline obeyed and was stunned to find herself in a schoolhouse. It was newly constructed, with desks, slates, books, and maps on the walls. If she had sat down and drawn a picture of the ideal spot for teaching, this was the exact scene she would have imagined.

At the front, a crowd was gathered around the teacher's desk: Stephen and Jo Price, hastily wed and with a babe on the way. The vicar, Ted Smith. Mr. Templeton, Mrs. Brookhurst, and other neighbors who had been friends of her parents, who had watched her grow up in Stafford.

Off to the side, there were several carpenters, wounded veterans from London who had served with the Price brothers. One was missing a foot. Another a leg. Another an ear. They were a rag-tag collection of lost souls brought to Stafford by the earl.

In the middle of the group, the earl, himself, Captain Nicholas Price, beamed fondly at her. He appeared regal, confident, larger than life, and on seeing him, she could barely keep from running over and falling into his arms.

He'd rescued her from Benedict Mason, had banished Vicar Blair to an unnamed location—supposedly to the penal colonies with Mason—then he'd left and had been gone for weeks. She hadn't known where he was or if he was coming back, and she hadn't asked. She wasn't in any position to inquire about him and had studiously avoided any gossip.

For some odd reason, he'd proposed to her before he departed, and she couldn't figure out why he had. She'd spent many sleepless nights mulling that peculiar encounter, recalling his shock at being rebuffed.

In light of how he'd tricked and deceived her, had he really thought she'd shame herself again? The notion had enraged her, and she'd kept herself centered and sane by envisioning him in London, chasing after every beautiful, rich debutante in the city.

Now he'd resurfaced as abruptly as he'd vanished. What did it portend?

"Surprise!" they shouted in unison.

"What is this?" she tentatively asked.

"It's a school," Nan explained. "Lord Stafford had it built—just for you."

Nell added, "All the children in the village will be required to attend. He's ordering them to learn to read and write, so you'll be happy."

"Oh."

"Isn't it grand?" Nan queried.

"Yes, very grand."

The three girls skipped away, and they rushed to Lord Stafford and hugged him, grinning as if he walked on water.

"You wore me down, Em," he said. "You nagged and nagged over your blasted school, and now you have it."

In case she hadn't noticed his largesse, he gestured around. It was a magnanimous, kingly motion that vividly reminded her of all that she had once loved and hated about him. He could be the kindest, most generous man in the world. But he could also be the most calculating and cruel.

She didn't want him at Stafford. She was still recuperating from her ordeal, and she couldn't abide the prospect of seeing him constantly and remembering how terribly he'd wounded her.

Suddenly, she realized that the room was very quiet. Everyone was gaping, waiting for her to comment. They were in a festive mood and had expected her to be, too. The earl had presented her with her life's dream, practically on a silver platter.

Why wasn't she celebrating? Why wasn't she spinning in joyous circles?

"Do you like it, Emeline?" Nell nervously broached.

It was too much for Emeline to absorb. The school and the earl and her memories.

Feeling unaccountably distraught, she mumbled, "Excuse me," and staggered out. Blindly, she raced down the street, out of the village and into the woods. She slowed to a stop and sat against a tree.

What was happening to her? All she did any more was weep and regret. She was overly emotional, prone to melancholy and maudlin reflection.

She wallowed in self-pity and couldn't move beyond what had transpired. Why not? She wasn't the only female in history who'd ever been duped by a scoundrel. Why couldn't she forgive and forget as was the Christian way?

To her eternal disgust, much of her misery was due to Jo's happiness.

Jo was pregnant with the baby she'd presumed she could never have. She had a husband she adored and a daughter she cherished. She was rid of her horrid brother forever and living in a beautiful house, Mason's old residence behind the manor.

Jo was brimming with elation while Emeline was more dejected than ever.

Gad, she was pathetic! She couldn't be glad for her friend, couldn't wish her well.

Every time she gazed at Jo, she was overcome by envy and

resentment. She and Jo had both dallied with the Price brothers, but at the conclusion of their illicit affairs, Jo had been blessed with every boon while Emeline was where she'd always been. Alone. Poor. No husband. No home. No change on the horizon.

Long before she saw him, his boots crunched toward her on the gravel. She could have predicted that he'd chase after her. He'd given her a wonderful gift, but she hadn't been sufficiently grateful, so he'd harangue at her until she responded in a fashion more to his liking.

At the prospect of quarreling with him, she was frozen in place, too weary to flee or fight.

He rounded the bend and kept coming until he was directly in front of her, until he was so close that the tips of his boots slipped under the hem of her skirt. With her seated and him standing, he seemed inordinately tall. The sky was so blue, the clouds floating by over his head, and the sight made her dizzy.

He was too handsome, too virile, too...too...everything.

"For months, all I heard from you"—he was in a temper, his color high, his eyes flashing daggers—"was *I want a school, I want a school.* So I build you a damned school, and when I give it to you, with the whole town watching, you have a hissy fit and run off. What is wrong with you?"

"Go away."

"Not 'til you answer my question. What is wrong with you?"

He plopped down beside her, a lazy elbow balanced on his knee.

"Don't you have to be somewhere?" she rudely snapped.

"Like where?"

"Oh, I don't know. How about with your regiment in the army? Weren't you recalled to duty?"

"I retired from the army. That's why I was away for so long."

"You what?"

"I resigned. I missed Stafford too much."

"You liar."

"I'm not lying. You insisted the property would grow on me, and you were correct. This spot is my home. It's in my blood, and I'm never leaving it again."

He was staring at her strangely, making her extremely uncomfortable. They were playing a game of cat and mouse, with him the cat and her the mouse. He was toying with her, leading her down a road she was sure she shouldn't travel.

"How about your fiancée?" she asked. "Why aren't you in London with her?"

"I told you I jilted her."

"What a gentleman," she snidely retorted.

"I did it for you. You should be thanking me."

"Thanking you!"

"I never should have proposed to her. My brother warned me, but I wouldn't listen."

"You seemed fairly *happy* that day she was here at the estate."

"I was just pretending. I'm relieved to be shed of her, although when I met with her father to work out the details of the split, I really got an earful. If you'd been there while he was shouting at me, you'd have enjoyed it."

"I'll bet I would have."

"I haven't had anybody yell at me like that since I was a fourteen-year-old private." He gave a mock shudder. "Do you feel sorry for me?"

"No."

"I'm not engaged anymore. What do you think about that?"

"I don't think anything about it."

"I'm free to wed whomever I choose. *You* for instance. I could marry you if I decided it suited my purposes."

"I already told you—never in a thousand years."

"Why is that, exactly? You used to be sweet on me. Where is your unbridled passion? You can't tell me it evaporated. I'll never believe you."

He leaned in and stole a kiss, and as he drew away, her heart hammered so hard that she worried it might burst from her chest. He was enormously pleased with himself while she was distressed, furious, and sad.

It hurt to look at him, hurt to hear his voice and see his smile. Didn't he understand? She'd been scraped raw, hollowed out. There was nothing remaining of the person she'd once been. He'd left her an empty shell.

She scrambled to her feet and hastened off down the lane. Of course, oaf that he was, he wouldn't let her storm off with any dignity. He came after her, his long legs rapidly covering the ground so that, shortly, they were strolling side by side.

She tried to ignore him, but she couldn't. He simply took up too much space.

"I've been gone for a while," he said, "and now that I'm back, do you know what I noticed?"

"No, and I don't care what you noticed, either."

"You've put on a few pounds."

"How kind of you to mention it."

"Your bosom is bigger, your tummy more rounded."

She halted and whirled on him. "Are you calling me fat?"

"No, I'm calling you pregnant."

She gasped. "What?"

"People claim you're overly emotional. You cry at the drop of a hat. You're constantly dizzy. You're pregnant, Emeline Wilson."

Could it be? Frantically, she counted the days, the weeks. It had been ages since she'd had her monthly flux, but she'd attributed the lack to stress and strain.

Oh no, oh no, oh no...

"If I had a gun," she seethed, "I shoot you with it."

"You ought to be a tad nicer to me. It sounds as if you need a husband." He smirked. "I'm available."

"Maybe I won't kill you. Maybe I'll kill myself."

"And do away with Nicholas junior? You never would."

He stared in that intent way he had, the way that had previously elated her. Once, he'd made her feel as if she was the most unique woman on Earth. Now she just felt tired. Tired and miserable and so very, very lonely.

He reached into his coat and pulled out a gold wedding band. He waved it under her nose like a talisman.

"What is that supposed to be?" she asked.

"What would you imagine it is?"

"I don't have any idea."

He clasped her hand and slid the ring onto her finger. It fit perfectly.

"Marry me, Emeline."

"What? No."

"Marry me," he said again. "You want to so badly. Stop fighting it."

"No." She repeated more firmly, but he was unfazed by her reply.

"Why not?"

"Because if I were to wed, it would be for love."

"I know that about you."

"You're focused on status and revenge. You want a Lady Veronica Stewart—it's all you've ever wanted—and you'll never convince me that you'd suddenly ask me instead."

"I have lowered my standards quite a bit, haven't I? I'm definitely scraping the bottom of the barrel with you."

It was the sort of sarcastic remark that once might have coaxed a pithy rejoinder from her, that might have garnered him a playful jab in the ribs. But she was exhausted and depressed and anxious to slither away so she could lick her wounds in private while she contemplated her pregnancy.

"Don't do this," she quietly implored.

"Don't do what?"

"You assume I'm increasing, and you've been overcome by some odd chivalrous impulse, but it will pass."

"You think this is an *impulse?*"

"I'm certain it is. Just leave it be, Nicholas."

"You called me Nicholas."

He flashed a devilish grin that had her heart pounding again, and a collage of images popped into her head: their first meeting in London, his initial visit to Stafford, the afternoon he'd caught her fishing in the stream, his kindness to her sisters, her developing infatuation, his ultimate seduction.

She'd been so happy then. She'd felt so vibrant and alive. How had that joy fled so completely?

"Let me share a little secret with you, Em," he said.

"Please don't."

"You want to marry for love. Well, what about me? What if I want to marry for love, too?"

"Then you should go find someone who loves you. You're wonderful, remember? I'm sure you won't have any trouble."

"I don't have to search," he insisted. "I've found what I need very close to home. It's been waiting here for me all this time."

To her consternation, he dropped to a knee and clasped her hand again.

"I love you, Emeline."

"Nicholas, no, don't you dare—"

"Hush," he soothed, "and listen to me for once."

"Why should I turn over a new leaf at this late date?"

His eyes were so very blue. A woman could get lost in those eyes. *She* had gotten lost in those eyes. She tried to glance away but couldn't.

"When I first came to Stafford, I hated it."

"How could I forget?"

"You made me love it. You made me love *you.* You've ensnared me, and you can't simply walk away. It would be too cruel."

"You're mad."

"No, not mad. Just in love. With you." He stroked his fingers across her stomach, reminding her that there might be more at stake than pride and hurt feelings. "You need a husband, Em. Let it be me."

When he assessed her like that, when he spoke in that soft tone...

"I don't know what to do." She started to shake. "I don't know what's best."

"*I* am best. I am precisely what you need. Say you'll have me."

"But...but...a few weeks ago, you were engaged to somebody else."

"A huge mistake on my part. I admit it."

"You can't have changed your opinion so quickly."

"Can't I have? I'm a man, Em, and a particularly thickheaded one at that. It never dawned on me that I was in love. I couldn't figure out what was wrong with me. Guess what I realized."

"What?"

"I love you so much, I'm dying with it."

"Oh, Nicholas."

"I'm not much of a catch. I'm vain and stubborn and intractable, but I'm also loyal and faithful. I will always stand by you and be your staunchest ally. You'll never be alone again." Overwhelmed by sentiment, he had to swallow twice before he could continue. "Take a chance on me, Em. You'll never regret it."

Voices echoed down the lane, and they peered over to

discover that the people from the party had come looking for them. Jo and Stephen Price, her sisters, Annie Price. The new vicar, the carpenters.

"Get up," she urged, trying to tug him to his feet, but he wouldn't budge.

"No. The entire town should bear witness to my proposal."

"I don't want you to be embarrassed."

"Silly Em, you could never embarrass me."

His brother called, "Have you worn her down yet?"

"No," he replied. "She doesn't think I'm worth having."

"I didn't say that!" she huffed.

"You didn't say *yes*, either." He kissed her ring again. "What's it to be, Em? We're waiting for your answer."

She gazed at him, at her sisters and friends. Their expressions told her she could have it all. The husband who adored her. Children. A father to care for them and keep them safe. A home where she was happy and cherished.

"Swear to me that you mean it," she demanded.

"Yes, I mean it. I swear."

"Swear to me that you'll stay at Stafford. You won't be off gallivanting, where I'm panicked and fretting over where you are and if you're all right."

"I wouldn't want to be anywhere but here."

"Promise me that it's forever."

"Forever..." He nodded. "I like the sound of it."

She couldn't refuse him. Not with spectators studying their every move. Not when he was offering her exactly what she craved.

The sad, pathetic fact was that she still loved him. She always had and always would, and she could have him for her very own. She could have him for the rest of her life.

"Don't ever lie to me again," she warned.

"I will if it's for your own good."

She scoffed. "You're impossible."

"Yes, I am. Impossible and conceited and possessed of every other bad trait. Now what's it to be? Will you have me or not?"

"Yes, Nicholas, I will have you."

He grinned a sly grin. "I knew you couldn't resist me." He stood and faced the crowd. "You heard her, folks. I'm about to become leg shackled."

"About time," his brother muttered.

"Isn't anybody going to congratulate me?"

They clapped and cheered. The girls rushed over, hugging them and squealing with delight.

Nicholas soaked it all in, and she watched him, realizing how much he'd changed from the angry, solitary man he'd been when they'd first met. She'd given him this. She'd brought him this contentment, this sense of belonging.

She sighed with satisfaction.

"Let's go back to my school." She smiled—just for him. "I want you to show me everything."

"You better gush over it," he advised her. "You better spend the whole day telling me how marvelous I am."

"I'll definitely tell you," she said. "I'll tell you and tell you, and I'll never stop."

About the Author

Cheryl Holt is a New York Times and USA Today bestselling author of thirty novels.

She's also a lawyer and mom, and at age 40, with two babies at home, she started a new career as a commercial fiction writer. She'd hoped to be a suspense novelist, but couldn't sell any of her manuscripts, so she ended up taking a detour into romance, where she was stunned to discover that she has an incredible knack for writing some of the world's greatest love stories.

Her books have been released to wide acclaim, and she has won or been nominated for many national awards. She is particularly proud to have been named "Best Storyteller of the Year" by the trade magazine, Romantic Times BOOK Reviews.

She lives and writes in Los Angeles, and she loves to hear from fans. Visit her website at www.cherylholt.com.

Oh, the delicious peril of deception...

What the Mistress Did
© *2011 Anya Delvay*

Lady Marianne Gillingham has no intention of ending her affair with David Dunscombe, Earl Harrington, despite his pending nuptials. She craves his attentions, and he satisfies her deepest yearnings.

Yet, when his fiancée, the sweet, innocent and oh-so-very young Annabelle Frazier, appears on her doorstep to demand the end of the association, Marianne realizes she does not wish to be second in David's affections. She also cannot resist issuing a warning. The earl will bed his wife with tedious regularity, but never reveal his more *unusual* desires.

To Marianne's amusement, her prediction comes true, with a surprising twist. The countess is back with a new demand: repair the problem her prophetic words created. Taking pleasure in imagining the other woman's fear and horror, Marianne rekindles the affair to demonstrate exactly how to fulfill David's lascivious desires—while Annabelle secretly watches from the shadows.

She never expected Annabelle to prove so resilient and surprisingly easy—not to mention delicious—to corrupt. Or that the ensuing erotic tangle would be impossible to put right without heartbreak.

Warning: Loosen your stays and have your fan at hand. Plumes and floggers, along with some other leather devices, were employed in the creating of this erotic tangle. Contains Georgian ladies behaving badly, often with each other. M/F/F, M/F, F/F action herein.

Available now in ebook from Samhain Publishing.

SAMHAIN
PUBLISHING

It's all about the story...

Romance

HORROR

www.samhainpublishing.com

12/12=7 **WITHDRAWAL**

For Every
Individual...

INDIANAPOLIS PUBLIC

Renew by Phone
269-5222

Renew on the Web
www.imcpl.org

For General Library Infomation
please call 275-4100

CPSIA information can be obtained at www.ICGtesting.com
Printed in the USA
BVOW030838130612

292550BV00002B/2/P

9 781609 287054